Miss
OPHELIA

Miss
OPHELIA

a novel

MARY BURNETT SMITH

William Morrow and Company, Inc.
New York

It is the policy of William Morrow and Company, Inc., and its imprints and affiliates, recognizing the importance of preserving what has been written, to print the books we publish on acid-free paper, and we exert our best efforts to that end.

Library of Congress Cataloging-in-Publication Data

Smith, Mary Burnett, 1931–
Miss Ophelia : a novel / Mary Burnett Smith.—1st ed.
    p.   cm.
ISBN 0-688-15234-1
I. Title.
PS3569.M537738M57   1997
813'.54—dc21   97-7055
                                                          CIP

Printed in the United States of America

First Edition

1   2   3   4   5   6   7   8   9   10

BOOK DESIGN BY SUSAN DESTAEBLER

In memory of my mother

Acknowledgments

Thanks to Flora Eikerinkoetter, who listened to my early manuscript and helped me with authentic details; to Monique Smith and Pamela Amos, who listened and asked important questions; to Susan Fleming, who read and offered sensible advice; to my editor at Morrow, Tracy Quinn, for being patient and thorough; to my agent, Ray Lincoln, for her faith and helping me to keep the faith. Also my gratitude to my dear friend Pat Pollard, who put a fire under me and started me to writing again. And my heartfelt thanks to my husband, Snowden, for helping me through four months of illness so I could meet all my deadlines.

On days like this I think of Miss Ophelia. Long summer days when the late afternoon sun shines through the leaded glass window onto my piano and I watch the dust motes dance up the beam, as I am doing now. I look at my fingers, puffy with age, and I think of hers, then long and slender, covering mine to position them on the keys.

Ebony on brown.

On days like this, sweet, lazy days when I dallied at the piano, Miss Ophelia would gently touch my shoulder and say, "Perhaps now would be a good time for me to play, Isabel. Go sit on the porch and I'll play a waltz for you."

Until I met Miss Ophelia, everyone called me Belly; Isabel was the introduction to a verbal rap on the knuckles. *Isabel Anderson! Are you talking again? Isabel, keep on scuffin up those shoes. Money don't grow on trees.* But with Miss Ophelia it was an invitation to a pleasant interlude.

Isabel. Time to listen.

I would jump up from the mahogany stool at the piano and head for the glider on the tiny back porch and listen while she played an étude by Chopin or Liszt or a rag by Scott Joplin; the music would ripple through the window next to the piano, and I would swing and dream, lost in a haze of music and shadows.

Then she would take the piece that I was working on and call through the window for me to note a particular passage where I was having difficulty, and she would play it again. Soon she would join me on the glider with the music book in her hand; she would take the passage she had just played and make me name the notes as she hummed them softly in my ear.

There was always a pitcher of iced tea and a plate of homemade sugar cookies. And always the smell of roses: delicate tea roses, white and pink; prickly red and yellow roses with velvet petals that climbed the fences and hedges and filled the small backyard and Miss Ophelia's tiny parlor with their perfume.

Miss Ophelia Love. I sit here now and whisper her name slowly, softly. Miss Ophelia. Miss Ophelia Love. I whisper her name and remember a summer when I was eleven.

Mason County, Virginia, was nothing but country in 1948. Country roads, dirt or graveled, and country people with country ways. I lived in an area of the county known as Pharaoh, a small community of colored people who had settled there before and after the Civil War on parcels of land sold to them by the white farmers who owned the farms where they worked. Many such communities were scattered throughout Mason County at that time. Communities named after a hollow or a creek or a grove of trees. You could not find their names on a map, even today. To reach them you had to go to Lambertville, a little town ten miles from us, which white people had begun with a post office and a flour mill. There was by that time a main street with a few other establishments: a supermarket, a drugstore, a movie house, a furniture store, and a five and ten. If you wanted to get in or out of Lambertville, you took the Trailways bus that ran through twice a day. Tickets were sold in the gas station at the bottom of the road that led into the town.

Lambertville had a few colored businesses as well. Joe Jennings's barbershop (crowded with the men from the surrounding colored communities) and his pool hall above the barbershop, Nate Robinson's funeral parlor, and Gerald Butler's restaurant with a speakeasy in the back run by the Butlers, who also ran a thriving taxi business for the colored people who wanted to come into Lambertville to get their Saturday groceries or their monthly haircuts or a meal and a few drinks.

Summer in Mason County was a time God set aside for children: mud slides and wading in the branch for guppies and tadpoles and dodgeball and hide 'n' go seek. And every year in August the excitement of the Silas Green Show and the churches crowded with people down for homecoming on Third Sunday. And the food! Tables loaded down with fried chicken and cold ham and greens and potato salad and peach pies topped with vanilla ice cream spread out on snowy cloths under the three giant poplar trees that stood between the church and the graveyard.

That was the summer my best friend, Teeny Gibson, was going to teach me how to swim. The promise had been made the year before when she had pushed me into Pine Run and I'd almost drowned. I had promised not to tell if she taught me how to swim. But not now, I'd said, shivering in my wet dress. Next summer. Next summer when the fright had worn off.

Next summer had come. School had been out a week and it was the first Sunday in June and it was warm. Warm enough to talk about learning to swim. So after Sunday School I looked for Teeny to remind her of the promise. When I did not see her immediately, I knew just where she had gone. Down to the church graveyard to make goo-goo eyes at that Mitchell Looby. Her mother better not see her. She knew what she'd get. In front of Mitchell, too.

But as I approached the little cemetery I knew that Teeny would not be there. Not today. It was the Sunday after Memorial Day, and people who had not been able to come on the holiday were now tending the graves of long-gone relatives or straightening headstones and putting flowers on the graves of those more recently deceased. Uncle Willie and I had come on Friday and tidied up the graves of my grandmother and grandfather. On Saturday Mama and I, dressed all in white, and Uncle Willie, in his navy blue suit, had knelt and prayed and placed flowers at all the stones of every Walker buried there.

Now it was Sunday and church was over and Teeny had disappeared. Where could she have gone? I went to the fence at the edge of the graveyard and looked into the next field. There was a big oak tree there where she and Mitchell met sometimes. But I did not see her there. It seemed that she had vanished.

The next day I waited until midmorning, when the tall grasses in the field between my house and Teeny's were dry enough for me to run through. I sneaked by Uncle Willie, who was painting the porch furniture, and climbed through the barbed wire fence that separated our property from the Gibsons'. The grass was up to my chest, and wild and scratchy; I had not been through the field very often this past spring, and I had to make a new path. The sun was hot by now, beating down on my head, and I was sweaty and itchy when I ran up onto her porch. The front door, which was usually open, was closed. I opened the screen door and raised my hand to knock, but the door opened and Teeny eased out and greeted me, leaving the door ajar. I did not see her mother, but I sensed that she was near, watching and listening.

Teeny and I were a study in contrasts. At thirteen she was a beanpole. At eleven I was as tall and thin as she, but while Teeny was slim and reedy, my Uncle Willie reminded me every day that I was thin, and horsey. Her hair, which she braided in four plaits that she kept pinned against her head, was long and kinky. Mine was long and straight, almost down to my waist. I wore it in the way easiest for me to arrange—one long braid secured with a rubber band. Her skin was coffee-bean brown, mine pale as buttermilk, but darkened every summer by the hot sun. That morning she was wearing a big dusty gray smock, probably her mother's, while I had squeezed into one of my old dresses, tight across the chest and gathered at the waist, which had somehow climbed up to my bustline.

Head lowered, Teeny avoided my eyes and sidled over to me and we sat on the edge of the porch to talk. Usually we went walking in the field or climbed a small hill behind her house where an unused outhouse still stood, but Teeny said she could not leave the porch.

Oh, I see myself now, legs dangling over the edge, bare feet red from the silky dust, leaning forward, bending my head against the bright sun, letting Teeny unbraid and braid my long plait, prattling happily about the things we would do that summer. For some reason I do not mention what I had come to talk about, the swimming lesson. I am babbling away; she is unusually quiet, not joining in as usual, but my enthusiasm blinds me to her reticence. Finally I notice her gloominess. I wind down. I look at her anxiously. "What's the matter, Teeny? You got the cramps?" Whenever she was this quiet her monthly visitor was usually the reason.

I became aware that Teeny had been blessed with the state of womanhood two years before, early one morning on our way to the school bus stop. The poor girl had grabbed her stomach, dropped to the road, and writhed, teeth bared, as if she were being metamorphosed into a savage beast. "My period's on," she'd moaned.

I had looked at her in confusion. At the time the only period I was acquainted with was the full stop at the end of a sentence.

"I got the cramps. I think I'm gonna throw up." She crawled to the side of the road and vomited in the grass.

Should I run for my mother, I cried.

She shook her head and pulled herself up to a fence rail and hung there and retched again.

I sat nearby and pulled at my socks and begged God not to let it happen to me.

Miraculously, a few moments later she was standing again, but weak as a newborn colt. By the time we reached the bus stop she was smiling.

I am sure now that this is her problem this morning. What other reason could she have for not smiling? Teeny, unlike me, always had a smile on her face.

"You feel sick in the stomach?" I say again now.

She won't look at me. She shakes her head. "It's something else," she whispers, twisting the corner of her dress.

I lean forward. "What?" I whisper.

Now comes Miss Myra's voice, low, reproving, behind the screen door where she has been lurking like a giant spider. "Teeny. These breakfast dishes still in the sink."

Teeny frowns, jerks herself up, lays her hand on the doorknob. "See you, Belly." She opens the door. Goes in.

I say goodbye, I pick up my shoes and jump off the porch. I hurry down the driveway and run along the road. The gravel stones hurt my feet and I hop onto the grass under the big maple that signals the beginning of our property. I stand there letting my feet sink into the cool soft grass. I lift one foot, then the other. I sit down on gnarled roots that dig into the ground like the talons of a giant bird. I bend over and rub one foot, then the other where the stones have left their bruises. Frowning, I study my feet. I listen to the rustling leaves. I look at the long, fine grass. I touch the ugly roots and shudder. I feel the coolness of a slight breeze on my neck.

Pictures explode in my mind. The brightness of Teeny's porch. The dark inside the doorway. The slump of Teeny's shoulders as she enters the house. Suddenly I am embarrassed. Teeny had been keeping something from me. A secret. And I had suspected nothing. Kept talking like a fool until her mother got rid of me as if I were a stray cat. Oh, God. My face burns. I slip on my shoes and jump up and start running. The pictures jumble and disappear. My face cools.

We lived in an old farmhouse, my mother and my uncle Willie and I, the same house where they grew up and where my mother and I had remained after my father was killed in the war. Her family, the Walkers, had status in the community. William Senior was a farmhand. He worked from dawn to dusk every day and was a deacon at Pharaoh Baptist Church. My grandmother kept house; occasionally she did day's work for extra money and was a member in good standing at Pharaoh as well. There were three children living: Aunt Rachel, my mother, and Uncle Willie, who got an itchy foot one day and joined the army because he wanted to see some of the world before he died. Even if he got killed to do it.

The house stood in a field almost a quarter of a mile from the road. Two maple trees stood nearby, one in the front, one in the back. The house had weathered clapboard siding and rose straight up two stories high. Inside were four bedrooms, a real bathroom recently installed with part of the money from my father's GI insurance, and three rooms downstairs: a parlor (closed off most of the time), a dining room (which my mother used as an ironing room), and a large, roomy kitchen that ran the width of the house. This was where we spent most of our time.

Around two sides of the house ran a narrow porch, much like a veranda. At the back of the house was a little screened porch where my mother kept the washing machine in favorable weather.

My mother had once kept a few chickens and a big garden. Without my father, it became too much for her, so when Uncle Willie came back from the South Pacific, he moved in with us. He had been big and young and jolly when he left for the war, and never drank anything stronger than apple cider, so Mama said. He came back a nervous slip of a man who spent a lot of time sitting on the front porch (where the breeze was best) leaning back against the house in a ladder-back chair, listening to his phonograph, eyes half closed, with a cigarette hanging from his lip and half-pint of whiskey on the floor by his chair. But he never got drunk. If I had never seen the bottles or smelled it on his breath, I would never have known that Uncle Willie drank whiskey.

When I ran up the driveway he was reared back in his chair listening to a record by the Ink Spots. Uncle Willie loved those Ink Spots. I hopped onto the porch and flopped, hot and sweaty, on the top step. "Whew!" I wiped my face with the hem of my dress. "It sure is hot!"

"Shuh. You ain't been hot til you been to New Guinea. You been to New Guinea, you think this is the pleasantest weather in the world."

"Well, it's hot to me."

"Where you been anyway," he said, knowing very well where I had been.

"Up the road."

"At that Gibson gal's house."

"What if I was. Anyway, Mama said I could go."

"I didn't hear you ask her."

Ask her. I rolled my eyes at him.

Uncle Willie brought his chair down and stood up. "Well, your mama got somethin to tell you."

I squinted up at him. "What?"

He opened the screen door. "Go on inside. She tell you. She in the kitchen."

I jumped up. "Why can't you tell me?"

" 'Cause I ain't supposed to."

"I'm never gonna tell you anything I know anymore."

"Hah! Everything you know spill out like water over a dam."

"That's a lie and you know it."

Uncle Willie jerked my plait. "Watchit, now. Respect your elders."

I slapped his hand, stomped into the kitchen, and he stomped along behind me, still pulling my plait. My mother was not inside but in the yard hanging up clothes. She was a lean, brown woman, the color of an oak leaf in winter, of above-average height, with arms and shoulders made strong from lifting and wringing out heavy wet clothes. That morning she was wearing a sleeveless, faded blue housedress that tied behind her back. Around her waist was strung a big denim pocket filled with clothespins.

I hopped from the top step into the yard. "Mama! Make Uncle Willie stop pullin my hair!"

Uncle Willie was right behind me. " 'Mama, make Uncle Willie stop pullin my hair!' "

My mother could put up with a lot of silliness, but she had hazel eyes that she used like weapons of war, and when she was not in the mood for foolishness, she could squelch it with a glare more effective than a blade across the throat or a bullet to the head. From the set of her back and shoulders I could tell that this was one of those times to keep quiet. Without turning from the line she said, "Willie, I've told you to stop teasin that gal. You'll have her evil as the day is long." She bent over the basket at her feet. "Here, Belly. Stop screechin and help me finish hangin up these clothes."

"It's too hot out here." Oh, I was a whiny, fresh child.

Mama turned toward me then. "Like you gonna melt."

Before I could move, Uncle Willie jumped to the ground. "Your mother done spoiled you rotten. Too much mouth and lazy to boot." He raised his hand. "Get on over there before I swat you on that round Walker behind."

I swung around. "I'm an *Anderson!*" My hands went to my hips. "And you better *not* put them Walker hands on me, neither!"

"Belly!" Mama's voice was rising. "Git over here! I swear, I don't know who's worse! You or Willie! What in the world's got into you!"

Uncle Willie grinned at me behind his hand. "She mad 'cause I won't tell her about you-know-what."

Mama's hands went to her hips. "I swear, Willie, your mouth need a zipper on it."

"What you gonna tell me, Mama?"

"I'll tell you after dinner."

"Awww."

She handed me a shirt. "As soon as you finish, come in the house. And"—her eyes narrowed—"no more of this jumpin up and goin down the road without askin."

Ask. That word again. First Uncle Willie, and now Mama.

Before that day I had never asked to go anywhere around home. I just went. But the words from Uncle Willie on the porch and those from Mama just now hinted that a radical change was about to occur in the quality of my life. And I did not like it. I muttered to myself as I hung up the clothes.

Ask.

The word is like a pebble in my shoe. I frown. Something is wrong. Like Miss Myra not letting Teeny off the porch. I feel a queasy flutter in my stomach. Slowly I pin the rest of the shirts to the line. Glumly I pick up the basket and head for the house.

After dinner, after the dishes were washed and put away, after the red country dust was swept up and the linoleum floor damp-mopped, Mama sat at the table with me and Uncle Willie, who had plopped himself in a chair across from me. "Now." She took an envelope from her apron pocket. "I got a letter from your Aunt Rachel. She's comin down here day after tomorrow."

I shuddered. "But—it's only June!" Aunt Rachel never came until August for homecoming.

"She's goin to have a operation and she want you to come and stay with her for a while after she leave the hospital."

My mouth fell open. I stared at the envelope as if a rat had jumped out.

"Look at that face!" said Uncle Willie. "I told you, Lizzie!" He leaned on the table and jabbed at me with his finger. "All summer you gonna wear shoes, comb and brush your hair at least three times a day, take a bath twice a day, and eat at regular times. And no rippin and runnin around like you do here. You goin to Jamison with them uppity town folks who spend all their afternoons spruced up on the front porch gossipin." Uncle Willie made a final jab. "Yessir. She gonna keep you inside doin dishes and washin off clothes and cookin and rubbin her back and feet."

"Hush up, Willie," said Mama. "Ain't nobody goin there to be no housemaid."

I shook my head. "I don't want to go, Mama. It's borin at Aunt Rachel's."

"She'll probably give you some money so you can buy some clothes for school," said Mama. "You goin to the seventh grade. To the high school. You know you could use some new skirts and new shoes."

I looked down at my dusty feet.

"Outgrown your good shoes and wore out your old ones," said Uncle Willie. "And shoes for them *Anderson* feet cost money."

I shook my head again.

"And you talkin about it bein dull in Jamison, well it gets borin here in Pharaoh, too," said Mama. "I don't want to hear no moanin later on this month about how you lonely or there ain't nothin to do," said Mama.

"But it's my vacation! Me and Teeny, we made all these plans for when her cousins come down, and she's gonna teach me how to swim."

"Mmmmm. Them Baltimore cousins," said Uncle Willie. "I don't expect you'll see them this summer."

I looked at him, a question in my eyes. I looked at Mama, the same question there.

I got no answer. She got up and went to the screen door and looked out into the yard. "You see Teeny today?"

There is something in her voice, something lurking in the question, something I can't catch, tied in with something she has said earlier. I try to remember. I can't. "Yes, ma'am," I say.

"Was Miss Myra home?"

"She was in the house. I think she was mad at Teeny because she wouldn't let her come off the porch."

"Wouldn't let her come off the porch, hunh," said Uncle Willie. Now something in his voice, too, the same as my mother's.

I shook my head. "No. She told her to come in and do the dishes."

"That's a lazy-ass woman," said Uncle Willie.

"I'm gonna stay with Teeny," I said.

My mother came and sat back down across from me and tried to catch my eye.

I looked away and parroted Uncle Willie. "Aunt Rachel ain't gonna get me in her house sweepin and scrubbin and dustin just because she's sick in the bed." Then I added softly, "And she's mean."

We sat silent. Nothing more to be said, it seemed.

But Uncle Willie couldn't let the subject rest. "Yeah, dust make Rachel nervous, all right."

Mama threw him a look like a thunderclap. "Keep talkin like a fool, Willie Walker."

Uncle Willie shook his head. "The gal spoke the truth, Lizzie, and you know it. Rachel's my sister, but that woman ain't got one bit of joy in her body."

Mama snorted. "The only joy in yours come from that bottle you keep in your back pocket."

"I told *you* and I told *Rachel* I'd come stay with her," said Uncle Willie. "I can help her out better than a eleven-year-old child, even if she is big as a he-horse. Rachel get out the bed to go to the bathroom, fall down, Belly sure can't help her up."

"Well, she sure don't want you there. You know Rachel don't stand for no drinkin in her house."

"She sick, she can stand a lot she can't stand if she's well. Hell, if I *didn't* drink, she'd drive me to it in a week."

Mama had enough and chased him onto the porch, where he sat with one ear at the window so he could hear every word she said. "Well," she said as she came back and stood at the screen door. "I can't make you go. I can only tell you to think about it." Her voice was soft, her shoulders slumped like Teeny's had been on the porch.

Guilt squeezed my heart. I was willful and loud, but just below that surface was the sensitivity that I had learned to hide in response to Uncle Willie's constant teasing. "Don't be mad, Mama," I whispered.

She took a deep breath. "Belly, I'm not mad. I understand why you don't want to go stay with Rachel. Now I know she ain't the easiest person to get along with. And I know there ain't much for you to do in Jamison. But you could always read. That's what you do all the time anyway."

"Aunt Rachel always fusses when I read. Talkin 'bout how I always got my head in a book."

"I know, Belly," said Mama. "But sometimes, well . . . sometimes we have to help other people, whether we want to or not."

She opened the door and went out.

My eyes misted. I sat a moment, looking at the table, the floor, listening to the tock-tock of the clock on the mantel. Then I got up and went to the door. Mama was sitting in a chair next to Uncle Willie. I wanted to go out to her, sit by her side, feel her hand on my head. But guilt held me back.

I stood pondering. I wanted to say something, make peace with her, so I blurted, "What kind of operation is Aunt Rachel gonna have, Mama? Like that time when I got my tonsils out?"

"Oh, Belly," said Mama with a sigh. "Somethin like that."

"Only they ain't goin down her th'oat," said Uncle Willie.

Mama leaned over and tapped him on the head. "I told you to mind your business, fool."

"Tonsils." Uncle Willie cackled and slapped his knee. "Hee hee. Tonsils."

My father's name was Tyler Beatty Anderson. My mother said he used to laugh at all his names, which were the surnames of his white relatives, his burden to bear since he was the last of the male Andersons. His father, William Beatty, was from a large family of Andersons who had lived in Pharaoh since before the Civil War. They were "white" colored people: they looked white but possessed the few drops of Negro blood that classified them otherwise. Near the end of the last century most of them decided to acknowledge the white side of their family. They left Mason County to join that great mass of hopeful souls migrating to the Wild West, where it was a shooting offense to question a man's background. A few of them stopped in Ohio, and one by one William's children left to join their aunts and uncles there and live the lives of free white men. William was the last of his tribe to go; he had remained in Pharaoh not for noble purposes but because his wife was too brown to be anything but the Negro that she was. When she died he persuaded my father, who was eighteen at the time, to go live in Ohio with the rest of their family. But Tyler Beatty Anderson was still crazy about Isabel Walker, his childhood sweetheart since the second grade. And in spite of his white skin he found it impossible to maintain the deception that his family practiced among the white people where they lived. After seven years in exile, he told his father and his other relatives that he missed being around colored people and colored food. He was raised colored and he was going back to Pharaoh and be colored. If any of them wanted to come visit he would be happy to see them; he would not stay in Ohio and spoil things for them. So at the age of twenty-five he returned home and married Mama and lived with her and my grandparents and hired out as a farmhand along with my Uncle Willie.

I was four years old when the United States entered World War II, five years old when Uncle Willie and my father left for the army, and still five when my father was killed six months after reaching the South Pacific. Before they left, my grandmother had died. While they were gone, my grandfather died.

So in 1942, at the age of thirty-two, my mother was a widow with a five-year-old child and had to earn a living. Most of the colored women in Pharaoh did day's work—cleaning house, the entire house, top to bottom, inside and out, as well as cooking, washing dishes, ironing, and any kind of labor that could be found for a colored woman to do around the house in a day's time. When my father and Uncle Willie first left, my mother tried it for a while; I howled every time she left me at the house of an obliging neighbor and she gave it up. But luck was with her. One summer morning she was in the backyard hanging up clothes when the Northern Virginia Power Company made its way down to our end of the earth; as she watched the men raising the poles and stringing the wires my mother got the idea of getting an electric washing machine and taking in laundry. She hooked up to the line and in one day we leaped from the nineteenth century into the twentieth. From an old galvanized tub used for washing clothes and bathing to a motorized wringer washer, from unwieldy flat irons to a sleek electric appliance, from oily-smelling kerosene lamps with smoky shades to electric fixtures with sunlight captured in a glass sphere. All the eerie shadows that leaped up the walls of my room at the whim of a flame jumping in a kerosene lamp suddenly were gone, and I was no longer afraid to go to bed at night.

One afternoon that same summer we had visitors. It was an afternoon so hot that the heat rose in waves from the earth and the leaves on the maple hung limply from the branches and the grass in front of the house curled over the terra-cotta ground in shock. My mother was on the front porch ironing. I was busy on the shady side of the house chopping weeds and making mud cakes for my dolls, who were propped against a box watching me with unblinking eyes.

"Somebody's coming, Belly," said Mama.

Enveloped by the waves of heat, the shimmering figures of a woman and a child, small in the distance, were moving up the dusty driveway, growing larger and larger until they stood at the fence that enclosed the yard. The woman, Brazil nut brown and alley-cat scrawny, wore a loose dress and a floppy straw hat that shaded her thin face; the girl, a little taller than I, was in a loose dress like the woman's. Her eyes were too big for her face; four skinny black pigtails curled out from her head.

My mother set the iron on its heel and went down to the fence. The women stood there and talked. All this time the strange woman had held the girl's hand tightly, shaking her when she tried to pull loose, but now she relaxed it and the little girl slipped her hand free and hung on the lower rung of the fence peeping at me; she eased a leg through, then her body, and suddenly ran toward me, but a sharp word from the woman jerked her back as if she were on a leash, and she shrank in such a way that I wanted to run over and hit the woman with my fist.

My mother called me over for introductions. The woman's name was Miss Myra Gibson; the child was her seven-year-old daughter Teeny. They had moved into the house across the field where Miss Clara Bell used to live. "Remember Miss Clara, Belly?" Miss Clara had been ill for the last twenty years with a "wasting" disease and spent the last ten years of her life in bed. My mother had taken me along on many of her visits, but all I had ever seen of the sick lady were two sunken eyes and a fragile, claw-like hand. My mother went on to explain that Miss Clara was Miss Myra's aunt, and now that she was gone, Miss Myra and her little girl had come from North Carolina to live in her house.

"Now you'll have a little friend to play with," said Mama. "Give her a hug."

Our mothers pushed us toward each other. Stiffly we pressed cheeks and limply hung our arms around each other. Then my mother pushed me toward Teeny's mother. "Don't you have a hug for Miss Myra, too?"

I had just seen Miss Myra's *other* side, and I would rather have kissed an adder than put my arms around this skinny woman in the floppy straw hat. I drew back against my mother and scowled. "She's mean."

"Belly!" gasped Mama. She gripped my shoulder, shook me.

Miss Myra did not seem offended. She looked down at me with a sour smile. "Yes, *ma'am*, Miss Belly. You right about that, I guess. Now we understand each other, there won't be no trouble."

In spite of this unfavorable beginning, Teeny and I were inseparable from that day on, and I managed to control my impulsive behavior around her mother.

Miss Myra did day's work three times a week, and three times a week Teeny was under the supervision of my mother. Just after sunup the colored drivers in the long black cars would pick Miss Myra and Teeny up at their house and drop Teeny off at our driveway and she and I would charge toward each other like wild things let out of a cage.

Just after dark the colored drivers in the long black cars would return and stop at the driveway and out would slip Miss Myra, foot and leg first, then her purse with the two dollars she had made that day tucked inside. Teeny would run to meet her while I waited on the porch. They would embrace, and Miss Myra's arm hugging Teeny to her side, they would walk up to the house.

My mother always had a cup of coffee ready, and she and Miss Myra and sometimes Uncle Willie would sit and talk for a while. Then Uncle Willie would drive Miss Myra and Teeny home.

In order to supplement her income, Miss Myra "did hair" two days a week in her kitchen. For seventy-five cents a head, she washed, straightened, and curled the hair of a select group of women who met her stringent requirements: hair not too nappy, not too short, not too long. Hair that would look "good" with a minimum amount of attention. Most important of all, the women must come at least every two weeks to ensure her a steady income.

She could not persuade my mother to accept money for taking care of Teeny, so she got around that by various donations throughout the year. Every spring she would send Teeny and me into the fields for dandelions, which she made into a delicious wine. Three jugs went to Mama and Uncle Willie. Throughout the summer she made jams and jellies from the blackberries that we picked; she also canned tomatoes and green beans that came from a small garden on the side of her house. My mother, not to be outdone, presented her with pan rolls, biscuits, and cakes, which Miss Myra greatly appreciated; her rolls were like rubber balls, her biscuits like hardtack, her cakes like dried sponges.

Through the years proximity made her and my mother companions, almost friends. But Miss Myra was a tippler and a gossip, too, and my mother discouraged her in those efforts by grunting or keeping silent. This was very effective; Mama's grunts were like slaps, her silences like dashes of cold water.

Those days that Teeny was at my house were among the happiest in my life. Those were the days when we roamed the fields and picked wildflowers and visited Miss Janie Green and played on her piano and went to the swimming hole. Then, abruptly, they ended. When Teeny was ten years old, Miss Myra determined that she was old enough to stay at home by herself. She did not need to come to my house anymore after school.

Teeny was even afraid to stop by our house after school. For the life of me I could not understand how someone could be with you constantly for four years, then abruptly be removed like an uprooted tree.

"But Miss Myra won't know you ain't home," I cried one afternoon after this nonsense had been going on for about two weeks.

Teeny shook her head. "She call on the phone. Every day, different times. She say she want to make sure I'm all right, but she checkin to see if I'm home."

At supper that night I complained to my mother about it. How Teeny was not allowed to come to see me. How her mother checked on her by telephone. Mama had not said anything when Miss Myra first told her that Teeny was old enough to stay alone. Now she pressed her lips together as if to refrain from any negative comments; but not Uncle Willie.

"Gotta watch people who check on their kids so close like that," he said. "They was probably devils when they was kids."

"Maybe Myra just wants Teeny at home," said Mama. "It's her right." That's all she said that night.

But the next day she said more.

Although Miss Myra had stopped Teeny from coming to our house, she continued to have the chauffeurs drop her off at our driveway after work three days a week, and while Teeny was at home alone Miss Myra continued to sit and pass time with Mama, enjoying as usual her little pick-me-up (a lot of whiskey and a little water) along with her cup of coffee. That evening when she stopped by Mama put the bottle of whiskey on the table, but did not put a glass in front of Miss Myra as she usually did. She sat down at the table, something else she did not do unless something was on her mind. She looked Miss Myra in the eye and dove right in. "Myra, how come Teeny can't stop by when her and Belly come home from school?"

Miss Myra's eyes bucked.

"Belly been asking her every day to stop in after school. They used to do their homework together, which I think was a good thing. But Teeny says she can't stop. Has to go home."

Miss Myra flicked a glance at me. "She got chores to do at home. I guess she want to get them done."

Now we all knew that Miss Myra had been loading Teeny down with all the housework from the moment she was able to reach the sink and hold the carpet sweeper, but Mama had never interfered. One day when I had remarked about it (I was always helping Teeny clean so she could come out and play with me) she shut me up with the observation that she didn't give me enough to do.

"Ain't nothin wrong with chores," she said now to Miss Myra. "Of course, I don't give Belly too much to do around the house when she's goin to school. Her homework and readin is her chores then. And this did not just come up. When did her work get done before?" said Mama. Miss Myra tried to answer, but Mama didn't give her a chance. "Teeny been here with us for four years. She's almost like a daughter to me. And she's like a sister to Belly. Then all of a sudden she don't come anymore. Like we did something you don't approve of. Something *wrong*." Mama got up and went to the sink and returned with a glass half filled with water and plunked it on the table.

"Indeed, Lizzie. You know better than that," said Miss Myra, eyes on the glass. "I just didn't want to take advantage. And now that Teeny's bigger and can stay home I didn't want her gettin on your nerves."

"My nerves is fine." Mama opened the bottle. "So if that's the only trouble, then I guess she can come after school then." She held the bottle over the glass of water and waited for an answer.

"Oh, yes, indeed," said Miss Myra.

Mama poured the whiskey into the water and Miss Myra picked up the glass and gulped the whiskey.

So Teeny came to our house again, but things were not the same. She always left before her mother came. More and more often, she passed my house and went straight home. If I wanted to see her for any length of time I went to her house. Like a horse or a cow, Teeny had been effectively tethered.

And it seemed that now my mother wanted to do the same to me.

Although I felt bad about not yielding to my mother's request to stay with Aunt Rachel after her operation, Uncle Willie's lighthearted treatment of the subject convinced me that it was not serious, and I went to bed with a clear conscience.

The next morning the sound of voices in the front yard woke me. I got up and went to the window. Miss Myra and Mama and Uncle Willie were standing beneath me in the yard. For some reason my mother looked up at the window. I drew back into the room. I heard the truck start up, and when I looked again, I could see Miss Myra in Uncle Willie's truck rattling down the driveway.

I heard the clap of the screen door shutting, then my mother's voice calling up the stairs. "Belly! You up?"

"Yes'm!"

"Come down here, then."

A moment later I was at the kitchen table sitting across from my mother, eating creamed dried beef and biscuits. She never fixed such a breakfast during the week. My regular fare was cornflakes or oatmeal and a cup of cocoa. I glanced at her occasionally while I ate. She was usually cheerful in the morning, singing, ironing, laughing. This morning she was subdued, preoccupied, stirring her coffee again and again, looking at me, then away, as if she had something unpleasant to tell me.

I didn't know what to think, except that it must have something to do with Miss Myra's visit. She never stopped at our house that early in the morning when school was out. I dawdled over my food, waiting for my mother to speak.

Finally she did. "Maybe you should go see Teeny this morning, Belly. You can go after breakfast."

That's why Miss Myra was here. She came to say that Teeny could come out today. But was it necessary for me to go this morning? "I was going to wait until later. Sometimes when you get the cramps, you don't feel good in the morning."

Mama looked at me oddly. "Cramps?"

"I thought that's why Teeny's sick."

Mama looked away from me, out of the window. Finally she said, "Teeny ain't sick, Belly." She hesitated, then, "I might as well tell you because you'll know sooner or later. Miss Myra's sending her away."

"Away!" That's what Teeny had been trying to tell me on the porch the day before. That Miss Myra was sending her away. "Why?"

"Miss Myra don't want you to know, but I'm tellin you anyway. "Teeny's goin to have a baby."

"A baby!" I had warned Teeny. I had warned her. Last fall when she started skipping Baptist Young People's Union meetings and going to the graveyard with Mitchell Looby. But she had dismissed me with a laugh and the arrogance that a thirteen-year-old holds over a girl two years her junior.

Mama slid me a look. "Did you know it?"

"Me!" I was outraged. "No!"

"Now don't get excited. I just thought she might've told you somethin since you two are together all the time."

"She didn't tell me *nothin*!"

My mother had asked me the wrong question. If she had asked if Teeny had been doing anything that might get her pregnant, I would have told her the truth, for however rough I was, I was not a liar. But perhaps it didn't occur to her to ask me such a question since she had never spoken to me about what girls did to get pregnant. My knowledge had been gleaned from giggling whispers in the schoolyard and one embarrassing conversation with Uncle Willie, which I had promised never to repeat.

We were digging up the garden one morning in April.

"Poppin out there, aintcha, gal. Any of these boys touchin your butt or tryin to feel your breasts?"

Mortified, I crossed my arms over my chest. "No!"

"Don't get your hackles up. Just askin. They gonna try it soon. And if they do, just kick 'em in the balls, hear?" He pointed to his crotch. "Put your foot right there, or if not your foot, put your knee right there as hard as you can."

My mouth was still open.

"Close your mouth. And no need to tell your mother what I been tellin you. Trouble with women is they always wait until too late to tell their gals how to protect theirselves." He closed one eye and put a cigarette in his mouth. "Teeny doin anything like that?"

I suspect now that he must have noticed Teeny's thickening body, which I had not. I shrugged.

"Mmmm hmmm. Well, just don't you do nothin like that, you hear me? Girls do stuff like that, they end up with diseases that'll set you on fire so you'll be walkin around gap-legged and scared to sit down. You want somethin like that to happen to you?"

I shook my head violently. "No, sir!"

"Just keep your body to yourself and you'll be all right."

The garden soil was worked into a fine silt that morning. And heeding Uncle Willie's advice, I kept that talk to myself.

Now I asked my mother, "Why's Miss Myra sending Teeny away to have the baby?"

"Oh, I don't know, Belly," said Mama, annoyed. "Because she's sick about it, I guess, her being the church mother and everything, she don't want people to know. Anyway, this morning she's sending Teeny to her brother in North Carolina."

That didn't make sense to me. "Everybody's gonna know about it when she comes back with it."

"Well," said Mama, "I guess Myra will cross that bridge when she comes to it." She collected the dishes and took them to the sink.

Suddenly I felt very sad. "She ain't gonna let her bring it back, is she, Mama." Every girl in the schoolyard knew that when girls got "in trouble" (no matter how they tried, that secret always got out) they were sent away to visit relatives, and when they returned their "troubles" were gone.

"Some people think children can't be raised right without a mother and a father," Mama said softly.

"I don't have a father."

"You have a father, Belly. Even if he's dead, you have a father. You can be proud of him and tell everybody who he is and that he died for his country. Teeny's baby won't be able to walk around and talk about its father. Oh, he'll know who his father is if he's raised here in Pharaoh, because everybody will whisper about it and the kids will tease him in school. But he'll be made to feel ashamed of his father and Teeny, too."

Ashamed. Suddenly I pictured myself the day before on that porch, rattling happily on about my plans for the summer. I remembered Miss Myra in the kitchen, listening, and Teeny's silence, too. Blinking, I ducked my head and pushed dried beef into my mouth. Oh, what a fool I had been.

I hated them both.

My mother was still at the sink. Now she turned to me, "Willie took Myra up to town to buy a few things for Teeny and get the tickets. Teeny's home alone now, and if you want to see her you can go now before Miss Myra gets back."

But my heart had twisted into a knot.

"And don't stay too long. I told Willie to bring Miss Myra by here first when they come back."

"I don't want to go see her." The words were like ice.

"Why not?"

"Because." I stared at the table. "Teeny knew she was goin away and she didn't even tell me."

My mother said quietly, "Teeny didn't know she was leavin. Myra and I just discussed it this mornin."

"She knew she was gonna have a baby and didn't tell me!"

"I guess Myra told the child not to tell you."

"She still could'a told me."

"Myra left her home crying. Seeing you before she leaves would make her feel better."

I kept looking at my plate.

My mother came and stood by my chair. "It's up to you, Belly. It's nine o'clock now and Willie and Miss Myra been gone almost an hour." She pressed my face against her stomach. "Go see her, honey. Go see your friend before she leaves."

I hesitated, then I jumped up and slipped into my shoes and was across the field on wings, my dress billowing in the wind. The grass was wet from a light rain the night before and my hem was wet when I arrived a few moments later on Teeny's porch. I slipped off my muddy shoes, then knocked on the door. A moment passed, a crack appeared, and I whispered into the opening, "It's me. Belly."

Two eyes peeped out at me. "Mama don't want me to see you!"

I was furious. "Well, I didn't want to see you neither! Mama made me come because we're supposed to be friends!" I pushed open the door and explained to her about Uncle Willie and my mother's plan to keep Miss Myra away. But we were too frightened to talk in the house. We locked the front door and ran through the house to the back, crossed the yard and climbed the hill where the giant oak tree stood, so that in case Miss Myra did appear, we could see her coming and Teeny could get back in the house in time.

We sat with our backs against the tree and stretched our legs out on the soft grass. I put my shoes in the sun to dry. We were high up, facing a forest with a small creek running through it, and just across from the trees was a steep cliff, as if the earth had been sliced away from the flat ground at the top. I looked down the hill where we sat, green and gently sloping, and remembered other days when we hunted tadpoles in the branch or rolled down the hill screaming with fright.

"We had a lot of fun rollin down this hill," I said.

"I know *I* ain't doin no rollin no time soon," said Teeny.

I looked over at her and laughed.

Yesterday morning I had noticed nothing different about her, but today she looked different, this round-bellied girl who sat beside me on the grass, her stomach resting on her lap as if she were holding a large melon under her dress. The dress she had worn before had been overly large. In this cotton smock she looked more adult, womanly. Her face seemed rounder, her chest fuller. The gathers just below her bust emphasized the roundness of her stomach.

I tried to make a joke. "I ought to call you Belly now."

Teeny grinned down at her stomach. "It is pretty big."

"When you gonna have it?"

She counted the months off on her stubby fingers. "Uh . . . July or August."

I did a quick mental calculation. "How do you know you got it in January?"

"I didn't *get* it in January. I got it in December. At Cora Looby's Christmas party."

My mother wouldn't let me go to that party. Those Loobys were loose, she had declared. And randier than a bunch of billy goats.

"Right in Mitchell's room," said Teeny.

"Weren't you scared you'd get caught?"

"Everybody was all drunked up."

"Bet that's not where you got it," I said. "Bet you got it in November in that shed in back of the church."

Oh, that shed, that shed. I glanced at Teeny, then away, still embarrassed by the memory. It rushed back, the musty smell of the church basement, the little group of girls and boys sitting in the basement of the church, Miss Myra's voice calling for Teeny from the top of the stairs, my panic, then the hurried dash out the back entrance, running across the narrow field, slipping on the gravels, across the rutted driveway, back to the graveyard and the shed, looking in the window. God. Teeny leaning back on the table, resting on elbows, Mitchell standing between her legs, her legs wrapped around Mitchell's bare behind, his pants and drawers around his ankles, her pink ones on the dirt ground . . . him thrusting, gasping, thrusting. Aghast, I shut my eyes and rapped on the window, then ran around to the door and pushed it open to call in, "Miss Myra lookin for you, girl!" And later, on the way home in a neighbor's car, Teeny's lie—"We was out lookin at the graves . . . Me and Belly gonna be buried right next to each other, ain't we, Belly?" And I, later, on her porch, in a state of fury, whispering, "You said y'all was only *neckin.*"

And now look at her. All my talking had been to no avail.

"Naw." Teeny shook her head. "I got my period after that. And I sure didn't go back to that shed no more. It was *cold.* And that table was *hard.*"

I looked at her stomach. "Well, how'd you hide it all this time? Your belly wasn't out like that last week. Now you look like you gonna pop open."

Teeny shrugged. "Mama trussed me up in a old girdle."

I was horrified. "Didn't it squash the baby?"

"Naw. Just pushed him back. He's okay. Feel." She took my hand and placed it on her stomach.

"I don't feel nothin."

"Wait."

Suddenly I felt a fluttering, a ripple. I snatched my hand away. "Ugh!"

Teeny doubled over laughing.

"Don't it make you sick, wigglin around inside you like that, like a tadpole?"

"Naw. I'm used to it."

I was still disgusted. "I wouldn't never get used to somethin like that." I leaned back on my elbow. "Miss Myra gonna let you keep it?"

"Sure I'm gonna keep it." Teeny's eyes narrowed. "What you ask me that for?"

I shrugged. "When Callie Tibbs had her baby her mother made her give it away."

"She didn't *make* her. Billy Miles' mother wanted it 'cause it was his, and she didn't have no grandchildren. And Callie didn't want no baby anyway. But ain't nobody gettin my baby."

"Well, you're only thirteen."

"So what?"

"So how you gonna take care of it?"

"Mama will help me."

"Miss Myra don't even want you to have it." I lowered my voice. "It's a wonder she didn't send you away before so you could get rid of it."

Teeny frowned. "Get rid of it."

"Well, ain't that what everybody does? If they can?"

"Maybe some girls do. But Mama don't believe in that. She say you git a baby, you gonna have it. Period."

"Okay, so if she's gonna let you keep it, why's she sendin you to North Carolina?"

"She don't want me to be around Mitchell, that's why."

"Is that what happened after Sunday school the other day? Miss Myra took you home?"

She didn't answer.

I changed my line of questioning. "You want a boy or a girl?"

"A girl. She's gonna have straight hair just like yours and Mitchell's. And even if it ain't good as yours it's gonna be curly and she gonna have real fine hair at the back of her neck, not no nappy kitchen like mine. I'm gonna let it hang in curls, and put pink ribbons on it. And put little gold earrings on her."

"You gonna pierce the baby's ears?" I grimaced and rubbed my earlobes. "Won't it hurt?"

Teeny didn't know. Her ears, like mine, had not been subjected to this treatment. "But lots of little babies in Baltimore have their ears pierced. It's the style. And they look so *cute*." Our discussion continued until we saw Uncle Willie's truck coming down the road with Miss Myra. Up we jumped and hurriedly said goodbye. There was no time for sadness or tears. Teeny gave me a quick hug and ran down the hill and into the back of her house. I made my way down the opposite side of the hill and ran along the ground by the little creek, then climbed up to the road. When I got near my house I waited to hitch a ride with Uncle Willie on his way back home.

At the supper table that evening Teeny was the main topic of conversation, and naturally I repeated her statement about piercing her baby's ears.

"Cute!" Uncle Willie dropped his knife. "I always knew them Gibsons was stupid, but this takes the cake. The way babies move their hands around, suppose it grabs ahold of that thing and gets a bloody ear. And suppose another little baby grabs it. Then she'll be the first one ready to fight that baby's mother."

I added fuel to the fire. "Teeny says it's the style in Baltimore."

"The style!" said Mama. "I didn't know babies was supposed to be in style. But punchin holes in a baby before it can drink out of a cup shouldn't have nothin to do with no style."

I knew a little bit more about style. "In the *National Geographic* I was readin about a tribe in Africa that puts pans in the babies' lips and the pans get bigger and bigger and their lips get longer and longer."

"That was the Ubangis," said Uncle Willie. "They started that for a reason. To stop other men from stealin their women and makin slaves out of them. And so now in their society to them that's a sign of beauty. The ones with the longest lips."

I stretched my bottom lip until it hurt. "I'd rather be a slave."

"A slave," said Uncle Willie. "Negroes done come a long way in this country when we can laugh about slavery. You wouldn't want to be one even if you had to cut them lips off."

"I was only jokin, Uncle Willie."

"Some things you don't joke about."

For a moment we ate without talking, but it wasn't in Uncle Willie's nature to stay angry for long. He returned to the subject we had been discussing. "And talkin about style, you should see what some of them natives in New Guinea do."

"What?" I said, happy to be on his good side again.

"They take this tree bark and make quinine out of it and put it in their hair to turn it red and blond. You should see some of them. Now they sure look weird, runnin around with that mahogany skin and that frizzy hair bleached in all kinds of ways. Hair on one head brown, red, blond. That to them is style."

"Well," said Mama, "*they* are heathens. But I don't know what this world is comin to when civilized Christian people take the chance of infectin their babies' ears just for style."

"Sure do make you wonder," said Uncle Willie.

Aunt Rachel was coming; we rose at dawn to get the house in order before she arrived. What *time* she was coming my mother was not sure, but she was coming *that day*; everything must be ready for white glove inspection before the sun was up too high.

"Rachel know what kind of house you keep, woman," grumbled Uncle Willie. "She been here often enough. Long as she got a clean bed to sleep in and a clean plate to eat off, she shouldn't be expectin too much more. You ain't got time to run around dustin and scrubbin like she do. You work for a livin."

I swept and dusted the middle bedroom, the one that had been Aunt Rachel's before she left home. I must not forget to change the bed. Even though the sheets were clean, Mama thought they smelled musty. Who liked to climb into a musty-smelling bed?

My mother cleaned the bathroom. She wanted to be sure it was thoroughly cleaned. We laughingly called it Aunt Rachel's other room; it was she who had persuaded Mama to have it installed four years earlier. Up until that time we had no indoor plumbing. We used the outhouse or a chamber pot; we took baths in the tin washtub: in the yard during the hot weather, in the kitchen during the winter.

But one summer day Aunt Rachel had retired to the outhouse to peruse the Sears catalog and stayed too long. A swarm of hornets, resentful of her lengthy intrusion, attacked her. Out she bolted, drawers looped around her ankles, screaming like a stuck pig. She swore she would never visit us again until a toilet was put inside. The following spring Uncle Avery, Uncle Willie, and Miss Janie Green's son Malachi added a bathroom onto the house.

At eight o'clock Mama and I paused in our housework to eat breakfast, Uncle Willie to take a bath and gulp down a cup of coffee before taking Teeny and Miss Myra to the bus station.

He glanced at me from the corner of his eye and said hesitantly, "Anything you want me to tell Teeny?"

I shook my head, unable to speak past the burr in my throat. I excused myself from the table and went up to my room and cried a little. When I came back down he was gone.

My mother glanced at me, then away. She seldom used words to comfort me. Her answer for most of my problems was work. Handing me the Dutch Cleanser, she said, "The tub has to be cleaned again, honey."

I swelled up in protest. "You just cleaned it!"

She laughed. "Before Willie took a bath."

I groaned and climbed the steps breathing fire. Uncle Willie, no matter how often he bathed, always left a black ring around the tub as if he sweated crude oil instead of water. Muttering and scrubbing, I bent over the tub. Misery turned to anger and washed away with the perspiration pouring down my face. I stood back and inspected the tub. Gleaming white for Aunt Rachel.

I was on the porch reading when Uncle Willie returned and flopped into his ladder-back chair.

"Whoo!" He picked up his bottle from its place at the side of the house and took a swig of whiskey. "Well, Teeny's gone."

I stopped rocking. My stomach quivered. The misery was still inside me after all. "I don't care."

"Oh, I see. You mad at Teeny, hunh. She ain't your friend no more."

"Nope."

" 'Cause she havin a baby."

I exploded. "No!" I sat for a moment, stiff. Tears stung my eyes. Mortified, I took a deep breath, and in a voice almost a whisper said slowly, "It's just . . . we made all these plans for this summer, and now she spoiled everything!"

Uncle Willie lit a cigarette. "Now how'd she do that, Belly."

"After the baby comes, she ain't gonna have no time like we did before." I bent my head to wipe my eyes with the hem of my dress, hoping Uncle Willie wouldn't notice and tease me. "And I'm not gonna go see her when she comes back, neither."

After a moment Uncle Willie said gently, "Well, maybe you'll change your mind."

"No I won't."

"Teeny's older than you, Belly. Right now she's a little ahead of you. It's like you and her was out for a walk, and she runs ahead of you and turns a corner. You don't see her for a couple of seconds, and you're mad and callin her name. But you catch up to her and you see her again. And you're so glad to see her you forget you were mad."

I stared down at my book. "No, I *won't.*"

"Soon as she get back you'll be right here holdin her baby."

How could Uncle Willie be that dumb. "She ain't gonna have no baby when she comes back," I said scornfully.

"Teeny tell you that?"

"No. She said Miss Myra's gonna let her bring it home. I didn't say nothin, but I bet she ain't. Everybody knows that when a girl goes away to have a baby she comes back without it. She usually leaves it with some cousin or aunt or somebody."

Uncle Willie leaned forward. "Why do you think Miss Myra won't let her bring it home?"

I repeated the answer my mother had given me. "*Because.* People would talk about her. And that would be embarrassin. And Miss Myra wouldn't like that. Mama says she's real upset."

"Oh, she is that, all right," said Uncle Willie. He blew out a stream of smoke. "Well, with Teeny gone, ain't gonna be nothin to do here 'cept stay home and read or walk up and down the road and get dusty. And your mama ain't gonna let you do too much of that, considerin."

I swelled up and started rocking. "I don't know why people always think that because somebody's friend did something, they're gonna do it too."

"Most kids do what their friends do. You know that, Belly."

"Well, what happened to Teeny won't happen to me, no matter how much I walk up and down the road. You gotta have a boyfriend to get a baby, and I ain't thinkin about no boys. And if I did have a boyfriend, I wouldn't do nothin to get a baby. Having a baby without being grown up and married is dumb. And I ain't dumb."

"No, you sure ain't dumb." Uncle Willie's eyes were steady on my face. "How'd you get to know so much?"

I stopped rocking. "I got eyes, don't I? I got a brain, don't I?" I started rocking again. "I got ears, ain't I? I hear what people say about girls who have babies if they ain't married. They call them whores and call the babies little bastards."

"Yes, ma'am, Miss Belly."

He only called me that when I was being fresh, but I didn't think I was being sassy. "It's true."

He nodded. "I know. But since you're so smart and Teeny's so dumb, maybe it's better you won't be friends no more."

My mouth opened, then I snapped it shut. After a while I said, "I didn't say we wouldn't be friends no more. I just said I was mad at her, that's all."

"Oh, is that what you said," said Uncle Willie.

I scowled and rolled my eyes, then jerked my elbow onto my knee and clapped my chin into my hand. We sat in silence. Uncle Willie stared into the distance. After a while I leaned back and listened to the creak of the chair as I rocked, rocked, rocked.

By midmorning the house was beginning to smell like a holiday feast: baked ham, turnip greens, macaroni, lemon custard pie. Dough for the rolls was rising in a crock near the stove. The kitchen table was covered with a pearly white damask cloth; as I laid the napkins under the forks next to the good china plates, my mother stood back and, hands on hips, looked around the kitchen and nodded. The house was ready.

"Well, I'm worn out," she said. "I'm goin on the back porch and take a nap."

I was exhausted, too. I went into the dining room and fell into a chair and fanned myself with an old newspaper and watched Uncle Willie getting ready to make his daily rounds delivering the laundry that Mama took in. Twice a day Monday through Friday he picked up and delivered the freshly ironed clothes, neatly folded and stacked in wicker baskets, to the ladies who used my mother's service. Weekends he reserved for himself, conceding on Saturdays to chauffeur my mother and (more often than not) Miss Myra to the stores and me to the movies in Lambertville, and on Sundays me to Sunday school and Mama to church whenever we felt the need to attend. Since Miss Myra *lived* in church she made separate arrangements with members of the congregation for that service. This morning he was working hurriedly: because of that side trip with Teeny and Miss Myra to the bus stop, he was a little later than usual, and Uncle Willie became crotchety whenever he was thrown off schedule.

"Can I go with you this morning, Uncle Willie?"

He was tucking a cotton coverlet into the sides of a basket where my mother had carefully stacked the clothes she had ironed.

"I guess so." He threw a coverlet at me. "Here, tuck this over that basket and I'll be ready to go. Just tell your mama you goin with me."

I ran to the back porch. My mother was asleep on a little cot, her mouth open, snoring lightly. "I'm goin with Uncle Willie," I whispered from the doorway. I was taking no chances. If I woke her up, she might tell me to make the pan rolls. I dashed out to the truck but Uncle Willie made me go back inside for my shoes. I ran back with them in my hands and a few minutes later we were bouncing down the highway.

"We goin by Mrs. Chapman's?"

Mrs. Chapman was a wealthy white widow who lived on an estate on the other side of Mason County. Uncle Willie had been the Chapmans' gardener before he joined the army. Although he got along with her well enough, many of the colored people who worked for the family did not hold Mrs. Chapman in high regard. Among the litany of reasons were these facts: that she was nothing but a piece of white trash from New York City who had latched on to Bill Chapman Junior one night when he was drunk, that his father had almost died when Bill Junior brought her home as his wife (and did pass away the following year), and that she didn't know which side of the plate to put a knife and fork on. None of that mattered to me since Mrs. Chapman was a prime source of the books that filled the shelves in my bedroom.

"You know we goin by Mrs. Chapman's," said Uncle Willie. "That's why you asked to come along."

"No, I didn't."

"Yes, you did."

"I read most of the books she gave me the last time."

"Well, she gonna ask you about 'em."

We delivered her laundry last; we drove up the long tree-shaded driveway, then around to the rear of the house. Uncle Willie got out and went to the back door and rang the bell. A large colored woman opened the door. Miss Josephine Butler, known throughout Mason County for her wagging tongue as well as her cooking, which, from her size, indicated she loved to eat as well. She was round as an apple, with skinny legs and arms and feet so long they looked like paddles.

"Mornin, Willie."

"Mornin, Miss Pheeny. I got the laundry."

"You a little late."

"Yeah. Got sidetracked."

"Come on in." She held the door open for him. "I'll get Mrs. Chapman."

I slipped on my shoes, got out of the truck, and walked around behind Uncle Willie. "Hi, Miss Pheeny."

"Hi there, Belly! My, ain't you gettin tall. Then all them Walker women is tall."

"Yes'm."

"How's your mother?"

"Fine."

Uncle Willie went in with the basket. Miss Pheeny held the door until I passed through. "Got a piece of caramel cake for you."

Miss Pheeny made caramel cakes that melted in your mouth. I squeezed into a seat behind the big oak table, ready for the treat.

"Don't forget to cut me a piece," said Uncle Willie.

Miss Pheeny laughed deep in her throat. "I ain't lost my mind yet, Willie Walker."

Uncle Willie went into a room off the kitchen to set the basket down. In a minute he returned and sat down. Miss Pheeny put a slice of cake on a butter plate in front of him, then another in front of me.

"Well, how's everybody down your way," said Miss Pheeny. She leaned against the stove and crossed her arms across her bosom in the stance of a woman ready to engage in gossip.

"Still kickin," said Uncle Willie.

Such a generous slice of cake deserved a better answer than that. "Aunt Rachel's comin to visit today," I said through a mouthful of caramel goo.

"Oh? Thought she usually came in August for all day meetin," said Miss Pheeny, shifting her eyes from me to Uncle Willie.

"Changed her schedule," he mumbled.

Her eyes shifted back to me. "How long she gonna be?"

I felt Uncle Willie's eyes. I was walking on eggshells. "I don't know."

" 'Bout a week," said Uncle Willie.

Eyes back to Uncle Willie. "Maybe I'll get down there before she leaves." Miss Pheeny could keep that promise; unlike most colored women in Mason County she did not have to depend upon the mood of her husband or a gracious neighbor to go places. Miss Pheeny Butler *drove*. She was the only colored woman I knew for a long time who had a car at her disposal, thanks to the family taxi business. "Anyway, ain't seen Lizzie in a while."

"Welcome anytime," said Uncle Willie.

Mrs. Chapman came in. Those attributes that had caused the downfall of Bill Chapman had long ago wrinkled, drooped, or withered away. She had once been tiny and tantalizingly round; now she was short and unpleasantly plump. The bloom on her cheeks was replaced with pink rouge; her eyes, once large and brown, sank into her face like watermelon seeds pressed into floured biscuit dough. Her hair was silver blond, from a bottle, her lips very, very pink, from a tube.

And she gushed like a geyser. "Good mornin, Willie! And hello there, Belly! Well, Pheeny, I wasn't going to have any of your cake, but now that I see it, I just can't resist! Just a tiny piece." She sat down across from Uncle Willie. "Now, Willie, I believe that's five dollars I owe Lizzie. I hope she hasn't lost anything this time. Last week it was a satin slip. With lace at the bottom. I'm sure I sent it to her. I've looked all over the house and it isn't here." She nibbled at the cake. "Pheeny, this cake is simply out of this world! We need to commercialize your recipe. You'd make a *fortune*!"

Miss Pheeny laughed. "I don't have no patent on that recipe. Everybody I know use the same one."

Mrs. Chapman winked at me. "Don't you think it's delicious, Belly?"

"Yes'm."

Uncle Willie folded the money and put it in his shirt pocket. "I'll tell Lizzie about the slip."

"I'm not saying that anything is *wrong*. It's just that I can't find it and I'm sure I sent it out last week. I always wear it with my beige chiffon and I wore that dress to Mrs. McClellan's soiree last Tuesday and if I wore the dress I had to wear the slip and if I wore the slip I certainly sent it out to be washed."

She subsided a moment. Then, "Have you been readin those books I sent you, Belly?"

"Yes'm," I said.

"She stay buried in them," said Uncle Willie.

"I've read a lot of them."

"Which ones?" said Mrs. Chapman, winking at Miss Pheeny as if my words were suspect.

I rattled off the names. "Well, *Uncle Tom's Cabin, The Five Little*

Peppers, A Little Princess, The Secret Garden, Otto of the Silver Hand—"

"My goodness!" said Mrs. Chapman.

Miss Pheeny was also impressed. "You read that many books since you was last here?"

"More'n that," I said. "I just can't remember the names." I frowned, trying to remember. "Unhh, *The Little House on the Prairie* . . . I think that was the name of it."

"Oh, she reads, all right," said Uncle Willie again.

"Do you *remember* all those stories?" said Mrs. Chapman.

"Yes, ma'am."

"Tell me about *Otto of the Silver Hand*. I've never heard of it."

"Well, it's about mee-dee—" I stumbled. "Medi-*e*-val days. About knights and lords and ladies. And castles. And this boy, Otto, he's a son of a noble. And he—somehow he gets his hand cut off in a battle when he's tryin to escape from a castle and they make him a silver hand and he becomes a great knight."

Mrs. Chapman's eyebrows ascended to her blond bangs. "My! Your uncle Willie should be very proud of you." She stood up. "I'm very happy to give you all our old books, Belly. The children have moved so far away, and I haven't any room for them. I always thought they'd want them for their children, but"—she laughed—"I guess I'll never be a grandmother. So you're welcome to them, dear." She headed for the room where Uncle Willie had set the basket of clothes. "I have them in here, Willie. In these boxes."

After they left the room, Miss Pheeny came over and hugged me. "Mmmmm! You sure showed that hussy. She didn't believe you read them books. You keep it up. Show all these folks." She sniffed. "Hmph. Commercialize my cake recipe. I could put all the ingredients in a box and if I let her mix it, the cake wouldn't even rise. It's the *person* doin the cookin that makes the cake taste good, not the writin on the box. That's what they don't understand."

Uncle Willie came through the kitchen with his first box of books. There were two more, he said. I waited outside while he got them, and giddy with anticipation, I thanked Mrs. Chapman and got into the truck. Uncle Willie revved the motor, and just before we took off, Miss Pheeny ran out and pressed a waxed paper package into his hand. "For Lizzie," she whispered. "Tell her that slip was here *yesterday*. I seen it with my own eyes. Don't let that woman bamboozle her. Wore it to a *swahray,* my foot." She touched her head and whispered. "She ain't been right since *he* died."

C h a p t e r **5**

The summer after Miss Myra had started keeping Teeny at home, I was hard to live with. It was the first time in four years I had no constant companion. I slunk around the house slamming doors, feeling sorry for myself. And Teeny herself, who was then eleven, was not as much fun as she used to be. She had turned away from running in the fields and picking blackberries and wading in the creek and was inclined to stay on her porch and read *True Romance* or those silly magazines that contained the latest gossip about her favorite movie stars. I was not interested in either subject, so I spent less time with her and more time at home and drove my mother and Uncle Willie to distraction.

Uncle Willie had found an answer to my dilemma. Occasionally he cleaned out cellars and hauled the trash to the landfills in Mason County. Magazines and books were often tossed out with old mattresses, broken furniture, and discarded toys. One Saturday morning he found in a trashy cellar piles of tied-up books that he decided might be put to better use. He threw them into a box and brought them home and dropped the heavy carton onto the porch and yelled into the kitchen where I was ironing handkerchiefs for Mama. "Belly! I got somethin for you!"

I ran outside and saw the boxes and dropped down next to them. "What is it?"

"Somethin to keep you busy," he growled. "And keep you from drivin me and your mama crazy."

"Must be a miracle," said Mama, who had followed me outside.

Uncle Willie had tied the boxes up tightly with heavy cord. He took a penknife from his back pocket and cut the cord on the first box with a snap.

I quickly opened the box. Inside the box were blue books, green books, yellow books, tan books; I opened them eagerly and looked inside. Books with large and small print, books with pictures and without pictures. Dusty, musty, mildewed books, many of the pages still uncut. My mother dusted them and wiped them with water and bleach. I split the pages with Uncle Willie's knife.

From that day on I became an avid reader. Uncle Willie kept me amply supplied with stories and novels from this century and the last. At first he culled discarded books and magazines from his trash collections, but soon many came from the well-to-do white people in and around Mason County who heard of his requests for books and saved them out for him. He had recruited Mrs. Chapman as a donor one day when he was delivering laundry; along with some other trash she had asked him to take to the landfill she had included a box of books. He had inquired if she had any more she wanted to get rid of, and ever since she had donated books of her own and those she collected from the households of various acquaintances.

Soon books were stacked in piles in my room. They had to be shelved. On one trash pile Uncle Willie found a rickety bookcase. He brought it home and brushed it off and nailed a few boards across the back to strengthen it, then anchored it against the wall in my room near my bed and filled it with books; as more came he added more shelves until I was surrounded by walls of books. And I retreated to this room to read and dream; and strangely enough, Teeny and I became closer again, for she would come and read her magazines uninterrupted (Miss Myra seemed to think that romance, fiction or otherwise, might have a corruptive influence on her), and we spent many peaceful hours lying across my bed reading and eating peanut butter and jelly sandwiches.

As soon as we got home from Mrs. Chapman's that day, and Uncle Willie had set the last box of books on the porch, I dropped down and sat cross-legged near one so I could inspect my treasures and make a pile of those I intended to read first. My method of selection was simple. The thick books with long, unbroken paragraphs of tiny print I returned to the box. I would read them later. Next to the box I stacked a pile that consisted of books I inspected for pictures that piqued my interest; they nearly always had an exciting story. If the book had no pictures, it must pass another print test: larger print meant an easier story.

Then I would read for content: the first page, a few pages from the middle, and the last few paragraphs. I liked happy endings; fortunately most of the books met that requirement. If I could ascertain that they did not, I tossed them back in the box for those desperate times when I would run out of reading matter. Finally I finished. I inspected my pile of first selections and arranged them neatly on top of the other books in the box.

For my first reading session of the summer I chose a thick book called *The Pink Fairy Book*. It was loaded with pictures and long stories. The princesses were beautiful, the princes handsome, the ogres more hideous than any I had ever seen. I stood up, pushed the box carefully against the side of the house so the books would not fall off, and started to head for the back of the house to read belly down on the cot in the screened porch.

The sound of a car coming up the driveway stopped me. I turned to look. A black sedan was rolling toward the house with two stiff figures in the front seat. Aunt Rachel and Uncle Avery.

I searched hurriedly for my shoes. Not finding them near the boxes, I ran into the dining room, where my mother was ironing, talking to Uncle Willie. "Mama! Aunt Rachel's comin'!"

"Uh, oh." Uncle Willie got up from the table and headed for the back of the house.

My mother set the iron down and smoothed her hair and headed for the front porch.

I laid my book on the table and ran upstairs to look for my shoes, then remembered I had left them in the truck and galloped back downstairs into the kitchen, intending to run around the side of the house to the front, where the truck was.

Uncle Willie was sitting on the back step. One of my shoes dangled from his finger. "Lookin for these?"

I grabbed my shoes and headed for the front door.

"Don't I even get no thanks?" called Uncle Willie.

I ran back. "Thanks, Uncle Willie." Still carrying my shoes, I hopped off the back stoop and ran around the house to the front.

The sedan was in the yard under the maple tree. The trunk hood was standing up, and someone, Uncle Avery, I supposed, was setting suitcases on the ground.

My mother and Aunt Rachel were standing on the porch talking. Aunt Rachel was taller than Mama, but she also had the lean body of every Walker I ever knew. Her skin was a lighter brown than Mama's, but both had high cheekbones and crimpy black hair that straightened out with a bristle brush, water, and Dixie Peach hair pomade.

I sidled up to the porch and hopped up to put on my shoes.

Aunt Rachel caught me from the corner of her eye. "What you carryin them shoes around for, Isabel? And what you sneakin around for out there in this hot sun? Come on up here and give me a kiss."

I dragged myself up onto the porch and suffered a dry peck on the forehead along with a few observations about me directed to my mother. "Well, Tyler sure named her right when he named this child Isabel after you. Just like you when you was her age."

"I wasn't that tall when I was eleven," said Mama. "But then, her father was tall."

"Gonna be big as a he-horse," said Aunt Rachel, inspecting me as if I were on the block. " 'Course, her hair's straight. And she done lightened up considerable since I last seen her. 'Course every time I see her she been out in that hot sun blackin up for three months."

"And her daddy looked white," said Mama. "So what do you expect the child to look like."

"Sure ain't no pale-skinned Walkers. Papa took care of that. And she got your eyes. And that same look—bold."

Uncle Willie stepped onto the porch with two suitcases. "Let the gal alone, Rachel. Belly, open the door so I can take these bags in. They ain't full of feathers."

"Well," said Aunt Rachel, turning her attention to the porch. "Your furniture looks nice. This old wicker holds up pretty good." She sat down in a rocking chair.

"Yes, it does," said Mama. "Willie keeps it painted nice." She sat down next to Aunt Rachel.

I quickly got out of their way and retreated to a chair on the side porch, out of eyeshot, but within earshot. I was sure that Mama and Aunt Rachel would be discussing me at one point or another. I opened my book and pretended to read in case anyone suddenly came upon me.

"Well, when's she comin," said Aunt Rachel.

Already! I scrunched down in my chair and scowled.

I strained to hear Mama's answer. "She ain't made up her mind yet."

"Made up *her* mind," said Aunt Rachel, sounding as if she had swallowed a fish bone.

"Yes, *her* mind," said Mama.

"I wish a child of mine would tell me what she's gonna do or not do at her age."

"She ain't a child of yours," said Mama.

And that's just why I ain't comin. You too mean.

"When *do* you think she'll make up her mind."

Never!

"School's just out. She'll get bored soon."

Never.

"Well, I got to know as soon as possible. Else I'll have to make some other arrangements."

"When do you have to know by?"

"I can go in the end of July or the middle of August. I'd rather go in July and get it done with. I'll call Myra by the end of the month. You should know by then. Why that Chesapeake and Potomac can't get a telephone line down in here, I'll never know. Worse than the pony express."

"Cost too much for them to come any further for just one house. Only reason a telephone's in Myra's house is because Miss Clara was sickly."

"Hmph. If you was white you would have one."

Rocking sounds, then Aunt Rachel. "Avery! You need to move that car from under that tree before the birds doodoo all over it! Stuff will bake to clay out there in this heat!"

"That's a new car, ain't it?" said Mama.

"Avery got it last winter. The other one was fallin apart."

"It's nice."

"Don't know why you and Willie don't get a car instead of drivin around in that old truck."

"If we get anything new it'll be another truck. Else how am I gonna deliver my laundry."

"In the back of the car."

"Truck's better. Ain't nobody but me and Belly."

"Hmph."

Sounds of rocking, then Mama. "Avery finished takin out the livin room walls yet?"

"Yes, indeed. He finished that last March. Got new carpeting, too. And some furniture."

"Must look nice."

"You'll see it if you come."

"How's things in Jamison," said Mama.

"Still kickin."

"How's Miss Mattie."

"You tell me. I seen her in the Safeway the other day buyin food enough for six people. And ain't nobody in that house but her. Still cookin like she got a house full."

"That's a habit hard to break," said Mama.

"I don't know what Avery's wipin that car off for," said Aunt Rachel. "Avery, why you wipin that car off now? Why don't you wait til this evenin when it's cooler?"

From a distance, Uncle Avery, plaintively. "Rachel, I think I know if it's too hot to wipe the bird mess off this car."

"Told him not to drive it under that tree when we come up the drive," said Aunt Rachel. "Got a head like a rock."

"What man ain't," said Mama.

More rocking. Then, "Thought you'd come to Jamison more often since your friend is still there," said Aunt Rachel. "You all was so close when you was in school."

"Friend! Who?"

"Ophelia Love."

"Ophelia. She still in Jamison? I thought she went back to New York right after her father's funeral last November."

"So did I. But Mattie said she's still there. Sick. Somethin with her heart. From that rheumatic fever when she was small."

"Well, this is news to me. I sure did not know that."

"Neither did Avery. He usually know everything that goes on in Jamison. Mattie says she been stayin there now until she can straighten things out. I think she wants to sell the house. Though I don't know how she thinks she can if nobody even know she's there and wants to sell it. I knowed she was there for about a month after Deacon Love died because I seen her in church a few times last winter. But when I didn't see her no more, I was sure she left. She sure don't come out of that house. Mattie says she only come out at night onto that back porch. Hmph. Livin like a skunk."

"And how do Mattie Hearns know that."

"Don't she live right next door? The only way she knows somebody is alive in there is when she hear the piano. 'Course, after Ophelia been in New York *City* all them years, I guess ain't nobody in Jamison sophisticated enough for her to bother with. Anyway, when Mattie went over to see if anything was wrong, she come to the door and opened it a crack and said she didn't need any help. Wouldn't even let Mattie in the house. At least that's what Mattie said."

"I guess that makes it gospel, if Mattie Hearns said it."

"I don't know about no gospel. It's just unhealthy, stayin there cooped up like that. Wrappin herself up like she in a cocoon. She sure ain't gonna turn into no butterfly."

"Well. When I bring Belly over, I'll stop by and see her."

Me!

"Thought you just told me she wasn't comin," said Aunt Rachel.

"I didn't say no such thing," said Mama. "I said she didn't make up her mind yet."

"Same thing," said Aunt Rachel.

"You ever take time to make up *your* mind?" said Mama.

"*I'm* forty years old," said Aunt Rachel.

More rocking sounds.

"Belly." Uncle Willie's voice came from the back of the house. I turned. He was standing at the corner. "Come here," he said, and disappeared.

I got up and went back. He was sitting under the maple. He pointed to a chair. "Sit down."

I rolled my eyes, but I sat down without a word.

"Listenin to people's conversations again. I done told you about that. One day it's gonna get you in trouble."

"Well, don't nobody ever tell me nothin!"

"Some things you don't need to know."

"Well, they wasn't talkin about nothin anyway."

He got up. "Well, you sit here and read your book. Not on the side porch where they can't see you listenin to every word."

"Mama knows I was there."

"Sometimes your Mama ain't got the sense of a horsefly."

"I'm'a tell her you said that, too."

"Maybe I'll tell Rachel you was listenin."

That shut me up. Uncle Willie turned to go, but before he left, I wanted to appease him, and I knew exactly how to do it. Pass along a bit of gossip. "They was talkin about somebody named Ophelia Love. Aunt Rachel don't like her."

Uncle Willie started. "Ophelia Love?" He came back to his chair and sat down. "What was they sayin about her?"

I had him, and I was going to make him work for every bit of information I gave him. I shrugged. "Nothin."

"You just said they was talking about her."

"They was." I stopped.

He studied me, nodding and chewing on his upper lip. "Mmm hmmm, you want to play games." He stood up. "I'll just go ask them and say you told me."

"No!" I said. "I mean Aunt Rachel said she was still in Jamison and that she was gonna sell her house."

Uncle Willie eased back into his chair. "Why do you say Rachel don't like her?"

"The way she was talking. Like she don't never leave her house except at night like a skunk and she think she's too grand to be around the people in Jamison."

Uncle Willie nodded reflectively. "All that sounds like something Rachel would say about Ophelia."

"Well, who is she?"

"Well, Ophelia used to live across the field when we were kids. Her and your mother was good friends. Kind of like you and Teeny."

I was curious. I did not recall hearing that name before.

"Sure you did," said Uncle Willie. "Lizzie went to Ophelia's father's funeral last winter and you wouldn't go to Jamison because you didn't want to stay at Rachel's and she had to take the bus because I had to stay here with you, remember?"

I remembered now, but Uncle Willie was adding a new twist to the story. The fact was that Miss Myra had volunteered to keep me while Uncle Willie drove Mama to the funeral and came back, but he had refused to go because he didn't feel like going. Mama threw pots around the kitchen for three days and swore she would take the bus before she asked him to take her anywhere again.

"Anyway," Uncle Willie was saying, "Ophelia's house burned down when they was in high school, and the family moved to Jamison. Then Ophelia went to stay in New York City with her aunt to finish high school and go to college."

"Did she ever come back?" I said.

"Once in a while, to see her mother and father. And when she did Jamison is far enough away that she only got to see your mother once or twice. Then they just lost touch."

I sighed.

Uncle Willie lit a cigarette. "It's hard to make friends down here in Pharaoh. Hard for your mother as well as you. Unless you stay in that church, you don't get to see many people. And you can't blame folks for not lettin their girls come down here after school. Like comin to the end of the earth. So it's mighty lonely, sometimes, I guess."

I threw my head back. "*I* don't get lonely. I don't like none of them old fresh girls at school anyway. Teeny's the only friend I need."

"Sometimes that's good to have just one friend, sometimes it's not." Uncle Willie stood up. "Well, I'm goin around the front to talk to Avery. "And you come along." He went toward the back steps. "I gotta go in the house a minute. When I come out, I want to see you on the front porch, not the side porch."

I went slowly to the front of the house, thinking about what Uncle Willie had just told me about Mama losing her friend. I was beginning to realize that I had not appreciated Teeny all those years. Now I was going to see how it was without her.

It is common knowledge that many of the mixed children in the South were the result of the slave masters' sexual peccadilloes among their female slaves; however, many of these children were the products of romantic liaisons between black and white men and women. Black/English and Black/Irish mixed breeds with skin tones from pink to plum were sprinkled liberally throughout Mason County. At the end of the century many an uninformed census taker walked into a yard of colored folks, looked at them, and recorded them as white, then in the course of taking other vital information discovered otherwise and had to scratch out "white" from his records and write "colored" underneath.

Uncle Avery was the child of a romantic liaison. His father was Henry Swann, a colored farmhand; his mother was Helen Carville, daughter of the farmer he worked for. Their story was as tragic as those found in the gothic romances that abounded then and now, but unlike the heroes and heroines in those stories, their passions could not be quenched by quick kisses, liquid looks, or soulful sighs.

One spring afternoon about a year into the romance, Farmer Carville went into the barn to tend to a sick cow and heard suspicious moans coming from the hayloft. Upon investigation, he found his daughter and his colored farmhand thrashing around in the straw. Right after the birth of the child, at the fiery urging of the local Klan leader and over the objections of the Carvilles, who had made plans for shipping the father to the hinterlands with his offspring, Henry Swann was hanged from an oak tree on the edge of the Carville prop- erty, near a well-traveled road so that all who passed could see what happened when a nigger took advantage of a white man's daughter.

After the hanging, Lena kept Avery with her. Mr. Carville loved his daughter and eventually became attached to the child who had his daughter's gray eyes and elfin face; he looked as much like a Carville as the other grandchildren at his knee. He was a suntanned replica of himself when he was a child. When Avery was four years old, his grandfather died of a heart attack. Lena's brothers, ever mindful of their children's property rights and their own status in the community, sent the boy to live with Henry Swann's mother. Lena visited the child for a while, but eventually she moved away and word got back that she had married and had other children. Avery clung to the memory of those visits by the gentle mother who smelled like roses; but with time, like all memories, they faded.

I remember Uncle Avery as a quiet, handsome man, tall, lean, and suntanned with curly gray hair and eyes that were more gray than blue. He must have been almost fifty years old that summer. *Old*, by the standards of an eleven-year-old. He smoked a pipe that he held clamped between strong white teeth. He removed it when he talked, which was seldom. He was a man of long silences and few words.

When I was younger I counted Aunt Rachel's visits as one of those temporary unpleasantries that people must suffer in this world, like a toothache or the mumps. As I grew older and observed her and Uncle Avery together, I began to wonder why someone so diplomatic would marry someone so brash. That thought had been in my mind as I lis- tened to her nagging him about the bird mess on the car, and I remem- ber leaning forward in the rocking chair to look at him, waiting to see what he would do. Now as I came around the side of the house from the backyard I could see that he was still under the maple tree, and having silently dismissed Aunt Rachel's advice, had followed his own inclination and was steadily polishing the black sedan with a large yellow cloth.

Now Aunt Rachel's voice again, surprised as if something new had caught her attention. "What in the world!"

I hurried around front and saw Aunt Rachel standing over the boxes of books sitting at the edge of the porch. She touched one with her foot. "What in the world is this?"

My heart sank. Since she had not noticed the books when she first came, I was hoping that Uncle Willie might get them upstairs without any comment from her. But I could see that I was not going to escape without hearing about the slothful habits that reading engendered. I ran up onto the porch and stood behind my mother.

I think Mama had also had enough of Aunt Rachel, for she sounded irritated when she answered. "Books, Rachel. What do they look like?"

Uncle Avery had come up to see what Aunt Rachel was exclaiming over. He took his pipe from his mouth. "Looks like books to me, Rachel."

"Any fool can see they're books," said Aunt Rachel. "I mean it's so many of them. Where in the world did they come from?"

At that moment Uncle Willie came out of the house. "What? Oh, them books. I just took them off the truck. I ain't had time to take them up to Belly's room yet."

"Belly's room!" Aunt Rachel's laugh crackled like cellophane. "Where's she gonna sleep? Last time I was down here there was books piled from the floor to the ceiling."

"She got bookshelves," said Uncle Willie.

Aunt Rachel grunted. "She must keep her head in a book." She looked at me. "Ain't you got nothin else to do? You big enough to be cookin and cleanin and helpin your mother out with the washin and ironin."

I scowled. I couldn't say I did those things with any regularity so I said nothing.

Mama laid her hand on my shoulder. "She does all those things when I tell her to."

"Hmph." Aunt Rachel, looking away from me back to Mama. "You still ain't said where they come from."

"Mrs. Chapman," said Mama. "Willie was out there one day last year and Mrs. Chapman was clearin out her attic. He seen all these books she had boxed up and said Belly would like to have them. So she keeps givin him books."

"Today Belly told her how many she read, and the woman's eyes bucked out of her head." Uncle Willie pulled my plait. "Told me I should be proud of her."

"She was right about that," said Uncle Avery.

"Ain't nobody said she shouldn't read," said Aunt Rachel. "Just need to find other things to do as well so she can be useful when she run out of books."

"Well, maybe she won't run out of books," said Mama quietly.

"If she do she can read them again," said Uncle Willie.

"How many books you think are there, Belly?" said Uncle Avery.

"About a hundred, I bet."

"Tell you what. Every one you read, you mark it down. Give you a nickel for each one."

"A nickel!"

"But you got to tell me the story so I know you read it."

That would be no problem. "Yes, sir!"

"She'll give your ears a real workout," said Uncle Willie.

"Well, I'm used to that," said Uncle Avery.

Aunt Rachel looked at him. Didn't say anything. Just looked.

Uncle Avery didn't seem to notice. Just drew on his pipe, but it was out. He took it from his mouth and knocked it against a post and said to Mama, "Well, Lizzie, what you got for lunch?"

It was in times like those that I wished that there was more to our family than Uncle Willie and Mama, that there were other sisters that Aunt Rachel could visit. But the Walker family had petered out with Uncle Willie, and Aunt Rachel was childless. No sisters or brothers, and, of course, since Uncle Willie had not married, no Walker cousins for me. None that he cared to acknowledge, in any case. And none (acknowledged) on the Anderson side of my family. So without a cousin I could name, I was subjected to the undiluted attention that childless aunts and uncles bring to only nieces, and Aunt Rachel and Uncle Willie continually jerked me around like children fighting over a rag doll; Uncle Willie was determined that I should be a free, informed spirit; Aunt Rachel that I be a credit to her vanity.

After lunch I went to my room to read. On the dresser was a picture of my mother and father. He was holding me on his arm. His arm was about her waist, they were smiling into the camera. My dim memories of him, his laugh, his teasing smile were of a man in a dream, a man who would be forever young and happy. Would he and Mama, if he were here now, act like Aunt Rachel and Uncle Avery? As much heat in that relationship as comes from a cold stove, Uncle Willie had observed more than once.

I flopped onto my bed with a scowl. I wasn't ever going to get married. I sighed and opened *The Pink Fairy Book.* Ugh. An ugly little bowlegged man with poppy eyes stared at me. I turned to the middle of the book and began reading. Eventually I fell asleep.

A few hours later I awoke feeling sweaty and groggy. The heat in my room had intensified. I sat up. Where was my fan? Then I remembered. Gone to the middle room for Aunt Rachel and Uncle Avery.

Voices drifted up to my window, voices laughing, talking. The voice of a woman, familiar, but one I could not immediately identify. I grabbed my book and slipped into my shoes and went downstairs and looked at the clock in the kitchen. Five o'clock. I went back through the hall and stood at the screen door.

They were grouped in the front yard under the maple tree. Uncle Willie was standing propped against the trunk. My mother was sitting with her back to me. Uncle Avery was leaning back in his chair, one foot resting on his knee. Near him was Aunt Rachel, facing Mama. And next to her Miss Pheeny Butler. It must have been her voice I heard. She had said she was coming to see Aunt Rachel, but I had not expected her so soon. I stayed inside and watched them, unnoticed.

". . . so you won't be down to Third Sunday this August," Miss Pheeny was saying.

"Not this year," said Aunt Rachel.

"Well, that's a first," said Miss Pheeny with raised brows.

I was surprised, too. The third Sunday in August was *the* big event at Pharaoh. People scattered far and wide returned home to Mason County like salmon swimming upstream back to the place of their birth. Aunt Rachel never missed the opportunity to gossip with friends and listen to them swap success stories, which were, according to Uncle Willie, a bunch of bald-faced lies. Even a few Andersons sneaked back from their far-off places to meet with childhood friends, leaving their white children and spouses behind.

Another reason that Aunt Rachel came was to keep her membership in Pharaoh Baptist current so she could take her final sleep along with the rest of the family in the church graveyard that was crowded with the original Walkers and their descendants. It was as if she took comfort in the fact that she and Uncle Avery, no longer alone, would lie with the rest of the family, united in death.

Mama had no patience with this attachment to Third Sunday. When she went it was only because she was tired of Aunt Rachel nagging her to go. So now she countered Miss Pheeny's statement with "Pharaoh Baptist will be there next August."

If Miss Pheeny had been able to gauge my mother's moods she would have dropped the subject of Pharaoh Baptist, but her mind was intent on gossip. She cast forth tidbits of news as if she were dispersing corn in the barnyard, waiting for the chickens to gather around her feet pecking and clucking for more.

"Gonna lose one of our deacons," she began, almost primly.

Uncle Willie pushed himself toward her with his elbow anchored against the tree trunk. "Which one," he said.

"You know all about it, Willie," said Miss Pheeny.

"Swear to God I ain't heard nothin," said Uncle Willie.

"Who," said Aunt Rachel, turning her full attention on Miss Pheeny.

"Dick Thompson," said Miss Pheeny in triumph.

"Dick Thompson," said Mama.

"And I bet I know what for," said Aunt Rachel.

"A dollar says you don't," said Uncle Willie.

"Let us not profit from the misfortunes of others," said Miss Pheeny.

"Think it's proper for us to hear this, Pheeny?" said Uncle Avery.

"There you go, Avery, bein a deacon," said Miss Pheeny. "We ain't in church, you know."

Uncle Avery grunted and puffed on his pipe.

Uncle Willie turned to Mama. "What did he do, Lizzie."

"I don't *know* nothin. All I *heard* is they tryin to put him out of the church. At least, that's what some of them *tryin* to do."

"Who?" said Uncle Willie.

"Don't know that," said Mama.

"What for?" said Uncle Willie.

Uncle Avery began to jiggle his foot.

"Now you have to ask the deacons that," said Mama. "That's all I heard."

"You mean *Myra* didn't tell you why?" said Uncle Willie.

Miss Pheeny came to attention. "Myra Gibson? The church mother? I hope she ain't spreadin church business around."

"Myra didn't tell me nothin," said Mama. "But I guess you can spread it around, since you ain't the church mother, although I guess you wouldn't mind bein it."

"Well," said Miss Pheeny, "it would be a lie if I said I wouldn't mind. But since I ain't, it's somethin I think members of the church should know about, since he's your deacon and it's your church."

"Not mine," said Mama.

"Hush, Lizzie," said Aunt Rachel. "What did he do, Pheeny."

"Lizzie *knows*, I'm tellin you," said Uncle Willie.

"I don't go to Pharaoh enough to know any of that business up there," said Mama.

"You still a member," said Miss Pheeny. "I don't see why you don't come to church more often."

"Because I found out that's where all the devils are," said Mama.

"Whoooh," said Uncle Willie.

They were silent, as if waiting for Mama's hot words to cool.

"Well, it must've been a pretty big sin," said Aunt Rachel after a moment.

"Pretty big is right," said Miss Pheeny. "They havin a meetin at Pharaoh Sunday after next. Clear it all up."

"Only thing I can think of is gettin somebody with a baby," said Aunt Rachel. "Dick Thompson's famous for that."

"A man got to live up to his name," said Uncle Willie.

"Got the wrong one with a baby this time," said Miss Pheeny.

Everyone hung silent, waiting for the next words.

Miss Pheeny took her time answering, took a sip of iced tea first, then, "Esther Lee's daughter. Lila."

"That little yallah bird," said Uncle Willie. "Not even out of the nest. Ha, ha, ha." He laughed softly high in his throat.

"Fool," said Aunt Rachel. "Ain't nothin funny."

"Esther Lee was the fool," said Mama. "Takin a man into her house and she got a teenage daughter. Bad enough when you got a *husband* and a daughter that ain't his."

"You mean—he was *livin* with Esther?" said Aunt Rachel.

"Ha, ha, ha." Uncle Willie laughed again.

"Well," said Miss Pheeny with a wink, "he lived at her house. Payin room and board. She say nothin was goin on, but you know how that is."

"Mmmph, mph, mph." Uncle Willie shook his head. "Double dippin from the same trough."

"Fool oughta be drawn and quartered," said Aunt Rachel.

"He sure should've known better, I'll say that," said Miss Pheeny.

"All them deacons at Pharaoh fool around. Put a skirt on a sow and they'd jump her," said Mama. "What did the woman expect."

"We know they all fool around, Lizzie," said Miss Pheeny, laughing, "but even *they* got limits."

Everybody laughed except Uncle Avery.

"No disrespect, Avery," said Miss Pheeny.

Uncle Avery smiled and shook his head.

Uncle Willie leaned back and looked up into the maple tree. "Tree, if you could talk, *you'd* have a story to tell."

Aunt Rachel was still laughing when Uncle Willie said that. When she heard it, she jerked her head down and snapped her mouth shut like a snapping turtle snaps up a dragonfly. She stared balefully at Uncle Willie.

Mama stopped laughing, too. "What's wrong with you, Willie."

"Nothin. Them leaves flappin overhead, sounds like they got somethin to say."

"Well, we don't need no interpretations," said Mama.

"I call it Rachel's tree," said Uncle Willie.

Aunt Rachel turned pistachio green.

"Why's that?" said Miss Pheeny.

"She planted it when we was little," said Mama.

Uncle Willie strangled a laugh.

It got very quiet. Miss Pheeny sat a moment, looking up at the sky as if searching for another subject. "Seems Lucy Jenkins' daughter Katie was in the hospital about two months ago. Come out fifteen pounds lighter."

"What was she in for," said Uncle Willie.

"*She* said it was her gallbladder," said Miss Pheeny. "*I* say it was Mitchell Looby."

Mitchell Looby. I put my hand over my mouth.

"Mitchell Looby," said Mama. "Now I gave him more credit."

"Junior," said Miss Pheeny. "Not his father. He just followin in his father's footsteps. And Senior got some woman with a baby over in Riverton last year. Remember how he had three girls with a baby at one time back when we was in school? And I heard the son has the Jenkins girl and *another* one swelled up." She looked around slyly. "They won't say who, though. Anyway the Jenkins gal found out and tried somethin crazy."

"Tree, tree, tree," said Uncle Willie.

"Well, ain't Mitchell Senior a deacon?" said Mama, talking over Uncle Willie.

Aunt Rachel was sitting silent, listening.

"Last time I was in church he was," said Miss Pheeny.

"Well, why ain't somebody puttin *him* off the deacon board?"

"Ladies." Uncle Avery crossed his leg and tapped his pipe

against the side of his shoe. "Can't we find something uplifting for discussion?"

A laugh burst from Mama. "Seems to me they did."

"Hooh hooh!" said Miss Pheeny.

"Watch your mouth, there, Lizzie," said Uncle Willie. "No dirty talk in front of me."

Miss Pheeny, still hooting, said, "Like the stuff you men talk about, I guess."

"You don't want to talk about what men talk about," said Uncle Willie. "Least, not the men I know."

Uncle Avery stood up. "Well, maybe I'll go sit on the porch and talk to Belly. I see her standin at the screen door."

"Soakin up every word of her mother's dirty talk," said Uncle Willie.

I opened the door and stepped onto the porch.

"Well, Belly, see you again today," said Miss Pheeny.

"Yes, ma'am."

She nodded at the book in my hand. "Started on your readin, I see."

"Yes, ma'am."

By this time Aunt Rachel had regained her composure. "Avery promised her a nickel for each book she reads."

"She'll be rich by the end of the summer," said Mama.

Uncle Avery came up onto the porch. I sat down and opened my book, then looked up when Miss Pheeny called me again.

"Where's Teeny?" said Miss Pheeny. "Seems strange to see you without her at your side."

Uncle Willie looked up into the tree again.

I looked down at Mama. She wasn't looking my way, so apparently it was safe for me to answer. "She's away."

"Away? In Baltimore? I thought her cousins came down here every summer."

This time my mother answered. "She went to Carolina this year. I think Myra's sister sent for her."

"Probably sick," said Miss Pheeny, sucking her teeth.

"Wasn't none of my business, so I didn't ask," said Mama.

On the porch, his back to them, Uncle Avery smiled. Then he said, "What's the book you're startin, Belly?"

"The Pink Fairy Book."

"Oh, fairy tales."

I nodded.

Uncle Willie came up onto the porch and whispered in Uncle Avery's ear. "Watch this." He chuckled and went inside.

"Which one are you readin?" said Uncle Avery.

" 'Beauty and the Beast,' " I said.

" 'Beauty and the Beast.' " He took the book and leafed through it. "I remember the teacher readin that to us in school."

Music from the Victrola, turned up loud enough to be heard throughout the county, poured through the window and the screen door. The familiar sound of the piano interwoven with the strums of a guitar introducing an Ink Spots number, then:

Why do you whisper, green grass?
Why tell the trees what ain't so?

The women in the yard eyed each other then the house.

Whispering grass, the trees don't have to know

"What is that fool Willie up to now?" said Aunt Rachel.

No, no. Why tell them all your secrets,
Who kissed there long ago

Uncle Willie came through the door, arms raised, swaying, singing along with the music.

Whispering grass, the trees don't need to know

He hopped down from the porch and danced over to Aunt Rachel.

Don't you tell it to the trees
They will tell the birds and bees

He swayed back, arms wide.

And everyone will know because you
Told the blabbering trees

He danced around to Miss Pheeny.

Yes you told them once before,
It's no secret anymore

Miss Pheeny got up, indignant. "Willie Walker, you the biggest fool that ever walked."

Whispering grass, don't tell the trees,
For the trees don't need to knoooooow

Flushed and flustered, Miss Pheeny swiped at him but he jumped nimbly to her side. "I'm leavin this crazy place, Rachel. See you soon, Lizzie." She turned to go. Her dress, like those of many overweight women, had caught up in her behind.

"Oops!" said Uncle Willie. He bent over and pulled at her dress.

"Man! You crazy?" Miss Pheeny turned and got a good slap on his head.

"Woman!" Uncle Willie fell to the ground laughing and sat loose-jointed, knees up, pant legs flopping over his skinny shins.

"He was only freein up your dress, Pheeny," said Mama.

Miss Pheeny tugged at her dress. "Well, he shouldn't act so damn simple about it." She went over to her car and got in, slammed the door, and with a wave, took off in a cloud of dust.

Mama followed the car with her eyes. "I can't stand that woman."

"I don't blame her for not puttin up with that foolish brother of yours," said Aunt Rachel.

"Hmph," said Mama. "Them Butlers always was too free with their hands. One of these days she gonna hit the right one and get knocked on her fat behind."

"She know I'm a gentleman," said Uncle Willie. "That's why she took a swipe at me."

"Lizzie here gettin all upset," said Aunt Rachel.

"Ain't nobody upset over her smackin Willie. I'm talkin about why she came by here in the first place."

"She come to tell you about that slip of Mrs. Chapman's," said Aunt Rachel.

"Willie told me about that slip. Probably stole it herself for that fat daughter of hers. She just come by to be newsy. Find out why you're here and then pass on somethin she done heard and probably ain't even true."

"How do you know it ain't." Aunt Rachel folded her arms.

"Mash that whole Butler family through a strainer and you won't get a teaspoon of truth," said Mama, swelling with righteousness. "And two things I can't abide, a liar and a gossipmonger. Tryin to worm somethin out of Belly. 'Oh, Belly, where's Teeny? *Baltimore?* I thought her cousins came down here every summer.' Tryin to get somethin on Myra so she can be church mother, that's all."

"Can't get somethin on her if there's nothin to be got," said Aunt Rachel.

Mama shot her a look hotter than a sizzling poker. "For that matter, I guess there ain't none of us that ain't did somethin that we don't want nobody to know. And you and Willie just as bad as Pheeny, both of you out here eggin her on like your lives are as clear as a glass of spring water." She marched up onto the porch past Uncle Avery and me and *bang* went the screen door behind her.

"Well!" Aunt Rachel looked around at Uncle Willie, then up at Uncle Avery and me. "What the devil's wrong with her?"

Uncle Avery shrugged and puffed on his pipe.

I kept rocking.

"Don't ask me," said Uncle Willie. He looked upward and pointed. "Ask this tree."

The week of their visit was perfect vacation weather. The first two days Uncle Avery and Uncle Willie went fishing. They rose before dawn and disappeared until after sunset, and no matter how I begged they would not let me go with them, since the purpose of the trip, Uncle Avery whispered in my ear, was to dust the cobwebs from their brains and get away from gabby women. When I pointed out that I was not a woman, they contended that I still fell into the female category.

The first night they cleaned their fish and cooked them over an open fire. Uncle Willie put up a table under the maple tree so we could eat outside, but the flies were too numerous and bold. We finished the rest of our meal inside. After dinner Uncle Willie put his phonograph outside under the maple tree and played his records and hopped around and when he was tired of that he told jokes. Everybody laughed, even Aunt Rachel. The rest of the week the men pitched horseshoes in the backyard and played croquet on the close-cropped grass on the side lawn that Uncle Willie kept in prime condition for Uncle Avery's visits. He loved the game and grinned widely as he beat Uncle Willie every time. I played once, but I did not have the grace to be a good loser, so I watched instead. At night we sat on the porch and watched lightning bugs and listened to a cicada orchestra. Uncle Avery puffed on his pipe and chuckled at Mama and Aunt Rachel and Uncle Willie as they told stories about times when they were young.

"Remember when Willie broke his leg and was hoppin on crutches, and Rachel asked him for a hop, and he told her no, and she took a crutch and hit him over the head and ran? She didn't come back until midnight."

"I was out in the field, scared to death to come home."

"I saw stars when that gal hit me. Papa should've kill her."

"Lord. Mumma tried to hold me down on the bed so she could beat me, but I kicked and screamed so hard I wore them out."

They giggled and laughed like children; the black velvet nights enfolded them and their prickly thorns; like perfume from the night-blooming cereus, their sweet stories filled the air.

And we sang. Hymns. Uncle Willie and Mama had been members of the Pharaoh Baptist choir almost as soon as they could stand. Uncle Willie had favorites that we sang over and over again. That wonderful, pulsating music filled the night with its sweet sound. Uncle Avery and I sang along, his voice deep and clear, mine strong and sincere. They supplemented the hymns with other traditional songs. "The Old Oaken Bucket," "Londonderry Air," "Long, Long Trail," "She'll be Comin' Round the Mountain," so many songs that are now almost forgotten. And when we tired of singing, Uncle Willie would play his records and we would sit in the dark and listen to his favorites. Billie Holiday, Billy Eckstine, Sarah Vaughan, the Ink Spots.

Seven days after their arrival Uncle Avery and Aunt Rachel rode away. Contrary to my expectations, the week had been a pleasant one. I was almost sorry to see them go. But I was also puzzled. Neither my mother nor Aunt Rachel had mentioned Jamison to me. There had not been a hint.

"Rachel know Lizzie said it's up to you to go to Jamison," said Uncle Willie. "And she know *you*. She ain't fool enough to wave a red flag in front of a bull."

"I ain't no bull."

"No. You a heifer. But sometimes you act like a bull."

• • •

The first three days after their departure I read. The pile of "first reads" on the floor in my room rapidly dwindled. Every day I stretched out on an old blanket under the maple tree in the backyard, and with three or four books beside me, plowed through them page by page. *The Blue Fairy Book, The Green Fairy Book,* and a hilarious novel called *Miss Minerva and William Green Hill.* It kept me laughing so hard that I got stomach cramps and rolled on the ground clutching my sides, tears running down my face.

My mother and Uncle Willie came running out to investigate, mystified at the sight of me kicking and screaming with laughter on the grass.

"Can't nothin be that funny," said Uncle Willie.

After a few moments I managed to sit up and wipe the tears that were streaming down my face. "Yes, it is."

"You been readin for three days straight, Belly," said Mama, looking concerned. "Don't you want to go over and see Miss Janie and play on her piano?"

"Before you get brain fever," said Uncle Willie.

"You ain't been over there for a while," said Mama.

She had apparently forgotten that before Teeny left she had ordered me not to go away from the house without her permission because she didn't want me running up and down the road, but I did not remind her of that temporary lapse of good sense. I merely nodded and stretched out on my blanket and said, "I will. Tomorrow." And I went back to Miss Minerva, who was determined to bathe her goggle-eyed charge with a scrub brush and a bar of Octagon laundry soap.

Miss Janie Green was our only other neighbor within a mile. She was almost eighty years old and in the grips of rheumatoid arthritis. She lived with her bachelor son, Malachi, and I had been going to see her whenever I wished since I had been able to make my way through the tall grass. Lately, since Miss Janie's memory had been slipping, my mother had been happy whenever I went to visit her, especially since Malachi worked all day and Miss Janie was alone. I had deliberately stayed away since Teeny left to show my mother that I had no inclination to "run up and down the road." That decision had been hard on me, since Miss Janie's was the only piano within walking distance.

Miss Janie not only possessed a piano. She knew how to use it. She had taught music in the colored high school and had given lessons on the side. Mama and Uncle Willie had taken lessons from her when they were children. The magnificent walnut structure had stood in her parlor for decades. On that old and well-used instrument she had taught me how to read music and play simple songs. But I suspect that Malachi had grown tired of me coming over and banging on the piano whenever I felt like it; now the piano stood on her porch, where he had moved it a month before.

"He probably gonna get rid of it," Uncle Willie had said when he heard about it.

"It's his mother's, not his," said Mama.

"Maybe that's why it's on the porch and not in the trash."

"Well, I'm gonna see if I can get it for Belly," said Mama, and I had shivered with delight at the thought of having my own piano in the parlor.

Whatever happened, it had been on the porch for a month. And I had been running over to her house every day to play on it until Teeny got pregnant and my mother decided to keep me close by.

There were two fields that separated our house from Miss Janie's, each enclosed in barbed wire fences. They both belonged to the Walkers. My grandfather used to keep a few cows in one of them. He let the Greens use the other. Miss Janie kept a garden there when all her children were at home. Corn, tomatoes, cabbage, carrots, squash. Pumpkins. All kinds of vegetables, Mama used to say. But the children grew up and left home and she grew old and the garden was too big for her. My grandfather died and Mama and Uncle Willie sold the cows. Weeds and wildflowers and blackberry bushes reclaimed the fields.

Miss Janie's house, like ours, was made of clapboard that once had been white. Time and weather had turned it dull gray and it stood gaunt and weary in the midst of Miss Janie's flowers, which had become her avocation after she gave up her garden. Several trees that stood on her property blocked the sun at different times of the day and the flowers had been planted accordingly. Near the house were her impatiens and other flowers that were partial to the shade. Along the fence were her multicolored zinnias and yellow tea roses and, further down, her lavender petunias and sweet alyssum, which loved the sun. From the porch hung baskets of purple-leafed begonias with pink flowers. When I climbed over the fence she was watering them with a long-spouted garden watering can.

Miss Janie had snow white hair so thin you could see her pink scalp. She was slim, veins like cords in her hands, and was bent over with a dowager's hump. "Well, Belly, child, I haven't seen you for a *while*." She set the can on the porch. "I heard that Teeny went away."

"Yes, ma'am." I went up on the porch and sat down.

"Heard your Aunt Rachel was down. I was beginnin to think that maybe you went back to Jamison with her."

I grimaced. "Oh, no, ma'am."

Miss Janie laughed. "Don't take much to Rachel, hunh. Well, she has her brighter side." She came and stood next to me. "You want to play somethin?"

I nodded, and she and I began to play a duet, "Heart and Soul," but her arthritic fingers gave out after the first six bars. She sat in her rocking chair and bobbed her head while I played a tune from one of her elementary music books. After a half hour of uninspired plunking I gave up and plopped myself morosely on the step, chin in hand, and stared out across the field.

Miss Janie stopped rocking and lowered her body carefully to sit next to me. "So you miss Teeny, do you?"

I nodded.

"Well, why don't you write to her?"

"Write?" I turned and looked into those old gray eyes enfolded in layers of drooping, wrinkled skin.

"Surely you can write," said Miss Janie. "People do it all the time. I'm sure Teeny would be glad to get a letter from you. I re-member when I was about your age, my sister Phoebe went away one time to visit our oldest sister when she had a baby (she was old enough to be our mother), well, she wrote me a letter and I was so happy. I declare, it was better than havin her home with me because we was always fightin. Least that's what my papa used to say. And you know we wrote each other twice a week for three months." She gazed into the distance and spoke as if recalling a dream. "I swan, that was a long time ago."

Write. Such a practical suggestion, yet one I would never have thought of. I jumped up and hugged her. "Thanks, Miss Janie! See you tomorrow!" I ran across her yard and hopped the fence and was flying across the field ready to write a letter the moment I got home.

I ran panting into the hallway and stopped dead. Miss Myra's voice. She was in the kitchen with my mother. I had not seen her since Teeny had gone, and I did not want to see her then. I tipped toward the stairs, but my mother's voice stopped me.

"Belly? You back?" She came to the kitchen doorway. "Come on in here and speak to Miss Myra."

I went to the doorway and greeted Miss Myra.

She was sitting with one arm resting on the table. A bottle of whis-key was near her arm, her little "taste" held loosely in her hand. "Good afternoon, Belly. How are you?"

"Fine."

"How's Miss Janie?"

"Fine."

It was Thursday. Why wasn't she at home doing hair? And why did Mama have to tell her all my business, telling her where I had been? I looked over at her. Reading my expression, she was watching me apprehensively, not knowing what would pop out of my mouth. "Miss Myra brought me some wine," she said and nodded toward three corked jugs in the corner.

"I guess you two been playin on the piano," said Miss Myra. "Teeny say you and her play together."

"It ain't no fun without Teeny. Miss Janie's fingers are too stiff."

My mother frowned. Ordinarily that would have stopped me in my tracks, but if I was to follow Miss Janie's suggestion, I needed Teeny's address, so I blundered on. "Where'd Teeny go?"

"Go—" Miss Myra's eyes blinked like a startled chicken's.

"Belly," said Mama, "now don't you go bein fresh."

"I only asked where she went so I could write to her." I caught Miss Myra's eye. "Can't I write to her?"

"Why—" Miss Myra blinked again. My direct attack had disconcerted her. She was probably wondering how much I knew. But having sworn my mother to secrecy, she had to assume that Mama had kept her promise and told me nothing.

While we were all eyeing each other like roosters in a cockfight, Uncle Willie came into the kitchen. "Afternoon," he said. He spotted Miss Myra's glass. "Well, think I'll join you." He got a glass from the cabinet, then sat at the table, then, as if suddenly aware of the tension, said, "Oops." He looked around at our faces. "I fall into some woman talk or somethin?"

No one answered.

"Well." Uncle Willie waved his hand. "Y'all go on back to your talkin then."

I asked Miss Myra again. "Can't I write to Teeny?"

My question had knocked her off balance, but she had time to regain her composure. "Well," she said, "she went to visit my sister Betty in Baltimore."

Uncle Willie, just having sipped a bit of whiskey, leaned over and sputtered. He looked, but said nothing.

"You remember Nigel and Lucilla."

I did. They were Teeny's cousins and had been coming down to stay for a week every summer.

"Well, I got a phone call from Betty sayin how they were movin and they couldn't come down this summer, and so Teeny asked me if she could go up and visit them in Baltimore and she begged so hard I let her go. Now I don't remember that new address by heart, but when I go home I'll look for it, and if I can't find it I'll see if I can reach them. I don't know how, though. They don't have a phone yet."

Uncle Willie closed one eye and looked in his glass at the whiskey. "You drinkin the same stuff I am, Myra?"

My mother shook her head and kept ironing.

Miss Myra, unabashed, continued her verbal odyssey. She didn't know why Teeny hadn't told me that day I was on the porch that she was going away the next day. "Maybe she thought you might be lonely and then she wouldn't go and she really wanted to go." She shrugged and took a sip from her glass. "I don't know."

Uncle Willie stood up. "I'm goin out of here before somebody gets struck by lightnin and goes up in smoke."

"All right, Willie," said Mama.

"I think I'll go out back and read," I said.

"But when I get that address," Miss Myra said in a reedy voice, "I'll come right over and give it to you soon as Betty call."

By then I was so disgusted with the woman I might have said something else if Mama hadn't diverted my attention. "Here, Belly. Take this wine and put it on the back porch and then go on outside."

I lost respect for Miss Myra that day. I had never liked the woman from the moment I met her; I tolerated her because she was Teeny's mother. But like my mother I hated a thief and a liar and at the dinner table I said as much.

"That woman *lies!*"

"People aren't perfect, Belly," said Mama. "We all have faults."

"Why do you like her then? You said you can't stand Miss Pheeny because she's a liar."

Uncle Willie winked at Mama. "Mmm hmmmm. Let's see you get out of this one."

But Mama was not ruffled. There were different kinds of liars, she explained. Some people lie to protect themselves. Some people lie to keep secrets. Other people lie to get other people in trouble or find out their business so they can spread it around. Myra had lied to protect herself. "She thought you didn't know about Teeny havin a baby. And she doesn't want you to know."

"In other words," said Uncle Willie. "There's times when lyin is all right, and times when it ain't."

"That's not exactly what I said, Willie."

"Sounds to me like it was."

"Well," I said, "if she brings me Teeny's address, I'll know she's a liar, because she'll be in North Carolina, not in Baltimore."

"Oh, liars are inventive," said Uncle Willie. "Myra will find some way to get around that. Wait and see."

$$\mathscr{C} \quad h \quad a \quad p \quad t \quad e \quad r \quad \mathbf{8}$$

One afternoon during those dark weeks of June when I was missing Teeny terribly and barely tolerating Miss Myra, Miss Pheeny Butler stopped by again. Mama had just sent Uncle Willie off to deliver his second load of laundry, and she and I were on the porch relaxing.

"I swear, that looks like Pheeny Butler's car comin up here," said Mama, frowning at the green Chevrolet crunching up the drive. "Now why in the world is she comin back here again."

She stopped in a cloud of dust and stepped out of her car, accompanied by her thirteen-year-old niece, who had come down from Baltimore for a week's visit. "No girls around my way, and I knew Belly was alone over here, and Philice was lonely, too, so I thought I'd bring her over for a visit."

Philice. Daughter of Alice (Miss Pheeny's baby sister) and Philip Rhodes and whose name, Philice (File*ese*), was a combination of the given names of her parents. Her physical appearance denoted no such compromise. Like all the Butlers, she was big and fat, and looked enough like Miss Pheeny to be a younger sister.

Miss Pheeny, remembering her last visit with us, looked around suspiciously and inquired about Uncle Willie.

"He's gone to deliver laundry," said Mama.

"Fine with me," said Miss Pheeny, and ignoring Mama's tight-mouthed look, plopped herself into a chair.

But this visit was not fine with me. They had come while I was starting a new book and I was expected to stop reading and entertain my unexpected guest. I took her up to my room and soon discovered that for Philice intellectual pursuits were a repulsive pastime. "Books!" she said when she entered my little library, and she drew back as if she had stepped into a room filled with six months of unwashed socks. "Who wants to read books when they ain't in school!" She whirled and clomped back downstairs.

I followed her meekly into the parlor, where she spied Uncle Willie's record collection. She put one on and jumped around the parlor to the music with hips wiggling like watery Jell-O. The floorboards groaned under the strain, but she sat down only when Miss Pheeny yelled in for her to stop shaking the house down. She kept sighing and fidgeting. I did not know what to do to make her comfortable. I offered her a few of Teeny's old movie magazines piled on a shelf nearby, but she rejected them with a sniff. "I read them last year. What you keepin old magazines around for? You backwards."

I smarted from her barbs, but I was determined to be polite. "What do you do for fun up in Baltimore?" I asked politely.

"We go to the movies, for one thing."

We had a movie theater in Lambertville but it wasn't open in the afternoons, I explained.

"That's what I mean. You all *backwards*. We go to the movies anytime we want, night or day. On Sundays, too. And now I can go to dances when my brother goes," she continued, "and sometimes we go downtown to the band concerts." On and on she went about the fun children had where she lived.

Baltimore sounded like the place for someone like her. But if she had so much fun there, why did she come to the country, I wanted to know.

"To meet my relatives. My mother is from down here. And I don't blame her for leavin. I hope she don't think she gonna get me down here again."

It was my fervent hope as well. Suddenly I had an inspiration. My mother had made a chocolate cake that morning. Everybody I knew liked chocolate cake, and judging the size of Philice, I thought she must spend a lot of time eating. I stood up. "Want a piece of cake?"

She smiled and nodded and followed me into the kitchen and in a few minutes we had eaten half the cake. While I washed our dishes, Philice went to the doorway of the back porch and looked around curiously. At the cot. Who slept there, she asked. Anybody who felt like it, I replied. The washing machine was old-fashioned, she noted. My mother liked it, I answered. She took two steps into the porch. She was staring at something in the corner. I went onto the porch behind her. "What's that?" She pointed to the jugs of wine that I'd set on the counter when Miss Myra had brought them over a few days before.

"Dandelion wine," I said.

"Oooh, what's it taste like?"

"I don't know," I said with a shrug. "I just pick the dandelions."

"And you mean you ain't never had none?"

"Never wanted any."

"Never even *tasted* it?"

"Nope."

"I sure would like a taste."

Giving her cake without my mother's permission would have been considered good manners, but giving her wine was taboo. Wine could turn people into fools. Many times Mama and Uncle Willie would talk about the effect it had on their father. He would fill up a mason jar to the rim with blackberry wine and drink until he rolled off his chair onto the floor and would sleep there all night, then wake up moaning about his aching back. These stories were indirect warnings: the contents of those jugs was not for me or my friends. "I can't give you any wine," I said to Philice. "Not unless I ask Mama."

Philice rolled her eyes. "Why you gotta ask your mother? All she gonna do is say no."

"If she says no, then you can't have any."

"She ever tell you not to drink any?"

"No."

"Then she don't care if you drink some."

I still made no move toward the jugs, but Philice knew how to provoke a saint. "You just *scared*."

My hands went to my hips. "No I ain't," I declared. I got two glasses and went to the wine closet. I did not use one of the jugs on the counter, for they were not properly aged; I took one from the cabinet below, as I had seen Mama and Uncle Willie do many times before.

I pulled the cork with my teeth and poured the wine into the glass. It was clear; I tasted it. To my surprise it was like a fruit drink. I drank two full glasses. Philice had three and wanted another, but I told her no, this was not cake we were eating, and put the cork back in the jug. But the wine was making her foolish. She grabbed the jug and tried to wrest it from my hands, but the wine gave me strength. I pushed her back and put the jug in the cabinet and reeled to the back steps and sat down.

Philice followed me. "Why can't I have another glass?"

The wine made my tongue loose, too. "You a pig, that's why."

"Don't you call me a pig." She pushed my head with her foot.

Not a kick, but a push, an act that indicated she considered me an easy conquest in a fight. I was a blabbermouth, but not a fist fighter. When Teeny and I were younger, we fought once, but my mother and Miss Myra had gathered some switches and impressed upon us the consequences of settling our differences with our hands and teeth. From then on if we had any disagreements we left each other's company in a huff.

The touch of Philice's foot sparked the resentment that had been building inside of me for the past hour, and I exploded. I leaped off the porch and grabbed her leg and pulled her down to the ground. We both fell down with a thud and jumped up. She grabbed my plait and swung me down to the ground. I went down swinging and flailing. Philice was fat around the torso; I punched her a few times in the middle, but my blows had no effect. She had my neck in the crook of her arm, punching me on the back. My face was pressed against her leg. Desperate, I bit her on the thigh. She let go of me and sat up screaming. I jumped on her and she went on her stomach with me on her back. I was punching her in a blind rage when Uncle Willie came around the corner of the house.

"What the hell is goin on back here!" He grabbed my arms and pulled me off Philice and threw me on the steps. "Lizzie! Pheeny! Come around here and see what these gals is up to!" He glared at me, then at Philice, who was on her knees brushing grass from her hair. "What is you all fightin about!"

"She called me a pig!" screamed Philice.

"You are!" I screamed back. Oh, I felt good. I threw myself back on the porch and laughed. "She is a pig, Uncle Willie! She drank three glasses of wine and got mad because I wouldn't give her no more and she put her foot on my head so I knocked her on her big fat ass!"

"Belly!" said Mama who had come around the house.

"Her foot on your head!" said Miss Pheeny, glowering.

"Wine!" said Uncle Willie. He threw up his hands and went inside. Miss Pheeny apologized to Mama and me, grabbed Philice and pushed her around to the car, and left. I went upstairs to my room to rest. The bed was rocking as if it were afloat, but I dove onto it and fell asleep. I woke hours later with a headache and a sour taste in my mouth and a bottom lip doubled in size.

When Uncle Willie saw me he snorted. "Next time you wanna fight, you better pick a welterweight. That gal got muscles in her arms bigger than Joe Louis. Looks like she was tryin to do you in worse than he did Jersey Joe."

"I didn't want to fight," I said, painfully working the words through my swollen mouth. "She started it."

"Well," said Uncle Willie. "You better learn when to fight and when to run."

Putting an ice pack on my mouth, Mama lectured me on the evils of wine. "Belly, of course we know you didn't suggest drinkin the wine. It's here all the time and you ain't never drunk any," said Mama. "But even just one glass of wine will loosen you up, and two glasses, *water* glasses, will make you do things you would never do if you hadn't drunk it. And you're gonna meet up with a lot of people who will say things just to get you mad, especially if you been drinkin and they been drinkin, just to get you to do things you ain't got no business doin. Philice know how to use words to goad you. You *backwards*. You *scared*. Look out for those words. Especially *scared*."

"You know, maybe it's good that somethin like this did happen," said Uncle Willie. "So your mama can warn you. I just hope you learned a lesson."

I hung my head and in a wobbling voice whispered I had, and my mother told Uncle Willie to say no more about it.

Uncle Willie had another question he wanted answered. "What I don't understand is what Pheeny Butler come here for in the first place. After the other day I thought we wouldn't see her face no more 'til next year."

"She said she was bringing her niece to keep me company," I said past my puffy lip.

"Some company she was," said Uncle Willie.

Mama snorted. "That was just some of that Butler camouflage. What she really come for was to tell me that the meetin on Deacon Thompson was changed from the end of this month to this Sunday comin. Asked me if I was comin."

"Her and Myra sure is determined to get you back in church," said Uncle Willie.

On reflection, I realize that my mother was probably an outcast in Pharaoh simply because she did not attend church. In Mason County there was a church wherever you could gather a group of ten. Pharaoh Baptist was the glue that bonded the community together. The daily and social life of "decent" people revolved around the church, and they did not relish my mother expressing her opinions when she pleased and to whom she pleased, especially those opinions about a few unsavory souls who went to church every Sunday yet continued on their wayward paths because the congregation tacitly condoned their illicit conduct.

To support her accusation she often referred to the antics of my grandfather, who had been the head deacon at Pharaoh. Until the day he dropped dead he was an unrelenting, whiskey-swilling womanizer who was famous for wringing his sins out to dry in front of the congregation every Sunday only to keep on sinning Monday through Saturday. He chilled his children's souls and broke their mother's heart.

Uncle Willie lost the remnants of his religious fervor in the steamy jungles in the South Pacific. It was also during the war (after the death of my father) that Mama stopped going to church regularly. She confined her visits to funerals or weddings or the times when there was a noted guest minister. Or any other occasion that she deemed special. No urging by Miss Myra or Miss Pheeny could get her to change her mind. She preferred to talk to God without a man in the middle, I often heard her tell them.

In recent years, however, Pharaoh Baptist had begun to keep its eyes and ears attuned to the indiscretions of its members and address them with considerable speed. And Miss Pheeny Butler had speedily brought the news of Deacon Thompson's impeachment to my mother's attention and urged her to see with her own eyes that Pharaoh Baptist was taking its sinners to task. Uncle Willie was almost correct in his assumption that she was trying to get my mother back in the church. But Miss Pheeny did not give a fig about the redemption of sinners. Her mission was more earthly.

The change of philosophy at Pharaoh was primarily due to the new pastor, Reverend Sykes, a college-educated, ordained minister from Atlanta, Georgia. He was a tall brown man with a balding head, a booming laugh, and an infectious personality. At that time he preached at Pharaoh Baptist two Sundays a month and would have been unavailable on the date originally scheduled for the hearing on Deacon Thompson. The meeting had been moved forward so that the congregation could avail themselves of his electrifying presence in so important a matter as the chastisement of Deacon Thompson. Otherwise, the associate pastor, Reverend Monroe, would have officiated. That would have caused a conflict of interest, since he had been pastor almost as long as Pharaoh had existed and was on drinking terms with every man on the deacon board.

The personality of the new minister had attracted people from other communities to Pharaoh Baptist. One of them was Henry Binns. Sometime the previous spring my mother had attended a funeral there. Henry Binns had seen her and (in his words) had fallen like a fifty-foot pine that has been struck by a powerful bolt of lightning. Every week he looked for her at church or at different church functions, but he had not seen her again. He was beginning to think he had imagined her. Then he remembered he had seen her talking to Miss Pheeny Butler and asked her about Mama. Surmising his state of mind from his obvious embarrassment, Miss Pheeny set about seeing that he and my mother would meet. Had I known about this, I might have thought less of Miss Pheeny, for I had no desire to have another man around the house. Especially one who might want to take the place of my father.

My first sight of this man was in the churchyard when we arrived at the meeting for Deacon Thompson. Mama and Uncle Willie and I were standing to the side waiting to go into the church. The regular service had just ended and the members who were not staying for the meeting were leaving the area. Those who were remaining were stand- ing around talking excitedly. I noticed a man next to Miss Pheeny Butler who kept looking over at us.

Uncle Willie noticed him too. "Watch out, Lizzie. I think you got an admirer. He's standin with Pheeny, but he's lookin mighty hard over this way."

Mama was wearing her blue voile dress and a floppy white hat and white shoes. She looked very pretty that day, as she always did when she dressed up. She looked toward Miss Pheeny and the man, then tossed her head. "Willie, stop talkin foolishness and come on into this church."

The church was almost full. The whisper of fans and the soft voices of the women and the smell of Evening in Paris perfume filled the air. Miss Myra, who had come for the service as usual, waved us to her pew, where she had saved us seats. Women in hats adorned with flowers, necks stretched, gazed around to see who was present. Mama and Uncle Willie drew stares and whispers. *Miss Lizzie and Willie!* Miss Myra, basking in the unaccustomed attention, smiled and nodded at various members.

A few moments later, Reverend Sykes entered and went behind the pulpit to open the meeting. We rose and soon the church was throbbing with a few verses from a hymn chosen for the occasion.

I once was lost in sin, but Jesus took me in,
And then a little light from Heaven filled my soul.
It bathed my heart in love, and wrote my name above
And just a little talk with Jesus made me whole.

"So let us have a little talk with Jesus," sang Uncle Willie, head bobbing. "Let us tell him all about our troubles."

I stood on my toes to see the object of this musical petition. In a front pew were standing Esther Lee and her daughter, Lila, and Lila's boyfriend, who had been pointed out to me by Uncle Willie before we entered the church. Across from them were the deacons. I scrutinized each one, hoping to spot the culprit, but not one of them standing there looked guilty or ill at ease.

The singing over, everyone sat down and waited for Reverend Sykes to begin. The man was a powerful speaker. His modulated tones rose and subsided on waves of emotion ever and always ascending until that climactic moment of his sermon when his voice paused, then thundered and bounced off the walls. Although many of his words were over the heads of the congregation, the worshipers always left the service uplifted, secure in the knowledge that they had just heard the words of God.

"Which one's Deacon Thompson?" I whispered to Uncle Willie.

"He ain't up there," he replied.

How could they have a meeting about him if he was not there? I was about to ask Uncle Willie, but at that moment the Reverend Sykes began to speak. "Bretheren. The business before us today is serious and goes to the heart of our mission in the Christian community. There's been a lot of gossip"—he stopped and looked the congregation over a few seconds—"innuendo"—stopped again—"and some out and out lies that have been swirling through Pharaoh Baptist and Mason County over the last few months. Things have got so bad that we have deacons and church members not speaking, both sides making wild accusations and some even demanding that the head of the deacon board be made to step down."

A unified gasp from the congregation.

"I have even been accused of showing favoritism"—gasps—"and of being derelict in my duties as minister of Pharaoh Baptist"—gasps. "I have decided to bring the entire matter before the membership this afternoon so you can decide for yourselves the gravity of the matter and I will take the appropriate action."

Silence.

"The facts are these." Reverend Sykes lays them out. "One. Deacon Thompson rents a room with Sister Esther Lee." (Coughs from the congregation.) "Two. Sister Esther Lee has a daughter Lila." (Coughs.) "Three. Lila Lee became pregnant and had a child." Pause. "Now those," he thunders, "are three facts!"

Silence.

"The speculations are these." Reverend Sykes lays *them* out.

"Lila Lee has a child. The child looks like Deacon Thompson." (Titters.) "Ergo, Deacon Thompson is the father." (Guffaws, glares, silence.) "Now THAT is faulty reasoning!" thunders Reverend Sykes. "Now if we take these speculations as truth, what are we really saying about this girl? About this man, Deacon Thompson?" He waits.

Oh, the people begin gabbling and gabbing and pointing and whispering. *There's Lila Lee, up front, standin next to her boyfriend. See. He light-skinned with good hair. She light-skinned. Hair down her back. There's the baby. Black. Like Deacon Thompson. And like all them other little Thompsons sproutin up in the congregation ever since he been here.* Oh, they talked. They were beyond reason.

Up stands Miss Esther Lee. Did they think she would let something like this happen in her house?

Didn't have to happen in your house.

Did they think she would have Deacon Thompson still renting a room there if she thought he was runnin with her daughter?

Woman, sit down.

Down she plops, sobbing.

More people pop up and down, for and against Deacon Thompson. Then someone demands that the deacon himself stand up and give his version of the events, but the deacon is not present.

Gabblegabble, babblebabble.

A tall, dignified man in the front pew stands up. The man who had been staring at Mama. He turns and speaks. "Reverend Sykes has laid out the facts. But it is also a fact that Deacon Thompson is not here to speak up for himself. Is that the action of an innocent man? Reverend Sykes spoke about speculation. In my opinion, we don't need a head deacon or any deacon who is open even to speculation. A deacon should set the example, head and shoulders above the rest of us." He sits down.

"Now he sure is right about that," says Uncle Willie.

Within a few minutes it is all over. A little man in a middle pew stands up and recommends that the congregation take a vote by voice. All in favor of Deacon Thompson stepping down, aye. The ayes fill the air. He does not sully his lips with the word "opposed."

Reverend Sykes says a few more words. The church empties out.

Outside Miss Pheeny Butler was waiting for us. "Good afternoon, everybody," she said. "How's your head, Belly?"

"Fine," I whispered.

"Belly and my niece got into Lizzie's dandelion wine," Miss Pheeny said to Miss Myra.

"Belly! I'm surprised at you!" said Miss Myra.

"Yes indeed. She come down from Baltimore for a couple days." Miss Pheeny looked at Miss Myra with narrowed eyes.

Miss Myra smiled nervously.

"She live right around the corner from your sister Betty. Goes over there all the time."

"Oh," said Miss Myra.

"She knows Nigel and Lucilla. Cilla, she calls her. Funny, I asked her if she knew Teeny. Said wasn't no Teeny up there."

I felt sorry for Miss Myra, who was looking as if Miss Pheeny had caught her in the henhouse stealing eggs.

But Mama drew herself up and said, "I don't know why you're rakin over old coals, Pheeny. I told you in the yard the other day that Teeny went to visit Myra's sister in Carolina."

"Oh, I thought Belly told me Baltimore," said Miss Pheeny.

"I didn't tell you nothin," I said.

"No, she sure didn't, Pheeny," said Uncle Willie. "I remember that day perfectly."

This discussion ended abruptly when the man who had been standing with Miss Pheeny earlier gawking at Mama appeared on the church steps with Reverend Sykes. Miss Pheeny saw him and waved him over. He and the minister came over to us and after a short discussion of the meeting, Reverend Sykes left and Miss Pheeny introduced the stranger.

I frowned at the man. He looked dazed, as if someone had struck him with a bat. Or else he'd had too much to drink.

Mama smiled nervously and took my hand.

Mr. Binns talked to Uncle Willie about the meeting, all the while keeping his eyes on Mama. Finally we went home and Uncle Willie teased Mama all the way.

"His eyes was glazed," I said. "Like he been *drinkin.*"

Uncle Willie laughed. "That's how it strikes you sometimes."

"What?" I said.

"Willie, just hush up," said Mama.

Miss Myra was at our house every day for a week after that. For the first two days she talked incessantly about the injustice of voting against Deacon Thompson when he was not there to defend himself. "It just seems so unchristian, to judge a man that way."

"Preacher asked them to vote," said Uncle Willie.

"He could've been there," said Mama. "Where was he?"

"Out somewhere pluckin out his right eye," said Uncle Willie.

"Don't make fun of the Bible, Willie Walker," said Miss Myra.

I wondered why she wasn't at work or at home doing hair instead of sitting at our kitchen table moaning about Deacon Thompson. The proceedings at the church, either that meeting or her conversation with Miss Pheeny, seemed to have thrown her into a state of hysteria. But after two days her spirits rose and I would come in and find her laughing and talking with Mama.

I was still angry because she had not given me Teeny's address. I had promised Mama not to bring it up again, so I decided to avoid her. Whenever she came I confined myself to the back porch or my room. Her loud laugh, usually in response to some story my mother or Uncle Willie was telling, offended me so much that I would slam my book shut, snort, and glare at the wall and smolder at the good feeling emanating from the porch or the parlor or wherever my mother was working that day. I would sometimes stomp downstairs for iced tea or water; they would stop talking, look over at me and smile, then go back to talking and laughing, ignoring me. I would stand hesitantly by; they would stop again, eye me as if I were intruding. I would mumble that I was going outside or upstairs or over to Miss Janie's.

In my own house I was suddenly de trop.

I fumed with anger. I smoldered with resentment. I wallowed in self-pity. I could understand Mama needing company, someone to talk to besides Uncle Willie and me. But did Miss Myra have to come *every* day? Did Mama and Uncle Willie have to enjoy her presence so much?

By the end of the week, Miss Myra's visits combined with Teeny's absence made me think about an action I would not have considered the week before. I would go to Jamison. Yes. If that repulsive woman kept coming to my house, then I would leave and go stay with Aunt Rachel. Anything was preferable to her insufferable presence. Even the boredom of Jamison. Even Aunt Rachel.

My mother had not mentioned that subject again and I did not know how to bring it up, but Miss Myra provided the opening when I came panting into the kitchen one particularly hot afternoon with my arms full of music books. She was at the table as usual with a whiskey glass at her elbow.

"What in the world, Belly," said Mama.

"Music books." I plopped them on a chair. "Miss Janie gave them to me."

"My niece Nettie have enough of them to open a music store," said Miss Myra.

"Nettie?" said Mama. "When did she start playin the piano?"

"Last January. Right after they moved to Jamison."

"Jamison! You have a niece live there?"

Jamison. I looked over at Mama, who would not look at me.

"She not *really* my niece. She the daughter of a good friend of mine. We like sisters."

I rolled my eyes. Another lie.

"She can have these books," I said. "I sure can't use them."

"She don't need no more," said Miss Myra.

"You might be able to use them someday," said Mama.

"How. I don't take no lessons." I picked up one of the books. "This says 'Easy Piano' and I can't read nothin in it."

"You play from the 'Book I' Miss Janie gave you," said Mama.

Miss Myra took a sip from her glass. "You should take lessons from a real piano teacher, Belly."

"Miss Janie was a real piano teacher until she started forgettin things. Anyway, I don't even have a piano to practice on if I did take them."

"I guess you right about that," said Miss Myra.

"Who gives Nettie piano lessons in Jamison?" said Mama.

Miss Myra had difficulty with the name. It was unusual, she said. She frowned, thinking, then, "Ophelia, I think she said."

Mama stopped ironing and looked at Miss Myra, surprised and pleased. "Ophelia Love?" said Mama. "My sister told me she was still in Jamison, but I didn't know she was givin piano lessons."

"That's right. Your sister do live in Jamison."

"Ever since she been married," said Mama.

Miss Myra looked at me over her glass. "Maybe you should go visit your aunt Rachel. Then you can take lessons all summer."

Then a bolt from the blue. "And she has a piano," said Mama.

I stared at her. "You didn't say nothin about a piano."

"Wouldn't have made no difference," said Mama, keeping her eyes on the shirt she was ironing so intently. "You said you wasn't goin to stay with her no matter what."

I sat back, frowning. What were these two up to? Miss Myra was talking as if she did not know Aunt Rachel was getting an operation or had asked me to come stay with her. But surely during these afternoon visits my mother had told her.

It sounded suspicious to me. Did Miss Myra really have a friend in Jamison? Could this entire week, including this very conversation, be part of some conspiracy to get me to go to Jamison? Mama had told Aunt Rachel she'd let her know by the end of June. And it was almost here. I, who had been on the verge of asking my mother to let me go to Jamison, now dug in my heels like a mule and decided that I was not.

I scowled. "I bet Aunt Rachel's just sayin she has a piano."

"Now why would she do that?" said Mama.

"She can't play it," I said, "so why would she buy one?"

"She didn't buy it, Miss Know-it-all. One of the ladies she used to work for a long time ago gave it to her. She's movin to California with her children so she gave it to somebody she knew would take good care of it." Mama laughed. "And she's right. Rachel might not play it, but she sure will dust it to death."

"Then she probably don't want me to even touch it."

"We'd have to cross that bridge when we come to it," said Mama. "*If* you went to Jamison."

"Surely Rachel wouldn't mind if you played soft, Belly," said Miss Myra. "And since she live in Jamison, you could take lessons where Nettie take hers. From Miss Ophelia."

Liars. They were liars, both of them. I stood up, looked from Miss Myra to Mama. "Well, I still don't want to go." Out to the front porch I marched. Into the rocking chair I flopped. Who did that Miss Myra think she was, trying to tell me what to do. Just because she made Teeny go away didn't mean she could make me do what she wanted. Probably in cahoots with Mama. Mama could try every trick she knew. And Aunt Rachel could get all the pianos she wanted. And that Ophelia lady could give lessons until her fingers fell off.

I wasn't going anywhere.

For another week I maintained this position. I made a chart for my reading and taped it to my wall. Twenty books so far. I sighed and sat in a chair and looked out the window, then started reading again. Then, one afternoon, sated with words and bleary-eyed from reading them, I closed my book and went into the parlor and told my mother that I was ready to go. It was one week before Aunt Rachel was slated to go to the hospital, but I asked if I could leave the following day. My mother, poor woman, probably thinking my brain had deteriorated from those marathon reading sessions, agreed, and immediately sent Uncle Willie to Miss Myra's to call Aunt Rachel and tell her I was coming.

Miss Ophelia

• • •

The following Monday, early, soon after Uncle Willie watered the garden, early, while the dew was still on the grass and the sun still an orange glow just behind the hills, Uncle Willie's truck turned onto the gravel road that ran by our house. We rode, bouncing and rattling, splashing dust onto the roadside weeds, swerving to avoid sluggish racoons and skittish rabbits, finally reaching the paved highway that veed into the distance, a long black thread woven through a tan, brown, and green tapestry of rolling fields and cows grazing and horses standing behind fences with black barbs, like spiders on black strings. Alone on the landscape, we rolled toward the sun, past fences. Past fields. Cows in fields. Cornstalks. Orchards. Fields. Horses. Cows in fields. Past farmer dolls on toy tractors. I stared at the monotonous black ribbon of road; I nodded off and on, then came fully awake sixty miles later when the truck jolted, then jerked as Uncle Willie shifted gears for the steep climb up to the town.

The town of Jamison was on a hill. The road into town ran up to the main street, crossed it, and ran back down to the other side of town. At the top of the hill, on Fitzgerald Street, stood the courthouse, a magnificent white building with smooth round columns and wide steps where a few colored men passed the afternoons in warm weather gossiping and soaking up the sun and tipping their hats to people of note who went by. Afternoon, Dr. Allen. *Sure miss Dr. Dewberry. Well, he gotta start somewhere.* Afternoon, Sheriff Palmer. *Wife done left again. Third time, ain't it?* Afternoon, Reverend Smith. *Man sure can preach. Too loud for me.* Others who were rising to prominence received a slight nod or a desultory wave.

We chugged into the town while it was still drowsing, while the sun's rays livened the treetops with apricot frosting and slanted brilliantly across the roofs of the low brick buildings and bounced from the storefront windows. Down Fitzgerald Street we drove, past the white barbershop where the colored barbers cut white men's hair; past the drugstore that had a soda fountain where colored people could not sit; past the brick post office on its green lawn that was tended by the only colored worker; past the Safeway Supermarket just opened the year before, where colored shopped but could not work; past the Fitzgerald movie theater, where the colored went up to the balcony by way of a back staircase; on to the other end of town, where the colored community lived: three streets, none of which was paved, touching the main street.

Aunt Rachel lived on Randolph Street, first of the three. Narrow white clapboard houses, railroad-car style, stood side by side, ten feet apart, two stories high, flat roofs. They stood on concrete blocks and were separated from the street by narrow strips of grass. Dirt paths led up to wooden steps that led up to wooden porches with wooden railings.

When we pulled up, Aunt Rachel was sweeping her porch. My mother was the first out of the truck. "Mornin!"

"Mornin," said Aunt Rachel, hand on hip. "I guess y'all must be hungry."

"You said it," called Uncle Willie from the back of the truck. He dropped my suitcases to the ground and jumped down.

I got out of the truck and stood at the side.

"Ain't nobody worried about you, Willie Walker. You're always hungry," said Aunt Rachel. She raised her voice to send it over the cab of the truck. "What you standin down there in the street for, Isabel? Come on up here out of that sun before you turn into a raisin."

I slunk up onto the porch for the dry peck on the cheek. Aunt Rachel opened the door and we stepped inside.

"Well, Rachel," said Mama, standing by the door, "this looks diffent in here now!"

Uncle Willie set the suitcases down and looked around. "Avery knew what he was doing, I'll give him credit for that. Good job he did. Good job."

The room was much different from the last time I had been there. Then it had been like our parlor at home, dim and unappealing with a dark flowered carpet, a stiff horsehair couch with a coffee table stacked with magazines, and two chairs, both with doilies on the arms and backs. Perhaps that had contributed to my unhappiness whenever my mother said she was going to visit Aunt Rachel, for she had usually banished me to the gloomy front room to read magazines while she and Mama talked in the kitchen. The dining room, which had been separated by a wall, had been even darker, for the one window in the side wall caught the light only in the late afternoon.

Now the wall had been knocked out and the room was flooded with light from a large window that replaced the narrow one overlooking the front porch. The two rooms that had once been cramped now were opened to give an airy feeling of space. The dark carpet was gone, replaced with two long beige carpets that almost covered the entire floor. The old sofa and chairs were gone. New ones in flowered slipcovers were arranged around the coffee table. Drapes to match covered the windows.

And there against the wall where the old sofa had stood was the piano, a graceful walnut spinet, shining in its glory.

"It's like a flower garden, isn't it, Mama?" I said.

"Without the bugs," said Uncle Willie.

"It's very nice," said Mama. "I'll have to get Avery down to the house and have him and Willie knock out our wall."

Uncle Willie drew back. "The damned house would fall in."

We laughed. Aunt Rachel started toward the kitchen, but Mama stopped at the dining room table and looked back to the living room. "I don't know, though. I don't know if I'd like my house so open that when you come in the front door you could see me eatin my dinner."

"Hmph," said Aunt Rachel. "How often do you eat in that dinin room now. Table piled up with clothes. That's why you don't want it open. Have to keep it neat."

"Look, I didn't come up here for no discussion about decoratin," said Uncle Willie. "I need to get somethin in my belly before I pass out. We didn't eat before we left, or did you forget."

"Shut up, Willie," said Mama.

In the kitchen a large round table was set for a light meal: cold sliced ham, potato salad, rolls, iced tea, and chocolate cake. While we ate, Mama and Aunt Rachel discussed the conditions of my servitude: light housework (dusting, vacuuming) and serving lunch on a tray (Avery would bring breakfast and dinner). No washing, no ironing, no scrubbing. I was already regretting my impulsive offer to come.

"Most'n gen'ally, I just need somebody here with me in case I have a relapse," said Aunt Rachel.

"Who'll know if that happens," said Uncle Willie, talking around his ham sandwich. "And how will Belly know what to do."

Mama looked at me doubtfully. "Belly ain't had any experience in this kind of thing."

I looked at them as if they thought the world was still flat. "Aunt Rachel got a telephone, don't she? All she got to do is put the right numbers on a tablet by the telephone."

Finally we got around to my needs: movies, reading, and piano lessons.

"Piano lessons," said Aunt Rachel.

"Uh-oh." Wiping his mouth with a big white napkin, Uncle Willie stood up. "I'm goin on the porch before I get a earache."

Aunt Rachel eyed him. "Earache, my foot. You mean a throat ache. And not for no *water*, neither. Remember, Mr. Walker, you got to drive your sister back home. And just remember whose front porch you sittin on and whose neighbors are outside."

Uncle Willie threw up his hands and went out back.

Aunt Rachel turned back to Mama. "Movies and books is fine if that's what she likes to do, but I don't know about no playin the piano."

"Well, I told Belly she could take piano lessons, and if she's gonna take lessons she got to practice," said Mama. "And what's the use of havin a piano in the house if it never gets used? My God, Rachel, it'll only be about a half hour a day for about a month. And she won't play loud. Will you, Belly?"

I had just taken a large bite of chocolate cake, so I could only shake my head.

Aunt Rachel thought a moment. "Well, I'll have to call Reba Lomax and see if she got time."

Reba Lomax? I looked at Mama. She shook her head slightly.

Unaware of this byplay, Aunt Rachel continued. "Avery don't get home from work until seven o'clock, and he might not feel like driving this child out to her place. That's seven miles out and seven miles back."

"I wasn't thinkin of Miss Reba," said Mama. "I was thinkin of somebody who Belly can walk to."

"Walk to!" Aunt Rachel drew in her chin. "Who in this town is giving piano lessons? Not nobody colored. And if they is, it's news to me."

"Ophelia," said Mama.

"Ophelia." Aunt Rachel frowned, then, "Ophelia Love?"

"That's the only Ophelia I know," said Mama.

"And the one *I* know don't give no piano lessons," returned Aunt Rachel.

"Well, Myra Gibson told me she does," said Mama.

"Myra Gibson. What's Myra Gibson know about what's goin on over here in Jamison."

"Her niece lives over here and she told Myra that she takes piano lessons from Ophelia."

"Well, I ain't heard about no lessons," said Aunt Rachel, as if they could not occur without her permission. "Didn't I just tell you a couple weeks ago that Mattie Hearns said the woman was sick? So how's she gonna be givin some piano lessons? And I don't believe it noway. That prune-faced hussy think she too good to give piano lessons. Mouth all turned up and talkin so proper, tryin to be cute."

"Now you know Ophelia ain't never been like that," Mama said quietly.

"Givin piano lessons and nobody even knew she was in that house." Aunt Rachel was so beside herself that she sliced herself a second piece of chocolate cake, an act she normally considered gluttonous. "And if she was givin lessons, I wouldn't know about sendin this child there with her bein sick. Might fall over dead or somethin while Belly's there."

"If she gets sick when Belly's there it might be good. She could call somebody."

"Hmph," said Aunt Rachel.

We sat for a few moments. Mama and Aunt Rachel drank tea. I had another piece of cake.

"Well," said Aunt Rachel finally, "I'll talk to Avery when he comes in. He might not mind the ride out to Miss Reba's. He's got some cousins out that way and always complainin he never gets out to see them."

I was disappointed. I had heard so much about Miss Ophelia I felt I would be cheated if I did not make her acquaintance. But I dared not express a choice, for I had figured one thing out about Aunt Rachel; she was contrary. If I said I wanted to go to Miss Ophelia, she would insist I go to Miss Reba.

My mother was probably considering that side of her, too. "Miss Reba or Miss Ophelia, it don't matter," she said, warning me with a look. "As long as Belly gets her lessons."

Aunt Rachel shrugged. "Well . . . I don't know. I'll see about it this evening. It probably would be better all around if Belly could walk instead of botherin Avery."

And so it was settled. If Aunt Rachel was true to her word, I was to go to this Miss Ophelia for piano lessons. I would meet this friend of Mama's from New York City who had a weak heart and only came out at night, like a skunk. I shivered in anticipation.

Aunt Rachel and I went onto the porch to see Mama and Uncle Willie off. Then Aunt Rachel went inside and got a needlepoint canvas to start for a footstool and brought me *The Pink Fairy Book,* which I was reading for the second time, but soon I had to stop and nod politely and often to a stream of curious members of Randolph Street and others in the colored community who had heard that Miss Rachel was going to the hospital (Operation? Well I declare . . .) and her niece had come to stay with her for a while. (Her sister Lizzie's daughter. She married Tyler Anderson. You remember Tyler Anderson. Killed in the war.)

All the time their heads twisted on necks of rope, looking up at me, then Aunt Rachel, but no one was invited up onto the porch for more detailed information. No matter. Someone would find out and they would all know within twenty-four hours and cluck and speculate for twenty-four more.

Unsettled by so many interruptions, I was about to ask Aunt Rachel if I could be excused when the door to the porch next door opened and a woman stepped out.

"Stay right there," she said to someone behind the screen.

A whiny protest began. The woman slapped the screen with a large flyswatter.

"Mornin, Ella," Aunt Rachel called across the alleyway.

"Mornin, Rachel." The woman came to the porch railing. She was small and wiry. "Looks like we're gonna have a lovely day." Her voice was reedy.

"Looks like it," said Aunt Rachel. She pushed me toward the railing. "This is my niece, Belly. The one I told you was comin."

"How do you do, Belly," called Miss Ella.

"How do you do," I called back.

"Miss Ella moved here last year," said Aunt Rachel. "She got a little boy. Jimmy."

"And he's a devil, too," said Miss Ella. "That's him at the door wantin to come outside, but he's on punishment again. Went out of that backyard when I told him not to."

"Miss Ella's gonna cook dinner for you and your Uncle Avery while I'm gone," said Aunt Rachel.

"Now is that Friday, Rachel? I know you mentioned it . . ."

"Saturday. Belly came a week early."

"Well . . . that'll give her time to get used to us before you go." She leaned over the banister and called to Aunt Rachel in a low voice and she went over to listen. "I was talkin to Nola this morning. About her problem." She paused and raised her eyebrows. Obviously her news was not suitable for the ears of pubescent girls. Aunt Rachel took the cue and dismissed me to the back porch, where I was only too happy to go and read my book.

C h a p t e r 10

"**H**ey, girl."

I was reading, stretched out belly down on Aunt Rachel's wicker settee. I looked around, but I did not see the face that belonged to the voice. I went back to my book.

"Whatcha readin?"

I didn't answer.

"You deaf, girl?"

"A book!"

"What's the name of the book?"

Again I didn't answer.

"Cat got your tongue?"

I rolled my eyes and scowled. "I wish you'd leave me alone."

"You Miss Rachel's niece."

Exasperated, I sat up and closed the book. On the porch across from me a boy was hanging on the railing peeping through the balusters. He must have been the boy Miss Ella slapped at behind her screen door a few minutes before. He seemed determined to live up to his mother's description, for he was grinning devilishly. "What's the name of the book?" he asked again.

Again I didn't answer.

"You prob'ly don't even know."

"I bet you better shut up."

"I don't shut up, I grow up, when I see you I throw up, the only reason I don't throw up is I'm 'fraid you might lick it up." The words flew from his mouth like bullets from a machine gun.

I stared over at him.

He stared back, then stood up. He was short, but he was able to throw one leg on the railing, swing himself over, hold on, dangle, then let go and fall to the ground.

I flopped back down on the settee and pretended to be reading. A moment later he was standing near the top step of Aunt Rachel's porch. I looked over at him. His head was round as a cantaloupe, his nose so flat its tip almost touched his top lip.

I crossed my legs at the ankles and turned back to my book. I did not see him ease up onto the porch and stand next to me. "You read all that?" he asked, pointing to my book with a pudgy finger.

Angry, I swung up and around. "Yes, I *did*."

His eyes met mine. Dark brown eyes that turned up at the corners like a cat's.

I frowned. "I want to read the rest, but you can't read when people keep interrupting you."

My exasperated tone didn't seem to bother him at all.

"What's it about?"

I studied him a moment, wondering what it would take to get him to leave. "I'll tell you if you go away."

"Okay." He sat on the edge of a chair across from me.

"It's about this real ugly beast."

"Is that him there? He's ugly!"

"Do you want me to tell you or not?"

He nodded.

"It's a story about this old man who passed through the woods and got lost and tired and saw this castle. And then he went up to it and went inside and ate and slept. And then this beast, who the castle belonged to, but he was really a prince under a magic spell by an old witch, he told the man he'd kill him for eating and sleeping in his castle."

"Did the beast kill him?"

This was my third reading of the story, but I looked into his eyes and lied. "I haven't finished reading the story yet."

"Will you tell me the rest when you do?"

"Maybe."

He came over and sat down next to me. He waited a moment, then said, "My name's Jimmy Diggs. I'm eight."

I wasn't about to reveal my age to this impudent boy.

"What's your name?"

"You said you would go if I told you the story."

He lowered his voice and whispered, "Can I tell you something first?"

I hesitated.

His eyes narrowed shrewdly. "You gotta promise not to tell."

"What."

"Miss Rachel goin to the hospital on Friday."

"That ain't nothin to tell," I said contemptuously. "Why do you think *I'm* here? To take care of her when she comes out of the hospital. And she's going Saturday, not Friday." I stood up and shook my dress out and went to the screen door and opened it.

"That ain't all." He edged toward me and looked past me into the kitchen, then stepped back and crooked his finger. "C'm'ere."

I kept my hand on the doorknob and leaned forward. "What?"

He edged forward and tipped his head back to whisper in my ear. "She gonna git her guts took out so she can't have no more babies." He turned his head and looked up at me from the corner of one chocolate eye.

My jaw dropped.

He drew back from me and nodded slowly, then added in a rush, "But she can't have no babies no way 'cause she already had one a long time ago but it was born dead."

Holding his eyes with mine, I walked over to the swing and sat down.

He followed and sat next to me. "And she *mean*. And my mama says that's probably why she can't have none because God don't like people to be mean to babies." He leaned closer. "And my mama says—"

"Jimmeee!"

We jumped.

Miss Ella was standing down in her yard waving her fly swatter up at us.

As if jerked by a string, Jimmy jumped up and galloped down the steps of our porch and across our yard to his own and began dancing and ducking to avoid Miss Ella's slaps on his legs.

"Didn't I tell you not to go out of this house! You got a head like a rock . . . over there botherin Miss Rachel's niece! Probably talkin your head off about things you don't know nothin about. Git up here!" Whap! Jimmy scuttled past her and ran screeching up the porch steps. "I'm'a tear your behind up!" She ran up after him and got him again on the legs. He ran screaming into the house. She stopped for a breath and called over to me, "I'm sorry he come over there and bothered you, honey. Rachel said you was out here readin . . . If he come over there botherin you any more, just holler for me or his father. That boy know better. He got a head like a rock."

Perversely, I sided with her son. "He wasn't botherin me," I said. "I was tellin him a story."

"Oh," said Miss Ella, deflated.

Aunt Rachel's voice came through our screen door. "I thought you come out here to read, Belly. Who you talkin to?"

"Miss Ella." I nodded toward the porch next door.

Aunt Rachel opened the door and leaned out. "Oh, there you are, Ella. I was wonderin why Jimmy came shootin out onto the front porch like a bat out of hell."

"That boy got the hardest head in creation. I put him on punishment and he think he gonna do what he want. I tell him to stay in the house and he come outside anyway. Out here on your porch botherin the child while she was readin."

"Belly didn't mind," said Aunt Rachel.

"Well, even if *she* didn't, *I* did, and he's goin to bed with no supper tonight!" She slammed her screen door open and took off like a witch on a broom.

I opened my book. Aunt Rachel stood at the door. I felt her eyes on me, but I did not look up for fear she might take a notion to have me join her again on the front porch. But after a moment she said, "It's almost time for Avery's lunch. He'll be comin in and I won't have it ready and I guess he'll think I've gone crazy."

Uncle Avery never appeared for lunch. He came home from work just as I finished setting the table for supper, carrying a black metal lunch box. "Evenin, Rachel. Belly." He set the box on the counter next to the sink and began to wash his hands.

Aunt Rachel looked at the box. "Oh, you *carried* your lunch today. I fixed lunch and me and Belly sittin here waitin while the food got cold."

Uncle Avery soaped his hands and said quietly, "If you remember I told you last night I wouldn't be home for lunch today, I had a busted pipe at the school and it would probably take us all day to fix it." And he went on to say if she had been up this morning when he left he would have mentioned it again, but he did not want to disturb her.

Aunt Rachel did remember. And she had meant to get up and pack his lunch, but she was feeling extra tired. Probably due to her condition and her impending operation.

Uncle Avery nodded sympathetically and turned to me and smiled as he dried his hands. "Well, now, who's this stranger? Could this be Isabel Anderson?"

"Yes, sir," I said, grinning, from relief because the tension was easing, but mostly because he was smiling at me.

"Done any more readin since I seen you last?"

"Yes, sir."

"Lizzie said she wore her brain out," said Aunt Rachel.

"Are you keepin a list of your books?" said Uncle Avery.

"Yes, sir." I could never think of much more to say to Uncle Avery.

He pulled out a chair and sat down at the table. "Sit down, Belly. Can't eat standin up."

I went to sit in a chair Aunt Rachel pulled out for me. "You sit here, Belly. Across from your uncle Avery."

He spread his napkin across his lap. "I didn't realize you were so tall, Belly. How old are you now, twelve?"

"Eleven."

"And big as a he-horse," said Aunt Rachel.

"I'll be twelve in November," I mumbled, as if those four months would diminish my size.

Uncle Avery winked at me. "Well, we all go through that awkward stage."

"Yes, sir."

"Put your napkin on your lap, Belly," said Aunt Rachel.

Flustered, I shook out my napkin and reached across the table for a roll, unaware that Uncle Avery had bowed his head for the blessing. By the time I noticed he had begun.

"Lord we thank Thee for the food we are about to receive for the nourishment of our bodies, in Christ's name, amen."

I dropped my hand and lowered my head. I did not look at Aunt Rachel, but her eyes were on me, I knew.

We ate in silence, breaking it only to ask for the salt, the pepper, bread, or the butter. I finished quickly. At home I would have excused myself and gone outside to sit on the porch, or upstairs to read, but that night I sat, hands folded, and watched my aunt and uncle consume the meal of broiled lamb chops, mashed potatoes, and peas bite by bite, pea by pea. At last it was over. Uncle Avery wiped his mouth and rose.

"Oh, Avery," said Aunt Rachel, as if she had just remembered, "tomorrow when you go cut Miss Mattie's grass, see if she can get hold of Ophelia Love."

"Ophelia Love?"

Aunt Rachel had risen and was now clearing the table and scraping the dishes. "I want to talk to her about givin Belly piano lessons."

"Piano lessons." There was something about Uncle Avery's voice, the way he held his body, like a cat when it sits very still in the grass, slightly moving the tip of its tail, watching something only it can see.

Aunt Rachel's attention was entirely focused on her after-dinner ritual. Uncle Avery was not in her sight or on her mind as she repeated the conversation she'd had that afternoon with Mama. She was unaware, when she mentioned Miss Ophelia's name, that his body had stiffened, his hand had gripped the back of the chair so hard that the knuckles turned white; or that his face had changed color. I was aware, however, and curious.

He recovered quickly and smiled at me. "So you want to play the piano, Belly? I thought you were a champion reader."

"I do like to read. But I want to play the piano, too."

"Well, I guess it would be nice to go someplace where you could walk to." He pushed his chair under the table. "I'll ask Miss Mattie about it tomorrow."

I would have followed him into the living room to talk about my ambitions, but Aunt Rachel stopped me with a sharp "Isabel." Uncle Avery had worked hard all day and liked to be alone to listen to the news, she explained. Meanwhile I could take the dish towel and dry the dishes.

Afterward, we went upstairs and she gave me soap and a towel and showed me the new shower. I was not used to water pouring over my body or getting my hair wet unless it was being washed, and a hasty sprinkle was more than satisfactory.

I went back downstairs and sat on the porch and smelled the sweet smoke from Uncle Avery's pipe and listened to the chigchig chigchig of the locusts and Aunt Rachel and Miss Ella talking softly to each other across the alley between the porches. I wondered if she would have confided so easily in Miss Ella had she known her real opinion of her or that she discussed their conversations in the hearing of an eight-year-old blabbermouth.

I went to bed earlier than usual. Perhaps that explains my inability to get a good night's rest. I remember that I lay awake for a long time. Then, too, it was my first time away from home for an overnight stay, and the room and the bed were unfamiliar, but finally I fell asleep.

Sometime in the middle of the night I sat straight up in bed, my heart thumping, wondering where I was. I remembered and lay back on my pillow and stared into the dark and listened to the silence. The clock in the kitchen chimed the half hour. I crept out of bed and sat at the window and looked at the moon gleaming in the sky like a large honeydew melon. A veil passed over it. It shimmered, then gleamed again, translucent, whole. I stared at the sky and I wondered.

I wondered about Miss Ella and Jimmy and why she smacked him so often with a flyswatter; I wondered how long I would be able to tolerate eating dinner in this house; I wondered about Miss Ophelia, why Mama liked her and why Aunt Rachel held her in such contempt; and I wondered about Uncle Avery's reaction when Miss Ophelia's name was mentioned. I wondered about that most of all.

"Do you know Miss Ophelia?" I whispered to the moon.

But the moon only gleamed and shimmered.

The next morning Aunt Rachel led me through the house to show me a few things she wished I would do while she was in the hospital. We started in the kitchen with the large white refrigerator. This she wiped out once a week with Clorox and water. In the dining room she pointed out the gleaming walnut tabletop and the gleaming walnut china closet and in the living room the gleaming walnut spinet that needed dusting every other day. She gave me a demonstration. It looked dustless to me, I pointed out, but the idea was to keep the dust off, not to let it collect, then wipe it off. And dust *after* you run the vacuum cleaner.

The stairway had not yet been remodeled and, as in all those houses, was dark and steep. I followed her up to the bathroom. Uncle Avery would take care of cleaning the floor, but I must be sure to wash out the sink and tub after I used them. And of course I would be responsible for keeping my own room neat. This was the end of the tour. I was dismissed. Aunt Rachel went into her room.

With a silent whoop I ran down the hall and galloped down the steps. Suddenly, my feet were in the air and I was on my behind, bumping down the steps, where I fell to my knees on the landing.

Aunt Rachel ran down behind me and pulled me up by my arm. "Jesus wept! Gal, is you crazy? Gallopin down them steps like a fool! Break your neck and then there'll be two of us in the hospital." Supported by her arm, I limped over to a chair, where she eased me down. "Here. Let me look at that knee." She pressed the area with strong fingers. I winced. "Just swolled a little, that's all. Sit there while I go git a wet towel." In seconds she was back, kneeling, wrapping it around my leg. "Lord, Lord. I hope you ain't gonna be more trouble than you worth."

Uncle Willie or my mother might have reacted with words as harsh or even harsher than those Aunt Rachel said to me that day, but I was familiar with their ways, rough and soft. I only knew Aunt Rachel's rough side, and her unsympathetic words cut like a whip. I burst into tears.

"Now you too big to be a crybaby," said Aunt Rachel. "Ain't nothin broke and you ain't dead."

There was a knock at the screen door. Miss Ella was peering at us from the other side. "Rachel? Is everything all right?"

"We're still alive." Aunt Rachel went and unlocked the door.

Miss Ella followed her in. "I was outside and heard this boomaloo-maloom and I said to myself, 'Oh, my God, somebody done fell down the steps.'"

"Belly." Aunt Rachel grunted. "Here she is mooin like a sick cow."

Miss Ella came over to me and felt my head. "The child had to hurt herself fallin down the steps."

"That's the only way she gonna stop gallopin down the steps. If it was fun, she'd try it again."

Miss Ella bent over me to look in my face. "You all right, honey?" When I nodded, she went to a chair and sat down. "Now it's easy to fall down the steps in these houses, even when you take your time. They all too steep and crooked and dark. Can't see your hand in front of your face. I fell down mine last winter and almost broke my back. Soon as I get the money, I'm having mine opened up." She stopped to look around the living room enthusiastically. "I declare, this is the first time I got a good look at this room. It sure is beautiful since Avery knocked that wall out. Opened up the whole place. I done talked my-self hoarse tryin to get Jimmy Senior to do ours." She rose and went to the window. "And look at how Avery fixed this window."

"A picture window," said Aunt Rachel. "Lets in more light."

"Well, I declare, it looks like a picture in here," said Miss Ella, arms folded, making a complete turn in her seat. "Just like them pictures in the *Ladies' Home Journal.*"

They had forgotten about me. I sat back and relaxed.

"Well, I didn't need no magazine to teach me how to decorate," said Aunt Rachel. "I started workin for rich folks when I was ten years old. Polishin silver. Cleanin. Cookin. Bein in their houses you just naturally see the way some of them fix up their homes, you see the way they live. You learn their manners." She lowered herself to the piano bench; Miss Ella, still on the chair, looked attentively into Aunt Rachel's face, encouraging her verbal strutting with nods, smiles, and expressions of awe.

Now, Mrs. Guilford, the first one she worked for, when she found out she was redecorating, had given her that club chair in the corner. Mrs. Remington gave her that dining room suite when she got her new one. And that Chippendale sofa came right from the living room of Dr. Dewberry when he was gettin ready to move. And those drapes, they were made from the *same* material Mrs. Granville had her new slipcovers made from. Didn't she ask where she could buy some, and didn't Mrs. Granville give her six yards for a gift? And this needlepoint stool, she covered that herself. Old Mrs. Remington taught her to do needlepoint when she was thirteen years old. Every young girl should have something useful to preoccupy her time, she used to say. Of course she was sick in bed at that time and Rachel was nursing her, else she would never had time to learn no needlework. Woman died with a needle in her hand . . ." She paused, thinking, then turned to me. "I might teach you to do needlepoint, Belly. Before I go to the hospital. We got time."

I did not think I would like that at all, but I nodded.

Miss Ella was ecstatic over the idea. "That is such a practical thing. And it will give her something to do. Things get very boring for these young girls here in Jamison. If more of them knew how to occupy their hands and minds, they wouldn't get into *trouble*." I deciphered that as pregnant. She raised her eyebrows and looked slyly at Aunt Rachel in the same manner she had the day before. Another piece of gossip.

Aunt Rachel promptly settled me in a wicker chair on the back porch with my leg propped up on a stool, my book in my lap, and four Social Tea cookies folded in a napkin on the table next to me. I began reading.

"Psssst!"

That nosy darned boy again. I tried to ignore him, but he had the persistence of a cat stalking a bird. In a flash he was over the railing and on our porch. "I know your name. Belly."

"Isabel." I shot back.

"Mama told me to stay in the house today."

"Don't she *ever* let you out?"

"When I'm good."

"Why she keepin you in this time?"

"Because I come over here and bothered you yesterday."

"I thought that was why she beat you yesterday."

"No. That was for leavin the *porch* yesterday."

"Well, ain't you worried she might catch you and keep you in some more?"

"Be in the house anyway." He was looking at my leg. "You break your leg or somethin?"

"Nope."

"I broke my leg once."

"You keep hoppin over that railin and you're gonna break it again."

Now he was looking at my cookies. "Can I have one?"

"One." I handed him a cookie. If you have ever eaten a Social Tea cookie, you know that they are tiny and dainty and melt almost immediately on contact with the tongue; that one is merely a tease and whets the taste for another and another and another.

The cookie was gone as soon as it was in his mouth, and he looked at the last one on my napkin. I showed him no courtesy. I popped it into my own mouth. "You better go back before your mama gets home and you get in trouble."

"You said you was gonna tell me the rest of that story. About that prince who was a beast."

I sighed.

"Please."

I tried another ploy. "I forgot where I stopped and I ain't startin at the beginning again."

Without blinking he repeated almost word for word what I had told him the day before.

I hurriedly related more of the story. "Well, the beast told the old man he could go home if he sent him one of his daughters to stay with him, and the old man was upset, but what could he do, so he went home and told his daughters one of them would have to go to the beast or he'd be killed and the only one who would go was his youngest one, who was very sweet and so pretty that her name was Beauty. So she went to save her father."

"Did the beast kill her?"

Before I could answer Aunt Rachel's voice said, "That's who she's talkin to. Jimmy." She opened the screen door and stepped onto the porch. "I thought that fall might've affected your head and had you talkin to yourself."

Miss Ella stepped out behind her. "Jimmy, didn't I tell you not to come over here again?"

Jimmy's mouth flapped but no words came out. I took pity on him and answered instead. "He didn't come over. I saw him on the porch and I called him over so I could tell him the rest of the story I was tellin him yesterday."

His mother glared at him. "Did she finish? Because I better not catch you over here no more unless I tell you."

Jimmy darted a look at me.

"No, ma'am," I said. "I didn't finish. I told him I'd tell him the rest tomorrow so he could go home now before he got in trouble."

Miss Ella smiled. "See, boy, here's the kind of friend you need. Somebody who'll look out for you."

Aunt Rachel bent over to look at my knee. "Don't look like she can take care of herself, much less look out for somebody else."

They went back inside.

I looked at Jimmy speculatively. "Can you do dishes, boy?"

He nodded vigorously. "And I can dust, too. I help Mama a lot."

"Good," I said brusquely. "Now you better go before you get into more trouble." I ignored his sorrowful look and went back to my book.

At bedtime that night I had more than a sprinkle-shower. After dinner Aunt Rachel inspected my knee. She suggested that I soak in a long, hot bath and she came with me to make sure I did. I was embarrassed to undress in front of her but I quickly got over any modesty about being naked in her presence.

"You ain't got nothin I ain't got. Least, I hope you don't." She went into a cabinet next to the sink and took out a jar and a bottle. From the jar she sprinkled Epsom salts into the tub for the soaking. The bottle contained shampoo. "Here's some Breck shampoo. Mrs. Guilford used it all the time. I know you ain't washed that hair in a blue moon. Dull as dishwater. This will make it shine." She unscrewed the cap and pushed the bottle under my nose. "Make your hair smell good, too. Now get in."

I stepped into the tub of warm water and she gave me my instructions. Run more hot water into the tub until the water got so hot I almost couldn't stand it. Then soak for twenty minutes. Soap myself good. "Especially where the sun don't shine and the air don't hit."

Twenty minutes later she returned and wet my hair, poured on shampoo and worked up the suds. "Now stand up, let the water out, turn on the shower, and rinse your hair and shampoo it again. Then you're done." I turned on the shower and this time stayed under the water so long Aunt Rachel came back in. "I didn't say drown yourself. I said wash your hair. Now get out of there and dry your hair and go to bed."

That night I fell into bed and slept straight through until the sun's rays woke me the next morning.

Uncle Avery's hobby was cutting grass. I call it that since he did it on a regular basis without pay and seemed to enjoy it. I suspect it was also a legitimate reason for him to get out of the house and away from Aunt Rachel's nagging. On Saturdays he cut the grass at Canaan Baptist Church; during the week he took care of his own yard and those of the widow women on Randolph Street. Old widow women. Randolph Street was full of old widow women. Women whose children had moved far away; women who had no adolescent grandchild or the son of a friendly neighbor to mow grass or chop wood or replace rotting porch boards or do other odd jobs that crop up in the upkeep on an old house.

Yes, Randolph Street was an old street with old people. If there were any younger people, they worked six and a half days out of the week and had little time for such chores. So the old widow women became dependent upon the generous spirit of their neighbors' husbands or other men in the community who would work for a minimal fee, or, in the case of Uncle Avery, free.

Miss Mattie Hearns was one of Uncle Avery's widows. On Tuesday after dinner he pushed back from the table and said, "Want to take a little walk, Belly? Walk some of that dinner down." He looked over at Aunt Rachel. "Goin to Miss Mattie's."

I thought for sure Aunt Rachel would tell me I had to do the dishes first, but she nodded instead and I jumped up to go, but not because I wanted to get any exercise. My reason was a selfish one. Since Miss Mattie lived next door to Miss Ophelia, I hoped to get a glimpse of the mysterious woman who might be my music teacher. I was very curious about this person who aroused such contempt in Aunt Rachel and such disquiet in Uncle Avery.

We went down to the back gate and stepped into a paved alleyway that ran behind all the backyards on our side of Randolph Street. The alley was overgrown, like a path through a forest, bushes and wild hedges entangled with honeysuckle vines on either side, narrow, a little wider than Uncle Avery's lawn mower. At some yards, the bushes were trimmed back for an entrance, but most back fences were overgrown with foliage.

"Don't touch none of these weeds," warned Uncle Avery. "Some of them's poison ivy."

I held my arms close to my body and slipped sideways behind him. Soon we came to the end and Uncle Avery entered the gate of the last yard. We stepped into a yard like all the others on Randolph Street, long, narrow, enclosed with a fence. This yard, unlike Aunt Rachel's, was bordered with large green-leafed plants and flowers. A woman was sitting on the porch. She stood up. She was bent over, hand on hip, not standing up completely.

"Hullo there, Avery!"

"Hullo, Miss Mattie!" said Uncle Avery. "How's that arthritis this evenin?"

"Comes and goes when it wants. Today it decided to hang around."

She held on to the railing and leaned toward us. "Who's that you got with you?"

"My niece. Somebody for you to talk to this evenin."

"Your niece." She cocked her head like a little bird. "This must be Lizzie's child. Bring her on up here so I can get a good look at her."

We went up onto the porch. Miss Mattie was old, but not as old as Miss Janie. Her hair was slate gray and pulled back in a tight bun. Her eyes sparkled like bright black beads in her smooth brown face. After Uncle Avery introduced us, she offered him a cup of coffee.

"Think I will, Miss Mattie. Give me a little boost." Uncle Avery sat down and crossed his leg while she poured it for him.

Then she offered me a cup. I loved coffee. In the mornings my mother let me have a cup laced liberally with milk, but she never let me have it at night. Aunt Rachel, a tea drinker, never touched the stuff, and even if she did, would never have given it to a child. I looked over at Uncle Avery for permission.

"Don't look at him, child," said Miss Mattie. "I'm askin *you* if you want some coffee."

"Yes, ma'am."

"I know, people say it will keep you awake all night. Won't do you no harm if you put a lot of milk in it. And sugar. My mother let me have it, mornin or night. Always kept a pot on the back of the stove. Got so strong it could melt nails. And I bless her to this day." She settled in her chair. "Yes"—she was like a tabby cat purring in the sunlight—"there's nothin like a good cup of coffee. In the mornin with a buttery biscuit, in the evenin with a piece of cake." She handed me a slice of pound cake. "Nothin like a good piece of cake."

Uncle Avery sat on the edge of the little porch and placed his cup beside him. He studied Miss Mattie's yard. "Well, your grass looks okay, a little dry. Flowers need a little weedin."

"My back been givin me a little trouble lately. I been thinkin of gettin that little Jimmy Diggs down here. He asked me the other day at church if I had somethin for him to do. I didn't then, but I never thought of that. Give him a chance to get out from under that whinin mother of his."

"Be good for her, too," said Uncle Avery. "And he'd probably do a good job. Maybe Belly can bring him down here one mornin and show him how to weed the flowers."

She asked me if I would and I nodded. "Yes, ma'am."

Uncle Avery finished his coffee and went down to cut the grass. I drank coffee and ate cake and listened to Miss Mattie. "That's a good man down in that yard. A good man. Comes by here every week. Cuts my grass. Keeps my impatiens so beautiful."

I was familiar with impatiens but not the plants with the large green leaves. I pointed at them. "What are those?" I asked.

"That's called hosta. Next month green stalks will rise up and lavender flowers will grow on them. Real delicate flowers, like little bells. Then the fat bees crawl up in the flower and it closes around them and while they're all snug in there they suck out the sweet juice. You ever see them do that?"

"No, ma'am."

"Well, I guess I didn't either when I was your age. But when you get older you see these things. You have time to sit around and see things you didn't see when you were young. I used to have a garden full of sage and marigolds and begonias and petunias. All kinds of flowers. But I couldn't keep up with 'em. The impatiens and the hosta's enough for me. And the honeysuckles on the fence. They give a lovely smell. That's all I need. A little grass and one or two sweet-smellin flowers. That's all I need."

"Whose hedges are those? They need cuttin." I was referring to a row of privets between her property and the house I assumed to be Miss Ophelia's. They were at least eight feet high.

"That's the way poor Deacon Love let them grow, poor soul. Sick the last couple of years before he died. Let it all go. Avery told him he'd trim them for him, but he said no. Avery cut them once, but he got real upset. Wanted his privacy, he said. Uh-huh. Privacy from who. Me? His mind was gone, poor man. But you can't just go choppin on people's hedges if they don't want you to. Well, maybe when the house is sold the new people will cut them lower. Avery cuts this side for me when they get to lookin too wild."

I had heard that the house was to be sold. That was not new. I pumped Miss Mattie for new information. "Don't some lady live there? What about her?"

"Deacon Love's daughter," said Miss Mattie. "Ophelia. Nobody but her now." She grunted. "And she sure ain't strong enough to cut them bushes. No indeedy."

I almost blurted out about the piano lessons and Miss Ophelia, but I remembered in time that Aunt Rachel had told Uncle Avery to have Miss Mattie arrange things. I did not want to do or say anything that might get me into trouble.

"You're Lizzie's only child?"

"Yes, ma'am."

"You look like her when she was your age."

"Yes, ma'am."

"Willie livin with her, I understand."

"Yes, ma'am."

"He's never married, I understand."

"No, ma'am."

"Just as well."

"Yes, ma'am."

"Guess you ain't lookin for no stepfather."

"Oh, no *ma'am*."

A dry laugh. "Uh-huh. Don't blame you. Not one bit."

Uncle Avery came back up on the porch. "Well, not much more I can do today. This hot weather done burned out a lot of the grass. I'll let it alone for a while. Now I pulled the weeds over by the fence on the side and back."

"Looks like a different yard," said Miss Mattie.

"Looks a little better," said Uncle Avery.

"Oh, it looks much better, Uncle Avery," I said. "And I can even smell the honeysuckle better."

Uncle Avery smiled and said to Miss Mattie, "Water the flowers tomorrow morning before it gets too hot." He picked up the coffee cups. "Here. I'll take these inside for you."

They went into the house. Now he would ask her to see Miss Ophelia about the piano lessons. I sat on the edge of the porch and put my arms around my knees and smelled the sweetness of the honey-suckle and gazed at the flowers in the yard and I suddenly realized that Aunt Rachel had no flowers in her yard. No plants around the borders. Merely grass, neatly mowed. I looked over at the tall hedge. What was on the other side? Maybe I could take a peek. I got up and went toward

the steps but sat quickly back down when I heard the door open behind me. Uncle Avery and Miss Mattie came back out onto the porch.

"Let's go, Belly," said Uncle Avery.

"See you soon, Little Lizzie," said Miss Mattie with a wink.

The house I had come to was very different from my own. Our house
was always filled with sounds and smells. My mother singing, cooking,
Uncle Willie talking, laughing, yelling, the washing machine, the radio,
the record player, the pungent smells of boiling cabbage and percolat-
ing coffee, frying onions and old boots, and the mustiness of an old
house after it rains. In Aunt Rachel's house was the overwhelming
sound of silence along with the hum of the vacuum cleaner, the clink
and clatter of silverware and dishes, the smell of furniture polish. The
smell of food was confined to the kitchen by a door with fifteen window
panes. Words and laughter were rare as pearls.

In a few days I learned to lower my voice, quiet my feet, and control
my laughter. By the end of the week I was moving and talking as if I
had been born and bred in that bastion of civilization.

Sometime during that week Aunt Rachel taught me to do cross-
stitching. From her canvas bag where she kept her own work she took
a small linen square and needle threaded with blue floss and started
me out making large X's. Within two hours I could make several rows
without sticking my fingers. Within two days I was embroidering a
border for my first sampler. When I was ready to stitch the verse, Aunt
Rachel chose a verse from the Bible and inscribed it in ink on the
linen square. *Blessed Are the Meek.*

I was determined to make it a work of art and worked at it diligently
every afternoon on the front porch while she inspected the work with
a practiced eye, making me undo and restitch until my fingers were
numb and the letters were almost perfect.

As I stitched, I thought about my piano lessons. Whenever I passed
the piano, I longingly touched the keys, hoping that Miss Ophelia or
Miss Mattie would call that day. Finally word came on Friday, the day
before Aunt Rachel was to leave for the hospital. She called me from

the back porch, where I was working on the last part of the border. Miss Ophelia had called. Since we were going to Woolworth's to buy embroidery thread we would stop by her house and make arrangements for the piano lessons.

I was elated. A few days earlier I would have jumped up with joy. Instead I anchored my needle into the linen and laid it in the bag Aunt Rachel had given me. "Go upstairs and throw some water on your face and brush your hair," said Aunt Rachel. "When you go out on the street you should make sure you are neat and clean." Up in the bathroom I inspected my face in the mirror; no dirt was on my face and not a hair was out of place. I shrugged and did as I was told.

A few minutes later we were on Miss Ophelia's porch. Aunt Rachel opened the screen door, knocked, and waited. We listened for a moment. No sound. "She said the door would be open, but I just don't like to walk into people's houses." She knocked again.

"Come in, Rachel."

Aunt Rachel turned the doorknob. We stepped inside. The room was dim, much like Aunt Rachel's living room before it had been remodeled. But even less light could make its way through the heavy drapes so that the room appeared to be nothing but shapes and shadows. It was early afternoon, and the sun had passed over the house to the rear; I could see into the dining room, where the light filtered into a narrow window and threw more shadows. The faint odor of roses was in the air.

Someone was descending the stairs carefully and slowly. A woman. I could not see her clearly, but Aunt Rachel, who saw her first, spoke. "Well, good afternoon, Ophelia."

We were standing at the door, now we went further into the room. My eyes were growing accustomed to the dimness. I could see now that the room was small, cramped. A round table stood in a corner cluttered with photographs and a pile of music books. The piano, a mahogany upright, was placed against the wall across from me, and in front of it sat a claw-footed stool with a rose velvet cushion.

"Good afternoon, Rachel." The voice was soft and low. The woman went over to the piano stool and sat down. I looked at her, trying not to stare. She was a dark-skinned woman, the color of wet coffee grounds. Black, Aunt Rachel had called her. Her hair was also black, plaited into two long braids that were brought from the back of her head, wrapped up around her head, and pinned up at the top. She was wearing a blue cotton dress, smocked at the shoulders. It fell in loose folds around her body and draped down to the floor so I could only see the tip of one shoe. She folded her hands in her lap and smiled across at me.

"Well, this must be Isabel."

"Yes," said Aunt Rachel, pushing me forward. "Isabel, this is Miss Ophelia."

"How do you do." I held out my hand.

She took it in hers. "Lizzie's girl." She studied me a moment. Her eyes were large and luminous, like a doe's eyes. She looked over at Aunt Rachel. "Doesn't she look just like Lizzie when she was this age, Rachel."

"That's what everybody says," said Aunt Rachel.

She looked back at me. "And you want to take piano lessons."

I nodded. "I have a piano—"

"Belly, now you know you don't have no piano," said Aunt Rachel.

"Yes, I do! Only it's on Miss Janie's porch! And Mama says if I do good with Aunt Rachel and you, she'll see if she can buy it. And Aunt Rachel says I can practice on hers while I'm here if I don't play too loud."

"Good grief, Belly," said Aunt Rachel. "Nobody asked you for a long story. All you had to do was nod your head."

But Miss Ophelia encouraged me to continue. "Do you know how to play?"

"I know how to play a little. Miss Janie taught me how to read notes and play 'Chopsticks' and 'Heart and Soul' and—" I was about to tell about my music book collection but Aunt Rachel's frown stopped me.

My hand was still in Miss Ophelia's. It was soft and warm. She gently placed her other hand on mine and said, "She's enthusiastic, Rachel. That's a good sign. She'll have to be very determined if she wants to play the piano. It can get to be *very* boring after a while."

I shook my head. "Oh, I won't be bored." I thought of the needle-work sampler waiting for me when Aunt Rachel and I got home and blurted, "Can I start now?"

Aunt Rachel began to scold me for being so forward, but Miss Ophelia tilted her head and smiled. "Why not? You can show me what you know. Then we can make arrangements when you finish." She looked at Aunt Rachel. "Is that all right with you?"

Aunt Rachel was perched on the edge of a chair like a bird ready to take flight. She stood up. "That's fine with me. I think I know what color embroidery thread to pick out." She would stop by on her way home from Woolworth's.

She and Miss Ophelia went to the door and stood a moment talking softly. I went to the piano. On the rack was a book, *Grade 1*. I opened it to the first page. There in the corner my name was written in a fine script. Isabel Anderson. I felt a thrill. She was expecting me. Carefully, I placed the book on the holder and was picking out the tune when Miss Ophelia returned. She pulled a chair up beside me and I dropped my hands into my lap, embarrassed.

"You really can read notes, can't you!" She stood behind me and lifted my right hand and placed it on the keys, her hand over mine. "Like this. Fingers curved." She removed my hand from the keys and played a scale. "So you know Miss Janie Green. I took lessons from her when I was a little girl. She must be very old now. How is she?"

We talked a while about Miss Janie and her arthritis, then she showed me how to play the scales. "Raise each finger high, still curved . . . that's right . . . now bring it down firmly on the tip . . . no, not enough force . . . like this, see? That's right. That's right. Now slowly . . . but forcefully, bring down each finger. What key is this? C. The key C. That's right. Now we're only going to practice with one hand . . . and I'll play up here while you play there. Try to keep pace with me."

Oh, so much trouble to play five notes! Up and down. Firmly, slowly. Fingers curved. On the tips. Over and over. Now. The second hand. Up and down.

"I know how to do this already, Miss Ophelia. Miss Janie showed me." I was beginning to get impatient.

"But you are not doing it correctly," Miss Ophelia said firmly. "And if you practice incorrectly, you will play the same way. We will practice two hands together now, and I will play along with you. Remember, not fast . . . but firmly, on the tips. Together now. Cee Dee Eee Ef Gee, Gee Ef Eee Dee Cee. Up, up, up we go. Down, down, down like so."

I scowled. I was not going to like piano lessons.

But Miss Ophelia knew when to stop and work her magic. "That's enough, Isabel. Now, look at this." She opened a fat music book and pointed to a page. "Read the title."

" 'Waltz,' " I said.

"Who wrote the music?"

"Johannes Brahms."

"His name is pronounced Yo-hah-Ness Brahmz. Say it." She waited until I did, then, "Suppose I asked you to go to the music store and get this piece for me. What would you ask for?"

I thought a moment. " 'Waltz,' by Johannes Brahms?"

"But he wrote many waltzes." She waited a moment, I suppose waiting to see what I would do.

I leaned forward and stared at the page. The notes were difficult, three on a stem. I picked the top notes and tried to hum them, but the music was unfamiliar and I had difficulty.

Miss Ophelia laughed. "Yes, you could hum the music to the person in the store. I've done that and gotten a sheet of music if I didn't know the name of the piece. But suppose the person waiting on you doesn't know the music either. And it happens a lot. Do you see anything on the page that gives you a clue?"

I looked more intently at the page and fixed my eye on the words under the title. "Op thirty-nine dash fifteen?"

Miss Ophelia nodded. " 'Op' means opus. Latin for 'work.' So when you say 'Opus 39–15' the store clerk will know which waltz you mean, and so will anyone who plays a lot of music." She ran her hands up the keys in a ripple of notes. "Now"—she pointed at the music—"do you know how this sounds?"

I shook my head.

"Well, sit down and lay your head back and close your eyes and listen. And you will see why even though you think today's lesson was enough to make you stop taking lessons, you will want to continue."

I sat in a big armchair under the step. Miss Ophelia began playing. The black notes came to life. The music rose softly, the little cramped room disappeared; I was filled with the sound of the music. When it stopped, I opened my eyes and looked at Miss Ophelia. I said nothing. I got up and went to the piano and touched the keys. "Will practicing my scales help me play this?"

"And much more," she said softly.

"Will it take me long?"

"The more you practice, the shorter the time will be."

She picked up the *Grade 1* and checked off two pages. "Play your scales ten times. Both hands. And practice this little piece. Can you read it?"

I nodded.

There was a knock at the door. Miss Ophelia quickly penciled a few instructions in my book and whispered, "Monday, same time." She hurried me to the door and closed it softly behind me.

Aunt Rachel was on Miss Mattie Hearns's porch engaged in conversation with Miss Mattie. I sat down on the top step of Miss Ophelia's porch and opened my music book. I could read most of the exercises up to page nine. I placed my hand on my knee and pressed each finger against my knee as I said the notes. The conversation next door became louder; words drifted past me like wisps of smoke. "Lessons . . . well, I think . . ." The voices dropped, then rose. "Thread . . . needlework . . . start this dinner . . ." They stopped. Aunt Rachel started down the steps.

I closed my book and stood up.

Aunt Rachel was on the bottom step.

"Now you let me know if you need me in any way, Miss Rachel," called Miss Mattie. She waved at me. "Hi there, Belly! So you gonna be a piano player!"

I walked to her pavement and stood next to Aunt Rachel.

"Yes, ma'am."

"Rachel tells me you're learnin to do needlework, too."

"Yes, ma'am."

"You goin to be a busy child."

"Yes, ma'am."

"Well, now, don't forget to stop in to see me when you come for your lessons."

"Yes, ma'am." By now perspiration was pouring down my face, for at that time of day the heat from the sun was intense, but I could not be impolite and end the conversation.

Aunt Rachel, who was beginning to sweat more than a little herself, ended it with an exclamation. "Lord, Mattie! This child will burn us to a crisp here down here talkin to you in this hot sun." She pushed me toward home. "And me and Belly don't need no more sun, thank you."

Miss Mattie waved us away with a laugh. "Tee-hee. I guess none of us need that."

Uncle Avery drove Aunt Rachel to the hospital on Saturday morning. There was a new hospital in Jamison but she had chosen one about fifty miles away in Juniper City.

And she had chosen Juniper City for one reason: privacy. Several colored people who lived in and around Jamison worked at the new hospital as janitors and cooks, and of course the colored patients were housed in the colored section. No one went into the hospital if he had something he wanted to keep to himself. Colored people working there could easily find out just by keeping their ears open why a certain patient was there. Or someone in the bed next to you might even be so bold as to ask you what you were in for. That was the information Aunt Rachel had conveyed to Miss Ella one day when she asked her why she was going to Juniper City.

"Shuh," she had grunted, "I go up to Jamison and nosy-bodies will have it all over town why I'm goin in the hospital, and it really ain't none of their damned business. They don't want to know so they can make my life easier, they just want to know so they can have somethin else to talk about when they playin cards or flappin their mouths over the telephone."

I wondered why she thought her secret was safer with Miss Ella, to whom gossip was an elixir more potent than Miss Myra's dandelion wine. I knew that, and I had scarely known her a week.

"Seems so far for Avery to drive every day," said Miss Ella. "Workin all day, then drivin a hundred miles in the evenin."

"What's a car for but to drive," said Aunt Rachel. "All it do is sit outside and get dirty. Give him somethin to do."

Since Miss Ella was going along with them, Aunt Rachel made provisions for Jimmy and me to go to the Saturday afternoon matinee at the movies with a warning to go straight home when it was over and wait on the back porch for Miss Ella and Uncle Avery if they had not returned by then.

Miss Ella also delivered a stern warning to Jimmy. No misbehavior in the movies. "Stay with Belly! And no hangin over the rail with those rough children throwin peanuts and candy wrappers down on them white people!"

By the time Jimmy and I arrived, everyone had already entered. I went to the main door, but Jimmy pulled me back. "Colored people can't go in there! We got a separate door!"

I fell back, embarrassed, and followed Jimmy to a door I had passed. In Lambertville colored and white people went through the same door into the lobby and formed separate lines. There was one booth with one ticket seller who sold tickets to white and colored. Then the colored people went to the left with their tickets, gave them to the usher, and went up to their seats in the balcony while the white people went straight into the main part of the theater.

Here in Jamison it was different, I discovered after Jimmy pulled me back and we went inside. Instead of a roomy lobby, we had entered a grimy little hallway with a booth on our right and a stairway straight ahead. A white girl took our money. There were no tickets. We paid and went straight up the steps to the balcony. The show had not started so the lights were still on. It was a dim, dismal, cramped place, almost like an attic, with a slanted roof and no windows so the air was hot and close and funky with the smell of old unwashed clothing. The floors were bare. The tiers of wooden bleachers were crowded with laughing, talking, eating children. A few adults were scattered among them, scowling at the noise but powerless to do anything about it.

Jimmy knew quite a few of the children. He waved and called them by name, and a few of them called to him, waving him down to the front rail where they were sitting, but I grabbed his hand and made my way up to the center, back where I could see more.

"Why can't we sit down front!" said Jimmy after we had worked our way up to our seats.

I pushed him onto a seat. "I ain't goin down there, and neither are you. Miss Ella said so before we left."

Just then the lights dimmed; the show started and his attention turned to the screen. *Looney Toons* was on; protected by the darkness the audience became even rowdier, yelling, clapping, and whistling. Then came the serial: *The Lone Ranger*. Halfway through the episode, a voice two rows down started yelling at the screen. "Watch out there, Lone Ranger! He's hidin behind that rock! I told you! I told you!"

I leaned forward to discern an old woman in a straw hat.

"That's Miss Laura Bell," whispered Jimmy. "She always come here and do that. Every Saturday. She crazy."

The heavy air in the balcony was now being invaded by a more powerful smell: that of a heavy cologne. I looked for the source. It seemed to come from a couple five seats to my left, sitting against the wall. The girl had her arms wrapped around the boy's neck and was kissing him so hard his head seemed to be mashed into the wall. I nudged Jimmy. "Who's that?"

He leaned across me to look, then sat back. "That's old Althea Robinson. Her mother swear she a angel. You see her, don't you."

I waved my hand in front of my nose. "Phew!"

"That's her mother's Evenin in Paris perfume," sniffed Jimmy. "She put it on every Saturday and come up here courtin. She got a new boy every other week. Everybody say she gonna git a baby if she don't watch out."

"It sure does stink."

Jimmy shrugged. "She better wash it off before she go home."

I studied the lovers a moment longer. "As close as she is to him she ought to wear it off in here."

"Or else he'll lick it off," said Jimmy.

I turned his head around to look at the screen. "Little boys shouldn't see stuff like that."

"That ain't new. Them girls be neckin every week."

After the Movietone News and the previews came the main picture, *History Is Made at Night,* with Jean Arthur and Charles Boyer. It was an old movie, but in Lambertville old movies, along with Westerns, were the backbone of the Saturday matinees.

Jimmy was now ready to leave. He had seen the preview of this film the week before. "All they do in this movie is *kiss* and make goo-goo eyes. That's why I wasn't even comin to the movies until Mama made me come with you."

I was familiar with the dewey-eyed Jean Arthur and the suave Charles Boyer, and I knew I was going to see a good love story. "I'm not goin. I want to see the picture!"

Jimmy folded his arms and snorted. Then he said, "Can I go down front, then?"

I didn't answer. My eyes were on the screen. Most of the audience seemed to agree with Jimmy and were talking instead of watching. I leaned forward to concentrate and soon was lost in the affairs of Charles Boyer, Jean Arthur, and her unsympathetic husband. And just as she put her arms around Charles Boyer and he embraced her and they began to dance, I became aware of a lot of noise coming from down front. I looked around for Jimmy but he was gone. I looked back down front. In the dim light I could see him, some boys, and the usher in an argument. The usher grabbed Jimmy's arm and escorted him out of the balcony. A few of the boys followed. I jumped up and ran after them. Down in the little hall there was a lot of shouting between Jimmy and the usher and the boys. Someone had thrown peanuts and candy wrappers down on the white audience below. This itself was not unusual. But someone had also "spilled" some cola and thrown the bottle down as well.

The usher, a tall white boy with red hair, bent over Jimmy. "Y'all kids keep it up and there won't be no matinees at all for coloreds!" said the usher.

"I didn't do it!" cried Jimmy. "I didn't have no sodas or nothin when I come in the movie, did I, Belly!"

I shook my head. "He didn't have anything, honest."

The usher was adamant. "Well, these boys sittin up front said he did. Said they gave him some soda pop, and he poured it over the balcony. It's his word against theirs. And he's been in trouble before up here."

The boys nodded. "He threw it. He did."

"I didn't!" yelled Jimmy.

In the end, Jimmy was banished from the movie for the rest of the summer. And he had to leave the theater immediately. Of course I had to leave with him, and I was so angry I could have killed him on the spot. I railed at him all the way home. "Just when it was gettin good! Now I won't see the end!"

Jimmy had only one concern. "You gonna tell Mama, Belly?"

"If I don't the only reason I ain't is because I ain't sure you did it. You should've stayed up there with me like I told you to. It's just like Miss Ella says. Your head's like a rock."

"But I asked you if I could go down there and you didn't say not to."

I blew out my breath in disgust and stalked ahead of him. "Listen at that. This dumb fool is tryin to blame it on *me.*"

On Sunday morning I awoke to a new smell in Aunt Rachel's house. The smell of bacon and coffee. I jumped up and tipped down to the kitchen. Uncle Avery was at the sink in his bathrobe, beating pancake batter and looking very relaxed. When he saw me, he winked, patted a spot on the table, and wordlessly, I sat down to a breakfast of pancakes, scrambled eggs, bacon, toast, and, to my delight, he pushed a cup in front of me and filled it with coffee and milk.

Oh, I could tell the next two weeks were going to be adventurous ones, the days much different from the last few that I had spent eating healthy meals and laboring over perfect X's on a cross-stitch sampler.

It had begun Friday morning with my first visit with Miss Ophelia; it was continuing in this abrupt switch from whole-wheat toast and cornflakes to buttery toast and crunchy bacon.

Poor Aunt Rachel. At the moment I gave no thought to her operation, her condition, her suffering, or the fact that she might succumb under the anesthesia. I only knew that she was gone and would be gone for two weeks and I felt as if I were standing on a cliff overlooking a deep valley brilliant with sunshine and green hills and blue haze. Something wonderful was about to happen. Why I felt this way I did not know. But I now suspect that fragments of human behavior, a glance, an involuntary movement, a raised eyebrow, are caught unknowingly by the eye and stored in our subconscious, later to emerge in our dreams or flash across our minds in unguarded moments or in times of deep meditation. I was unaware that things I had seen or heard since I had been in Jamison had led me to this state. I did not know why, but my imagination, piqued by fairy tales and fanciful plots of early-twentieth-century novels and romantic movies from the thirties, was as titillated as a butterfly trembling on the petal of a morning glory.

After breakfast we went to church. Uncle Avery left early to open the building and throw up the windows to stir the air. I was going with Miss Ella and Jimmy. I had just finished tying my hair back and twirling it in a long curl when a tap tap at the door announced them. I opened it and there they waited on the porch, Miss Ella in a black straw hat with a white band and a polka-dot voile dress and white gloves, Jimmy in a navy blue suit and starched white collar and black shoes polished to a spit shine. I was feeling overdressed and gangly in a blue organdy dress that Aunt Rachel had purchased for the occasion, white kneesocks, and patent leather shoes.

"Well, don't you look nice, Belly," said Miss Ella.

"You look beautiful, Belly!" Jimmy grabbed my arm and we strolled around to the white clapboard building two blocks away. We entered, walked down the aisle. Heads turned, fans were raised to mouths, lips whispered. *Miss Rachel's niece. In the hospital. I declare.*

I slid into a pew and shrank down next to Jimmy. Much to my

relief, the congregation's attention soon focused on the deacons as they began the devotional chant. I drew myself up and looked for Uncle Avery, who was seated near the pulpit with the other deacons, singing and patting his foot.

The service was long; the sermon was loud; the choir was reedy and weak. The air was hot and close. I fell into a drugged sleep. Jimmy shook me awake and with the enthusiam of a wilted violet I followed him and Miss Ella outside. We found a bench under a shady tree while Miss Ella made her way through the crowd laughing and gossiping and throwing glances my way. Finally Uncle Avery appeared; the women flapped their wings and clucked around him as if he were scattering corn. Words of advice and sympathy floated toward us.

Finally we left for home. Uncle Avery fixed a light lunch of ham sandwiches and iced tea; afterward he and Miss Ella went to the hospital to visit Aunt Rachel. "I would send Jimmy over to keep you company," said Miss Ella, "but his father took him down in the country someplace. Are you sure you're going to be all right? They don't allow no children in the hospital, but maybe you can wait in the car if you want to."

Uncle Avery nodded in agreement. "You can read while you wait," he said.

The last thing I wanted to do was sit in a car and read. Especially when I could stay home and practice on the piano without anyone around to express their annoyance. "I'd rather stay here and play on the piano."

Uncle Avery was happier with that idea. "Good! That's much better than sittin in a hot car in a strange town. And we'll be back before you know it."

As soon as they left I went to the piano and practiced my scales. Ten times, two hands together, being especially careful to watch what Miss Ophelia called the "prepared" thumb. Then I practiced the short exercises she had checked off, making sure I read the information presented with each exercise. They were simple exercises in the key of C major. I started slowly, as she had instructed; I played the pieces over and over. Within a half hour the work seemed too easy and I decided to keep on in the book. By the time I was up to exercise thirteen my fingers wanted to go more quickly, but I held them back. I marked where I stopped and went onto the back porch and flopped on the glider and read. I fell asleep and awoke to see Uncle Avery sitting across from me smoking his pipe.

I sat up. Then, casting around for something to say, I blurted, "How's Aunt Rachel?"

"She's in good spirits."

"Is she operated on yet?"

"Tomorrow mornin."

"Will it be—dangerous?"

He puffed a moment, thinking. "No, I wouldn't say it's dangerous. Anytime you go under ether it's a chance. But most people come out all right if they have a strong constitution."

A little while later Miss Ella fluttered over and fixed supper. Jimmy ate dinner with Uncle Avery and me and shared his medical misadventures with us, from the standard measles, mumps, and chicken pox to a frightening appendectomy. "These men in white masks was leanin over me and they put this thing over my face and said 'breathe deep' and I did and I didn't see them no more." We must look at his scar. He lifted his shirt to show us. I turned my head, looked at him in disgust, and told him we didn't want to see his old stomach while we were eating. Uncle Avery regarded him with amused affection like a man with a lot of experience with mannish little boys.

After dinner I saw to it that Jimmy lived up to his boast of being an experienced dishwasher. I put a stool in front of the sink and wrapped a dish towel around his waist and told him to stand on the stool and wash and rinse while I dried.

He began to question me about my visit with Miss Ophelia. "When you goin back for another lesson?"

I slid him a look. "Why?" I asked suspiciously.

"Can I go with you when you go?"

I scowled.

"Please, Belly. I ain't got nobody to talk to *all* day. And Mama don't even let me go out the yard. But she'll let me go with you. She say you pretty and nice."

"Your mother didn't say no such thing."

"She said so on the porch this mornin. And I heard her say so to Miss Mattie at church today."

She had said something like that on the porch. I stopped drying a dish and looked him in the eye. "You too newsy to go with me. Always askin questions."

He raised a sudsy hand and made a cross on his chest. "I promise I won't ask nobody *nothin*."

"What're you gonna do while I'm practicin?"

His brown eyes gleamed at me. "Nothin. Just listen," he said softly.

"Well—"

"*Please, please,* Belly."

"If you do, you better not make fun of me, boy. Or I'll put you in Miss Mattie's yard and make you pull weeds all day."

His shoulders went up to his ears. "Oh, I won't make fun of you, Belly. Honest."

"And no jumpin around like you did in the movies!"

He crossed his heart. "Oh, I won't, Belly, I promise."

I was soon to discover that Jimmy's promises had no more substance than a mouthful of hot air.

The following day Jimmy and I appeared on Miss Ophelia's doorstep at one o'clock. I was a little apprehensive about Jimmy being there since I had not asked her if he could come, but she welcomed him as if he were expected. Once inside, I headed for the piano, but she guided both of us to the back porch, where she had a pitcher of iced tea and two slices of angel food cake on the table. After we ate and talked for a while, she stood up. I started to follow, ready for my lesson, but she stopped me.

"Before each lesson, we listen, Isabel." She turned and went inside.

As soon as she disappeared Jimmy reached over to pour himself another glass of iced tea. I slapped his hand. "Boy! Don't be so greedy! You had three glasses already. And you know Miss Ella don't let you have no tea because it makes you go to the bathroom!"

"The cake done soaked up all my tea," said Jimmy.

"Well, I bet if you do have to pee, you better go home." I picked up another slice of cake and sat back to listen to the piece Miss Ophelia had chosen to play. Soon the porch was filled with music, soft, undulating, rippling, rising, louder, softer, disappearing, ending. A pause, then Miss Ophelia's voice.

"Isabel." She was at the window. "Come in now."

I pushed Jimmy in front of me. He settled himself in an armchair by the stairway while I sat on the rose velvet stool at the piano.

"It smell like roses in here," said Jimmy.

"There are some right next to you," said Miss Ophelia. "In the vase on the table."

He stood up and looked. "They pretty! Can I have one?"

"She didn't pick them flowers for you, boy," I said, irritated. "And you supposed to be quiet so I can get my lessons!"

"We can get you some later," said Miss Ophelia, laughing. "The backyard is full of them."

She pulled a chair up next to me and we began with the scales. I gave a competent performance. Then I played the exercises I had done the day before. I continued playing past those she had checked and Miss Ophelia said, "My!" She looked at me with delight. "How much did you practice!"

I explained about my time at home alone the day before.

"Well, you used it to your advantage, Isabel." She turned to a page in the middle of the book. "Let's try these." We tried a few. Miss Ophelia kept exclaiming as I read the notes and played awkwardly but accurately. She looked at the next few exercises. "This is a lot of repetition, Isabel. But I'm so afraid to skip anything because the future exercises in this book and more difficult pieces later will be based upon your mastery of the preceding work. Hmmm. This is a dilemma."

I made a suggestion. Since no one was at home with me all week, I could practice the new exercises and star the ones I had trouble with. Then she could help me with them when I came for lessons. "Like today, I'll be home all by myself, except when Uncle Avery comes home for lunch. Then after dinner today he's going to Juniper City to see how Aunt Rachel came through the operation. So I can practice a lot today."

"You don't want to wear yourself out."

"Oh, I'll stop when I get tired. Then I'll read. And when I finish reading, if I feel like it, then I'll practice some more."

Miss Ophelia smiled. "You *are* determined, aren't you."

I nodded. "I gotta learn as much as I can from you while I'm here. And I want to be able to read and play music in case I don't find a teacher when I go back home. And that will only be a month, unless Aunt Rachel has a relapse or somethin."

"Since your Aunt Rachel isn't home and you're alone much of the time, would you like to stay down here a little longer and practice? Then if you make mistakes, I can correct you and you might go along a little faster."

"Oh, could I?" Then I frowned. "But maybe . . . well, Uncle Avery might say I was takin up too much of your time and gettin on your nerves."

Miss Ophelia laughed. "Isabel, I wouldn't ask you if I thought you'd get on my nerves. As for your Uncle Avery, well, perhaps he might feel better if for a large part of the day you were under adult supervision."

I hadn't thought of it like that.

"You ask him for his permission this evening at supper. See what he says."

Suddenly we heard a series of bumps and a yell. I looked around at the chair where Jimmy had been sitting and I surmised what had happened. The tea had worked on his bladder and he had gone upstairs, against my specific instructions, to the bathroom. Miss Ophelia ran over to the stairwell, which was hidden by the wall, I right behind her. Jimmy was rising from the bottom step.

"Child! Are you hurt?" Miss Ophelia leaned over to get a look at him.

Jimmy shook the tears from his eyes. "No, ma'am."

Miss Ophelia looked up the steps. "It's that old piece of loose stair carpet," she said. "The whole thing should be taken up. It's practically worn to shreds."

I could dredge up no sympathy for Jimmy. He had disobeyed me and also ruined my lesson. "I'm not bringin you anywhere with me anymore! I took you to the movies and you got kicked out for the rest of the summer and now I can't go because Miss Ella might find out! And now look! Here you go fallin down the steps because you went to the bathroom without even askin!" Asking permission had nothing to do with falling down the steps, but I was beyond being logical. "You're the dumbest boy I've ever seen!"

"Oh, Isabel, don't say that," Miss Ophelia said. "Haven't you ever fallen down the steps?"

Her question should have shamed me, but I felt no remorse at all. The tongue-lashing I had received from Aunt Rachel the previous week when I had my fall made me not one whit more sympathetic toward Jimmy. "He didn't have no business up there!"

By now Miss Ophelia had him by the brighter light at the window and was murmuring softly as she bent over and examined his back and his legs. After a moment she straightened up. "Well, there aren't any lumps or bruises." She hugged him. "Like Humpty Dumpty, you had a great fall. Thank goodness you're not an egg!"

Jealousy is not green. It is red. Red hot. A searing red hot ember that streaks across your heart impelling you to strike out in unreasonable anger. "I'm'a still tell Miss Ella!"

My attitude shocked Miss Ophelia. "Isabel!" She stared at me in disbelief. "Don't be like that!" When I lowered my head, she spoke more softly. "We all make mistakes." She sat down and held Jimmy's hand. "Honey, I don't mind if you go to the bathroom, but you have to be very careful coming down those dark steps. I'm always catching my heel in that carpet."

Jimmy propped himself in the chair again and we resumed the lesson. But my enthusiasm was gone. Occasionally I rolled my eyes at Jimmy, who shrank from the heat of my glare. Miss Ophelia noticed. She said nothing then, but as we were leaving she held me back and whispered, "Isabel. No more about the steps now."

So on the way home I was silent, smoldering. When we got to Jimmy's porch Miss Ella was on the porch with her flyswatter. Someone had told her about Jimmy's misbehavior at the movies, she told him over the railing; she promised him he would not get out of the house for at least a week. Jimmy ran up the steps crying. I went into my house with a smile on my face.

Later when I told Uncle Avery what Miss Ophelia said about my remaining longer with her, he smiled quietly. "Well, I'm happy to see you've made a good impression on Miss Ophelia."

In light of my behavior that afternoon, I doubted that. The next day when Miss Ophelia opened the door, she reinforced that doubt.

She stood in the doorway and looked at me with an unmistakably un-happy face. "Isabel. Where's Jimmy? I hope you haven't stopped him from coming with you anymore."

For a moment I thought she was not going to let me in, since she was holding the door only half open, so I defended myself quickly. "No, ma'am! Miss Ella kept him home!"

"Oh."

She opened the door wider and I went inside, feeling very down-hearted. I told her about the incident at the movies and how his mother had found out and kept him home.

"I thought you might still be angry enough at him to make him stay home."

I told her the truth. "I was mad at him yesterday, and even a little bit today because he's always gettin in trouble. But I wouldn't leave him at home because he don't ever get out."

"I'm sorry I misjudged you, Isabel."

"But he does things to keep me gettin mad at him."

"He seems to like your company. Maybe you can influence him to modify his behavior."

I was very doubtful of that. "If Miss Ella's flyswatter doesn't make him behave I don't see how I can."

"Let's talk about it then," said Miss Ophelia. She turned and I followed her onto the back porch, where she had cake and this time a pitcher of lemonade. "I thought Jimmy was coming so I decided to have lemonade instead of tea. I suspect that's what sent him to the bathroom yesterday."

I agreed emphatically. "Miss Ella don't let him drink tea because he always has to run to the bathroom. But I forgot."

"Well, from now on there will be lemonade for Jimmy. And the ladies will have iced tea." She poured a glass of lemonade and handed it to me. "Now about Jimmy's behavior. I think you can help him. He looks up to you. You can have influence over him."

"Looks up to me. How?"

"He follows you around. He's attached himself to you."

"That's so he can get out of the house."

"If he didn't like you he wouldn't do that."

"Oh, I think he would."

"His eyes follow every movement you make. He doesn't take them off you."

"That's because he's *nosy*."

Miss Ophelia laughed. "Most little children are. But he likes you very much and he's a nice little boy. He can't be that bad, or you wouldn't help him get out of the house."

"I just feel sorry for him, that's all. I wouldn't like it if somebody cooped me up all the time."

Miss Ophelia sat back and smiled at me and shook her head. "Oh, Isabel, you are so determined not to let anyone know that you have a tender heart."

A tender heart. No one had ever accused me of that. I was so embarrassed I ducked my head and poured out my own glass of lemonade without asking. We sat quietly for a moment, then I asked a question that had been in my mind since I met her. "Why do you call me Isabel?"

The question seemed to surprise her. "Would you like it better if I call you Belly?"

"Oh, no! I like it. It's just that everybody calls me Belly, unless they're mad at me or somethin.'"

"Oh, I see. Isabel's such a beautiful name. And it sounds much nicer than Belly."

"Uncle Willie says it sounds like a pig. He goes Bellybellybelly when he wants to make me real mad."

"Willie is such a tease. He used to tease me about my name when we were young. He used to call me Feely."

"Feely!"

"Yes. And I hated that. Other kids called me Ofee and when the boys wanted to be fresh they called me Feelya."

"Ophelia." I said slowly. "I never heard that name before."

It was unusual, Miss Ophelia agreed. Her mother and her aunt Virginia had been close as sisters. Virginia went to New York City to college and became a teacher. "She never married. When I was born,

Aunt Virginia told my mother if she could name me, she would send me to college. Well, Mama agreed. And Aunt Virginia named me Ophelia because she loved a play called *Hamlet*. And the only other female in the play was the queen who was named Gertrude. She didn't want to call me that. And I'm glad she didn't, or else today you would be calling me Miss Gertie."

"You don't look like a Miss Gertie. You look just like an Ophelia." She asked me what I meant, but I did not know what I meant. I only knew that her name was exotic, although that word was not part of my vocabulary then, and suited her exactly that afternoon on the porch.

That day I saw her as I had not seen her that first time in the dim parlor. She was wearing a lavender dress that brought a soft glow to her face. A touch of rouge was on her cheeks; her eyes, which were hazel-brown, not dark as I first thought, shone oddly light in the dark face. Her lips were not full, but not thin. Her nose was not fat and not flat, but not sharp. Her hair was black and crimpy, not greasy. She spoke softly in a well-modulated voice, and I remember she smelled so wonderful, like attar of roses.

Oh, Miss Ophelia, Miss Ophelia. How I talked that day when she asked me to tell her something about myself. And how that woman listened. Her luminous brown eyes looked into mine and encouraged me to tell everything I knew; like a genie she worked her quiet magic and drew out my soul, nodding, smiling as words spilled up and over my tongue like water over a dam. How she laughed when I told her about Uncle Willie and Miss Pheeny and my books. "And what else does your uncle Willie do besides bring you books and pull your hair and tease the women around him?"

The smile left her face when I told her about Teeny, how we had never been separated for a whole summer, why she had been sent away, how angry I had been with her and Miss Myra because they had deceived me.

"Unfortunately, many young girls get pregnant," said Miss Ophelia. "Young girls should be kept busy at your age."

"That's what Uncle Willie says. That's why he started me on reading. I'll keep busy doing that, he said."

"And playing the piano. Don't forget that," said Miss Ophelia.

"Her mother's going to take her baby from her and give it away. Do you think that's right?"

"Right . . . I don't know."

"Well, I don't think it's right. I think she should let her keep it."

"But can a thirteen-year-old be a mother?"

"She can have it, can't she?"

"Physically. But is she prepared emotionally? Is she prepared to give up dating and dancing like all girls her age want to do? Does she want boyfriends? Does she want to finish school so she'll be able to take care of it? Can she do all that and be a mother, too? You have to devote a lot of time to *that*. Do you think Teeny's ready to do what I just said?"

I sat quietly, thinking, and said finally, "I don't think so." We got up and went inside. She sat at the piano, I sat in the chair next to her.

"And Teeny, are you still angry with her?" she said.

"No," I replied. "But if she had listened to me, she wouldn't have got in trouble in the first place."

"She definitely should have taken your advice," said Miss Ophelia with a wink. She began playing softly. An étude, she explained. By Chopin.

"But if she didn't go away, I might not be here right now," I said, dreaming along with the music. "I'd probably be right there in Pharaoh learning how to swim. And I like this much better."

"I'm glad you came, too, Isabel," said Miss Ophelia. Suddenly, as if tiring of our discussion, she swung into a sprightly tune. When she finished she turned to me. "Did you like that?"

I nodded.

"That was a little piece by Bach. Johann Sebastian Bach. We'll work on it for a recital piece for you."

"Recital! I ain't givin no recital."

"Someone might ask you to play something. You should have something in your repertoire." She leaned forward and touched me on the forehead. "A few pieces you can play almost from memory."

I shook my head. "Not me."

"Isabel, Isabel."

We exchanged seats. My lesson began.

I thought about what Miss Ophelia said about influencing Jimmy. I didn't believe I would make a difference, but the next day I knocked on his door when I was ready to go for my lesson. He opened it and looked up at Miss Ella, who was standing over him. "Well, I don't know, Belly. He was terrible in that movie and got put out. I don't know."

I told her I thought the other boys were lying so they wouldn't get into trouble.

"That's what he said. But he shouldn't have been up there in the first place. I told him that before he went!"

Jimmy's neck was twisting like a turtle's as he looked from his mother to me to his mother, then back at me with pleading eyes.

So I lied and told Miss Ella that he might have asked me if he could go down front and I might have said yes and Miss Ella, who seemed willing to accept any plausible excuse, finally gave in with her usual threats.

With a whoop he jumped out of the door and grabbed me around the waist. I pushed him away with another warning. "Boy, you heard what she said. First time you get out of line, I'm *tellin*."

Miss Ophelia was happy to see Jimmy. When he told her I was the reason for his being there she smiled and hugged my shoulder. "Good for you, Isabel," she whispered. That made me happy enough to smile over at Jimmy.

But his mind jumped around like fleas in a mason jar. No sooner was he seated in his chair than he started looking around for something for his thoughts to light upon. During a pause in the lesson, he brought a silver-framed photograph from the little table near the staircase over to Miss Ophelia. I had seen the picture before and was just as curious as he was, but I was old enough not to be intrusive. It was a portrait of a man with a narrow mustache. The picture was in sepia, but it was not hard to see that the man looked white.

"Miss Ophelia, who's this man?" said Jimmy, pointing.

"That's my father," said Miss Ophelia.

"Is he *white?*"

"Boy, there you go again, askin dumb questions," I said.

"That's not a dumb question," said Miss Ophelia with a laugh. "He's asking it because the man looks white. No, Jimmy. He's not white. He's a colored man."

"Oh, he's like Mr. Avery," said Jimmy. "I used to think he was white."

"How could Uncle Avery be white and be married to Aunt Rachel," I said in disgust.

"Now, Isabel," Miss Ophelia said quietly, "little children don't understand things like that. They have to be told. All they understand is that people who look like your uncle and my father look like the white people they see."

"Well if he lives with the colored people he has to be colored," I said.

"How'd you get so dark, Miss Ophelia?" said Jimmy. "Was your mother dark?"

"Boy!" I was appalled.

Miss Ophelia ignored my outburst. "Yes, she was, Jimmy," she said gently, and rose from the chair next to me and we followed her to the table. "This is my mother. She is my color."

I studied the photograph. The woman had an oval face with high cheekbones, and her hair was long, swept back from her face. Her lips curved into a slight smile.

"She's pretty," I said softly.

"Yes, she was," said Miss Ophelia.

"You look like your mother," said Jimmy. He leaned forward as Miss Ophelia placed the photographs side by side and studied them more carefully. "How old was they then?"

"These pictures were taken just before they were married. I imagine they must have been about twenty." She looked at them a moment, then she returned to the piano.

"How—" Jimmy began.

I pinched him, afraid that he was going to ask Miss Ophelia something else stupid, like her age. On the way home he confirmed my suspicions. "I bet you were gettin ready to ask Miss Ophelia how old she is, too."

"Well, she look older than the lady in the picture!"

"Of course she is! I declare. Miss Ophelia is *old,* can't you tell? Why I bet she's—I bet she's middle-aged!"

"She ain't got no wrinkles and no gray hair!"

"When that happens you're *real* old! And my mama went to school with her, so she must be at least . . . well, at least about thirty-five or forty years old." I stopped in the street and put my hands on my hips. "And you better stop askin questions or I ain't takin you with me anymore. I declare, you are embarrassin!"

"Aw, you wanted to know about them pictures, Belly. I seen you lookin at them. You just scared to ask, that's all."

"I ain't nosy like you. One day your nose gonna git you in trouble."

But trouble came to me. That day Miss Ophelia had given me my first exercise in Hanon, and the next morning as soon as Uncle Avery left for work, I gingerly approached the spinet, eased up the cover, and positioned myself in front of the keys. I placed the thumb of my right hand and the fifth finger of my left hand on the C keys an octave apart, then boldly began playing the scales, loudly, since Miss Ophelia had instructed me to lift each finger as high as I could and bring it down forcefully upon each key. Soon I was banging away with both hands.

Suddenly there was a pounding on the front door. I peeped outside. There stood a big-eyed, giggling Jimmy with a message from his mother. "Mama say stop all that loud noise this early in the mornin 'fore you wake up my papa."

His father. I did not believe he even had one. I had been there almost two weeks and I had never seen him. Not once. I told all this to Jimmy and banged the cover down on the piano.

Jimmy yelled through the screen. "Oooooh, Miss Rachel gonna git you bangin down her piano!"

"Get away from my door, boy!"

"I'm'a tell my daddy what you said, too!"

"And I'm not gonna tell you the rest of 'Beauty and the Beast,' neither! And I'm gonna tell her everything else, too!"

The rest of the morning I channeled my energy into vacuuming and dusting. That afternoon poor Jimmy trailed behind me as I stalked, nose in the air, to Miss Ophelia's. I refused to sit near him during the listening lesson. And as soon as I settled myself on Miss Ophelia's piano stool, I told her the reason for our falling out.

Miss Ophelia listened with raised brows. "But, Isabel, Mr. Avery leaves for work before seven! That's much too early to practice." And when I did play, which should be much later in the day, I must play more softly, she cautioned me. The keys on Miss Rachel's spinet required a lighter touch than was necessary for the ancient upright in front of me.

She had Jimmy and me shake hands before we left for home, and we were walking together when we got to his porch. There, standing arms folded, was a tall, husky man with a serious face. My heart fell into my stomach. I knew what was coming next. Damn that little rat. Told on me.

"Hi, Daddy!" Jimmy ran up to his father.

I stared at the big man on the porch. "Afternoon," I mumbled from the sidewalk.

"Afternoon."

"She the one play the piano," said Jimmy.

"Oh. Miss Rachel's niece, hunh," said the man.

"I-I-I ain't gonna practice anymore early in the mornings, sir," I said.

He said nothing. Merely nodded.

I skulked up onto my porch like a dog that had been smacked on its nose.

"See you later, Belly," called Jimmy.

I was too embarrassed to answer.

14

The following morning I followed Miss Ophelia's advice: I waited until nine o'clock before I went to the piano. I lifted my fingers only half as much, playing in a much more subdued manner. I had just finished my Hanon scales and had turned to a little waltz when there was a knock at the door. Thinking it was Jimmy with another message, I jumped up and threw the door open with a bang, ready to tear into him for getting me in trouble with his father the day before.

Instead of Jimmy, my mother and Uncle Willie were on the porch staring at me in amazement.

"Lord, Belly, what a scowl!" said my mother.

"Damn, gal." Uncle Willie gave me a gimlet eye. "You better be careful the way you treat Rachel's door. Who you mad at anyway?"

I quickly thought of a reasonable explanation for my angry response to the bell. "Aw, that little boy from next door keeps knockin when I'm practicin on the piano."

"We heard you playin," said Mama. She made a movement to step inside. "Ain't you gonna let us in?"

I moved. We stood inside by the door looking at the piano. "Well, you got a good workout this morning, Miss Piano," said Uncle Willie.

It is strange how we act when we have been away a few days from someone whom we have always known. We see them anew. Instead of my comfortable mother I saw a smiling, pretty woman, familiar, yet strange. Awkwardly I gave her a quick peck on the cheek.

Uncle Willie noticed a remarkable change in me. "Well, look at Miss Isabel. She ain't even been gone two weeks, and look. Got on some shoes, combed her hair and tied it with a ribbon." He spit on his finger and rubbed my arm. "And I swear the gal is clean. Most of that black on her musta been dirt. She done turned three shades lighter."

My mother pushed him into the house. "Willie, hush up and go on in the kitchen." I felt her studying me. "You do look different, Belly. More grown up or somethin." She ran her hand over my hair. "Your hair is so shiny and soft. Like silk."

"I wash it twice a week in the shower. And Aunt Rachel gave me some ribbons and a bottle of Breck shampoo."

"Hmph," said Uncle Willie. "Even that devil has a soft side."

"I stopped by Miss Ophelia's on my way here, but since you weren't there I said I'd stop on my way back."

"I'm sure glad you weren't there," said Uncle Willie. "If it was up to me, we wouldn't even have stopped here. We supposed to be goin to the hospital to see Rachel, not takin no detour to see how Belly's doin. Should've let Henry Binns bring you up here like he wanted."

Henry Binns! I stared at my mother; she avoided my eyes.

"You act like you had to go a hundred miles out of your way," said Mama. "What time do you go for lessons, Belly?"

"Not until one o'clock," I said. "Then we come back at about four or five."

"Four or five o'clock! Three hours!" said Uncle Willie. "And who is 'we.'"

"Me and Jimmy Diggs. He lives next door."

"If he so bad like you say, why do you take him with you?" said Uncle Willie.

"I don't want you worryin the woman to death," said Mama.

"But Miss Ophelia told me to come every day! And I don't play the piano the whole time. We sit on the swing and talk. And listen to music."

"Music," said Uncle Willie.

"Real music. Not that old stuff you listen to. We listen to beautiful piano music. Like Beethoven and Brahms and Cho-Chopin."

"Showpan. Hunh. Seem like Miss Ophelia doin more than just teachin you how to play the piano, hunh," said Uncle Willie.

"She's real nice," I said. "She's a *lady*."

"Well, Ophelia always was nice and lady-like, but she better be. She too black to be mean. Now if she was pretty she'd be hell on wheels."

My mother threw him a look.

"I know what you say, Lizzie. Beauty is in the soul. You can afford to say that because you pretty. But ugly people know it ain't true."

I leaped hotly to Miss Ophelia's defense. "Just because you black don't mean you're ugly! And there ain't nobody more conceited than you and you three times blacker than Miss Ophelia."

"It's different when a man is black. Ask the white man. That's why they always tannin themselves up layin in the sun tryin to look healthy when they stand next to them white women." He winked at my mother. "Now look at Belly. She look three times prettier since she shed some of that color she acquired down in the country, ain't she, Lizzie? Maybe Rachel need to keep her up here till she grow up."

My mother snorted. "Black or yallah, she's still Belly. And don't go spreadin no sour grapes in front of Belly about Ophelia. If I remember right, you was crazy about that black woman before you went into the army."

"That's where I got some sense."

"Sense, all right. In a bottle. That's why she wouldn't have you when you come back. Had to stay in New York City to get rid of you, and I bet if she crooked her little finger you'd be right there sniffin around. So let's leave black alone, hear?"

Mama's attack was unexpected. Uncle Willie's eyes popped; he sat very still, then, looking as if he'd been slit and gutted, he got up and slipped outside onto the little back porch. That day I felt sorry for him.

My mother did not often lay into him, but when she did it was always quick, sharp, and clean.

Face set, she sat a moment, then turned to me. "Do you have any iced tea? My throat's a little dry."

I got a pitcher of cold tea and a glass and sat down across from her. She poured her tea and we sat silent.

Usually I knew why she attacked Uncle Willie. He could be irritating. But I did not understand why she went at him so fiercely. He always called people black, even if they weren't. Usually Mama waved him away with a word or a look. What had made her so angry today?

Mama rubbed her forehead and sighed. "Don't mind me today, Belly. But Willie been actin contrary ever since I asked him to stop by here so I could see you. Been runnin his mouth all the way up the road talkin about what he got to do at home. Nothin. Nothin that can't be done tomorrow. He wasn't too bad until I said I wanted to stop in and see Ophelia."

Miss Ophelia again. What was it about her that caused such violent reactions in Aunt Rachel and Uncle Willie?

"I guess I shouldn't have jumped on Willie like that, but sometimes he says things he don't mean." She shook her head. "I thought he was over all *that*."

"All what, Mama?"

In a subdued voice she told me an amazing story. My Uncle Willie and Miss Ophelia had been high school sweethearts. Willie had every intention of marrying her. But then Ophelia's mother died and she went to New York City to live with her aunt Virginia. Virginia sent her to college. Willie went up a few times to see Ophelia, but Virginia kept after her to break off their friendship. Willie wasn't suitable, she said. Then the war, and Willie came back depressed and a drunkard. After a few disastrous visits with Miss Ophelia in New York City, he received a letter breaking off the relationship. Willie went deeper into his bottle.

Uncle Willie in love with Miss Ophelia! She had rejected him and now he hated her. Or did he? Maybe he had not taken Mama to Deacon Love's funeral last year because he could not face a woman who had hurt him so badly. His reaction to my remarks about Chopin and my condemnation of the music he preferred was comparable to mine when Miss Ophelia hugged Jimmy after he fell down the steps. Little red devils with red-hot pitchforks had jumped around inside his chest and pierced his heart, like mine. Could it be that he still loved her? "Poor Uncle Willie," I said.

"It's sad," said Mama. "And he's turned sour as a crab apple. But it's bad when people get so bitter about their life and run somebody down and don't let you know why they do it. Most of the times it's their fault, somethin they won't take the blame for." She stood up. "You don't want to be late for your lessons. And I'm goin to see Ophelia today. I don't care if this fool gets mad enough to swell up and bust open." She went to the screen door. "Willie, I'm goin down to see Miss Ophelia a minute with Belly. You goin with us?"

A negative mumble came from Uncle Willie, reminding her that they were on their way to visit the sick, not dillydally all day.

Mama rolled her eyes. "I'll be back in a few minutes."

Jimmy was leaning against the banister on the front porch, waiting to tell me in a trembling voice that he couldn't go. I wanted to call over and tell him I wasn't going to take him anyway because he had snitched on me, but Miss Ella came out and grabbed him by the arm. "What you gonna do down at Miss Ophelia's with those ladies? Keep your ears open? And then come home with your mouth flappin like a flag in the wind." She shook him and pushed him to the door. "Git in that house, boy."

A few moments later Mama and Miss Ophelia were down in the backyard talking in the little swing while I observed them from the glider on the porch. Mama exclaimed over the yard, especially a lattice bower with tea roses climbing over it. "This wasn't here before. And these roses are so beautiful! And they smell so good! Everybody should have roses in their garden." She looked around. "It's like bein in another world. So quiet and peaceful."

"Until we start banging on the piano," laughed Miss Ophelia.

"Who takes care of it, keeps it so nice?"

Miss Ophelia hesitated. "Avery. He used to come here and help Papa out when he was sick. And he still comes and does a few things when he cuts Miss Mattie's grass."

So what I had thought was true. Uncle Avery did take care of the yard. *Did Aunt Rachel know?* If so, why did she ask Uncle Avery to contact Miss Mattie about my lessons instead of directly going to Miss Ophelia? And, I wondered, what did my mother think of that arrangement?

If Mama thought anything was amiss, she didn't show it. "He does a good job. It's too bad Rachel don't like flowers. She always said they make her eyes water. I bet that border of begonias and sweet alyssum was your idea. Like the way your mother had her yard when you lived in Pharaoh before your house burned down. I used to love sittin on your porch smellin that sweet alyssum."

They sat there laughing and talking and for the first time I saw my mother as a person, someone who had once had a life before me. Friends. She and Miss Ophelia had been girls together, like Teeny and me, and like us, had been separated, too. Now here they were in Miss Ophelia's garden, talking and laughing like young girls, remembering old times. Their lives had taken different paths; Mama, a country life, marriage and a child; Miss Ophelia the city life of a spinster immersed in her music and plays. It seemed as if the intervening years, instead of dulling their affection for each other, had sharpened it. No, those laughing ladies were not middle-aged, as I had impressed upon Jimmy. Down in that garden the years dropped away; youth and beauty shone in their faces as they laughed and talked on the porch that day.

Suddenly my mother jumped up. "Oh, Lord, I told Willie I'd be right back."

"Willie," Miss Ophelia said quietly. "Is he with you?"

"Yes. He's waitin for me at Rachel's."

I followed them into the living room.

"How is Willie?"

"Fine as he can be. Still drinkin," said my mother. We reached the front door. "Belly isn't takin up too much of your time, is she? She says she's here until four o'clock some days."

Miss Ophelia laughed and put her arm around my shoulder. "No. Isabel's good company. And she's learning the piano very well. Next time you come you have to listen to her play."

"I will." At the door my mother stopped and hugged her. "And thank you for the other things you do for her, Ophelia."

"Oh, Lizzie."

"Down in those woods where we are she's not exposed to some of the things I'd like her to be. I can see a difference in her already. Maybe you can make a rose out of a dandelion."

"Dandelions are very useful, Lizzie. They make wonderful wine and delicious salads! And have you ever had them cooked in bacon grease? Better than turnip greens!" She squeezed my shoulder. "Not that Isabel is a dandelion. She's a—she's a wild rose. With little thorns. And she's just like her mother."

Mama laughed and kissed Miss Ophelia on the cheek. "That's what I'm afraid of. Thanks again." She grabbed me. "Gimme a hug, Belly."

A hug, another peck on the cheek, and she was gone.

There were no more complaints from Miss Ella. My days fell into a daily routine of housework, the piano, housework, reading, lessons with Miss Ophelia, more practice, more reading. And every night there was supper prepared by the admirable Miss Ella.

Aunt Rachel had left menus for two weeks. I had been directed to prepare the vegetables, not the entire meal. Aunt Rachel did not trust me with her gas stove lest I catch on fire and she'd have to take on Mama and Willie. I peeled potatoes and onions and shaved carrots and shelled peas and snapped green beans; the actual cooking was left to Miss Ella, who hopped back and forth between the two houses like a hen between two nests, preparing two meals at a time.

And Miss Ella cooked *meals*. Not boiled potatoes garnished with a sprig of parsley, but potatoes whipped with butter and milk and a dab of butter melting in the mound on your plate. Not cabbage steamed for five minutes and served as green as it was when it entered the pot, but cabbage with tender leaves, edges curled and browned from simmering an hour in the juice of onions and ham hocks. Not pale, unseasoned broiled chicken, but chicken dredged in flour and lightly salted and peppered and fried to a crisp with juices lingering just beneath the crust. Not a neat stack of whole-wheat bread on a dish in the middle of the table, but a pile of hot buttermilk biscuits in a bread basket covered with a napkin to keep them warm and fluffy.

Those two weeks that Aunt Rachel was away, there was food served well at that table. And in place of the long silences there was talk. Silly talk. And laughter. And sitting back and sighing after a meal, stomach straining, ready to burst.

I forgave Jimmy Diggs for his minor transgression; he stuck to me like a burr. I allowed him to help me with the dishes and was cantan-kerously grateful; he really did not mind drying them for me every night after dinner, but he wore me out with his endless chatter about people I did not know.

Miss Mabel Lawrence, she live across from Miss Ophelia, she was married three times. Her first husband died, and her last one, he left. She was runnin with Mr. Fred Lacey next door. He died in Miss Ma-bel's bed and Mr. Bill had to carry him out to the undertaker. And Mr. Rubin Harris, he live down the street, when he go to visit his kids in Boston, he pass for white. In Boston. All his children pass. That's why they don't come down here and visit him. And he pass on the bus, too. Mama say she got on one time in Washington, and he was already on, and he didn't change his seat to where the colored sat. He stayed in front. He seen her. But she didn't say nothin. He looked scared, too. Mama say he don't look that white to her. And more, more, more, delivered as if I had wound him up and started him off.

After these one-sided tête-à-têtes I would read aloud to him on the back porch. It was my way of thanking Miss Ella for those sumptuous meals. For an hour or two she could get away from her son and visit her neighbors without him trailing along. Reading to him was a defensive strategy; it kept him quiet, except for the questions he asked about the stories, which I did not mind.

One evening Uncle Avery joined us; he seemed to enjoy the fairy tale I was reading even more than Jimmy, who fell asleep halfway through the story. When I stopped reading, Uncle Avery waved me on, and when I finished, he lifted Jimmy up to carry him home. Jimmy looked up at him in sleepy surprise; Uncle Avery smiled down at him; Jimmy smiled and laid his head against his chest.

He went down the steps and stepped over the little picket fence that divided the yards, he went up on the porch and kicked at the back door; Miss Ella came to the door, her mouth opened in surprise, but she said not one word, merely held the back door open as Uncle Avery took the boy into the house.

When he returned he sat back down and lit his pipe and crossed his leg and asked me to read him another story, and I opened the book of fairy tales and read to the tune of the crickets and with the sweet smell of pipe smoke swirling around my head. From then on every time I read to Jimmy he sat with us and listened. And I puffed up with pride when he complimented me on reading so well with such wonderful expression.

There is one thing about playing the piano. You start to learn how hard it is to learn. I never remembered how I learned to read. It seemed that I always knew. I know I learned in school, but I did not remember having any difficulty. Perhaps the older we grow the more difficult it is to learn. I soon found that learning to play that piano was more than a notion. My hands would not work together. I had made mistakes when I played with Miss Janie, but I never went back and mastered a section of music. If my fingers had erred, I merely played another number, bumbling clumsily ahead. Perhaps that's why I was having a hard time now, explained Miss Ophelia whenever I grumbled. I had never played a piece until I could play it perfectly.

Moreover, I was especially tired of exercises, particularly Hanon, and expressed my dissatisfaction with a poked-out lip. "Why do I have to keep playing these baby exercises over and over, and the other scales over and over, too?"

Miss Ophelia was not perturbed. "When you play the piano, Isabel, you must play the same notes over and over and over until your fingers take over. By then the knowledge of the notes has traveled from your fingers up your arms into your brain and made a little rut." She ran her finger up my arm to my head and I giggled. "The notes are not a habit with you now. You are not sure. You're like a little baby is not sure when it takes its first steps. It falls down. But it pulls itself up again and starts walking again, over and over and over. When you walk, do you think of each step you take, hesitate before you put one foot in front of the other? No! You would never get anywhere! Now you look down at your fingers because you are not sure of the notes. But soon, practicing these 'baby' exercises will lead you to play as effortlessly as you walk."

Jimmy was watching us, chin in his hands. He nodded. I rolled my eyes at him and plopped down for my lesson.

A few days into the first week of my lessons with Miss Ophelia, when we took our break for lemonade and cookies, our laughter drew a visitor. Miss Mattie Hearns. Curiosity had brought her over, she explained. We seemed to be over here at Ophelia's having such a good time she thought she would see what was going on. She didn't know piano lessons were so lively. Of course she was happy because she hadn't seen Ophelia for a while and she had thought she was ill. She trailed off, not seeming to know how to continue, or more probably embarrassed, since Jimmy and I were staring at her as if she had flown in on a broom.

Miss Ophelia graciously welcomed her and in two days' time she was a member of our group whom we were especially happy to see: Jimmy liked the sugar cookies she brought with her; I liked her because she played dominoes with Jimmy and kept him busy while I practiced.

During the week we had another visitor: Uncle Avery. Since he had given me permission to stay with Miss Ophelia for most of the afternoon, I saw nothing strange in his visit. He came home every day for lunch so why not use that time to check on me? He appeared at one-thirty and said he had come to see how things were working out.

"Wonderful," said Miss Ophelia, who was, as I remember now, flustered and seemed to have lost her usual presence of mind. But at the time I thought she was surprised to see him on her doorstep. She prompted me to show him how much I had learned during the week. He sat in the chair where Jimmy used to sit (he was on the porch playing dominoes with Miss Mattie) and listened attentively as I ran through a few of the later exercises in *Grade 1*. To my astonishment I played without a mistake. He applauded lightly when I finished, patted my shoulder, and left.

Miss Ophelia clasped her hands and smiled like a giddy schoolgirl who has just received praise from her favorite teacher. She seemed overjoyed at my performance. "Oh, Isabel, you were perfect! No mistakes!" She leaned over and kissed me on the cheek. I looked up in surprise. I knew I had done well, but not so well that I deserved a kiss.

Uncle Avery's first visit was brief; however, the next lesson he came for fifteen minutes, the next a half hour, until finally his visits extended to at least an hour while he and Miss Mattie, on the porch, and Jimmy and I, on the swing down in the yard, listened to Miss Ophelia play the piano.

Those noon concerts were my idea. On one of those first visits when Uncle Avery came to evaluate my progress, I got up from the piano and suggested that he would rather hear Miss Ophelia play real music rather than listen to my banging. At first she declined, but when he smiled his approval of the idea, she yielded.

I went and sat on the step next to the chair where Uncle Avery was sitting. Miss Ophelia went to the piano and played "Romance," by Anton Rubinstein. I did not know the name of the piece then. It was so beautiful my heart ached. When she finished playing, Uncle Avery and I clapped lightly. Miss Mattie, who was out on the porch with Jimmy, called into the window.

"Play that the other way, Ophelia. You know, when you add in 'When I Grow Too Old to Dream.'"

"Oh, not now," said Miss Ophelia.

"Please," I said.

"Please," said Uncle Avery.

Again, she played "Romance," this time weaving in the other song in a way that I have never heard it done since, and Miss Mattie, on the porch, sang the words. I did not know them then, but I have sung them a hundred times since.

> When I grow too old to dream,
> I'll have you to remember.
> When I grow to old to dream,
> Your love will live in my heart.
> So kiss me, my sweet,

And so let us part.
And when I grow too old to dream,
That kiss will live in my heart.

Uncle Avery knew the words, too. He sang them softly along with Miss Mattie. And when Miss Ophelia turned at last from the piano, she looked over at him, and he must have looked back, and she became flustered, and hastily called me to the piano.

From that day Miss Ophelia would play for us every afternoon at lunchtime. Uncle Avery and Miss Mattie would sit on the little back porch. Jimmy and I would sit in the swing in the little rose arbor. The music would swell and surround us; Uncle Avery would lean his head against the pillow on the glider; next to him Miss Mattie would nod, and jerk her head up, then nod again; Jimmy would fall asleep as he usually did whenever he was still; I would close my eyes and fall into a dream fragrant with the smell of roses and sweet alyssum and the sound of music so beautiful that it transformed the little yard into a Garden of Eden. When it stopped, I would open my eyes, wanting the dream to continue. But Uncle Avery would rise and go in the house to thank Miss Ophelia, then leave for work, Miss Mattie would yawn and leave through the backyard to go back to her kitchen, I would jerk Jimmy's arm, pull him up, and we would go up onto the porch, ready to enter the parlor for my lesson.

I always talked loudly when we went up onto the porch. This was for a reason I did not want to admit even to my secret self.

That secret kept me awake at night, staring out the window at the stars or sniggling goofily under my pillow, thinking of what I had witnessed the week before. On the third day of Uncle Avery's visits, when I thought he had gone inside and through the house to go back to work, I started in after him to see if Miss Ophelia wanted me to come in for my lesson. Miss Mattie and Jimmy were sleeping, I went, barefooted, up to the window that opened onto the porch next to the swing, and peeked in.

My heart leaped up into my throat. Miss Ophelia and Uncle Avery were standing by the piano, her arms up around his neck, he bent over her with his arms around her waist in a tender embrace, and they were kissing. It was as if the characters from one of my romantic movies had appeared in Miss Ophelia's living room. I fell back from the window onto the glider. Miss Mattie sprang awake like a sleepy cat when a mouse scuttles in front of its nose.

"What's wrong, child?" she muttered, shaking herself completely awake.

"I fell up the steps!" I said loudly.

"You have to be more careful," she replied.

I got down on the floor and searched around. "I gotta find my shoes!"

"Why are you hollerin, child? I aint deaf."

I lowered my voice. "No, ma'am. I was lookin for my shoes so I can put them on when I play. I gotta go in for my lesson now."

"It looks to me like those are your shoes down there by the swing," said Miss Mattie.

"Oh, they are!" I ran down and put them on.

Jimmy was still sleeping and Miss Mattie had fallen asleep again. When I went into the living room, Uncle Avery was gone.

That night I lay awake and whispered tumbled thoughts into the darkness. Kissin! Suppose I had gone in before I looked in the window! Oh God. I turned on my stomach and pulled the pillow over my head. Suppose Miss Mattie! I squeezed my eyes tight. Suppose Jimmy! God! I turned over and stared at the ceiling. My God. They looked just like Jean Arthur and Charles Boyer in that movie *History Is Made at Night.* Embarrassed, I covered my face.

I gave not one thought to Aunt Rachel. I had tucked her into the recesses of my mind and had lived the days without her as if I had been whisked away to the land of milk and honey. But the picture of that kiss stayed in my mind until it was finally pushed aside by the thought of Aunt Rachel's impending return.

When I went for my lesson on Thursday afternoon, I covered my embarrassment by hanging my head and saying morosely to Miss Ophelia, "Aunt Rachel's comin home on Saturday."

Miss Ophelia took my hand. "Isabel. Don't look so downhearted. You should be happy your aunt is well enough to come home." To my relief she suspected nothing.

"I *am* happy she's well, but now I won't be able to come down here every day. She'll have me bringing up her breakfast, lunch, and dinner, and rubbin her feet and her back."

Miss Ophelia laughed until tears came to her eyes. "Rub her feet! Who in the world told you that."

I repeated Uncle Willie's wild predictions.

"Willie was always inclined to tease." She became serious. "Isabel, Miss Rachel is relying on you. She needs you."

"That's what Mama said."

"She's right."

"But I'll slip back in my playing."

"No, you're far enough along now to practice more on your own. Practice, practice, practice. You really only need lessons once a week. Practice on that beautiful piano of Miss Rachel's." She rested her hand on my shoulder.

"She probably don't want to hear the noise. That's just what she's gonna say."

Miss Ophelia was quiet a moment. Then, "I'm sure if you play softly she won't mind. And she might be pleasantly surprised to see how you've progressed in this little bit of time. And I'm sure you'll be able to get away twice a week for an hour."

"No she won't."

Miss Ophelia dropped to her knees beside me. "Isabel, I've never considered you to be pessimistic."

"Pessi-*what*? What's that?"

"*Gloomy*. A pessimist is a person who always sees the worst in everything. Instead of pluses they always see minuses."

I was determined to remain sullen. "Maybe they're right."

"Don't you see anything good that came from your visit except taking care of Miss Rachel?"

I lowered my head.

"You met Jimmy and made a new friend—"

"Lots of time he's a pain—"

"But not *most* of the time. And you seem to have a good time together . . . And then you met me . . . and I'm your friend, I hope."

I nodded.

"And for two weeks you've had a good time, haven't you?"

Oh, if she could only know how happy I had been. "Yes," I whispered.

"Well, you can't let yourself be overanxious about something that hasn't even happened yet. Try to look at the bright side. Why, if you do a good job nursing your aunt, and she hears you playing so well, why, she might even give you that piano!"

I looked up at Miss Ophelia. "She wouldn't ever do that!"

"Why not? You know, pianos are only dust catchers if you don't use them."

"Aunt Rachel don't mind dustin."

"That's the answer of a pessimist," said Miss Ophelia. "An optimist would think Rachel will give her the piano someday."

"What's an optimist?"

"The opposite of a pessimist. Now, I'm going to be an optimist. I bet one day you'll look up and that piano will be sitting right there in your parlor."

I shook my head. "I don't believe that will ever happen." The idea was so absurd that I smiled.

"That's what I want to see—that pretty smile." Miss Ophelia hugged me and stood up. "Now I can tell you something. I planned a little surprise for tomorrow. A picnic. Right here in our backyard. For you and Jimmy and me. And Miss Mattie. Would you like that?"

I nodded happily.

"Your Uncle Avery is coming too."

"Jimmy will like that. Then he won't be the only boy. And he likes Uncle Avery."

"A very optimistic answer," said Miss Ophelia.

On Friday I arose at dawn, went to the window, and rested my arms on the sill. I drew in a deep breath and smelled the honeysuckle. I lifted my head and listened to the birds. I felt strangely happy. It was not something I could put into words. I can't remember what I was even thinking at that moment. But I remember the sky, pearl mixed with rose. I remember the coolness. I remember the sunlight on my face, on my arms.

I took a shower and washed my hair and after dressing I tipped downstairs to sit in the sunlight on the back porch and opened one of the books I had brought with me. *Silas Marner*. It was a thick book with gilded edges, densely printed with long paragraphs and long sentences and long words and small print. I flipped through it; the etchings intrigued me: a group of old men with fat stomachs and pinched faces glowering at a younger man; a man staring crazily after he'd been robbed; near the end a pretty young girl in a bridal procession. I turned to the last page, read it quickly and tucked it under my arm. This book promised adventure and action with a happy ending. I perched it on my lap while I brushed my damp hair dry in the sunlight, and frowning and muttering and stumbling over the intricate phrasing, I slowly entered the world of Silas Marner. I had just finished the first chapter when Uncle Avery called me to breakfast.

"Well, Belly." He smiled at me across the table. "You were readin mighty hard out there. Must be mighty interesting."

I remembered he had asked me to be able to tell the story of the books I read, so I complied. "Well, I didn't understand all the words, but it was about this man whose friend called him a thief. That old friend of his, all he wanted was Silas' girlfriend, so he stole the money in the church and made it look like Silas did it so he could marry her and she didn't even come to him to ask him if it was true. Just believed what everybody said about him. Even the deacons in the church didn't believe him. They were a bunch of mean old men." I took a vicious bite from my roll. "If you ask me, her and him deserve each other anyway. Silas is a, a"—I searched for a word—"a goodhearted man and he'll be better off without them."

Uncle Avery seemed surprised at such a vehement summary. He pressed his lips together as if repressing a smile.

"Well, when you finish, you have to tell me what happened to Silas Marner."

Embarrassed, I nodded. I chewed silently for a moment, then, "You're a deacon, aren't you, Uncle Avery?"

He nodded gravely.

"Well, I hope you and the other deacons ain't as mean to people as they were. If people do wrong, they're supposed to help them be better, not be mean to them, ain't that right."

"Right," said Uncle Avery with an emphatic nod.

"You remember when Miss Pheeny Butler was at our house that day when you came to visit?"

He did.

"Well, I went to church to the meetin."

"I see. Pharaoh lets children come to the meetings now."

"Yes, sir. The new minister, Reverend Sykes, he says older kids should be allowed to come. Mama didn't want me to go, but Uncle Willie said I could because I heard it all anyway and I might as well get both sides of the story. But that's not what happened."

"It wasn't."

"No, sir. Because Mr. Dick Thompson never came. Just Miss Esther Lee and Lila Lee and her boyfriend and the baby. And all the people in church shouted at them and they sat down cryin. But the boyfriend, he didn't cry. Not even when people was whisperin about it couldn't be his 'cause he was light and it was dark. But even if it wasn't Deacon Thompson's, like they couldn't *prove* it, everybody still said Deacon Thompson had to go because he wasn't settin a good example. And you know what I think?"

"What?" said Uncle Avery after a puff on his pipe.

"I think they should've let the women alone like Mama said."

"Well," said Uncle Avery quietly, "they might have handled it in a more dignified manner."

"Especially since they were in church," I said and finished off my coffee in one big gulp.

There are moments in our lives that never pass from our memory. They reside in the recesses of our minds to be brought to life by a song, a word, or a quiet moment in a sunlit garden; we pause and close our eyes and see ourselves in a dream grown hazy with the passage of time, forever residing inside our hearts. So is my memory of that afternoon in Miss Ophelia's yard. I see the shadowy figure of Miss Mattie, smiling, happy, leaning over a table, I see the dappled light on the grass, I hear the muted laughter of the adults in the garden. I see Uncle Avery balancing a paper plate on his knee, I see his smile. I hear the music. I smell the roses. I see Jimmy sitting on the grass near Uncle Avery's feet, looking up at him with owl eyes, Miss Ophelia sitting on a nearby chair smiling quietly. It's later now, dusk. The air is fragrant with the sweet alyssum. It is almost chilly. Now Miss Mattie claps her hands once. She wants Miss Ophelia to play so we can sing. Soon we are singing *There's a long, long trail awinding, into the land of my dreams,* and *You are my sunshine, my only sunshine.* And finally, *When I grow too old to dream.*

Afterwards Jimmy and I went to help Miss Mattie carry home some food. Potato salad and chicken. Rolls. Cake. Enough to feed an army, Miss Ophelia had laughingly observed.

Feed me for a month, put it in my icebox, says Miss Mattie, and Jimmy and I load up and follow her home with it. In her little kitchen we have another piece of cake. Jimmy has to look at the big picture on the wall of Miss Mattie's family. Who's that, Miss Mattie? You? You was pretty. And who was that man? Mr. Hearns. He look like a nice man. You didn't have no children?

I finally get him to go. He leaps over the porch to the ground. I walk out the back gate and around. I'm gonna beatcha. I don't care. He runs down into the yard. I stroll slowly, then run breathlessly through the gate and around to Miss Ophelia's and through and onto the swing. I flop down next to him. We fall asleep.

"Belly! C'mere!"

I struggle awake. It is dark. Black.

"Belly!"

Jimmy is shaking me. "They kissin!"

I struggle out of sleep. "Kissin . . . who!"

"Miss Ophelia kissin Mr. Avery!"

God. That moment on the porch springs into my mind. I jump up. "Oh, they are not, boy." I hear music from the record player inside. Jimmy is pulling me to the porch. We are up there now. God. I don't want to look.

He whispers, "Shhhh!"

He peeps in the window. Where I had peeped. Where I had seen. "See!"

Reluctantly I look in. Uncle Avery is indeed near Miss Ophelia. His arms around her. Hers around him . . . Music is playing. His face is on top of her head. They are swaying to the music. I know the song. It's one we sing in school. "Smoke Gets in Your Eyes." A woman is singing in a soft, haunting voice.

I could not stand the sight. I fell back, desperate, trying to think of a plan to help those love-soaked fools out before this blabbermouth alerted his mother and all of Jamison before the next day was over. "They ain't kissin, dummy," I said as nonchalantly as I could. "They're dancin."

"Dancin."

"Yeah. Dancin. Ain't you ever seen people slow dance? Hear the music? It's slow music . . . and they're dancin to it. See?" I grabbed him and put my arms around him. "Put your arms around me. Now. You go like this. I sang as I danced. " 'I of course replied, something here inside, cannot be denied. They said some day you'll find . . .' "

Jimmy and I swayed. I laid my face on Jimmy's head. "See? You sway back and forth . . . then you move your feet."

"Mmm hmmm," said Jimmy. He laid his head on my bosom.

I stopped and pushed him away. "Well, that's dancin."

"Can we dance some more?"

"Heck no. I'm tired. I'm gonna swing." I plopped myself on the glider, hoping that by now they were aware we were on the porch. I pulled Jimmy down next to me and we went back and forth in silence, listening to the music.

Now laughing friends deride tears I cannot hide,
So I smile and say when a lovely flame dies
Smoke gets in your eyes.

The music ended, faded like the smoke in the song. I laid my head back and said into the silence, "And don't you say nothin to nobody about them dancin neither, boy. Or else you ain't never gonna come to another picnic with me or nothin else."

"I won't, Belly," said Jimmy. Then, "Can we dance again sometime?"

"Boy!" I got up and yelled from the porch into the window, not daring to look in, "Uncle Avery, me and Jimmy are goin home now!" I started toward Jimmy, who was waiting by the gate to the alley.

Quick as a shot Uncle Avery was at the door. "Wait, Belly. You all can't go up that alley by yourself. You might get poison ivy."

He took a few minutes to say good night to Miss Ophelia, and then the three of us went out onto Randolph Street and home.

I pretended to be very sleepy when we got in the house and I went right upstairs to my room, took a quick shower, and went to bed but I couldn't sleep; the music still lingered. For a while I listened to the silence, then, still restless, crept out of bed and sat at the window. There was no moon and the sky was filled with stars that sparkled more brightly as if to celebrate her absence.

I stared into the night and suddenly I became very sad, my eyes filled with tears. I laid my chin on my hand and gazed at the moon. Water trickled down my chin and leaked between my fingers. I shuddered, then took a deep breath and went to bed.

Later that night I was awakened by a sound. It was easy to hear sounds in that quiet house. I sat straight up, not afraid, wondering what it was. I got out of my bed and went into the back bedroom and looked down into the yard. Whatever it was, the sound was moving from the porch down into the yard. I stared into the night. It was pitch black. I could not see a thing, but something was moving.

I shrugged. Could be a cat. They were always moving around our house at night. Onto the porch, finding comfort in the pillows on the seats of the rocking chairs only to be kicked awake by Uncle Willie early the following morning. I waited a moment. The movement stopped and there was only the chinkchinkchink of the crickets. I started for my room. I passed by Uncle Avery's room, then I stopped. The door was slightly ajar. Had he heard anything? I went back to the door and listened for the sound of his breathing.

I heard nothing. Curious, I pushed the door open. "Uncle Avery," I whispered.

No answer.

"Uncle Avery," I whispered again, louder.

Nothing. For a moment I felt foolish. What would I say if he woke up? That I was scared? No! I would say that I heard a suspicious sound. What was wrong with that?

Nothing. But in the back of my mind was another thought. He wasn't there. But I was cautious. I did not turn on the bedroom light. I went back into the hall, turned on the light, and went back to Uncle Avery's room and peeped in. The bed was empty.

And I knew where he had gone.

I went back to my room. But I did not go back to bed. Almost as an unconscious decision, I got dressed and went downstairs and unlocked the back door and slid onto the porch, drawn by what I do not know, but drawn by some intensity of feeling of needing to see, to validate, my suspicion. If Uncle Avery had gone, as I suspected, to Miss Ophelia's house, I had to see it with my own eyes. How I expected to achieve this I did not know. I did not want to go down that black alley, filled with creepy vines and scurrying sounds, but I could not go down Randolph Street and take the chance of being seen. A few moments later I was in the alley, hunching my shoulders and arms forward to avoid as much as possible coming in contact with the bushes and vines, some of which would surely be poison ivy. I could not see my hand in front of my face, but I knew when I was at the gate of Miss Ophelia's house. I opened it and stepped into the yard and stopped and listened. They might be in the glider on the porch, or even in the swing down in the yard. I strained my ears in the darkness, listening for the sound of a creaking swing or the swishing glider, or the murmur of voices.

Nothing.

Cautiously I inched my way to the porch. A yellow sliver at the window indicated that a light was on inside. I went over. The window shade had been pulled down, but not all the way, to let in some air, I suppose. I knelt on the floor by the glider, being careful not to touch it, and peered through the crack.

I smile now as I remember that eleven-year-old girl out on a back porch in the wee hours of the morning peeping in a window, her eyes big as quarters, her heart beating as if it were trying to jump out of her chest. I had seen them kissing before, but oh, what I saw that night was the expression of love between a man and a woman, and I had nothing to compare it to, except those love scenes I had seen on the silver screen, where the man passionately kisses the heroine, and she moans his name and the kisses become more and more breathtaking and then the camera switches to waves crashing on the rocks, if they are kissing on a cliff, or to the flame on a flickering candle, if they are kissing in a bedroom.

But no waves crashed that night; no candle flickered and dimmed. The camera kept its eyes on the lovers. Miss Ophelia was again standing in Uncle Avery's arms and they were kissing, not as before, but passionately, then she was holding his head in her hands and they sank down, she into the armchair, yes that very chair where Jimmy Diggs propped himself almost every afternoon, and he went down to his knees, still holding her, murmuring softly and rubbing his face against her bosom. She was wearing a robe, a thin one, from what I could see, open in the front. He slipped it from around her shoulders, and they were bare, and he began moving his lips down her neck and down her shoulders, and she was moaning and murmuring his name, and then her bosom was bare and he began kissing her breasts and she was murmuring, "Avery, ohhhh, Avery." And he raised his face to hers and she bent her face to his and they went into a fit of kissing and fondling and murmuring. They had lost control of their minds; their emotions swept them into a frenzy.

I dropped to my knees, unwilling or unable to keep on looking. I crawled backwards across the porch and in my haste I knocked over a trash can. I froze, then jumped down the steps and under the porch just as the back door opened. I lay silent, waiting. Someone came onto the porch and lifted the can, then Uncle Avery's voice. "Probably a cat." I heard the door shut. I waited until I thought it was safe, then made my way carefully through the yard to the alley and ran as if the devil were after me, not caring about bushes or leaves or poison ivy. Halfway through, I stepped on a small limb. It smacked me in the shin. I pressed back a scream and limped the rest of the way home and sneaked inside and shut the door and leaned against it. "Whooh!"

I went up to the bathroom and turned on the shower, and jumped in, hoping to wash away any poison from the bushes that had whipped against me as I dashed back through the alley. As I leaned over to wash my legs, I saw the blood on my shin. I inspected the area. A small gash was bleeding. I stepped from the tub and packed it with toilet paper so no blood would get on the towel, then after I had completely dried myself, I poured some iodine, which I found in the medicine cabinet, onto my leg. It had stopped bleeding now. I found some gauze and taped it over the wound with a large bandage, jumped into my night-clothes, and went back to bed and pulled the pillow over my head. "Whooh!"

Then I lifted the pillow and stared at the window.

God.

What would I tell Uncle Avery in the morning about the bandage on my leg? My thoughts leaped from my leg to the scene I had just witnessed and my face grew hot. How could I face him or Miss Ophelia after what I had just seen? I thought about running away, but after that ridiculous impulse I settled my mind to saner thoughts. I had a late night. I would pretend to sleep late. When Uncle Avery got up, I would stay in bed. If he came to check on me, I would pretend to be asleep. I wouldn't have to look at him at all. As for Miss Ophelia, well, I had faced her before. I could do it again. Mind whirling, I soon fell asleep.

C h a p t e r **16**

The next morning when I awoke my aching leg reminded me of the night before. I moaned and pulled the covers over my head. Then I remembered my plan to "sleep late" in order to ward off any questions from Uncle Avery. I listened for sounds of movement downstairs. Nothing. I sat up and listened. Nothing. Probably outside. I swung my legs to the side of the bed and inspected the cut. The gash was small, but definitely a gash. Still no sound. I frowned. Could he have left already to get Aunt Rachel? I leaped out of the bed. After washing up and changing the bandage, I dressed and went slowly downstairs into the kitchen. Luck was with me. Uncle Avery was not there. I looked at the clock. Nine-thirty. Surely he had already gone to the hospital. I heard a sound from the porch and looked out the window. Jimmy Diggs was sitting quietly on the wicker settee unwrapping a chocolate candy bar.

I went to the door and opened it. "What you doin out there, Jimmy?"

Mr. Avery and his mother had already left for Juniper City to get Miss Rachel, he informed me, licking a sticky finger. "Mama told me to sit here til you woke up."

At that news my sour mood dissipated. Uncle Avery wouldn't see the bandage. Now I merely had to invent a reason for the bandage on my leg, which I knew, would be the topic of discussion for the first five minutes after Aunt Rachel got me in her sights. And as I stared at Jimmy, a plot formed in my mind. A plot as devious as one invented by any pulp fiction writer. Now it only remained for me to secure Jimmy's cooperation. While I ate my breakfast I worked it out in my mind, and afterward I got *The Pink Fairy Book* and went on the porch.

"What happened to your leg?" he asked when he saw me.

"Hit it on the steps last night."

I shunted aside further questions by reading him the entire story of "Beauty and the Beast" in one uninterrupted session.

"Will you read me another story?" he said when I finished.

"Not now." I snapped the book shut. This was the time to make him aware of my plan. I looked him in the eye and said, "Jimmy, I'm your friend, ain't I?"

He nodded as if I had asked him if he believed in God.

"You remember the times I told Miss Ella fibs to help you?"

He nodded again.

"Okay. So when Aunt Rachel and Uncle Avery asks me how I hurt my leg, I'm gonna tell them that you and me were playin catch with your dodge ball and it went in the alley and I went after it and stepped on a tree limb and that's how I hurt it. Okay?"

I sat back and waited for his next question, which I could have mouthed for him as he spoke. "Why don't you just say you hit it on the steps?"

"Well, you remember that day when you first saw me and I had hurt my leg? Well, Aunt Rachel yelled at me so loud because I was runnin down the steps. And she'll yell at me again if she finds out I did it again." I hesitated, then added, "Like Miss Ella yells at you."

He was mine. "Oh, I won't tell, Belly! Honest I won't! And I better go get my ball right now!" He jumped up and ran off the porch.

When he came back we went into the living room and he sat on the sofa and listened while I began to play one of the little pieces that Miss Ophelia had checked off for my repertoire.

MARY BURNETT SMITH

"I had a good time yesterday," he said. "Did you?"

I nodded.

"Mama didn't know Mr. Avery could dance."

I would have been less startled if he had pounded me on my back with his fist. I turned and gaped at him. "Did you tell Miss Ella about that?"

Jimmy's eyes were big as a newborn robin's.

"I can't trust you to do nothin! I wish I knew that before I read you a story! And now I ain't never gonna read you any more!"

I swung back to the piano.

"But she *asked* me!"

Bang! I slammed down the cover of the piano and stalked out onto the back porch. "I'm gonna read, and you better not say nothin to me the rest of the morning."

Miss Ella and Uncle Avery and Aunt Rachel returned shortly after that. As soon as they stepped from the car and before the flutter about my leg could begin, Jimmy ran down to meet them to stem the questions about my leg and within a few minutes had everyone convinced that the injury had occurred just as I had plotted it.

The house was busy after that with getting Aunt Rachel settled up in her room and answering the telephone (which had suddenly been shocked to life) and the door (on which neighbors were incessantly knocking). Miss Ella ran around trying to do the last two things herself. Finally she assigned me to the door with the instructions to tell everyone that Miss Rachel would be well enough see them all on Sunday afternoon.

On Sunday morning an announcement of her return was made in church, and all through the afternoon the house was filled with visitors eating and exclaiming like relatives and old friends at a wake. Members of the congregation had brought enough food to feed every family on Randolph Street for the following week. I was dizzy from passing out finger sandwiches and punch and cake; finally I found a moment to retreat to the back porch, where I flopped on the settee next to Jimmy Diggs, who was stuffing his mouth with caramel cake.

"It's like when somebody die," he said, licking his lips. "When my grandmama died, people come from everywhere, and all that food. And drinkin. I had a good time. Like now."

I looked at him in disgust. "You wouldn't if you were running around fetching punch and sandwiches and napkins. My fingers are about to fall off. I wish they'd all go home."

At that moment Miss Ella came onto the porch. If she heard my complaint, she acted as if she had not, for she grabbed my hand and pulled me protesting into the living room, which was crowded with adults sitting talking, standing talking, eating talking, and drinking talking, who all stopped talking to look at me when Miss Ella called for their attention. "Belly," that dreadful woman said, "we were all admiring Miss Rachel's beautiful piano, and I told them you were taking lessons from Miss Ophelia Love. And we were wondering if you wouldn't like to play something for us."

I was mortified. I looked around stiffly at the smiling, expectant faces. In those days it was a bold child who brooked the will of a group of adults, especially those dedicated to good purposes. But I had not been cast in a timid mold. "I only been taking lessons for two weeks and all I can play is the scales." I turned to Miss Ella. "You know, Miss Ella. That stuff I was playing that morning when you sent Jimmy over to tell me to stop that noise."

Everyone laughed, even Miss Ella, although with slight embarrassment, but she persisted in her purpose. Two weeks might not be enough time for a recital, she allowed, but she was going to look for one before I went home. She raised her eyebrows at Aunt Rachel; she smiled and nodded her approval.

By Monday morning the memory of the scene in Miss Ophelia's living room had begun to fade, and I had recovered enough to face Uncle Avery across the breakfast table without wincing, but he was hardly aware of me. He was his old silent self, subdued and preoccupied. It was as if a heavy cloud hung over the table. He took Aunt Rachel up a breakfast tray and went to work. When I finished eating I went up to collect it.

I knocked lightly and went into the room. "Mornin, Aunt Rachel."
She was sitting up in bed, reading a magazine. "Morning, Isabel."
"I came for the tray."

"Well, I'm finished. You can take it in a minute. Sit down."

I sat on the chair near the foot of her bed.

"Now." She looked me over carefully as she wiped her mouth with
a napkin. "I guess you know I can't go downstairs to stay for a few days."

I had not known, but I nodded.

"Miss Ella is going to come over and fix me some lunch and keep
on with the dinner for a few days, and you can bring the trays up
to me."

"Yes, ma'am."

"How is your needlework coming?"

I started guiltily. "All right." I had not touched the sampler since
she had been gone. "But I been practicin my piano lessons so I didn't
get much done on it."

Aunt Rachel nodded. "Well, you can work on it up here with me
this afternoon."

"When can I practice the piano?"

"Well, I suppose this mornin. How long do you practice?"

"Miss Ophelia told me a hour every day. I been doin it two hours."

Aunt Rachel was startled. "Two hours. No wonder Miss Ella complained about the noise."

"She only did that once. I can play better now."

"Still, I don't think two hours of practicing on the piano would help
my condition any."

All night I had thought about a way to get down to Miss Ophelia's
and now I saw the opportunity and seized it. "Miss Ophelia thought
of that, too, you bein sick and all, and she said if you want, I could
practice down at her house and not disturb you. Maybe while you're
takin a nap. Or maybe talkin to Miss Ella. Or doin your needlework."

Aunt Rachel frowned; apparently this was not a satisfactory solu-
tion. "Well . . ." She picked up the magazine she had been reading.
"I'll have to see. Right now, you can take the tray downstairs." She
opened the magazine.

I stood up. "Can I practice after I vacuum?"

She flipped a page. "Just don't wake up the dead."

I turned quickly to leave.

"And be careful goin down them steps with that tray. There's no way I can help your big behind up if you fall again."

On my way down I thought about her reluctance to allow me to practice. *I'll have to see.* Whenever my mother said that, it was a bad sign. It meant that I had to beg and cry and worry her for days on end to get what I wanted. Such tactics would not sway Aunt Rachel, I knew. She was determined to keep me in that house with her all day at her beck and call; I was just as determined to get out. Thoughtfully, I took the tray to the kitchen and washed the dishes and vacuumed, making enough noise to let her know that I was working.

Then I executed a plan that had come to mind while I was working. Instead of going to find some quiet activity, I went to the piano, took a deep breath, and began to play a lively little march (from my future repertoire), softly at first, then louder, more than loud enough to wake up the dead, and going quickly so as to make many mistakes.

After a few moments there was a loud thumping on the floor above. "Isabel!" Thumpthump. "Isabel!"

I stopped playing and went to the stairs. "Yes, ma'am?"

"Stop yellin up those steps and come up here!"

I tipped softly up the stairs with a big smile on my face. That afternoon (after Aunt Rachel called Miss Ophelia to make sure she did not mind if I came to practice) Jimmy and I were at Miss Ophelia's door as usual. Of course she immediately noticed my leg and Jimmy repeated the story I had concocted. This was the first time I had seen her since Friday, but I was not embarrassed as I thought I would be, perhaps because I had been in Uncle Avery's presence for two days and had managed to conduct myself without arousing suspicion.

Then I explained to her about my time being limited by Aunt Rachel. Miss Ophelia said she expected my visits to be shortened now that Aunt Rachel had returned, and she skipped the listening lesson and we went straight to the piano.

"Belly gotta give a recital, Miss Ophelia," said Jimmy as soon as I was settled.

Jimmy was hopeless. But instead of flying off at him, I sat resignedly at the piano waiting for Miss Ophelia's reaction.

She thought it was wonderful.

"No I ain't." I leaned around Miss Ophelia and glared at Jimmy. "I told your mother *no*."

Jimmy avoided my eyes. "Yes she is, Miss Ophelia. Mama and Miss Rachel said so. On the day she goes home."

"Well, we must see that you're ready," said Miss Ophelia.

I wasn't giving any recital, I mumbled. Besides, Aunt Rachel had probably forgotten all about it.

Miss Ophelia was adamant. Music was an art, musicians displayed their art through public performance, and besides, how proud my mother would be to see how well I had done. Didn't I want my mother to be proud of me?

She looked through several books and found three little songs for me to play. The first one, a minuet by Bach, I had been practicing all along. The second one was a little march. And the third one was a simplified version of a Chopin waltz. She played them all for me, and if I had been reluctant about giving a recital, now I could hardly wait to learn the pieces.

"I don't think I can learn to play the notes like you do."

Miss Ophelia dismissed my doubt with a wave of her hand. "You can do anything you have a mind to, Isabel. If I thought these works were too difficult for you I wouldn't have chosen them."

For three days there were no listening exercises. Jimmy still played dominoes with Miss Mattie, but there was no lemonade, no cake or cookies on the back porch. There was no time, explained Miss Ophelia when Jimmy complained about it. "Isabel can only come for an hour and we must concentrate on her recital music."

I, too, missed the afternoons on the back porch with Miss Ophelia. Since Aunt Rachel's return the quality of my life had deteriorated as quickly as if I had taken a bobsled from Paradise to purgatory. I sat on the back porch and worked on my sampler and contained my practice on the piano to fifteen minutes in the morning and fifteen minutes in the afternoon, when Miss Ella would visit Aunt Rachel.

I was determined to get Aunt Rachel to let me stay longer at Miss Ophelia's. On the third day an idea came to me, simple yet so logical that I felt no trepidations about advancing it to my aunt. One afternoon, after playing the piano for a half hour instead of the usual fifteen minutes, I went to the back porch where she was working on her needlepoint.

"Aunt Rachel, can I go to the movies tomorrow?"

The movies. She looked up as if she had been rescued from falling into hell. Did they show pictures during the week, she wanted to know.

I nodded. "Every afternoon. In the summers when the kids are out of school in Mason County sometimes they go every afternoon."

"I thought you and Jimmy was barred from the movies for the rest of the summer," she said.

"Jimmy was, not me. The manager just told Jimmy he couldn't come back."

She gave me her permission quickly, and on Wednesday afternoon, Jimmy and I appeared at one o'clock as usual at Miss Ophelia's. I told her I had permission to stay until four o'clock. She suspected nothing when I told her Aunt Rachel said I could stay a few hours extra for the rest of the week since I was getting ready for a recital.

And so passed my last few days with Miss Ophelia. Again I sat on her glider and continued my listening exercises and then went in for my lessons; Jimmy and Miss Mattie played dominoes and again Miss Ophelia and I stopped for a break and sat on her back porch and smelled the flowers and drank iced tea and lemonade and ate cookies and cake.

At Aunt Rachel's things were also back to normal. She was now able to negotiate the stairs several times a day. Uncle Avery now came home for lunch. Breakfast for me was cornflakes, orange juice, and milk. Dinners again were healthily steamed and broiled and served in the proper proportions and were eaten in comparative silence. Words again were as rare as pearls.

Uncle Avery's role as a quiet, dutiful husband could not have been surpassed by the most accomplished actor on stage or screen. The person he had been when he was with Jimmy and Miss Mattie and me at Miss Ophelia's had disappeared as effectively as if he had been poisoned and dumped down an abandoned well.

One afternoon Aunt Rachel and I were in the living room working on our needlework. I was now on my second sampler; another cross-stitch with a more complicated flowered border and a longer verse.

"That border looks nice, Belly," said Aunt Rachel. "The flowers are almost perfect. And you've got a good eye for color. You have a natural flair." She smoothed the piece of linen on her lap. "I've got some pieces you can take home with you." She nodded toward a bag at her side. "And you can take this bag with you when you go home. I've put some linen and floss in there for you, and some needles. You work on them when you get home. If you can get your head out of those books."

"Home." I hadn't realized the time was so near. I mumbled a few words of thanks.

"Your mother said she will be up this weekend to get you. Her and Willie."

This weekend. How could I leave this weekend? Today was Wednesday. That meant the recital had to be Saturday. How could I be ready in two days? How could I leave Miss Ophelia and my piano lessons? How could I go back to Mason County and be alone the rest of the summer? Suddenly a heretical thought crossed my mind. *Maybe I could stay a little longer.*

When I expressed my anxieties to Miss Ophelia she dismissed them lightly. "Isabel, the world isn't coming to an end. You'll be ready to give a recital by Saturday. You are ready right now." She hugged me. "And you have to go home and get ready for school. You're going into the seventh grade now. You'll probably want some new dresses, and Lizzie told me she's going to make you some new dresses. She has to have you home for that, doesn't she?"

I nodded dolefully.

I was sitting on the floor with my head resting on her knee. I heard

Miss Mattie and Jimmy Diggs on the back porch fussing over the dominoes. "I didn't tell Jimmy yet."

"Well, don't tell him until Friday."

I said nothing for a moment, then I looked up at Miss Ophelia. "But I won't have any piano to practice on." I felt my eyes filling. "And I'll miss you and all the fun we had."

"And so will I," said Miss Ophelia. Then she looked away. "I'm leaving, too, Isabel. I'm going back to New York."

"New York!" I burst out. "When?"

She took my hand. "Not before you go home."

"But . . . why?"

"That's where I live, honey."

Certainly I had been aware of that. But somehow it had never occurred to me that she would go back so soon.

She explained softly. "I have decided to rent the house and go back to New York until I decide what to do with it." She smiled. "Why, I might come back and stay forever and you'd have to take piano lessons from me the rest of your life."

"I would, too," I said fervently.

She smiled and pressed her cheek to mine. "Ah, Isabel, you are a joy."

I nodded in agreement; we both laughed and she sent me to the piano to play as if I were giving a recital. When I finished she put her hand on my shoulder and said, "Well done. You will be ready, Isabel."

She was standing behind me. I turned my head and smiled up at her. She patted my face. "Well, you're ready to play. And how are you going to look that day? How will we fix your hair?"

I looked at hers. Two braids wrapped around her head.

"Like yours. Then I can look grown up."

Flustered, Miss Ophelia touched her hair. "Like mine. These old plaits? No, Isabel, we can find something better than that."

I leaned back against her. "No." I shook my head stubbornly. "I want two plaits just like yours. Then I can take one of your pink roses and wear it on the side. Like you do sometimes." I turned my face. My cheek rested against her stomach.

Miss Ophelia stepped back.

But not before I felt a movement. A flutter . . . A ripple. I drew away and covered my confusion by shaking my head again, then I jumped up and began unbraiding my long plait. "No. I want it like yours. In *two* plaits." I did not look at her but at a small table near the stairwell where she usually kept a brush. "Oh, the brush isn't there."

What must she think of me! I looked over at her. Had she felt the movement? She had to. She was standing very still at the piano. Did she think I had noticed it? And even if I had would I have known what it was? I know that if I had not laid my hand against Teeny Gibson's stomach that morning on the hill I would have attributed the movement to a stomach gurgle. Gas, as my mother called it. But I had felt Teeny's stomach, and I had felt the same flutter then as I did now. And I knew what that flutter was.

But Miss Ophelia did not seem to notice anything unusual about my behavior. "I'll get the comb and brush," she said. "They're upstairs." And a few minutes later she was back with the brush and a few tortoiseshell hairpins. "Now. Let's see." I sat on the piano stool and before long she had arranged my hair like hers. "Well." She stood back. "You won't know yourself, Isabel."

I moved to stand up.

"Wait. Don't move now! I'll be right back." She went out to the back porch; I got up and looked into a little mirror near the steps. I stared. There in front of me was not Belly's face, but someone else's. Like me, but not me. I looked like my mother.

Miss Ophelia, followed by Jimmy, came in with a pink rose. "Goodness, Isabel, I told you that you resemble your mother when she was your age. But now with your hair up the resemblance is much more striking! You are Lizzie Walker personified!" She pinned the flower to my braid just above my ear and stood back. "Maybe you were right. That is a perfect hairdo for giving a piano recital."

"Belly, you look so pretty," said Jimmy. "You look just like a princess in *The Pink Fairy Book*."

The blood warmed my face. "You're so dopey, boy."

"Don't she look like a princess, Miss Ophelia?"

Miss Ophelia smiled. "Just like a princess, Jimmy."

A princess. I felt ashamed. A princess should be pure in heart as well as beautiful. During the last few days I had practiced enough deceit and told enough lies to turn my heart from true red to tattle-tale gray.

On the way back to Aunt Rachel's house I was quiet, disturbed by what had just occurred in Miss Ophelia's house. Something was happening that I did not fully understand, something I instinctively wanted to push down, away from conscious thought. No matter how much I wanted to deny it, the movement I had felt against my face was too strong to be caused by anything but the same force that I had felt when I laid my hand on Teeny Gibson's stomach, and I was filled with the same feeling of apprehension that I had felt that day on Teeny's porch when Miss Myra refused to let her come outside. Oh, something awful was going to happen, I knew.

I walked along slowly, head down, ignoring Jimmy, who was walking along beside me, puzzled by this strangely subdued Belly who seemed to be in a dream. Finally he gave up trying to get me to talk and hopped along beside me, talking to himself.

When we got home he saw his mother on Aunt Rachel's porch talking and rushed up the steps. "Mama, look at Belly's hair. Don't she look grown-up?"

I had forgotten about my new hairdo. Slowly I climbed the steps, bracing myself against the narrow-eyed scrutiny of the two women.

"I declare, she do look different, Miss Rachel!" exclaimed Miss Ella.

"Who in the world tied your hair up like a old woman's," said Aunt Rachel.

"I did," I said, determined to ward off any arrows that might be directed at Miss Ophelia.

"No she didn't," said Jimmy. "Miss Ophelia did. Belly want her hair like Miss Ophelia's for when she play at her recital on Saturday."

"Recital!" Aunt Rachel's eyebrows went up. "Recital where? And what's that hairdo got to do with it?"

When Miss Ella reminded her about the discussion in the living room the Sunday she came from the hospital, Aunt Rachel dismissed it with a wave of her hand. "Recital. Here it is Wednesday and Belly goin home on Saturday. Won't be no time to tell people about no recital. And I surely am not up to havin another house full of people swoopin down fillin their guts like crows in a cornfield eatin me out of house and home and leavin a thousand dishes to be washed. And who's gonna do all that cleaning and cooking to get ready for them. It's enough for me to do gettin ready for Lizzie and Willie."

Miss Ella dismissed Aunt Rachel's words with a laugh. "Now Miss Rachel, you know you keep this house lookin like a picture in a magazine. And people would be happy to bring something."

But Aunt Rachel would not hear of it. It would be too much for her just being home hardly two weeks.

I was relieved and embarrassed at the same time. All that practicing for nothing! To prop up my damaged ego, I stated that Jimmy had everything wrong as usual; that Miss Ophelia thought it would be nice for me to play the piano, not in a recital for a lot of people, but for Mama and Uncle Willie when they came after me, and for Miss Ella, so they could see how much I had learned while I was there.

I only succeeded in irritating Aunt Rachel even more. "Your Uncle Avery and me would like to see how much you learned, too, even though you didn't mention our names."

"Mr. Avery already know how Belly can play," said Jimmy. "He heard her lots of times."

I almost passed out.

"Lots of times," said Aunt Rachel, looking at me, then back at Jimmy. "When?"

My heart was jumping so hard I was sure the movement was visible under my blouse. I moved aside so I could nail Jimmy with a look. "I practiced every day," I said. "Didn't I, Miss Ella?"

"Yes, indeed," said Miss Ella, caught right up in my web. "I can sure testify to that! Mornin, noon, and night!"

"And since I'm going to play on your piano, you'll have to be here to hear me," I said. "That's the only reason I didn't say your name."

"Well," said Aunt Rachel, mollified. "I don't know who else's you would play on. I'm sure Miss Ophelia don't think your mother and Willie are comin down there to hear you." She looked at my head. "Though I don't see what a hairdo got to do with playin the piano any better."

"Now that's cute, Rachel," said Miss Ella. "She wants her hair to look like her teacher's. That's a nice tribute."

"Tribute." Aunt Rachel snorted. "Maybe it would be if her teacher had some hair of her own to fix."

That drew a gasp from Miss Ella. "Her own!"

"That's what I said," said Aunt Rachel.

"You mean, a *wig*?" whispered Miss Ella.

"Hunh. You'd be surprised at who wears wigs. I remember when I first started workin for the Ellises. She was a good-lookin woman, at least I thought she was. Well, one night Mr. Ellis was waitin for her to get dressed, they was goin out to dinner somewhere, they was always goin out somewhere, and he got tired of waitin and he come into the kitchen for some ice so he could make himself a drink, and he said to me, 'Rachel, I don't understand you women. You get stuff to smooth your skin from a bottle, the color on your lips from a tube, and your hair from some other woman's head.' And my eyes like to bucked out of my head but I didn't let him know how shocked I was, and then he says, 'And the men don't know a damn thing about it until they get married and their wives sit at the dressing table and start takin off their eyelashes and pullin out the cotton pads they've stuffed in their brassieres. And the final blow is when they start pullin off their hair.'

Lordy, that man had me laughin in that kitchen that night. And she didn't need no wig. She just wore it because she didn't feel like fixin her own hair."

Miss Ella lowered her voice and leaned toward Aunt Rachel. "But are you sure about Ophelia?"

"Of course I'm sure. I just said so, didn't I?"

I was stunned. "Miss Ophelia wears a *wig*?"

"You ain't deef, are you?" said Aunt Rachel. "So if you want to fix your hair like hers all you have to do is get one of them hairdressing books and send away for it."

"But it looks so real," said Miss Ella, still not recovered from the news.

"Probably is real hair. You can't tell it from their own hair. I know I never would've suspected Mrs. Ellis' hair for a wig. She wore it down long and loose and had it fixed in with her other hair. Now Ophelia, well, once I saw the back of her neck, I knew."

"The back of her neck!" said Miss Ella.

"The back of her neck," said Aunt Rachel. "I was wonderin what was so different about her. I hadn't seen her for such a long time. Then one Sunday in church she was sittin in the pew in front of me and she bent her neck lookin down at the hymn book, and I seen that nape. Child, that kitchen was coarse and knotty. Totally different from the hair on her head. Peas. And Lord forgive me, I almost laughed out loud right there in church."

"I swan," said Miss Ella, shaking her head. "It's gettin so that you don't know what to believe."

"Oh, she had hair at one time," said Aunt Rachel. "Until she was about six or seven. Thick, nappy hair. Could hear her screams all over Mason County when Miss Catherine combed her hair. She had good hair and didn't know how to comb that stuff on Ophelia's head. Then Ophelia got rheumatic fever, I think that's what it was. Well, whatever it was, her hair come out. And it never did come back strong."

"They say you always have some weakness after rheumatic fever," said Miss Ella. "It affects lots of people's hearts, you know."

"It did affect hers," said Aunt Rachel. "Least, that's what I heard.

2

We didn't see much of them after they left Mason County. But that's probably why she got sick. Mattie Hearns said it had something to do with her heart."

"You know," said Miss Ella, "that's probably why she was over in Greensboro at the hospital."

"Greensboro," said Aunt Rachel. "When was that?"

"About two months ago. Jimmy Senior was workin over that way layin pipes, and he thought he saw her comin out of the hospital. And I said to him why would she go forty miles to a doctor, as many doctors as we have here in Jamison. And he said he thought he saw her, it didn't have to be her, and I didn't think no more about it."

"Well, it wouldn't be no mystery if she was over there," said Aunt Rachel. "Dr. Dewberry was the only doctor in this town anybody would trust theirselves to if they wanted to stay healthy, and he moved over to Greensboro about three or four years ago to head up that new hospital. And everybody went to him for the heart. At least, that's what I hear he was good at. Heart problems. And forty miles ain't nowhere to go to a hospital. Not if you want to keep your business to yourself. Some people around here got ears and noses like elephants."

Miss Ella nodded. "That's true, that's true." She turned to where Jimmy and I had settled ourselves on the top step, listening avidly to every word. "Just like these two little pitchers sittin here."

"Well," said Aunt Rachel, "whatever went in better not come back out. Git up, you two, and go on out back."

At the supper table that night the usual silence was broken by another discussion of my hair. Uncle Avery began it with the comment that I had heard at least twice that day: how becoming it was. "You're the spittin image of your mother when she was a young girl."

"How could she look like Lizzie," snapped Aunt Rachel. "Belly's hair is stick straight. Lizzie's is crimpy."

"Lizzie used to wear her hair in two braids like that if I remember right," said Uncle Avery. "That's what I'm speaking of."

Why was Aunt Rachel arguing with Uncle Avery about whether or not I resembled my mother? Every summer she greeted Mama with the same observation: how much like her I looked.

She seemed obsessed with the way my hair was fixed. "Lizzie didn't wear her hair up like no old woman when she was eleven."

"Well," Uncle Avery smiled and winked at me. "Belly does look kind of old. Maybe about fifteen, even."

His humorous remark irked Aunt Rachel even more. "I don't know why Ophelia even fixed the child's hair that way. Wanted it like hers. It would be funny if it wasn't so pitiful."

The smile left Uncle Avery's face. "Pitiful how?" he said quietly.

Oh, I didn't want her to say that again. That Miss Ophelia wore a wig. Not in that sneering voice of hers. Not to *him*. But more than that, Uncle Avery had lowered his hand to the table; his body was still, tense, as it was my first night at their house, but now he seemed ready to leap. And I did not want him to. Oh, I did not want him to.

I jumped up. "I'm goin upstairs right now and take my hair down! I'm tired of everybody talkin about it!"

"Gal, I know you ain't lost your mind," said Aunt Rachel, looking at me as if I had. "Sit down and finish your dinner."

I sat down and hung my head. "Everybody don't have to keep teasin me about my hair."

Moments passed; the tension eased.

"No, we don't," said Uncle Avery. "Now finish your dinner."

Many years later I reflected upon that scene and wondered how much Aunt Rachel knew about Uncle Avery and Miss Ophelia. If she did not know anything, did she sense anything? But how could she not? Miss Ophelia had come back to Jamison in the fall of the previous year for her father's funeral and was supposed to return to New York City within the month. Why did she stay? Uncle Avery certainly had the opportunity to have contact with her since he was next door at Miss Mattie's house at least once a week. Also, Miss Ophelia had been a regular visitor at the church until the following spring when she had become ill. Aunt Rachel and Uncle Avery attended every Sunday. And what about the people in church? Had the congregation been blind to some involuntary glance, some unconscious gesture that surely must have passed between Uncle Avery and Miss Ophelia? Had nothing been observed by any member of the congregation and passed on off-handedly from one to another, as the wind warns a herd of unsuspecting cattle grazing contentedly in the field? *"Danger!"* whispers the wind, and the cattle stir and low.

"Love!" whispers the heart, and people watch and leer and nudge and whisper. But no one noticed anything. And if they did, they took it to their graves without saying anything.

And what about the neighbors on Randolph Street? What did they see and say? Did anyone suspect this dignified, handsome man, a man fifty years old, settled and seemingly contented, of jeopardizing his reputation, his marriage, to dally with a frail, quiet woman such as Ophelia Love? Some did, apparently.

Mr. Avery sure at Miss Ophelia's house a lot.

Mr. Avery at everybody's house on this block a lot, Mabel.

Yeah, but she a single woman.

And who ain't or wish they was.

He come to your house, don't he. You a widow. That's single.

I guess you right about that.

And if anything was goin on, Mattie Hearns would know.

And what do Ophelia Love have that he ain't got at home.

It sure ain't poontang, if that's what you tryin to say.

I ain't tryin to say nothin.

And what would a handsome man like Avery Swann want with somethin as black and shriveled up as Ophelia Love.

She don't look shriveled to me.

You look at anything in skirts.

You in skirts. I ain't looked at you. Then, my heart is bad.

Avery Swann and who! I declare, that's a terrible thing to be hintin about a man as nice and helpful as Avery. He been cuttin our grass and fixin our porches all these years, now people gonna try to run the man down because he cuttin the grass that he been cuttin for her father and her mother all these years. Now why would he stop cuttin it just because Ophelia's over there. He done knowed the woman since she was a young girl.

Well, now, young girls grow into women.

And her half sick from her heart.

Always was weakly.

Yeas, yeas.

Lord. Some people's minds just stay in the gutter.

A man that handsome could have his pick of anybody in Jamison if he decided to sow some oats. No, nothin goin on *there*.

These opinions of the people of Randolph Street were repeated through the years and easily overheard by my young ears. As for Aunt Rachel I have concluded that she also suspected nothing at the time of this affair, and if she did, dismissed the idea as something too absurd to consider worthy of thought.

I didn't go to Miss Ophelia's the next day. Aunt Rachel kept me at home ironing and cleaning and packing so I could go home on Saturday. But on Friday I returned to Miss Ophelia for my final lesson. Miss Ella in her infinite wisdom kept Jimmy at home. "Boy, you'll go to Miss Ophelia's house liftin up her hair tryin to see if it's real and then I'd never be able to face her again and I'd have to kill you and bring you back to life before your father came home."

In those two days a change had come over Miss Ophelia. When she met me at the door her face was drawn and serious. I followed her into the house and she sank down in the big armchair as if she were very tired. She seemed so worn I became anxious. I had seen my mother go through such cycles; sometimes she became so tired and snappish that Uncle Willie and I kept out of her way or skulked around the house until her mood had lifted. I had been warned that Miss Ophelia had a fragile constitution; now I was afraid that the stress of preparing me for my recital might have been too much for her.

"Miss Ophelia," I said softly, "are you all right? I don't have to play today if you don't want me to."

She managed a smile. "Oh, no, Isabel. I feel fine. Just a little frayed around the edges, I guess." She got up and went over to the piano and sat down to look over the pieces I was to play, and I am ashamed to say that while she bent over studying her notes on the music I did almost exactly what Miss Ella had feared Jimmy would do; I inspected Miss Ophelia's hair. I studied it at the temple, around the ears, at each side of her face where a little curl formed. I could detect nothing. I was so earnest in my inspection that while I was looking at the nape of her neck, I was leaning over her as if I were inspecting a dog for fleas. I found nothing to indicate that this hair was a wig. Nothing.

Miss Ophelia, probably feeling my breath on her nape, became aware of my scrutiny and turned to look up at me. I jumped back. "Is something wrong, Isabel?" She ran her hand over her face. "I feel as if I've suddenly developed warts."

"Oh, no, ma'am! I was just tryin to see how you do your hair so I can remember when I get home and do mine like it by myself."

"Well, it's a simple thing to do. Just make two plaits and bring them up around your head." She seemed irritated. "Now. I've checked my notes. There are a couple of things I want to check. Let's go through the three pieces you're going to play. Just as if you're there now. Begin."

I was not quite ready. "I don't know if I can do it, Miss Ophelia. I'm just so nervous."

"Every performer is nervous before he goes on the stage. But you will come through. You will sit at the piano and you will think how nervous you are, then as you begin playing, your fingers will take over, and you will play only needing the music as a guide. It will be like reading your books. The first time you read a story, it is strange, but if you read it over and over, what happens? You can tell the story by heart. Now let me tell you a little secret. If you make a mistake keep right on playing as if you hadn't."

"If I make a mistake, I'll stop playing. I know I will."

"When you're reading to Jimmy do you stop when you make a mistake?"

"No. But he doesn't know the difference."

"Neither will your audience when you're playing. Not unless they have played these songs themselves. And I don't think you need to fear that. If you stop, you will become embarrassed and lose your self-confidence. If you keep going, no one will be the wiser. Just throw in a few notes. Go back to the beginning again. Just keep going."

"Yes, ma'am."

The lesson was over too soon and it was time for me to go.

"Goodbye, Miss Ophelia," I whispered. My tongue felt thick, my throat felt tight. I forced out more words. "Thank you for the piano lessons."

Who can express the pain and sorrow of saying goodbye? Who can look at the trees in autumn and see the beauty of the red and gold leaves yet not feel a sense of dying? Yes, I could thank Miss Ophelia for the piano lessons, but I could not say thank you for femininity and beauty and love and tenderness and flowers and music and companionship, for I would not know for years that this is what I wished to say. And even if I had known, I would not have said it. It would have come out of my secret self, and we never reveal that, even to ourselves, except in our dreams.

"Goodbye, Isabel. Thank you for being such a good pupil." She walked me to the door. "I'll try to be there tomorrow to hear you play. But if I'm not, will you stop by before you leave? I'd like to see you and Lizzie before you go home."

There was nothing else to say. We hugged, then I slipped through the door and ran down the porch steps. It was over and I was going home.

My mother and Uncle Willie came for me on Saturday morning; my performance at the piano took place at two o'clock that afternoon. In attendance were my mother, Uncle Willie, Jimmy and Miss Ella, Aunt Rachel, and Miss Mattie, who delivered to me a box of cookies and a message from Miss Ophelia.

She was not feeling well and wouldn't be able to come hear me play, but said to remember what she had told me about keeping on if I made a mistake, and would I please remember to stop by on my way back home that afternoon.

Miss Ophelia had chosen two melodious tunes by Brahms and a simplified waltz by Chopin. I began nervously, but the patient instruction from Miss Ophelia and the hours of practice made the music flow from my fingers. I was playing the piano at last.

I played without one mistake. When I finished, there was a small silence until I stood, turned, and bowed my head as Miss Ophelia had instructed. Everyone clapped enthusiastically, Jimmy loudest of all. My mother came and kissed my cheek and whispered how proud she was of me. Uncle Willie looked at me with new eyes. Looking more embarrassed than I was, he shook my hand, then he, too, kissed my cheek. Miss Ella gushed that her eardrums had been soothed by such beautiful playing. "When you grow up and play in some grand hall, I'll tell everybody how you used to bang on that piano early in the morning and drive me crazy." Miss Mattie smiled and said she was going to tell Miss Ophelia how well I played. And Uncle Avery whispered in my ear that Miss Ophelia would have been proud.

Soon afterward we got ready to go home, rushed by Uncle Willie's yawns and hints about getting down the road while it was still light. He got my suitcase and the canvas bag with my needlepoint, then stood leaning against the door. "You all better come on if you want to stop by and see Ophelia. I know you gonna run you mouth for three or four hours and I don't want to be drivin home in the dark."

At that moment Aunt Rachel came in from the kitchen with an envelope in her hand. "You all sure do dance attendance on Ophelia Love," she snapped. "Wasn't no reason why she couldn't come up here and hear Belly play."

Mama snapped right back. "Miss Mattie said the woman is sick and I believe her. And after hearin Belly play I certainly ain't goin home until I thank her."

"You two can stay here and argue, but I'm leavin." Uncle Willie opened the door. "Come on, Belly. Avery can run your mama home."

"Man, shut your mouth." Aunt Rachel pushed an envelope into my hand. "Here. This is for you from your Uncle Avery and me. Don't open it until you get home."

Hardly giving me a chance to thank her, Uncle Willie jerked me onto the porch and we were finally in the truck and a moment later we jerked to a stop at Miss Ophelia's, and Mama and I jumped out and ran up onto the porch.

"Miss Mattie said she would leave the door open," said Mama. She knocked lightly and pushed it open. "Ophelia," she called. We stepped inside and closed the door. "Ophelia," she called again.

There was no answer. "She must be upstairs." She went to the stairwell and called up. "Ophelia! It's Lizzie and Belly!"

"Coming!" Miss Ophelia's voice became clearer as she neared the stairs. "I was wrapping a little gift for Isabel."

We went and looked up the steps. She was at the top landing. "Oh, you didn't have to do that, Ophelia," said Mama.

Miss Ophelia started down the dim stairwell. In one hand was a small package. "I was having trouble with my hair." One braid was down on her shoulder. She raised her hand to her head and stepped down.

"Don't bother with your hair. And you don't even have to come down. Belly and I are leavin—watch out!"

Miss Ophelia came tumbling down the steps, headfirst. The package hit the landing first, then Miss Ophelia, on her side, her foot twisted awkwardly under her body.

"My God! Ophelia!" cried Mama.

"Ohhhh," she moaned. "The rug on the steps, my foot got caught in it."

"Here, Belly," my mother was leaning over her, "Let's try to help her up." She tried to lift her by the arm. "Can you move?"

"No. No. It hurts. . . . No . . . don't lift me, Lizzie." Oh . . . she was holding on to her head. . . . Her hair . . . her wig had slid half off her head, and poor Miss Ophelia was embarrassedly trying to straighten it while Mama was trying to help her. "Oh, my God." She grimaced with pain. "Oh, Lizzie, help me . . . help me . . ."

"I will, honey, I will. Ophelia, we gonna have to take you to the hospital. I'll . . . Willie only got that truck. . . . I'll tell him to go get Avery, you can go in his car. . . ."

"No!" Miss Ophelia's voice was desperate. . . . She grabbed my mother's dress front . . . then . . . "Lizzie, Lizzie . . ." her voice lower now, she whispered to Mama.

My mother leaned over, listened, then turned to me. "Belly. Go

outside and get Willie. Don't go screamin and yellin out there like a
banshee, neither. Just tell him quietly to come in. And you go out and
stay on the back porch until I call you."

I don't know how long I sat on the porch. I don't remember what
thoughts ran through my mind. I do recall thinking about the wig and
the pain in Miss Ophelia's voice when she fell and her fright when
Mama offered to send for Uncle Avery. I remember Mama coming out
and running past me to Miss Mattie's and both of them running back
past me, without a word, then a few moments later Uncle Willie's
truck rolling up to the back fence, then he too dashing past me into
the house without a look or a word. I remember hearing their hurried
whispering and Miss Ophelia's moans and Uncle Willie's low exclama-
tions. Then the door opened and Uncle Willie and Mama came out.
Uncle Willie was carrying Miss Ophelia wrapped in a blanket. They
went down to the truck and put her inside. Uncle Willie got behind
the wheel, my mother came up onto the porch and told me I was to
stay with Miss Mattie until they got back.

We went over to Miss Mattie's kitchen. *Could it be the baby?* I
didn't dare ask. "Is she going to be all right?" I asked.

"She's going to be all right, child," said Miss Mattie, and no more.
I sat at the little round table and ate fried chicken and chocolate cake.
When I was finished I sat on the lumpy settee on her back porch and
fell asleep. I remember waking and watching the afternoon light turn
to dusk, then dark. I fell asleep again. Sometime later I became aware
that my mother had returned; she sat on the glider and put my head
on her lap and I heard her murmuring to Miss Mattie in the darkness.

Miss Ophelia was all right, the baby was all right, and it was going
to be a big mess, and Miss Mattie said who would have to know and
Mama answered that things like that always got out and Miss Mattie
told her that was true and Mama was wondering if I knew and Miss
Mattie told her she didn't think so, but I might. "You never know what
children know. They good at hidin stuff."

"That's true," said Mama. Then after a moment she said, "Well, it's
time to go." She shook me. "Belly, wake up."

"All right, all right," I said sleepily and swung my legs over and sat up and stretched and asked through a yawn, "Is it a boy or a girl?"

"Lordy," said Miss Mattie, her voice cracking with a laugh.

There was a moment's silence, then my mother's voice said softly, "A boy."

The next morning I awakened to brilliant sunlight slanting into my room. I sat up and hugged my knees, happy to be back home among my books. A new box stood under the window, but I did not rush over to inspect it. Last night was still on my mind.

What is it, I had asked. *A boy,* Mama had replied. On the way home not a word was said about Miss Ophelia or what had occurred, but I knew that Mama and Uncle Willie would question me this morning. As I dressed I went over what I would tell them. Not a lie, but not the truth, either.

When I got into the kitchen they were waiting at the table. Mama poured my cereal into a bowl, Uncle Willie began with the questions. "Well, from what your mama tells me, you know that Miss Ophelia had a baby yesterday."

I nodded. "Mmm hmmm." My mouth was full of cornflakes.

He waited until I swallowed. "How did you know she was goin to have a baby?"

I kept my eyes on my bowl of cereal. "Nobody *told* me. I heard Mamma tellin Miss Mattie about it last night."

My mother knew better. "Stop gettin around the question, Belly," she said impatiently. "Wasn't nobody born yesterday. You knew somethin or else you'd be down here drivin me and Willie crazy with questions about Miss Ophelia instead of us askin you questions. Now, I want to know what went on so I can know what to do about this situation."

"But nobody did tell me anything," I protested, angry because that was the truth and she didn't believe me.

Mama still persisted. What had I known about Miss Ophelia's condition? What had I seen? What went on in her house?"

Oh, I couldn't tell them what I had seen that night. That fevered kissing. And I couldn't tell that I had felt a flutter. Or else I'd have to tell about feeling Teeny's stomach; I'd have to admit that I didn't want to believe *that* about Miss Ophelia and Uncle Avery. I'd have to be embarrassed and explain it all. So again I took refuge in another lie, loudly, as if I were trying to convince the dead. "I didn't see nothin and I didn't see nobody! Nobody except Miss Mattie and Jimmy and Uncle Avery!"

Mama looked at Uncle Willie like a triumphant robin who has finally snapped a fat worm from the ground after much tugging.

I could have ripped out my tongue. But I remembered the advice Miss Ophelia had recently given me. When you make a mistake keep on going. So I told them about Miss Mattie and Jimmy being there every day when I had my lessons and how they played dominoes so he wouldn't get in the way. And I slipped in that Uncle Avery came a couple times to check on Jimmy and me.

Mama's and Uncle Willie's eyes swung toward each other. "Uncle Avery came?" said Mama, gently, as if she were trying to soothe a skittish pony.

"Yes, ma'am. He came a couple times during lunch to see how things were going and if me and Jimmy were annoying Miss Ophelia too much because we were at her house so long. But her and Miss Mattie told him we wasn't and he said all right and then he went back to work."

They exchanged glances again, but they asked me no more questions. I felt no obligation to reveal what I had not been asked. In fact,

I was pleased with myself because I had fooled them so easily, which would not have been difficult because they trusted me. They thought I was the same Belly that I was before I left for Jamison, Belly the champion of truth, Belly the despiser of deception and lies. How could they know that in those weeks at Aunt Rachel's house I had learned to be a sneak and a liar? That not only had there been a physical change in me, which they had immediately noticed, but also a psychological one? No, they did not know. And I had become living proof of the statement that Uncle Willie had made when I was so disgusted with Miss Myra's feeble attempts to deceive me about Teeny's whereabouts: "Oh, liars are inventive."

Sometime during that morning my mother told me that Teeny had returned home. She had meant it to be a surprise, that's why she had said nothing in Jamison the day before. With a shriek I threw down the new book I had started and a few moments later I was knocking excitedly on Teeny's door.

Miss Myra answered and smiled as if she were genuinely happy to see me. Teeny was up on the hill in back, she said. I flew around the side of the house and ran up the grassy slope. When Teeny saw me coming, she ran down and we grabbed each other and fell down laughing. Until that moment I didn't realize how much I had missed her.

We stood up and looked at each other. Teeny was thinner and darker than I had ever seen her.

"That Carolina sun ain't got no mercy. And guess what they had me out there doin. Pickin cotton! And I bet we ate rice morning, noon, and night. Rice for breakfast, rice for lunch, rice for dinner. I don't ever want to see no more rice as long as I live." She stood back, head tilted, grinning. "And look at you. I'm out there burnin up in the sun and you been kept in the house and turned three shades lighter. And I bet you must be two inches taller, Belly!"

We went to the top of the hill and sat on the ground and laughed and talked, pausing often to look at each other, then away, until finally she said, "Well, I guess you wonderin about the baby."

I nodded. "What is it?"

It was a boy, named after her uncle, who was going to adopt him.

"Leroy. Ain't that an awful name? Leroy Delevan Gibson. I wanted to name him Mitchell, but they wouldn't let me. And he looks just like Mitchell, too." Her voice stopped, I sat uncomfortable, not knowing what to say, then she continued. "You was right, Belly. About why Mama sent me away. They didn't say nothin to me at all about it. I had it in Uncle Leroy's house, and they just took him. Put him in the bedroom with him and Aunt Edna. Wouldn't even let me hold him or even nurse him. Put him right on the bottle. You know, if I'da known they was gonna try to keep him, I'da run away."

How, I said. You couldn't do anything.

"I was there a month before I had him. I had a little bit of money. I could'a jumped on a bus and ran away. Then I could've wrote to Mitchell and told him where I was." Her eyes filled with tears.

"Run to where?"

She shrugged. "Maybe to Baltimore . . . to Aunt Betty. She would've helped me."

I doubted it. Grown-ups always stuck together in matters like this, I told her. And Betty was her mother's sister. I snatched angrily at the grass and directed my rage at Miss Myra. How could she let them just take Teeny's baby? Didn't she care about her own grandchild?

Teeny wiped her eyes. "It ain't Mama's fault. It's mine. I should'a knew better. She's the church mother and they wouldn't let her be no more if they knew I sinned and had a baby."

And Pheeny Butler was trying her best to trip Miss Myra up. "I think a lot of people know you had a baby, Teeny."

"But they can't *prove* it. And as long as I ain't around showin it off in front of everybody, they ain't gonna do nothin. And anyway, I shouldn't be loadin no baby on Mama. It's hard on her. She could hardly raise me." She looked at me with sad eyes. "Ain't you never wondered where my own father was?"

I shook my head. I had never wondered because I was without one, and perhaps I assumed that hers might have been killed in the war, too. Besides, lots of children didn't have fathers around.

"Well, I don't have none. I mean, him and Mama weren't married. That's why Mama left Carolina. And you know, they put her out the church? So that's why she's so hard on me. She don't want to see another child raised up without a father. And Uncle Leroy didn't have no boys. He only had four girls. And his wife said she didn't want no more babies. And he wanted a boy."

"And she took your baby just because it was a boy? What would've happened if it was a girl?"

Teeny smiled. "Maybe she'd be here with me now."

That seemed a terrible injustice to me. A horrible stroke of fate. She lost her baby not because someone wanted to love it, but because they wanted a boy. "A boy." I snorted. I sat with my knees drawn up, and rested my chin on my arms. "Can't Mitchell do somethin about it? Can't he go git his own son? Can't you get married?"

Teeny shook her head. "We too young to get married without permission. And if he try to just go get him, they'll probably kill him." When I gasped Teeny nodded emphatically. "And they would too. And wouldn't nobody do nothin. He just be another dead colored boy."

"But—but what about *his* mother. She can git it if she wants to, can't she?"

"Hunh. She don't like me. She told me once she didn't want no little black hussies comin to her about no tar babies they say her son give them." She lifted her tear-streaked face. "But the baby ain't black. He ain't gonna turn black, neither. Aunt Edna, she looked at his ears and she said he gonna be light-skinned. He gonna look just like Mitchell. He light with straight black hair. It ain't curly or nothin." She put her head on her arms and cried softly. "He gonna call her Mama and Uncle Leroy Daddy and he ain't ever gonna know who I am."

She lay on the grass on that hill and cried and cried and I sat helplessly by, begging her to stop. Finally she did and we went back down the hill. At the bottom Teeny hugged me and looked at me through eyes swollen to a slit and said, voice quavering, "You're my best friend, Belly." She turned and ran to the house.

I ran across the field and halfway across sat down in the tall weeds and burst into tears of frustration and anger. I cried for a long time, then got up and headed home, wondering how I was going to explain my own swollen face to my mother and Uncle Willie.

•   •   •

Uncle Willie was on the porch so I ducked around the back of the house and into the kitchen. I splashed water onto my eyes but the mirror near the door told me it had not helped at all.

I heard my mother coming and tried to run up the steps before she saw me, but she stopped me. "Belly! How's Teeny?" When she saw my face she came and put her arm around my shoulder, which started me crying again. "Come on outside. There's a nice breeze on the porch. Come on outside and tell Willie and me about it. Then maybe you'll feel better."

If I knew Uncle Willie, he wouldn't say anything to make me feel better. He was true to form. "She'll get over givin the baby up," he said. "They always do."

I shook my head. "Miss Myra don't love Teeny or the baby. If she did, she would keep the baby. Even if she is the church mother."

"Well," said Uncle Willie. "She thinks she has to set an example for the women in the church. She thinks she's supposed to be upstanding. And her family, too. And if she ain't, then she thinks she has to give up her position. And I guess she don't want to do that."

"If them people at Pharaoh was real Christians," said Mama, "they'd ask Myra to forgive her daughter and take her child in instead of makin the girl feel more like a sinner than she is. Now everybody around here knows Teeny had a baby, but they gonna pretend she didn't so they can all go on pretendin that everybody is goin to heaven when they die. They gonna be surprised when they wake up on Judgment Day and see each other in hell."

"I feel like standin up in church and sayin it in front of everybody," I said ferociously. "Then see what she'd do."

Uncle Willie laughed so hard he fell out of his chair. "I don't know what the congregation would do, but Myra would jump over and snatch every bit of hair out of your head. Right there in front of Reverend Sykes and everybody. And then your mother and me would have to jump in and whip her black ass."

"Belly's just blowin hot air," said Mama. "And it's a bad habit. Don't start." She stood up. "Leave it to the Lord, honey. He takes care of everything."

"He can always use a little help," said Uncle Willie.

"Well, don't you go encouraging Belly to give Him some," said Mama. "For that she needs some wings, and I don't think she's ready for them yet." The screen door banged shut behind her.

Uncle Willie dragged on his cigarette. I sat and rocked. Then Uncle Willie sat back and looked up at the ceiling. "You know, Belly, some women forget what it's like to be young." He looked over at me, eyes squinched to a slit and cigarette bobbing on his lips. "Yup, some women just forget what it's like to be young."

I looked at him curiously. "You mean Mama?"

"Nah. I mean Myra. A hussy if there ever was one. Instead of her usin her experience to help Teeny learn from her mistakes, she act like she was born with a halo. Lookin down her nose when she see some-body doin what she call sinnin."

Before Teeny had told me that she was illegitimate, I could not imagine Miss Myra ever committing a sin. From the statement Uncle Willie had just made I assumed that he and Mama had been aware of her indiscretion all along, and now he was alluding to that fact for my benefit. Not revealing her secret, just hinting at it so if I ever repeated it, he could swear on the Bible that he never told me. Oh, I was wise to Uncle Willie's ways.

"If I didn't know better, I would think she was the type of woman to keep her nose in the Bible, never do nothin wrong. But when you see a woman workin her ass off to be a saint, well, watch out. They workin so hard because of somethin they did wrong in the past. They ain't workin to help other people out. They think they can erase their sins so they can get into heaven. And Teeny ain't doin no more wrong than Myra did when she was her age. Some people don't learn from their mistakes. They keep right on repeating them."

"Poor Teeny," I said.

"She'll be her old self soon."

But that was a slower process than Miss Myra or I could imagine. Teeny moped and cried around the house and got on Miss Myra's nerves so much that she let her come out more often. I tried to get her to do some of the old things we used to do for amusement. One afternoon we went down to Pine Run and sat on the bank and watched some children splashing around in the water under the fall where Teeny had pushed me in the summer before. But we only stayed a little while. Teeny got bored and we left.

"You were goin to teach me how to swim, remember?" I said.

"Don't seem like it's no fun, no more," said Teeny.

Nothing seemed to be fun anymore. We got back to her house and sat on the edge of the porch. We could hear Miss Myra and another woman laughing and talking inside the house. The smell of singed hair floated through the screen door.

"Phew!" I said. "Who's gettin their hair done today?"

"Miss Pheeny Butler," said Teeny.

"Miss Pheeny Butler." Now that was strange. "When did Miss Myra start doin her hair?"

Teeny shrugged. "I don't know. I think she just came today because she want her hair done and her hairdresser ain't in town. That's what she told Mama."

From my own experience, I thought that Miss Pheeny might be there for another reason: to gather news about Teeny's baby. "Did Miss Myra tell you about Miss Pheeny's niece from Baltimore?" I asked. When Teeny shook her head, I told her about Philice's visit and the fight. "You ever meet Philice?" I asked.

"Miss Pheeny's niece?" said Teeny. "No."

"Miss Pheeny's up to somethin," I said. I got up and went to the screen door. "Do you think Miss Myra would mind if I got a glass of water?"

Teeny looked at me oddly. "What's got into you, Belly? You know you don't have to ask no permission for water." She went ahead of me into the kitchen.

Miss Pheeny Butler's back was to us as we entered. Miss Myra had finished curling her hair and was now brushing the curls out for styling.

"Hi, Belly. You and Teeny back already?" said Miss Myra.

"Yes, ma'am," I said. "Hello, Miss Pheeny," I added..

"Why, is that Belly Anderson." Miss Pheeny tried to turn her head.

"Yes, ma'am," I answered.

Miss Myra put her hand on Miss Pheeny's head. "Pheeny, how do you think I can do your hair if you twist and turn!"

"I was just tryin to see the girls," said Miss Pheeny.

"See them when I'm done," retorted Miss Myra. She picked up a smoking marcel iron. "Else you'll have burns all over your scalp. This little bit of hair don't leave much room for error."

"Here's your water, Belly," said Teeny, handing me the glass.

"Stand over here where I can see you all," said Miss Pheeny.

Teeny and I went and stood at the back door.

Miss Myra started marcelling Miss Pheeny's hair and putting in clamps to hold the waves. "Well, you all didn't go far," said Miss Myra. "Used to be a time I couldn't get you in the house."

"They both young ladies now," said Miss Pheeny. "They don't find the same things fun to do that they used to do. How was it in Jamison, Belly?"

"Fine," I said.

"How'd you like Carolina, Teeny?" said Miss Pheeny.

Teeny hesitated, looked at her mother, and when she said nothing, answered, "It was hot down there. All I did was pick rice and cotton and turn black."

"Lost a little weight, too," said Miss Pheeny.

"How's your niece, Miss Pheeny?" I said. "The one from Baltimore?"

"Oh, she's fine," said Miss Pheeny, then quickly, as if to gloss over the subject, "How's Miss Rachel? Recovered and well?"

"Yes, ma'am," I said, then to Teeny: "Miss Pheeny's niece was down here when you left. She lives around the corner from Miss Betty. She said she didn't see you in Baltimore but I told her you were in Carolina."

There. Everything was out in the open. If Miss Pheeny wanted to have a conversation about Baltimore, now Teeny knew what to say if she asked her anything else.

Miss Myra, whose ears had been cocked with suspicion, now leaped into the conversation. "Oh, I forgot you told me you have a niece in Baltimore, Pheeny. Out on the church ground that time Belly and her got into the wine and had a fight. What's her name again?

Teeny will have to look her up when she goes up there. I was thinkin of sendin her up there soon for a little fun before school start. She didn't have no fun at all down in Carolina with my sister. They worked the poor child to a bone out there in those fields."

"Yes. You do look kind of peaked, Teeny," Miss Pheeny observed dryly. "You could probably do with some fun. Silas Green comin any day now. That oughta lift you up a little."

So. That was why Miss Pheeny was getting her hair done. For a special event. The Black Minstrel Show was coming to town. And Silas Green was a special event. So special that my mother, who never even went to the *movies,* went to see it, and once a year, on her only visit to town, Miss Janie Green went to see it. So special that Aunt Rachel and Uncle Avery planned their August vacation around it, and Miss Myra took a day off from doing other women's hair to make sure that hers was perfect the first evening and the last, when there was a dance in the pool hall over Jennings's barbershop.

I was overjoyed. Then I frowned. "I haven't seen any posters up sayin they were comin."

"I got ways of findin things out," said Miss Pheeny.

I did not doubt that.

"I declare, Pheeny, you do know just about everything that goes on," said Miss Myra.

"Trust me," said Miss Pheeny. "Very soon."

"Well," said Miss Myra, suddenly very busy pressing Miss Pheeny's hair against her head between two fingers to shape a wave, "Teeny just might not be back in time."

Back in time. I looked quickly at Teeny, who seemed as shocked as I was.

And that is when I learned that Teeny's crying was driving her mother to distraction and that Miss Myra was going to send her away again, this time to her sister Betty in Baltimore. Perhaps Miss Pheeny's unflagging interest in her affairs helped speed up her decision, I don't know. But the next day I said goodbye to Teeny again, this time at the bus stop, and I was secretly glad that she was going.

Once again that summer I was left alone, but now strangely happy to be. The house had become a haven, my room a sanctuary. Up there I read and slept and read and thought. Thought about Miss Ophelia and Uncle Avery with an ache in my heart, and about Jimmy and Miss Ella and Miss Mattie with a little smile. Around the house I was more subdued, restrained in my behavior. This kept Uncle Willie and Mama looking uneasily at each other, but saying nothing to me. Once I overheard him tell Mama that I was growing up. I think Mama took that to mean I must have started my period, for one day she tapped lightly on my door (which she had never done before) and came into my room and began to talk about it, but I reminded her I already knew what a period was and that mine had not come yet and I would let her know when it did.

She was very relieved, but wondered if I were unhappy, being alone, which I assured her I was not. "The Silas Green Show will be here soon. You'll have fun then."

"Well, I like bein up here in my room readin. And soon I'll be goin back to school. And then I won't even have time to think," I said. "So don't worry about me, Mama."

"Well, I do," she said. "I get lonely, too, sometimes."

She smiled and gave me a hug and then left my room, and I sat at my window and thought about what she said about being lonely. And I thought about Mr. Henry Binns and his dazed eyes when he looked at her. And I knew that it was because of me that she was lonely, that if I were not there, Mr. Henry Binns would be actively courting Mrs. Lizzie Anderson. I sighed and went back to my book.

One afternoon I was standing on the kitchen table so Mama could adjust a hem in a dress she was making for me to wear to school. "You haven't been over to see Miss Janie," she said through the straight pins she was holding in her lips.

I reminded her that before I went to Jamison she had told me I had to request her permission before I could go there.

"Turn around a little," she said. "Well, I changed my mind." She was worried about Miss Janie. Her mind was deteriorating before I left, but now she had taken to wandering and was almost hit by a car two weeks ago out in the road one night. "That triflin Malachi has his triflin nephew stayin over there with her until he can make some other kinds of arrangements for her. But I don't trust that fool Lewis any further than I can throw him. He ain't never had the sense of a horsefly."

Lewis Green was a fool. He was two years ahead of me in school and was always smacking his loose, juicy lips at the girls. From what I overheard in the schoolyard, he also had "Roman" hands and "Russian" fingers, terms that had nothing to do with geography but were a vulgar description of his manual dexterity by his silly, tractable girlfriends.

"Besides," Mama added casually, "when I told her you was comin home this week she said Willie and Malachi could bring the piano here for you. If you want it. Now since Teeny's gone, I thought Willie could bring it over here tomorrow and you'd have something to do."

I could hardly keep still until she finished the pinning, and a few minutes later I was hopping elatedly through the tall grass to Miss Janie's house. The path was still there but overgrown with bushes that whipped against my arms and legs. Panting and sweaty, I swatted at the gnats that swirled around my face. Finally I reached the fence at the edge of Miss Janie's yard and hung on it, panting, surveying the yard. Where was Miss Janie? I had expected to find her weeding the flower garden on the shady side of the house. But the petunias and begonias in the beds near the house were wild and overgrown with weeds. The grass in the yard was almost as tall as weeds in the field. Cautiously, I climbed the fence and went to peep around onto the porch. Miss Janie was sitting on the other end in her rocking chair. I started toward her, then fell back with a scream.

A dog had jumped out from nowhere, snarling and pawing the air, but it had been jerked back by a long rope and hit the ground with a thud. Now he was jumping around, still barking wildly. Most country children come into contact with dogs of all kinds, especially those leashed to a stake in the ground, as this one was, and I knew exactly what to do. I ran to the backyard and searched for a stick, found one, and ran back to the front yard. Brandishing the stick in front of me, I stomped up to the dog. "Who the devil you barkin at, you evil thing! You almost scared me to death!" He must have been well acquainted with sticks; immediately he stopped barking and lowered himself to the ground. "Bark at me one more time, and I'm gonna bring this stick right down on your nose!"

I stood for a moment, scowling down at him, then went to the porch where Miss Janie sat looking confused. She had not uttered a sound the whole time.

"Hi, Miss Janie!" I flopped breathlessly on the warped floorboards.

Miss Janie looked as if she had just jumped out of a sack. Her clothes were rumpled, her stockings hanging loosely on her legs. Her hair was white and wild like a dandelion pouf; she was wispy enough to be blown away. She turned her head and looked down at me. "Hello, child." Her eyes were glazed; she did not seem to recognize me.

"It's me, Miss Janie. Belly. I'm back from Jamison."

"Belly. Is that you, child?" Her eyes became more focused. "Come up here and give me a hug."

I climbed up by the chair. She raised her thin arms. I put mine around her bony shoulders. "When did you get a dog?" I wiped my face with the sleeve of my blouse. "He almost scared me to death."

"Oh, child. That's Lewis' dog."

"Why's he keep him tied up?"

" 'Fraid he'll run away, I guess. He beat him all the time." She pressed my arm. "I missed you, child. You back home to stay?"

"Yes, ma'am." I walked around and looked on the other side of the house. Nothing. No one. "Where's Lewis?"

Miss Janie fluttered. "Oh, he'll be back soon, he said . . . he went . . . I think he said he was goin down the road a minute . . ."

Something else was peculiar. "Where's your piano?" I turned to her. "It's gone."

Miss Janie started, then looked around. She lowered her voice. "I don't—is it in the house?" She rose, then sat back down quickly.

In the house? Malachi had moved it out at least three months before, I reminded her. Miss Janie did not remember. I started to smile at her. Instead I stared. A rope had become visible when Miss Janie started to rise from the chair. I moved forward and tugged at it and saw that Miss Janie had been tied to the chair. "Miss Janie! Who tied that rope on you?"

Miss Janie tried to rearrange her dress over the rope. "Oh, child. Oh, child."

I dropped down and looked at the rope. It was thick, like the one on the dog. The knots were too tight for me to loosen, even with the help of my teeth. I jumped up and ran to get a knife from the kitchen. But the doors were locked. I rushed back to Miss Janie. "You wait!" I said breathlessly. "You wait right here! I'm gonna go home and git Mama and Uncle Willie right now!"

Within a half hour we were rattling up the drive, and a few seconds later Uncle Willie was sawing at the rope with his hunting knife, muttering and cursing. "Wait'll I see that little bastard. Tyin this woman like a damned dog. I see his black ass before I leave here I'm gonna kick it all over Mason County."

Soon Miss Janie was on the front seat of the truck between Mama and Uncle Willie. I climbed into the back. Halfway down the driveway Uncle Willie stopped; I heard him yelling at someone. I jumped to the ground and looked around to see Lewis Green running back toward the road. Uncle Willie was hanging out the door of his truck. "You better run! I catch you in the next week I'm gonna skin your sorry hide like a rabbit! And you tell Malachi to come over to Miss Lizzie's house when he git home and see about his mother!"

Malachi came past that night, upset but relieved that we had rescued Miss Janie. He had been worried about her, but what was he to do, he had to work. No he hadn't known about the rope. He was going to take good care of Lewis when he could find him. His sister-in-law had told him what happened when he had gone there to see where his mother was. As for Miss Janie's piano, it was gone. Last week the boy and some of his friends had chopped it up and they had taken it away for firewood. He was sorry because he knew how I liked to play on it. In fact he'd been thinking of giving it to me.

"Your mother already told me Belly could have it and that's probably why that on'ry nephew of yours chopped it up," Mama said reproachfully. "Didn't want nobody else to have it." And what was Malachi going to do now, she demanded. He certainly could not leave his mother there with Lewis.

Flustered, Malachi turned his hat around with his long fingers. He had called his aunt in Baltimore and they'd agreed for Miss Janie to come live with her. He was going to take her to Baltimore in a few days and wondered if Mama would help him out until then.

"Help you out how," said Mama, arms crossed.

"Well, ma'am, I thought maybe Belly could come and stay with her until then."

"Belly! Belly ain't coming over nowhere with that big nasty dog in the yard and that crazy Lewis wanderin around."

"I ain't scared of that dog, Mama."

"That dog's too mean, Belly. It might get loose."

"You right, Miss Lizzie," said Malachi Green. "I don't know where Lewis got it from. Said it was a huntin dog and that's why he won't stay in the yard unless he tie it up. I told him to get rid of it."

Uncle Willie looked at him sourly. "Hell, that dog ain't huntin nothin but she-dogs. Got balls bigger'n a bull's. You gonna have to shoot that sucker, not turn him loose. Else every damn she-dog in the county'll be knocked up with his puppies."

Malachi Green nodded. "Tomorrow I'll ask around at work. One of the fellows is bound to take him." He looked at Mama. "If that'll satisfy Miss Lizzie."

"I don't care what you do with that dog," said Mama. "I still ain't lettin Belly stay over there alone with Miss Janie. Especially after Lewis and his friends choppin up that piano. They liable to come back."

"Lewis might be simple, but he ain't crazy," said Malachi. "He know better'n to go where I tell him not to."

"Well, I've already figured out what to do," said Mama. "I'm goin to bring Miss Janie here. Put her upstairs in the middle room. Belly might be able to keep her company, but she don't know about takin care of no old people."

So Miss Janie was assigned to our care, and the improvement in her physical and mental condition was immediate and apparent. Mama washed her up every morning and dressed her in a fresh house-dress. Then Miss Janie would sit in the parlor and watch Mama iron (she insisted on helping out by sprinkling and rolling the dampened clothes). Some mornings Uncle Willie would take us to Miss Janie's house so we could weed the garden; afternoons, she would sit on the porch and converse with Uncle Willie, who, I believe, would sneak her a sip from his bottle as they talked about old times. They seemed to do each other good.

"Old people need companionship, someone to talk to," observed my mother one afternoon when we were all relaxing on the porch and Miss Myra was remarking about the change in Miss Janie. "When you don't use your mind, it gets flabby, like your muscles. And your tongue, too, Miss Janie. Your tongue's like the handle on a pump. You push it up and down and the brain starts working, and the words, like the water, come gushing out."

• • •

Miss Janie had been with us only a few days when one morning just after breakfast Miss Myra came knocking breathlessly at the screen door and called Mama to the front porch. They whispered there for a few hurried moments. Mama called Uncle Willie from the table. Another hurried conversation, then Miss Myra rushed home, Uncle Willie came back to his cup of coffee muttering about "crazy damn women," and Mama came to the kitchen door and gestured to Miss Janie; they went upstairs. I looked over at Uncle Willie. He held up his hand. "Ask me no questions and I'll tell you no lies." He stood up, gulped down the rest of his coffee, and left the room. I heard him pounding up the stairs.

I finished eating and cleared the dishes from the table. Mama came back into the kitchen. She was scowling, lips pressed together. "Belly." Her voice was curt. "I've got to go out for a few minutes. While I'm gone go up and change the sheets on the bed in the middle room."

"But that's where Miss Janie—" I started.

Mama didn't answer, just went out to the porch. I followed her. Miss Janie and Uncle Willie were standing there waiting. Uncle Willie had changed from his work clothes to a clean shirt and pants; Miss Janie's suitcase was standing next to her. He picked it up, and threw it into the back of his truck. Mama helped Miss Janie off the porch into the truck, and without even saying goodbye they rattled off down the driveway, leaving me swelling up with anger and indignation. I had been abandoned without explanation.

Many years later when we recalled that day, I rebuked my mother for leaving me on the porch without telling me a thing. She was amazed. But she *had* told me. She had to go out for a few minutes. But everybody left, I answered. I was *alone*. She shook her head in amusement and said that I was old enough to be left alone, that I wasn't a child of five or six. My trouble was, she continued, winking at Uncle Willie, that I was angry because I didn't know where she was going or what was going on. And she and Uncle Willie chuckled over that all that afternoon.

What I did not tell them was that when they disappeared, I dropped onto the porch, ready to cry. Then angrily I jumped up, determined to find out something. If Miss Myra had come over, then that's where they went, I reasoned. They wouldn't take Miss Janie back to her own house. I hopped off the porch and ran across the field, stopping far enough from the house to see but not be seen. Yes, Uncle Willie's truck was there, and Mama was helping Miss Janie onto the porch. Uncle Willie came out of the house, he and my mother began talking excitedly, then he shook his head and got into his truck and drove off. Mama and Miss Janie went into the house. I ran back home.

I knew enough to piece part of the puzzle together. Miss Myra must have gotten a telephone message for Mama. It must have upset her and Mama. Why else wouldn't Miss Myra sit down and have a cup of coffee? She would always stay for coffee if she got a phone call that early in the morning. And someone was coming to stay at our house for a while. That was why Miss Janie had to go stay with Miss Myra. That was why I had to change the sheets. And Uncle Willie was going to get whoever was coming. And this someone lived in a town. Otherwise, Uncle Willie would have kept on his same clothes.

I nodded and hummed and whispered to myself as I changed the bed, somebody is coming, and I wondered who. I had an idea, but I would not admit it even to myself. It was too wonderful; if I thought about it it might not happen. I was sure it was Miss Ophelia. If Uncle Willie and my mother were troubled about the baby, others would be too. Miss Ophelia would come here to be away from prying eyes. I would see her again before she went away.

Mama came back within the hour and moved her ironing from the parlor to the front porch so she could see Uncle Willie when he returned. Still she gave me no explanation. Angry, I went up to my room to read. I could hear her as she went from the kitchen (to look at the clock, I assumed), then back to the front porch to her ironing. "Now where is that man," I heard her mutter. Or, "What in the world is takin them fools so long." Twice she came up to my room, which had the best view of the road, to look out of the window. The second time she seemed worried. "Lord," she said aloud, "I hope Willie's truck didn't break down."

I didn't answer. If I wasn't supposed to know anything, I'd be a dummy, not hear, not talk.

Just before dusk we heard the rattle of Uncle Willie's truck. If he had gone to Jamison as I had suspected, it would have taken him two hours up and two hours back. If, as I envisioned, Miss Mattie gave him lunch, that would take another hour. Then getting Miss Ophelia ready and into the car would be another hour. So I did not expect him until late in the afternoon, although Mama's actions and words indicated she had expected him much earlier. She had just gone back to the porch after another look at the clock when I heard the truck rattling up the driveway.

I jumped up and ran to the window. Mama was standing on the grass. The truck rolled to a stop. Uncle Willie pushed his door open, hopped down to the ground, and slapped his hat on his leg. "Lizzie, you better go help that woman out. She done stretched every last nerve in my body."

My heart dropped to my stomach. Miss Ophelia wouldn't get on Uncle Willie's nerves. As my mother went around the truck she called to the person inside, "What in the world happened? What took you all so long?" Apprehensively, I waited for the reply.

The voice that answered was too familiar and clearly not Miss Ophelia's. "This damn wreck broke down and we had to set at the side of the road for three hours . . ."

Mortified, I jumped back from the window.

That voice.

Those words.

Aunt Rachel.

She went directly to the middle room and stayed there for three days. She did not eat any dinner that first night; at breakfast the following morning my mother made her a tray. Uncle Willie, still not recovered from his sour mood of the day before, watched somberly as Mama loaded the tray with food to take it upstairs.

"Rachel sick?" he asked testily.

She still wasn't fully recovered from her surgery, Mama explained.

Uncle Willie's eyes flashed. He threw his fork on the table. "You must be tellin that lie to Belly, not to me. You know it ain't a thing wrong with Rachel that surgery had anything to do with. All that static she give me on the road yesterday wasn't from the mouth of no sick woman. Like I broke the truck down on purpose. And all that food on that tray looks like it's for a horse, not for no sick woman." He pointed his finger at Mama. "She's mad, mad about what she found out, and you might as well stop tryin to hide it from Belly. She's gonna find out soon enough what's really going on."

Mama's mouth dropped open.

"And don't stand there lookin like you don't know what I'm talking about. I'm sick of all this shilly-shallyin. And secrets. Maybe if you tell the gal what's wrong, she might tell you what she knows. She oughta hear it from you since you're her mother. But if you don't want to tell her, I will. Right here and now. And if you don't want to hear my version, get up and leave."

"I'm going, *Mister* Walker," said Mama, "but not because you tellin me to go." She swept out of the kitchen with the tray.

Uncle Willie dragged on his cigarette a few times, thinking, then said, "Wait." He plunked his chair down and signaled me to follow him. We went into the yard and sat under the big maple tree near our driveway. We sat on the grass with our backs to the house. He was going to tell me something, he said. Something that he didn't want Mama to overhear. But I had to cross my heart and promise that I would never reveal what I heard.

I did as he said and he began. "Remember you asked your mama about Rachel's operation and she wouldn't tell you nothin? See, now that's an example of what I'm talkin about. Keepin secrets. If you understood maybe you could've helped her better."

"Jimmy Diggs said she was gettin her guts out," I said.

"That's just the kind of thing I'm talkin about. Rachel think she keepin a secret, and you learn it from some little peanut-headed sucker livin right next door to her and he probably overheard his mother telling somebody what Rachel told her and it's too bad that's the main way kids have to find out stuff they should have explained to them by an adult." He took a long drag on his cigarette. "Only they wasn't her guts. Your aunt, she had what they call a female operation."

"What's that?"

"Every woman got some kind of sac inside them where a baby grows. The *wound*. Lots of women get an operation on it so they can't have any more babies. But some of them are sick. They git tumors and things there, and they get diseased." He took another long drag. "Now that's a fact of life. A female's life, anyway."

I wondered where this roundabout discourse was leading, but I patiently wrapped my arms around my knees and kept my eyes on his face as he continued. "When Rachel was about nineteen, she was wild. Mama had went up to Baltimore for a couple of months to stay with her sister Marcella who was sick, leaving us at home with Papa, who was gone most of the day workin and half the night drinkin. Well, at that time Rachel was liking Avery, in fact they was supposed to get married. But unbeknownst to him she also liked this boy down in Julep and at the time Avery was workin over there in Jamison cookin. So that give Rachel a lot of free time. And she got a baby by this boy from Julep. Right over there in that field you run through every day when you go see Miss Janie."

"Who was the boy?"

"Well, it ain't important now, but it ain't gonna hurt you to know. It was Mitchell Looby's father. Big Mitchell."

I gasped.

"Yep," said Uncle Willie, divining my thoughts. "That's just what I was referrin to under this tree that day. Thought it might shut her up."

"Did Uncle Avery know?"

"Wait. Let me tell you. Now the baby could've been Avery's. In fact she told him it was and he was in a rush to get married, but she come crying to me that she was scared to have the baby because it might turn out like Big Mitchell, who was black as my shoe, and then everybody would know it wasn't Avery's."

I was puzzled. "Why'd she think that? Mitchell Junior ain't dark. And he's got good hair, too. And all Teeny talked about was how her baby was gonna have good hair because it was Mitchell's baby."

"That's the whole point," said Uncle Willie. "Big Mitchell's mother was half white and his wife was high yallah. Now his mother didn't show up in Big Mitchell, but his wife and his mother all came together in his children. All of them are pretty light. Colored folks don't know what their children are going to look like, and Rachel should've knew that. After all, Avery's father was kind of dark-skinned. So Avery's baby could've been dark like Big Mitchell, but I guess she just wasn't takin no chances."

I shook my head in wonder. "I can't imagine Aunt Rachel being afraid of anything."

"She was scared Papa would find out, too, and beat that baby out of her. So to make a long story short, I took her to a woman and she give me some stuff to get rid of it. Old Nancy Grimes. Lived so far back in the woods there wasn't a road in five miles. Nothin but wagon tracks. But Rachel was still scared that the stuff wouldn't work by itself, so she climbed up that tree up by the house as high as she could and jumped out to make it look like a accident and me and Lizzie come runnin out thinkin that she done killed herself for sure. Bleedin like hell. Soaked all in the ground. Anyway, I figure she must've messed up her insides since she ain't never had any kids. And Avery, he didn't know nothin about Nancy Grimes, or nothin. He's thinkin Rachel really fell out of the tree. He was feelin mighty bad. Guilty. He was ten years older than Rachel, you know, and he felt it was all his fault. Anyway, he married her right after that. I don't know if he ever found out about Rachel and Mitchell Looby. If he did, he never let on. Not to me. But you know the way people talk. And them Loobys are famous for talkin. As well as some other folks around here."

Uncle Willie paused, took a drag on his cigarette, then exhaled a layer of smoke that drifted lazily away.

"Yep. I dug a hole in the side yard and we took up that whole bloody mess that she wrapped up in a sheet and we threw it into the hole and threw dirt over it to fill up the hole and then planted a rosebush there."

"I ain't never seen a rosebush on the side of the house," I said.

"There ain't one. Rachel would never water it or nothin. She only wanted it there as an excuse for why we dug a hole there. Mumma always said it was the wrong spot for a rosebush. Not enough sun."

Maybe Rachel didn't want to be reminded, I thought.

Uncle Willie said no more. He was finished. He got up and stretched out his hand and pulled me up. "Now your mother and me seen that baby of Ophelia's," he said, walking ahead of me. "It was pretty light-complected. And that's what's gonna cause the trouble. If it was dark like her, people would just shrug and pass it off as another hussy doin what comes natural."

Hussy! The word pierced my chest like a dart. I walked silently behind him, head bowed, looking down at the red dust powdering my bare feet. When we got to the house Mama was waiting for me on the porch and told me to come into the kitchen.

"I don't know what Willie done told you about Rachel bein down here, but I guess I better tell you what I know since you seem to be a part of it."

"Me!" I said.

"Seems like that little friend of yours next door is the one who stirred up all this mess. Seems like he went down to Miss Ophelia's to play dominoes with Miss Mattie. Said he been goin down there with you every afternoon and playin with her when you was takin your piano lessons. Anyway, Miss Mattie was over at Ophelia's helpin her out with the baby, and that little devil come in the back door and went sneakin up the steps and right into the bedroom where Miss Ophelia was and seen the bassinet and went right on over and looked in at the baby. Miss Mattie was about to choke him but Miss Ophelia stopped her. Talkin about some he had to go to the bathroom. Well, she scuttled his behind right on out. But it was too late then. He went home and told his mother, and she picked his brain. And when she finished she went over to tell Rachel what the boy told her. When Avery come home Rachel and him had a big argument and then the next day she packed her bags and here she is."

"Jimmy Diggs don't always tell the truth," I said.

"He said you and him saw Miss Ophelia and your uncle Avery kissin," said Mama. "Did you?"

I wanted to run and hide. I stayed and shook my head.

"What did you see?" said Uncle Willie.

Nothing, I told them. Only that at the picnic that's what Jimmy thought they were doing.

"What picnic?" said Mama, incredulous.

I explained about the picnic. How we sang. How Miss Ophelia played the piano. How I fell asleep on the backyard swing until Jimmy woke me and pulled me to the window. "They was dancin and he said they were kissin."

Mama sat back with a whoosh. "Lord."

Uncle Willie leaned back in his chair and stared at the ceiling.

"Belly, why didn't you tell somebody about this?" said Mama.

"About what? Them dancin? I didn't see nothin wrong. And anyway, Miss Mattie was at the picnic," I said.

"Lord, Lord, Lord," said Mama.

"What's wrong with dancin?" I asked.

They both sat silent, shaking their heads. Finally Uncle Willie brought his chair down easy. "The gal's right, Lizzie. Ain't nothin wrong with dancin."

I pointed out something to her that she had apparently forgotten. "And I heard Miss Ophelia tellin you that Uncle Avery did her grass. He had to come to her house to do that. And you didn't say nothin about it."

"Now this sure is the pot callin the kettle black," said Uncle Willie.

"But that just never came into my mind," said Mama.

"Or into Belly's neither," said Uncle Willie.

"Well," said Mama quietly, "it's Avery's baby. He ain't admitted it, but you seen that baby, Willie."

"I'm'a tell you like Papa told me. No man is ever sure who his father is."

My words tumbled out. "How could it be Uncle Avery's baby! Him and Miss Ophelia didn't do what Teeny and Mitchell did in the shed! They wouldn't do nothin nasty like that!" I could not bring myself to believe it, in spite of what I had seen.

"Jesus wept," Mama whispered.

Uncle Willie whooped and choked back a laugh, then jumped up and staggered to the sink for a glass of water. "Lizzie," he gasped, "I think it's time you had a talk with your daughter."

I flounced out of the kitchen in embarrassment and spent the rest of the morning lying across my bed thinking about Miss Ophelia, about Jimmy, about Uncle Avery. Pictures of Teeny and Mitchell and Uncle Avery and Miss Ophelia whirled around in my head. I groaned and pulled the pillow over my head and fell asleep.

That afternoon my mother came into the backyard and sat next to me on the blanket where I was reading. I was still embarrassed and hunched away from her, but she reached out and closed my book. I sighed and sat up, ready for a lecture that did not come. She seemed satisfied that I had nothing more to say about my time spent in Jamison; she posed a series of questions about Teeny and Mitchell, ending up with "But why didn't you tell me?" after I had graphically described their antics that day in the shed.

I tried to explain. "You would tell Miss Myra and Teeny was scared. And I didn't know she would get a *baby*." I kept my eyes down. "Then as soon as you found out you wouldn't let me go anywhere because you'd think I would get one too. But you didn't get one after Aunt Rachel did when—"

"God, I'm going to kill that Willie."

I looked up. "But I'm *glad* Uncle Willie told me about it. He said grown people shouldn't act like everything's a great big secret, that they should tell us things so we don't make the same mistakes you all did."

My mother turned her head and dabbed at her eyes with her apron and said, her voice quavering, "That damn Willie."

"Why didn't you, Mama?" I said after a while.

She was looking away from me, at the back of the house. "When I was growin up, if I did anything wrong, I got caught. I'd always get caught. Rachel, she would sneak out at night and come back in before light and nobody even knew she was gone. One time, only one time, I sneaked out to meet your daddy, and Papa caught me and tore my tail up. So I knew what would happen if I did *that*. I would get *caught*." She laughed through her tears. "Or go to hell in gasoline drawers."

I knew that it was more than that. But I didn't know how to express it, so I merely said, "Aunt Rachel's mad at me because I didn't say nothin to her, ain't she."

"What could you tell her, Belly? Like you said, I probably knew it, but didn't want to face it. Miss Mattie couldn't tell her nothin, and she lived right next door. No, what happened between Ophelia and Avery is between them and God." Mama stood up. "You just happened to be around at the wrong time."

I was thinking about the conversation I'd just had with Uncle Willie. Something he had said worried me, so I said before my mother could get away, "Mama, is Miss Ophelia a hussy?"

"A hussy? Now who said that?"

I hesitated, not wanting to give Uncle Willie away, then I said, "Well, like people said Lila Lee was a hussy."

"Some people might think she is," said Mama.

"Do you?" I asked.

"No," said Mama. She sat back down. "Do you think Teeny's a hussy because she had a baby?"

"No."

"Just because she's your friend?"

"No. I just think she was *dumb*."

"Well," said Mama. "Ophelia's my friend. So I don't think she's a hussy, either."

"Do you think she was wrong?"

"What's wrong for some people might not be wrong for others."

"Would you do what she did?"

Mama sighed. "Belly. All these questions."

"Well, would you, Mama?"

"No."

"Why?"

Mama looked me in the face and said softly, "It's wrong, Belly. Women know that they shouldn't fool with married men. If they do, they have to suffer the consequences." She got up. "Now. I have to get back inside to my ironing."

Later in the morning Uncle Willie went to Miss Myra's and brought her and Miss Janie back with him. They wanted to see Aunt Rachel. They climbed the steps as solemnly as two Pilgrims on their way to a funeral, Miss Myra clutching her Bible, Miss Janie hanging on to the railing to prop up her thin frame. I was hovering behind Miss Janie, ready to catch her in case she stumbled.

At the top, Miss Myra turned and whispered to Miss Janie, "After you tell Rachel your story, I'll read her a few verses from the Bible."

Her story? What story could Miss Janie possibly tell Aunt Rachel that would help her? I did not think my mother was in the mood for any more questions, so I went on the porch and asked Uncle Willie.

He shook his head. "Now, that Miss Janie's had a *life*. She could tell you some stories that would make your hair stand up. But I guess

Myra's talkin about the time Miss Janie was carryin Malachi. He's her youngest child. She had him when she was about the same age as Rachel . . . that would make her . . . let's see . . ." He squinted at his fingers, counting. ". . . about thirty-eight or forty. Anyway, Miss Janie had about a dozen kids at that time. Married all her life just about to Abel Green. But at the time she was carryin Malachi, Abel's other woman—"

"Other woman! Don't these men ever stay home?"

"Couldn't do it without the women," said Uncle Willie. "And stop interruptin. Anyway, the other woman was carryin his child, too. And she had it, a boy, just before Miss Janie had Malachi. Baby was the spittin image of Abel. Well, Miss Janie was mad, but it didn't kill her. And she was too much of a Christian to carry on like Rachel, but she got even with Abel. Now if you know your Bible, and Miss Janie *knows* her Bible, the Book of Malachi talks about treachery and infidelity. 'The Lord has been a witness between you and the wife of your youth, with whom you have dealt treacherously; yet she is your companion and your wife by a covenant—' "

"What's a covenant?"

"Well . . . a vow, like an agreement before God that can't be broken. Like when you get married. That's a covenant. And anyway, Malachi says, 'Let *none* deal treacherously with the wife of his youth.' So Miss Janie had the baby and it was a boy and she named him Malachi, and every time old Abel saw Malachi, or heard her call Malachi, or anybody talked about Malachi, well, he was reminded of his sin. And he knew he sinned. The fellows wasn't gonna let him forget that. They'd see Abel comin down the road with his kids, and they'd holler, 'Hooo, Malachi. How you doin, son!' Rub him all on the head. Give him a nickel. Didn't speak to the other kids at all. Ha, ha, ha. Old Abel, he was a deacon, too, you know. Ha, ha, ha. Anyway, maybe that's why Myra thinks that Miss Janie can help Rachel. She came out of it all right."

But what about Miss Ophelia, I wondered. Will she come out of it all right?

●   ●   ●

Aunt Rachel came downstairs later that afternoon. It was awkward between us at first. I mumbled a greeting; she nodded in return. She confined herself to the parlor, where my mother was ironing, so I did not need to worry about avoiding her. During supper and several games of Pokeno the tension was eased by the presence of Miss Myra and Miss Janie, who managed the conversation with the expertise of tight-rope walkers.

Before Uncle Willie took her home, Miss Myra promised Aunt Rachel she would come back the next day and they would read the Bible together. "Look to Jesus," she said. This was the only reference that was made to Aunt Rachel's problems.

The next morning after breakfast I was finishing the needlework I had started at Aunt Rachel's. I had not slept all night; guilt was squeezing my conscience like rollers wringing water from a sheet. Somehow I did not yet realize that the sin was not mine; that my presence had contributed nothing to the events that took place in Jamison; that the baby would have been born whether I had come there or not. But I had rejoiced in the illicit relationship between Uncle Avery and Miss Ophelia. And that I knew was wrong. I felt that if I showed Aunt Rachel the completed sampler, she would see that I valued what she had taught me.

Perhaps she would even forgive me.

Uncle Willie came from around the house and stepped up to my chair. "Hmph. Workin on that to please Rachel. I swan, the things people do to appease the devil."

Mama was at a table on the other side of the porch listing items of laundry and their prices on a sheet of yellow paper. "Leave Belly alone, Willie," she said without turning around. "She don't have no piano to play. She can't keep readin day in and day out. Ruin her eyes."

"Hunh. That needlework ain't no better." He sat on the edge of the porch. "When's Rachel goin home."

"I don't know," said Mama.

"Well, her and Myra and Miss Janie got their heads together in the back prayin and talkin. Myra may be the church mother, but she ain't up to no good. I'll tell you that."

"What makes you say that."

"Did Rachel tell you she seen that baby?"

"No," said Mama in surprise.

"Well, she did. I heard her 'confessin' to Mother Myra out back. And you know what she did?"

"What." Mama stopped working and turned around.

"When Ella told Rachel about the baby, Rachel took herself down to Miss Mattie's and when Miss Mattie wouldn't tell her nothin she went into Miss Ophelia's back door and went on upstairs to look at it herself. Busted into the woman's house."

"Lord," said Mama.

"Then that's when she had this fight with Avery when he come from work. Then the next morning she called you up." He jerked his head toward the backyard. "You don't believe me, go on back there. And if she don't tell you, Myra will."

Mama turned around. "I believe you. And if I didn't I wouldn't go back there and ask her. She'll tell me when she's ready."

"Lizzie, I hate to tell you, but there's lots of things Rachel will never be ready to tell you. Take it from me."

"Maybe it's best. I don't need to know all of Rachel's business."

"Well, when she's draggin you into it, you do."

Mama shrugged. "Come on over here and get these baskets for Mrs. Chapman. And don't lose this list. I wrote down everything and put the price by each one and then added it. And this time tell her to write down everything she sends. I'm'a break that white woman of that habit of tellin me I lost somethin." She pushed the list into Uncle Willie's hand. "Tell her I won't take the clothes if she don't make the list. Nip this stealin shit in the bud."

Uncle Willie put the list in his shirt pocket. "Gimme a pencil and some paper. I got a feelin I'm'a have to make this list. Or let Pheeny Butler do it."

"What makes you think she's gonna write down what's really there, if she can write. But I don't want you to make it. If Mrs. Chapman can't do it, she can keep the clothes."

Uncle Willie shook his head. "You a tough woman."

"Willie, hush up and go deliver that laundry so I can get my money." She walked over and looked at my sampler.

If I can stop one heart from breaking,
I shall not have lived in vain.

"That's very nice, Belly. Where did you get that?"

"From a poetry book Uncle Willie brought home."

"Well, I like that."

"Let me see," said Uncle Willie.

He read the verse out loud. "You might not turn out so bad after all."

Mama shoved him off the porch. "I'll buy you a frame so you can put it on the wall in your room."

"If you like I can make you one for your room, Mama," I said, feeling suddenly awkward.

Mama hugged me. "Oh, Belly, I'll like that a lot."

"Make two more, while you at it," said Uncle Willie. "Give one to Rachel so she can hang it over her bed."

In her role as church mother Miss Myra became a fixture at our house for the next few days. Now, what the duties of a church mother are I have never been certain, although through the years I have inquired of women who went to a church where there was one. The responses were similar. Well, there's the minister and the deacons, then the church mother. Oh, they could *name* church mothers: a neighbor, an aunt, a friend. But what were their duties? They varied from church to church. In one she would serve as an example to the younger mothers; in another, it would be a position of honor for one of the oldest women in the church, much like the top of the pecking order in the barnyard.

I doubt if Miss Myra saw herself in the role of example setter. Not as much liquor as she could put away at one sitting. And certainly not as one of the oldest women in the church. She plucked every gray hair from her head as soon as it appeared. No, I'm convinced that she fancied herself more as consoler and counselor, for she exerted herself mightily to console and counsel Aunt Rachel.

On Monday morning, a cool, bright morning, we were on the porch just after breakfast. Aunt Rachel had appeared for coffee and gone back upstairs. Uncle Willie was just finishing his coffee. My mother had given me a dress to hem. There came Miss Myra up the driveway, Miss Janie hobbling along at her side.

"Halloo!" called Miss Myra.

Uncle Willie brought his chair down with a bang. "What the hell," he muttered softly.

"She said she was comin to see Rachel," said Mama. "But I didn't think she was going to walk poor Miss Janie over here."

Exasperated, Uncle Willie set his cup down by his chair and jumped off the porch. "I'm goin to look at the garden. See if there's any more squash."

Mama went into the yard to help Miss Janie up onto the porch. I grabbed her hand; the poor old lady, panting and perspiring, fell into my rocking chair. I ran to get a wet cloth and a glass of water. My mother went into the parlor to iron; Miss Myra disappeared up the steps to Aunt Rachel's room.

As soon as I wiped her face with the cool damp cloth, Miss Janie fell into a dead sleep. I sat on the edge of the porch to finish hemming my dress. I heard Miss Myra and Aunt Rachel come down the steps; they stopped in the parlor and talked to Mama.

When Miss Janie woke she and I played dominoes. Uncle Willie appeared from the garden, where he had been hiding, and jumped in his truck and disappeared. Later in the day he returned with two baskets of laundry. Not long after that he took Miss Myra and Miss Janie home.

By supper time Aunt Rachel finally smiled. It was not very wide. It seemed a strain to draw her lips upward at the corners.

"So there's a human being inside that shell after all," noted Uncle Willie.

"Least it's in a shell and not a bottle," said Aunt Rachel.

"Yep. She's back to her old self," said Uncle Willie.

"You all are worse than two cats in a sack," said Mama.

Aunt Rachel turned her smile on me. "Lizzie said you finished the sampler you started at my house."

Happy that the course of the dinner conversation was about to change, I jumped up from the table and was back immediately with the canvas bag she had given me. I pulled out the sampler and laid it on the table.

Aunt Rachel inspected it. "This is nice work." She handed it back to me. "Your mama says she's going to buy you a frame so you can hang it in your room."

"I'm gonna make a wall full," I said.

"I hope you don't take to it like you took to readin," said Uncle Willie.

The next day Miss Myra came again, and again she and Aunt Rachel retreated to the backyard. Miss Janie went into the parlor with my mother. Uncle Willie went fishing. I sat on the porch and started a new sampler. At noon Malachi Green drove up and told Miss Janie that he was coming for her the next day; that she should be ready to leave early in the afternoon. Malachi went back to work; Miss Janie and Mama went back to the parlor.

That evening we had a celebration in honor of Miss Janie's departure. Mama and Aunt Rachel cooked a big dinner. Miss Myra made macaroni and cheese. Uncle Willie made peach ice cream. Miss Janie and I sat around and watched and tasted.

The next afternoon Uncle Willie brought Miss Janie over from Miss Myra's house. She waited on our porch with her suitcase. When she saw Malachi rattling up the drive she started to cry. A few moments later he rattled back down with Miss Janie and Mama, who went along to comfort Miss Janie. Suddenly, a foolish thought flitted across my mind. Miss Janie would miss the Silas Green Show.

When they had gone, Aunt Rachel, Uncle Willie, and I stayed on the porch. The day was warm but a gentle breeze cut the heat. We sat, not talking. I pulled my sampler out of my canvas bag. Aunt Rachel began to read the Bible. Uncle Willie sat back in his chair and nodded.

At that moment Miss Myra hallooed across the field.

"That woman got the eyes of a chicken hawk," said Uncle Willie. "Why the hell don't she stay home and do some work."

Aunt Rachel closed her Bible. "She's comin to see me," she snapped.

"Why don't you go to see her," Uncle Willie snapped back.

"I would if I was in a condition to walk," said Aunt Rachel.

"Your condition ain't stoppin you from runnin your mouth," said Uncle Willie. "And I guess you was in a better condition to walk over there than Miss Janie was to walk over here those last three days. And when you goin home anyway. Or you plannin on spendin the rest of the summer here."

I looked up from my sampler.

"I got just as much right here as you do."

"Well, this ain't no flophouse for discombobulated wives."

Miss Myra had reached the porch; now she looked up at Aunt Rachel and Uncle Willie with raised eyebrows.

"Ain't you got some houses to clean or some naps to fry?" said Uncle Willie.

I ducked my head and held back a giggle.

"Ain't you never heard of a *vacation*?" said Miss Myra. "And ain't nobody scared of you, Willie Walker," said Miss Myra.

"Woman, you ain't here to bother me. You here to gab with Rachel, or so she informed me. So you better go do it. And mention somethin to her about headin for home while you talkin."

"That fool's just tea'd up," said Aunt Rachel.

Miss Myra eyed Uncle Willie as if she agreed. Then she looked back at me. "Actually, I came over to give Belly a message from Teeny."

"Teeny!" I said.

"Yes. She said to tell you she'd see you tomorrow. She's comin home late tonight. Her Aunt Betty's drivin her down."

"Well," said Uncle Willie. "Maybe now you can find somethin else to do with yourself except needlework and readin."

"What else?" said Aunt Rachel dryly. "Get into trouble?"

"Well, there's enough of that to go around," said Uncle Willie.

Aunt Rachel didn't answer; she stepped up to the screen door and she and Miss Myra went into the house. Uncle Willie got up and looked in after them, then with a wink at me, he opened the door and tipped in. The familiar strum of an Ink Spots record, loud enough to wake the dead. Then:

Oooooooooooh . . .

Uncle Willie hops onto the porch and into his chair. He sits there, grinning. "They in the kitchen," he says. "Watch."

I can't show my face,
Can't go anyplace,
People stop and stare
It's so hard to bear . . .

The sound of feet rapidly approaching. The screen door bangs.

Everybody knows you left me,

Miss Myra and Aunt Rachel are now on the porch glaring at Uncle Willie.

It's the talk of the town . . .

Aunt Rachel speaks first. "Willie Walker, you no good, signifyin black scarecrow." She goes over and swipes at him, he leans over and falls out of his chair, laughing. He jumps up as Aunt Rachel kicks at him and misses, he hops onto the ground. Miss Myra has gone inside and turned off the Victrola; now she is back on the porch. Aunt Rachel has a stick now and is waving it at Uncle Willie.

"Watch out Rachel! Okay, woman!" His hands are over his head, now over his face, as he dodges her blows. "All I did is play the Ink Spots! Can't I play the Ink Spots in my own house?"

"No!" Another blow from Aunt Rachel. "Not when you gettin into *my* business! No." Another blow. "Keep on with your foolishness, hear? I'll raise a knot on your head so big you'll have to pay the barber double!"

"Go home if you don't want to hear my music!" Uncle Willie is now safe behind the maple tree.

Aunt Rachel throws down the stick and comes onto the porch.

"Damn fool." Breathing heavily, she shakes her head. "Come on, Myra. Let's go back in."

Bang! goes the screen door.

Uncle Willie climbed back onto the porch and into his chair. "Goin back there to sit and sip and smack their lips over that ham your mama baked yesterday," he muttered. "I know just how much talkin's goin on. Back there for three days eatin like dogs and callin on God in between bites. They ain't up to no good, believe me." He softened his voice, imitating Miss Myra. " 'Now you have to forgive Avery, Rachel. He's a man, and all men sin, but in the eyes of God he's your husband, and you made a vow til death do you part.' "

"You mean Aunt Rachel's goin to *leave* Uncle Avery?" I said.

"Nah." Uncle Willie lit a cigarette. "No matter how mad she git, Rachel ain't leavin her fine house to come down here in these woods. She got it *good.* Too good. And she know it. And Avery Swann ain't the first married man to cheat on his wife. And he won't be the last."

I shook my head. "If my husband went around with another woman I'd leave him."

"You eleven years old. What do you know about what goes on between a man and a woman. Especially when they married."

"If he did love somebody else besides me, well, I would want him to leave me and marry her."

"That's what you women don't understand. It's in a man's nature. In some countries, men have two, three, four wives."

"At the same time?"

"Sure."

"And they don't go to jail?"

"No indeed. It's the way their society is set up. But in this country, it's not set up that way. So I could guess you say it goes against a man's nature to have only one woman. So just because a man yields to temptation, that don't mean it's *love.* And it sure don't mean he's gonna leave his wife. Girl, you know what would happen if men left their wives because they playin around other women?" He laughed and shook his head. "Whooh! This would be a different world! Especially since most of them playin around with somebody else's wife. Musical chairs, that's what they playin. Musical chairs. A game. You go out the front door to work in the mornin and your neighbor or your best friend slip in the back door as soon as you out of sight." He shook his head again and chuckled. "Old Avery. Who would'a ever thought he had the moxie." He sat a moment, his expression that of a jeweler marveling over an unexpectedly fine diamond. "Well," he said. "It'll all pass. Rachel will get over bein mad at Avery and Teeny will get over givin up her baby. Two years from now, they won't remember nothin about it."

I was not convinced. I thought of Miss Ophelia in Uncle Avery's arms, of the anguish in Teeny's face, swollen from crying. I shook my head. "Nope." I shook my head again and threaded my needle with green floss and worked it rapidly through one of the leaves on my sampler. Uncle Willie was wrong. What I had witnessed might ease but it would not be forgotten.

That night when my mother was brushing my hair (a weekly ritual after I came home from school when I was eight with a head full of lice) I spoke of Uncle Willie's observations. Hers were partly contradictory. "Teeny will not forget that baby. Rachel won't forget that some other woman had her husband's baby. And Willie's right when he says that later it might not hurt so bad that they'll be bitter, although he sure ain't the one to talk about bein bitter. Just don't listen to that junk he tells you about men and marriage. He ain't never been married so he can only tell you what he's heard about it from men who are. And men tell other men what they want to hear so they won't call them stupid, or henpecked, or weak. The trouble with most of them is they want to tell their wives and children what's right and what's wrong but don't want to do right themselves. They don't want to set the example. Look at Willie. He had a fool for a father, and he's half a fool. Only reason he's not a complete one is he had a mother with some sense."

"Uncle Avery just seems so . . . Well, how could he do something like that?" He was almost as bad as Mitchell Looby.

"Avery is a good man, Belly. And Rachel ought to be talkin to him, not Myra. But most people can't talk to each other. *That* is the trouble."

"Even if they love each other?"

"Love gets in the way."

"Why?"

"I guess it's because people don't want to hurt each other's feelings."

"Did my daddy do that, Mama? Play around?"

"Your father was a jewel. He was a rare man. I guess he spoiled me for other men. After you have a diamond, you ain't satisfied with glass."

Early the next morning I made my way across the field to Miss Myra's; halfway through I saw Teeny coming my way. We did not run and grab each other and scream with joy as we did before. I stopped, apprehensive, and waited. The girl who walked up to me that day was still thin, but smiling broadly. My eyes fixed on her hair. The plaits were gone. Her hair was straightened sleek and glossy and combed straight down to curl under at the edges and frame her face. This was indeed a different Teeny. I stared.

Embarrassed, she touched her hair. "Aunt Betty did my hair yesterday. It's a page boy."

"It's pretty," I said.

"I told Mama you was up. She say, 'Girl, where you goin this early in the mornin! Belly ain't goin nowhere! Miss Lizzie think you crazy wakin them up this early!'"

Hands behind my back, I grinned. "Mama told me the same thing. I was comin earlier, but she made me wait on the porch for a whole hour."

We stood a moment, squinting at each other in the hot sun, then wondered aloud where we should go—to Teeny's house or mine.

"If I go back home," said Teeny, "Mama gonna find somethin for me to do. She don't believe in cookin and doin dishes when I'm around."

"Aunt Rachel's at my house," I said. "And her and Uncle Willie will probably start arguin like they did yesterday. Or start pickin with us."

We finally decided our old place on top of the hill was best. We could sneak around up the road and get up there without Miss Myra seeing us. Once settled in the grass we began to talk.

Teeny started first about her stay in Baltimore. Her cousins had a record player and they had all the latest records and they played records and danced every day. Also her uncle had taken her sight-seeing in Washington and she had visited the Smithsonian Museum, climbed the spiral stairs inside the Washington Monument. But best of all times was at home with her cousins. "Girl, I had so much fun. We went to the movie practically every day. And I met the *nicest* boy. He live around the corner from my aunt and he *cute*! His name's Robert Hawkins, Junior, and he got the whitest teeth when he smile. And he talk so soft and nice. And he's not fresh at all. Aunt Betty let him sit on our stoop in the evening, and girl, he can dance, and he taught me how to do the New York Bop and dance off-time. We had so much *fun*."

Watching Teeny's face, I saw no trace of the despondent girl who had left for Baltimore almost two weeks before. She seemed, as Uncle Willie had predicted the day before, "over it."

Had she forgotten her baby and Mitchell Looby, too? I seized on her admiration of Robert Hawkins to bring up his name. "What about Mitchell Looby? Don't you care about him no more?"

She dismissed the father of her child with a toss of her head. "Oh, him. He can't even *dance*."

Dismissed Mitchell Looby like a slap at a gnat.

"What about your baby?" I asked. "Do you still want to get him back?"

She looked down at the ground. "I had a long talk with Aunt Betty, and she said what Mama did was best, and that a baby needs a mother and a father, and that I probably shouldn't even tell anybody I *had* a baby. Especially if I want to meet some nice boy and get married someday. None of my cousins know I had a baby. My uncle neither."

As I listened to her rave about her good times in Baltimore I became more and more depressed. She had been on a vacation, seen new things, met new people, learned to dance. I, what had I seen, what had I done? Taken piano lessons and become involved in an intrigue that I was sure would not interest someone who had mastered off-time and the New York Bop. During a pause she asked me what I had done in Jamison, but I felt silly now. I mumbled for a few minutes about my stay there, ending desperately with, "I learned how to do needlework. I finished one sampler already. 'Blessed are the meek.' "

"Needlework. You mean make them little pictures that hang on the wall and say things like 'Home Sweet Home'?"

I nodded, waiting for a giggle, but instead, got a request. Would I show her how to do that? Robert Hawkins's mother did something she called needlepoint and had it all over her dining-room chairs and a footstool in the living room.

A few minutes later we were making our way through the tall grass to my house for my canvas bag. I thought about our earlier plans. "Then after I show you how to do a sampler, then maybe you can teach me how to swim."

"Swim." Teeny had been walking ahead of me. Now she stopped and turned. "I ain't goin swimming."

"Why not?"

"I'll get my hair wet."

"But you said you'd teach me this summer."

"You don't have to worry about your hair gettin nappy if it get wet. I do. Then I have to stand over the stove and sweat and heat the straightenin comb and burn myself . . ." She stopped and showed me two black marks on her face near the scalp. "See? And I can't keep straightening my hair every day. It'll break off."

She was finished. She turned and walked on. I followed, mulling over this new Teeny who danced and wore a pageboy and wanted to learn needlework. And never wanted to talk about me. Only herself and her problems. Who was not going to teach me how to swim because of some old *hair*. Resentment boiled up inside me. I wanted to make her feel as bad as I did. I could tell her about Mitchell Looby and the Jenkins girl. Even though she said she didn't like him anymore, it would hurt her, I knew. But I merely tramped along behind her and smoldered.

• • •

On the porch, under the surprised regard of Uncle Willie, I pulled out my canvas bag, and after showing Teeny my completed sampler, I gave her a first lesson, much in the way that Aunt Rachel had shown me. That first session did not go smoothly. Why did she have to make just plain X's, Teeny demanded. Why couldn't she start out on a proverb. Or a leaf. Or a border. Because she had to learn to do the cross-stitch, I explained, pointing out that she was having trouble with that. Teeny's fingers were stubby and awkward. Uncle Willie watched with amusement while she stabbed the linen and her fingers with the needle. "Hey, gal, that's a piece of cloth, you supposed to push the needle through, not punch your fingers and bloody up the material."

Exasperated, I said, "Uncle Willie, you keep botherin us and I'm gonna tell Mama."

Again Teeny pierced her finger. Ooch! She stuck it in her mouth and glanced sideways at Uncle Willie. He snorted. Up she jumped, shot him a look that cut off any comment, announced she'd see me later, and before I could say a word, hopped off the porch and ran for the fence.

"You forgot your needlework!" yelled Uncle Willie, holding it up and waving it.

I tried to work up my anger, speak in defense of my friend. But I couldn't. I was happy that she had failed, had become frustrated. Served her right for changing, for being happy. I watched her run across the field. "She don't even miss her baby. She thinkin about a new boy she met in Baltimore," I said in disgust.

"That's in the natural scheme of things," said Uncle Willie.

"Miss Betty said the baby had to have a father."

"That's just somethin she told her to make her feel better about lettin her uncle have the baby."

"Why would she say that?"

"Well, it's a boy."

So what, I wanted to know.

"Well, some people say a boy need a father."

"What if it was a girl?"

"She'd need a mother."

"Oh," I said.

I worked on my sampler. Mama was right; Uncle Willie didn't know what he was talking about most of the time. As I stitched, I thought of Miss Ophelia. With the new baby she probably didn't miss me at all. Then I smiled. I would make him a sampler, too.

First came the posters that mysteriously appeared every year. On the poles in town. On the sides of buildings and barns. On tree trunks outside of the churches. On a stake in someone's yard. Or perched lopsidedly in the grass along the roadside.

SILAS GREEN
FROM
NEW ORLEANS

The black minstrel comedy show was coming to Mason.

Then came the scouts. "Snoops," Uncle Willie called them. Colored men and women who insinuated themselves in the colored social life of Mason: the colored churches and the colored barbershop and the colored beauty parlor and the colored pool hall and the colored restaurants and speakeasies. They sang hymns and got their hair cut and their hair curled and shot pool and ate ham hocks and drank whiskey and danced. They mingled and listened. Listened to the gossip: who's cheatin on their wives or husbands; who's havin children out of wedlock; who's sinning in general. Listened to stories: who's seen something strange; who's seen something funny; who's been cheated, been mistreated, had an accident, caused an accident, made a fool of somebody, made a fool of himself. Who died: how much it cost, where the relatives came from and how they behaved at the funeral, the appearance of the corpse, family disagreements. These tidbits were tucked away to be later recalled and skillfully fashioned into skits for the amusement of the audience.

Then up went the tent the day before the show on a vacant lot just this side of the town limit near the railroad tracks. Near the colored folks, which was appropriate, since after all, it was a show *about* colored folks *for* colored folks.

"Silas Green comin Saturday," announced Uncle Willie one day after finishing his rounds. He had also been to the barbershop. He reeked of bay rum. "Seen the poster in town." He handed Mama her money from the laundry deliveries. "Ten dollars. Not bad."

"Not bad." Mama tucked the money in her bosom. "You hang over a washing machine and a clothesline and a iron in this scorchin weather and then you tell me not bad. And Silas Green comin, too."

"I think one of his snoopers was in the barbershop," said Uncle Willie. "Looks like that flat-nosed sucker I saw hangin around last year about the time they come to town. Never seen him agin til today. Called hisself readin the paper, but I could tell he was listenin. Never turned a page from the time he was in there."

"Did you say somethin to him?"

"For what?" said Uncle Willie. "I hope he hears all the dirt so I can have a good laugh."

"Hmph," said Mama.

On Saturday we rolled into town just before dusk. This was the first night of the show, and an hour before it opened the Silas Green Band always strutted down Main Street working their magic like a troupe of Pied Pipers. People on the sidewalks went mad from the music and crowded the street behind them as they strutted down to the carnival ground. In front of the tent two long lines formed, colored and white people standing one behind the other to pay for tickets, unmindful of class or color, waiting in line to see Silas Green.

But once inside the tent, all pretense at egalitarianism was dropped. The white people were guided to a special section that was roped off for them. These were the best seats, the grandstand seats that were in the front section of a large U formation, which formed a horseshoe. Colored people filled in the remainder of the seats on the outside of the U. A scramble for seats began as soon as people entered the tent. Teeny and Miss Myra had come in a taxi. I stood looking for them, and when I spotted Teeny waving wildly at me I hopped up the tiers and together she and Miss Myra and I spread ourselves apart to save seats for Mama, Aunt Rachel, and Uncle Willie. When they were seated, Teeny and I slid next to each other and surveyed the crowd. Everyone we knew in school was there, and we spent a few minutes standing and waving and yelling at each other until our mothers pulled us down.

Almost as soon as the grandstand was filled the show began. First the band played. The male performers, no matter how light or dark the skin, all wore blackface with chalk white exaggerated lips and white gloves.

Then Silas and Lilas with their skit, in the manner of Amos 'n' Andy.

SILAS: *Hey, Lilas, how much you charge for a polish? I got to look good for my gal tonight!*

LILAS: *(Looks at Silas's extra big shoes.) Well, I ain't never tackled nothin that big before.*

SILAS: *Not that! (Takes off green silk stovepipe hat to expose a completely bald big head.) This!*

LILAS: *I ain't never tackled nothin like that before, neither! (Smacks Silas's head. They tussle.)*

The audience howls.
Then Caldonia with the big shoes and her "sidekick."

SIDEKICK: *Caldonia, why you so evil?*
CALDONIA: *I just combed my hair!*

This time the audience screams and looks around at the women among them. The skit continues in this manner for ten or fifteen minutes. Then came the tap-dancing minstrels and showgirls. In between them, clowns. Finally came the long skit, the one that everyone had waited for all evening.

Out strutted a grinning minstrel across the stage carrying a sign. "The Dancing Deacon." Howls of laughter. Tittering and whispering in the colored audience. Then another minstrel with another sign. "Part I, The Picnic."

The skit proceeded. A tall, handsome young man with a devil's tail befriends two silly girls with their hair tied up in pickaninny plaits and pink ribbons. He flatters them into trying some of his red ripe watermelon. Some of their friends come up and chase him away and tease the girls for flirting with the devil. Whispering among the audience. Who? Who? Who? Chiiiild.

Scene II. Another minstrel struts across the stage. "Home." Two signs above two houses: "Church Mother" and "Sister Ruby." Much whispering in the audience now. Guffaws. People are leaning forward. I stare straight ahead.

In each house the mother is asking her daughter if she swallowed any watermelon seeds. They don't know. They rub their bellies. *That watermelon was so good.* Mother is frantic. What must she do? Call a deacon to help the daughter.

Scene III. "The Dancing Deacon." He dances into house number one and sends the mother away and questions the daughter with silly questions and then . . . throws her down and seduces her to get rid of the seeds. The audience goes crazy. He does the same thing with daughter number two in the next house.

Scene IV. "Praise the Lord." The daughters are rolling the babies in their coaches. They are prancing. People are looking, goggle-eyed, talking behind their hands.

"They sho' look like the Dancin Deacon!"

"Praise the Lord they didn't come here lookin like the devil!"

Screams and stomping from the audience. The show is over. We leave. On the way home there was much talk in the front of the truck where Mama and Aunt Rachel were sitting with Uncle Willie. I was alone in the back, but I could hear the talk, loud and argumentative as usual.

"If I was Myra, I'd've got up and left," said Aunt Rachel.

"What for? Then everybody'd know she thought they was talkin about her," said Mama.

"They know now," said Uncle Willie. "You didn't see Lucy Jenkins gettin up and leavin."

"They need to stop makin fun of the Lord, I know that," said Aunt Rachel. "Especially in front of all them white people."

"You mean it's okay for them to make fun of the Lord as long as it ain't in front of white people," said Uncle Willie.

"You know that ain't what I mean," said Aunt Rachel. "I mean they shouldn't make fun of the Lord, and they shouldn't tell all the colored folks' dirt in front of white people."

"Why not?" said Uncle Willie. "You think white people don't do no dirt? How simple can you be? You read the papers. You listen to the radio. All we hear and read about is white folks' dirt. And they sure don't give a damn if us colored folks see it."

"Willie Walker, you love to twist people's words around," said Aunt Rachel.

"You twisted them around before they left your mouth. I just repeated them." There was a pause, then, "And who you think told them minstrels all that stuff they put on in front of them white folks? Colored folks, that's who."

"I bet Pheeny Butler had her mouth in it," said Mama.

"I told you I seen them in the barbershop, and if they was in there they was in Butler's Restaurant," said Uncle Willie. "I think I seen her brother at a table whisperin to somebody the other day. Somebody else I never seen before."

"Well, nobody but some of us could've told that mess," said Mama.

"Poor Myra," said Aunt Rachel.

"Poor Myra my foot," said Uncle Willie.

•   •   •

I woke in the middle of the night sweating. The fan in my room had been loaned to Miss Janie, and when Aunt Rachel came, it had been reassigned to her. Again. The air in my room was hot and still: suffocating; it was as if I were stuck inside a pillowcase. I got out of bed and went to the window. No breeze. No moon. The night was like black velvet. I sat still a few minutes, listening to the snuffling sound of Uncle Willie's soft snoring. I went over and dragged a sheet and a pillow from the bed and quietly felt my way to the stairs. There was always a breeze on the front porch.

When I reached the front door I stopped. Aunt Rachel and Mama were out there talking softly. I turned and went into the parlor. There were two windows there and a cross breeze. I arranged my sheet and pillow under the window that faced the porch and eased down and stretched out. Cool air drifted down onto my face; I closed my eyes. Mama and Aunt Rachel were still talking softly, the murmuring voices rising and falling; now that I was still, the words that had been indistinct became clear.

"Did you talk to Avery about this?" That was Mama.

"Avery always wanted children. I just couldn't have none. And I sure can't have none now." That was Aunt Rachel.

"You just can't go take the woman's baby."

I had begun to drowse, but at those words I perked up. The woman's baby? What woman's baby? Frowning, I rose up on my elbow to hear better.

"I'm not takin just *any* baby, Lizzie. I'm goin to *ask* for it, ask for my husband's baby. The child gotten in sin." A pause. "She'd probably be happy to get rid of it."

A tart answer from Mama. "If she wanted to get rid of it, I'm sure she could've done that months ago."

"How's she goin to explain it to that uppity aunt of hers in New York."

"I'm sure she can."

Aunt Rachel again. "The child should be raised in a Christian home."

"His mother's a Christian."

"She's a loose woman. A sinner."

"The Lord forgives loose women. And sinners. And he also forgives adulterers. Like He'll forgive its father."

"The child should have a home with a married mother and father."

"Maybe she might get married."

A choking sound from Aunt Rachel. "Who in the devil would want to marry—" The words seemed to strangle her.

There was a little silence. I held my breath and stared intently into the dark.

The silence lengthened. A chair creaked. I heard the screen door open. They were coming inside. They went down the hall and up the stairs. I listened. They went to their rooms. I lowered my head to my pillow and stared up into the dark. After a moment I felt tears leaking around the back of my neck. I took a corner of the sheet and wiped it, then turned on my side. My eyes burned in the dark until I went to sleep.

A few hours later I woke up. It was almost dawn. Someone was moving around in the kitchen. I sat up and rubbed my shoulder. Uncle Willie came downstairs and went into the kitchen. I got up stiffly and followed him silently down the dark hall and stopped. "Well, we better get started before Belly gets up," I heard him say. "I don't want to hear her mouth this early in the mornin."

"Maybe we *should* take her along," said Mama. "It wouldn't hurt. Besides, I don't want to leave her here with Rachel all day."

That was my cue. I went into the kitchen rubbing my eyes, saying sleepily, "Mama, where you goin?"

Mama and Uncle Willie looked at each other. Uncle Willie shrugged and Mama said, "Ophelia's goin back to New York soon and we're goin to Jamison to get a few things that she said I could have, and I want to see the baby—"

I shrieked with joy. "Me too!" I waited to hear no more. I turned and ran up to my room and threw on my clothes and was back downstairs before they finished drinking their coffee.

"You ain't goin nowhere with me until you wash that face and comb that hair," said Mama.

I ran back upstairs and washed my face. I combed my hair in the truck as we rode along the highway.

"Gal's got a sixth sense, like a dog," said Uncle Willie. "Usually she sleeps until seven o'clock."

"I couldn't sleep! That floor in the parlor is too hard."

"Belly, you slept on the floor in the parlor?" said Mama.

I explained about the heat and my fan.

"Gal ain't got no fan," said Uncle Willie. "Got to sleep on the hard floor for some air because her aunt took her fan to keep comfortable because she too evil to be home with her husband."

"She might be back with him sooner'n you think," said Mama.

"If he take her back," said Uncle Willie.

"Avery's just givin Rachel time to cool off," said Mama.

I turned my face to the window to feel the breeze and let Uncle Willie and Mama think I was not listening to them. Then I rested my head on my shoulder and closed my eyes and wondered why Uncle Willie was now willing to face Miss Ophelia. Maybe taking her to the hospital had caused a change of heart.

A few miles passed, then Uncle Willie said, "You think the deacons will put him out of the church?"

"Why?" said Mama.

"Why! Fornication! You know they'll have a meetin about it."

"Shuh," said Mama. "I'd like to be a fly on the wall in that meetin. They'll tap dance around it hemmin and hawin because they do the same damned thing. Bunch of damned hypocrites. Just like Papa. When he was a deacon, he could quote every chapter and line that dealt with the sins of men. Especially lust and adultery."

"And wine," said Uncle Willie. "Don't forget that."

"And then would quote by heart the verse that lets them off the hook," said Mama. Then, imitating her father, 'And Ephesians say to put off the old man and put on the new man! Throw off the old man with his deceitful lusts! Put on the cloak of righteousness and the suit of new holiness! For you were in darkness, now you have come to the light! Brothers, let us help this sinner wrestle with the devil.' "

"Preach it, sister," said Uncle Willie.

A few more miles passed, then Mama spoke again. "I don't know where Rachel gets her nerve writin Ophelia a note like she did askin her for that baby."

"I bet Myra put her up to it."

"Myra couldn't convince her to do somethin she don't want to do. No, Rachel thought up that note by herself."

"Mmm hmmm," said Uncle Willie.

"Maybe I won't give the note to Ophelia. Rachel wants to send her a letter, let her mail it to her."

"Go ahead. Give it to Ophelia so she can answer it. And she can tell her *hell no* in writin. Besides, you already told Rachel you was gonna do it, and I don't want to hear no static about it when I get back."

Mama sighed. "I can't understand how a woman her age can be so *foolish*. And have such nerve. Askin that woman for her baby."

"Well, Lizzie. You don't like to think it, but your sister is spiteful. Plus she lives in a little town where people talk. And everybody know what Avery did. They talkin about it on the phone, in the street, at church. The deacons have a meetin, Avery won't be thrown out the church, so what is Rachel goin to do? How can she go to church or around town with her head up? Well, bein spiteful, she can turn her cheek like a good Christian and forgive her husband and take the baby and rub his nose in his dirt. And the other good folks will say what a good woman she is to do that, and she can walk around town and go to church with her head up. And have a baby to boot. And she ain't never gonna let him forget it. He'll be walkin around with his head on his chest the rest of his life."

Another mile or two passed.

"That would be a terrible thing if Rachel was to do somethin like that," said Mama.

"It's a terrible world," said Uncle Willie. "I learnt that when I went to war. First thing I learnt was there's more people like Rachel and Myra in it than you think."

"What's Myra got to do with it?"

"Aidin and abettin. Always doin good in the name of God and tellin you about it. The world is full of people like Myra. And Rachel, she sillier than a goose. Somebody like Rachel do somethin wrong, or is about to do somethin wrong, and Myra will tell her she's got the Lord on her side, and find some verse in the Bible to show her that He is. And then Rachel, she believe it and run around honkin about her Christian duty."

"You make Myra sound like a terrible woman."

"Well, if she the kind of woman that would give away her own grandchild, and the kind to tell another woman to take her own child's baby, what kind of woman *do* that make her? You tell me."

"Well, I can't tell you *that*," said Mama. "What I *can* tell you is you must've had an extra swig of whiskey from the way you're spoutin off."

"Well, I have had a drink. I'll say that, Lizzie."

They lapsed into silence.

Then Uncle Willie said reflectively, "But maybe Myra will change. After what them Silas Green folks did and said last night, I wouldn't put my head out of my house for weeks. And I wouldn't show my face in church for six months."

More miles passed.

I fell asleep.

C h a p t e r **23**

Many years later, when I was a young married woman and Miss Mattie was a very very old woman, we talked for a long time one evening on her back porch. I had come back to Jamison from Ohio for Aunt Rachel's funeral and was staying out in Mason County with my mother and her new husband and Uncle Willie. They had stayed at Aunt Rachel's right after the funeral to clean up and lock up. There was no one else to do it. Uncle Avery had died five years before and Miss Ella and Jimmy had moved away years and years ago to Pennsylvania (without James Senior).

I had not seen Miss Mattie for years. She came to the funeral, but not to the wake, and I was determined to talk with her one more time before I left for home. She was old and fragile, but the sparkle was still in her eyes. Naturally our conversation drifted back to that summer and how times had changed, especially times that we had shared.

And of course our talk turned to Miss Ophelia and what had happened that summer when I was too young to understand, not old enough to be told anything that might help me understand.

"You know, Belly, you and Jimmy Diggs were such a delight to me and Ophelia that summer. We were two lonely women and you children brought us companionship. And especially you. You brought with you the shining light of youth and a good mind eager to learn. Imagine! Here you come when Ophelia was so down and unhappy. She had closed herself up in that house since January and had shut all the windows and drapes like she was tryin to shroud herself in unhappiness. Then that afternoon I saw you on that sidewalk with your aunt, all elbows and legs, talking about learnin needlework and takin piano lessons and I said to myself, Lawd, don't let Rachel stop her from comin.

"You know," she continued, "that day was the first time Rachel Swann had a real conversation with me in three years. And she stopped to talk about you. Lord. And when you came, Miss Ophelia would say to me, 'Miss Mattie, she's so fresh and talks so much. And we talked and she poured her little heart out. Oh, I want to shake her and hug her and shut her up at the same time. And she is so bossy to that little Jimmy, and he just loves her to death. You should see how his eyes follow her around, and she berates him every five minutes. But here is a child who *reads,* Miss Mattie! Why she's read *Uncle Tom's Cabin* and *Oliver Twist* and *Little Lord Fauntleroy.* My God. And she's stuck down here in Jamison with all these *intellectuals.*' Oh, she was fond of you, Belly."

Eventually we got around to Uncle Avery. Miss Mattie spoke as if remembering a dream. "Well, I don't know when it started. Maybe when she come down that first time after her brother Eddie died in '46. He was livin here, you know. Then her father died the year after and it was hard on her. She used to go to church when she first came down here, you know. I guess Avery saw her there. Then when Deacon Love died, he come over to help her clean out things she gave to the church. But then she stayed on. Now what I understood was that she had some kind of attack. She had rheumatic fever as a child, you know. It was her heart, I think. I know she went to the doctor a few times. At first she didn't want no help, but I insisted. I've known the gal since she was sixteen. She was weak as a kitten.

"I do remember one time in church Avery asked me how she was, and I remember he dropped by one time, then again. 'How's the sick,

Miss Mattie?' And I didn't think nothin of that, him bein a deacon. That's their job, to comfort the sick. Of course, some of them send their wives, but Rachel never did like doin that. Comfortin the sick. Didn't like Ophelia neither. Said she was hincty. By the time you came she was obviously goin to have a baby. She didn't tell me right off, but I finally asked her about it and she told me she was. She didn't say whose it was, but I had an idea it was Avery, even though I never saw him over there unless I was there. But I was sure it was him from the way he acted when he came to see how you was doin that first week you started takin lessons. I guess it was a good thing they hid from everybody because if anybody ever saw them together they would know right away."

I knew, I told her. I saw right away. But I didn't know what I was seeing.

"Children see with different eyes than grown-ups. Innocent eyes. I knew what was goin on wasn't innocent. Was wrong. Was a *sin.* But it felt so good to be around them. We were all so happy, you and me and her and Avery and Jimmy. And I had something to get up for every day. Something to look forward to. Something to get up in the mornin for." She laughed. "I declare, Belly, life was *excitin* again. My blood tingled when I was around you all."

She hadn't told Rachel because it wasn't her business. "I wasn't her friend. Only time she spoke to me was when she wanted something. I wasn't her mother, or her sister. I was an old woman who lived next to the woman her husband was running with. Plenty of old women could say that about plenty women's husbands in Jamison. And can today. All it does is create enemies. Mind your business, I say."

She told me what happened to poor Jimmy, her voice cracking with laughter. "I could've killed that boy if I could. Run in here and saw that baby, then run home and tell his mother, who added the Lord knows what when she told Rachel. I ain't never heard Ella repeat a story without adding and adding to it so you don't almost recognize it when you hear it. Whatever she told Rachel, it set her off and she come stompin down to my house, come bustin through the *front door,* demandin to know what I knew about her husband and 'that black hussy next door' and called me a bunch of names I ain't never heard in my life. I told her I didn't keep tabs on her husband; that was her job. That sort of calmed her down, then she told me to go next door and get the baby and bring it to my house so she could see it, and I told her I wouldn't do no such a thing, then she swelled up like a bullfrog and busted through the back door and into Ophelia's house. Now Ophelia kept the door unlocked for me, you know, so I could get in and out without her always comin down, and that's how Rachel got in. Well, when she busted in, I was right behind her. Up them steps she ran like a whirlwind, and when I got up the steps she was in Ophelia's room lookin down at the baby in his bassinet. Ophelia, she was sittin up like she was lookin at a ghost. Rachel ain't said a word to her. Just kept lookin down at that baby, then she turned and pushed by me and busted on out of the house again. Lord, child, what a night. What a night." She sighed. "Lord, she gave the whole street enough to talk about for the next ten years."

Miss Mattie sighed again. "And of course, Rachel hadn't told your mother about that when you all came to see the baby. Else I'm sure your mother wouldn't have give Ophelia the note. Ohhh, that Rachel. Well, she's in the Lord's hands now."

In the Lord's hands. Well, Miss Mattie was sure of that, but I wondered about it. Surely she would have to beg Him a little to come into heaven if, as she always preached, our actions here on earth determine whether we pass unchallenged through those celestial gates.

During that long conversation I had expected to learn from Miss Mattie the answer to a question I had been asking myself for a long time. Why? Why had they fallen in love? And love it was, I had no doubt of that. I did not wonder about Miss Ophelia. She was a woman alone and vulnerable. It would have been surprising if she had not loved a man like Uncle Avery. But he was a married man, a man of integrity who did not give his word lightly. Was it opportunity? Proximity? I did not think so. According to Uncle Willie, many of the women on Randolph Street, as well as many in his church, had eyed Uncle Avery. He had as much opportunity to stray with them as he did with Miss Ophelia, if that's what he wanted to do.

Uncle Avery loved Miss Ophelia. My conversation with Miss Mattie merely confirmed that. But she had shed no light on the reason why, and I left her, my question still unanswered.

We arrived in Jamison that day early in the morning as we had done only two months before, and Mama gave Aunt Rachel's note to Miss Ophelia soon after we entered her house. She was in the living room getting ready to feed the baby. I went and stood over her, watching every move. "Can I feed him, Miss Ophelia?"

That's when Mama handed her the note. She took it and smiled at me and nodded. I guess she was wondering about the note and wanted to read it. "First sit down here in this chair, and I'll give him to you."

She nodded toward the chair where Jimmy always sat to watch me take my lessons. I sat down. Miss Ophelia handed me the baby and fixed my arms, one arm resting on the arm of the chair so that I held him close to my body, his head cradled in the curve of my arm. He was warm and soft.

"Don't be afraid to hold him, Isabel. He won't break." Miss Ophelia handed me the bottle. "Now put the nipple against the side of his mouth and he'll turn his head. See."

I did see. The baby had been squirming, whimpering. Now feeling the nipple he turned his head almost frantically and snapped it into his mouth and began sucking greedily. "You see him grab at the nipple!" I said with delight. "He acts like he's starvin!"

Miss Ophelia laughed. "He's always hungry." She stood above me and watched us for a minute.

"Do you like him, Isabel?" she asked softly.

I nodded.

"Well, I'm going out here to talk to Lizzie and Willie. If you need any help, just call me." She crossed the room and went into the kitchen to join Mama and Uncle Willie.

The baby had closed his eyes and was sucking contentedly now. I passed my hand over the silky fuzz on his head, traced my finger along his eyebrows, his lashes, his nose. I performed the time-old ritual of inspecting the tips of his ears, the skin on his little fingers at the base of his nails for the color there. Pink beige. He was going to stay light. I leaned over him. He smelled like baby oil and powder. His little hands were balled into fists; I inserted a finger in one, he grasped it tightly. Such a tiny hand. Love rushed through me, and a fierce urge to protect this helpless little body in my arms.

I leaned back and closed my eyes. Now I knew why Miss Myra's brother had not let Teeny nurse her baby, even hold it. If she had, he would've had to pry it away from her.

Things were not going well in the kitchen. I could hear Uncle Willie's voice, sharp, like a bark; Miss Ophelia was sobbing; Mama's voice was soothing, calm. I couldn't understand all the words, but apparently Uncle Willie was upset about something Aunt Rachel had done to Miss Ophelia.

Suddenly Uncle Willie stomped into the living room, Mama and Miss Ophelia right behind him. "Bustin into somebody's house. Hmph. I'm goin to see this man right now! He's gonna take that woman back home tonight, if I gotta bring her back here myself."

"Willie!" said Mama.

Uncle Willie was beyond reason. "Bustin into somebody's house. And he better talk some sense into her! If he don't, I will!" The front door slammed behind him.

Miss Ophelia ran up the steps. The baby whimpered. Mama came over to me. "Lord. Makin all that noise wakin this poor child." She took the baby up and held him to her shoulder. "Did you burp him, Belly?"

I shook my head.

"Get up, honey."

I stood up. Mama sat down and laid the baby on his stomach across her legs. She laid her hand on his back and pressed his sides. "If you don't burp him, he'll get gas and wake up and cry." She squeezed again. He belched. "See?" She held him up to me. "Take him upstairs and put him in his bassinet. Lay him on his belly."

"Can he breathe then?" I said anxiously.

"Of course, Belly. Just turn his head to the side. Sometimes after they eat they throw up and if they're on their backs they'll choke."

Such a wise, wise woman. I went softly up the stairs to carry out my mother's instructions. Miss Ophelia was in the bathroom; she came into the bedroom while I was settling the baby. Her eyes were red from crying. I pretended I didn't notice and said inanely, "Are you all right, Miss Ophelia?"

How could she be with eyes swollen into slits.

Miss Ophelia turned her face from me and nodded. I had an awful feeling that I was going to burst into tears. I stretched my eyes open as widely as I could and turned to leave.

"Belly." Her voice was hardly a whisper, but I heard it.

I turned back, wondering. "Yes, ma'am?"

She was sitting on the bed, her head lowered. "Please don't think that I'm—" Her words were lost in a snuffle, but I would have sworn I heard "loose woman" or "hussy."

Oh, she looked so pitiful sitting there, as if the world's woes were all on her shoulders. I went over to her and stood, not knowing what to say, not knowing what to do. "Oh, I don't think you're a loose woman or a hussy either, Miss Ophelia," I blurted. "And neither does Mama. And I'm glad you have a baby. And I bet Uncle Avery's glad, too. You wait. Everything will be all right."

She had been crying, but now she broke out in a laugh and grabbed me around the waist and pressed her face against me. "Oh, Belly. You make me want to laugh and cry at the same time."

I stood there listening to her cry. Finally she released me and took the edge of her bedspread and wiped her face and looked up at me. "I feel so silly. So silly. I've been acting so crazy I even called you Belly." She pulled my face down and kissed me. "You go on downstairs to Lizzie. I'll be all right now."

My mother was in the kitchen drinking iced tea. She poured me a glass. "Miss Ophelia all right?"

My throat was so tight I couldn't speak so I nodded.

My mother seemed to understand. We sat drinking tea, not talking. Just sitting.

Finally I stood up. "Can I go see Miss Mattie?"

"She's not home. She's visitin her sister over in Julep."

I sat back down. "Oh."

We sat on, not talking.

Finally my mother stood up. "I'm goin up the street to see what Willie's up to. You want to go? Then you can see Jimmy."

Before we left she went up to see Miss Ophelia. "She's almost asleep," she said when she came back down. "The baby's just been fed, so they should be all right for a couple of hours."

Miss Ella Diggs was elated to see us standing on her porch. "Lord! As I live and breathe. I know Jimmy will be glad to see you, Belly! Come on in, both of you. Jimmy's in the backyard. Go on out. Surprise him." As I tipped toward the kitchen, I heard her say to Mama, "How is Rachel, Lizzie? I saw Willie on the porch next door. I guess he caught Avery before he went back to work."

Jimmy Diggs was on the porch coloring.

"Boo!" I said through the screen door.

The poor boy jumped and knocked his crayons onto the floor. I pushed the door open and said, "Guess who?" I stepped onto the porch.

Jimmy stood up, mouth open. "Belly!" Then, shy, he stooped down and began picking up his crayons. "You made me break some of my crowns. I can't color with no stubs."

I got on my knees beside him. "I'll help you pick them up. Bet half of them were broken anyway."

In a few moments Jimmy was his talkative self again, and he gleefully related all that took place after I left for home. "Miss Ophelia had a baby!" he began.

"I know that, boy," I said. "And I know you told your mother that she did and started a lot of bad feelings. I told you about tellin everything you know."

"But—but—Mama already knew she had a baby. I didn't tell her."

"You told her it looked like Uncle Avery."

"No I didn't, Belly." His face was solemn. "I told her I seen it and she said what's it look like and I said he was light like Mr. Avery. That's all I said."

"Why did you have to say Uncle Avery?"

Jimmy was puzzled. " 'Cause it was a boy."

"Well, why didn't you say Mr. Rubin Harris? He live down the street. And you know him, 'cause you told me he's always passin for white when he leaves Jamison."

Jimmy shrugged. "I don't know. I just didn't think about him. Besides, he got red hair, and the baby's hair black like Mr. Avery's."

"That baby ain't got any hair, boy. It's just got fuzz."

Jimmy's lips drew together like a prune. "Well, I still didn't say nothin but he was light like Mr. Avery."

He looked as if he was going to cry, and I did not want him to do that before I heard more. I patted his shoulder. "That's all right. It don't matter anyway."

Encouraged, Jimmy continued in a low voice, keeping his eyes on the door in case his mother should appear. "One night I was out here and I heard Miss Rachel cryin so loud. Mama say she sounded like a sick cow. Mama had to go over there and talk to her five times a day at least. She was actin like a *wild* woman, Mama say."

I did not doubt that.

"Then one night her and Mr. Avery had a big fight. She was so loud. Not him, though. Then the next day, she disappeared. Everybody wondered where she went. Then somebody told Mama she went to your house."

"She sure did."

Jimmy put his hand over his mouth to hold back a laugh. "Ooooh. Was you scared?"

"Me! What do I have to be scared about!"

Jimmy worked his head up and down. "You know, Belly. You know."

"I don't know *nothin*, boy. Your imagination is workin overtime."

"Heeeeh. You know, Belly. You know."

"Anyway, Mama and Uncle Willie wouldn't let Aunt Rachel bother me. She's in our house. We're not in hers. And I already told them I didn't know nothin."

"Heeeeeh," said Jimmy Diggs.

"Oh, hush up, boy."

•   •   •

Mama and Miss Ella were having a long talk, too. But I was sure Jimmy had told me all that they were discussing. Within an hour Mama appeared at the screen door and told me it was time to go, that Uncle Willie had finished talking to Uncle Avery and we had to go check on Miss Ophelia again before we left. Jimmy tried his best to go with us, but his mother smacked him with the flyswatter and sent him howling up the stairs.

Halfway up he leaned across the banister and screeched, "You told me I could go stay with Belly for a while!"

"Miss Lizzie ain't got no room at her house right now! And even if she did, she got too much on her mind!"

Jimmy screeched louder. "You said I—"

Miss Ella leaped for the stairs and ran up after Jimmy. "You want another swat? Or do you want three or four more!"

Outside, Uncle Willie shook his head. "You wait. That boy gonna grow into the biggest sissy you ever saw."

"You sure do talk off the top of your head," said Mama. "Like you didn't get your behind whipped."

"A man whipped mine. Not no screechin woman."

"Hmph," said Mama.

Miss Ophelia was better when we returned. She gave us a shaky smile and began talking to Uncle Willie about moving things in the house: furniture, dishes, cooking utensils. "Lizzie, anything you see that you want, take. My aunt has a completely furnished house there, and it will all be mine when she goes." Aside from a few things that belonged to her parents, she was taking nothing. She turned to me. "Belly, I would offer you this old piano, but I don't know if you'd want it. It would probably fall apart if it was moved from that spot."

"I want it! I want it!" I cried out. "Can I have it, Mama?"

Uncle Willie went over to inspect the piano. He shook his head doubtfully. "She's right. It's rickety. But I'll try to move it. Me and Malachi Green and a couple of fellows can come up here one day. But I ain't promisin we'll get it home in one piece, Belly."

I was satisfied. They would try. That was all I could expect.

Before we left, Miss Ophelia gave my mother a letter. I supposed it was an answer to the note she had received from Aunt Rachel. Between the letter and any message Uncle Willie was about to deliver to Aunt Rachel from Uncle Avery, I was sure there would be no peace in our house that night.

The battle began as soon as we stepped onto the ground; the porch was the site of the initial conflict. My mother had brought along a few pieces of Miss Ophelia's furniture that she liked. Aunt Rachel, at the door, watched dourly as Uncle Willie moved them from the back of the truck to the porch.

"I'll put this stuff here until you decide where you want it, Lizzie."

Neck stretched, chin up, arms folded across her chest, Aunt Rachel fired the first shot. "What is that junk."

"Junk to you, not to us," said Uncle Willie.

"Some pieces that Ophelia said I could have," said Mama.

Aunt Rachel stepped onto the porch to investigate. "This stuff ain't been cleaned in years." She looked at a beaten armchair. "Woman must live like a dog."

"I can fix that like new," said Willie.

"Ophelia didn't live in the house, Rachel," said Mama. "Her father and brother did. And men ain't the greatest housekeepers. I guess they was doin well to cook and wash the pots and dishes and sweep the floors."

"Hmph," said Aunt Rachel.

"Everybody don't get the D.T.'s when they see dust, like you, Rachel," said Uncle Willie.

Aunt Rachel retreated. "I got dinner ready, Lizzie. And I made a peach cobbler."

She may have been part devil, but God must have guided Aunt Rachel's hands when she made a peach cobbler. No bruised peaches for her. She collected the fruit from the trees while the dew was still on them, then tenderly peeled and sugared them and laid them on the crust in the pan. A dab of butter and a dash of cinnamon and sugar on each layer and a healthy application on top. Finally the top layer of crust stretched over the top, pinched around the edges, and into the oven. Delicious odors filled the kitchen, and at last, the sweet gooey concoction was on a plate before you and you sank your teeth into the sweet goo floating in the chewy, tender crust.

Uncle Willie, however mad he was at Aunt Rachel, was well aware of her prowess in the field of baking, for when she said the words "peach cobbler" a wide smile stretched across his face. "Good!" He dropped a table to the porch. "I'll get the rest of this stuff out of the truck after dinner."

Then there was the skirmish at the dinner table while Mama was passing the Brussels sprouts to Uncle Willie, who started the attack.

"Avery said he'd be down here to get you in a few days, Rachel," he said, piling his plate with sprouts.

Aunt Rachel drew back, working her mouth as if she had lost control of the muscles in her jaw. Finally she got the words out. "*Avery* said! Who is Avery to be sending messages to me! And who are *you* to be bringing me messages from him!"

Uncle Willie popped a Brussels sprout into his mouth. "Well," he said, forcing his words around it, "last time I looked, Avery was your husband. As for me, I'm your brother."

They were at each other for five minutes. My mother and I stayed out of it, not saying a word. She poured iced tea into everybody's glass, I calmly pushed mashed potatoes around in my mouth.

"You goin back to him *some* time!" said Uncle Willie. "Might as well let him come next week and talk to you! That's what he said he wants to do. Talk, without a lot of screaming and yellin."

"I'll scream and yell as much as I want! He oughta be glad I ain't one of them women that don't say nothin, that just wait for somebody to go to sleep and then throw lye on his balls!"

"I guess Myra done put that shit in your head."

"Myra! Myra been tellin me to forgive him! To go back!"

"Why don't you listen to her then."

"I'll go back home when I'm ready, Willie Walker," snapped Aunt Rachel. "Not when Avery Swann's ready. Not when you're ready. And I'll never forgive him! He just better get used to that! Holdin me up to ridicule in front of the whole town. Havin a baby with that—" Her voice broke. She started crying, big heaving sobs. She got up from the table and went upstairs.

My mother went after her. Uncle Willie and I ate the rest of our meal in silence. I had two helpings of peach cobbler. Uncle Willie had three. That night I heard Aunt Rachel crying.

The next confrontation was at breakfast. Aunt Rachel came down, eyes puffy, and in her distressful state drank two cups of coffee instead of tea. I had finished eating by then so I got up from the table and went out back to read, but soon I heard Aunt Rachel and Uncle Willie and Mama, this time shouting. I went up to the house and sat under the window so I could hear.

This time it was about Miss Ophelia and the letters.

"You had some goddam nerve askin the woman for her baby anyway," Uncle Willie was saying. "If anybody should've asked for it, it should've been Avery! It's his baby. And yeah. Ophelia told me and Lizzie about you stompin into her house to look at it. Did you inspect his ears to see how black he'd turn? Did you look at his hair to see how nappy it would be? Did you open its eyes to see if it was wall-eyed? 'Cause the only reason you'd want it is if it's gonna be yallah with good hair. Well, she answered you right. She's keepin her son! That sweet pretty boy is goin to be raised by his black mama!"

"All right, now, Willie!" That was Mama.

Now Aunt Rachel. "You mealy-mouthed, liver-lipped, rat-faced, bucktoothed, boogey-picking, nappy-headed bastard!"

"Rachel!" Mama again.

"Hah hah hah!" Uncle Willie exploded into a laugh loud enough to dent the screen in the window above my head.

I exploded, too. I covered my mouth and rolled on the grass and laughed until my stomach cramped. When I was able, I sat up, wiping my eyes, and crawled back under the window.

Now Uncle Willie. "Got you where it hurt, didn't I! Right in the gut! 'Cause you know and I know what happened a few years back. Long time ago. When you jumped outta that tree! You didn't know whose baby you was carrying, but you jumped anyway!"

"All right now, Willie, all right now," said Mama. "Don't need to rake over dead coals.'

"Oh, yeah. Oh, yeah. We do. We do. We need to rake over all them coals, 'cause they ain't dead. Just smolderin. Avery might'a already had a son today! But you was so scared it might be black as that other good-time Charlie you was foolin around with and then Avery wouldn't marry you! And now that Avery got a son, you want to take it. But I don't think so, Rachel Swann. I don't think so. And if you ain't careful, when I'm drinkin too much and around Avery, I just might let that little bit of information slip right off my tongue!" He paused, then lowered his voice. "Talkin about forgivin, he might end up not forgivin you." He stopped again. "Better go on back to Avery, woman. While he still feelin guilty enough to take you."

I heard a chair scrape. I jumped away from the window and threw myself on my blanket under the maple tree and slapped my book open. A second later, Uncle Willie came out of the back door and stood on the stoop.

He stood, hands in his back pockets, looking straight ahead. He stood there a while, then sat down and lit a cigarette.

I could hear the voices of Mama and Aunt Rachel, Mama's low, Aunt Rachel's high, strident. What they were saying I could not understand. But Uncle Willie got the gist. Suddenly he got up and went to the window where I had been listening.

"Okay, Rachel, I tell you what," he yelled in. "Don't go back to him. Better yet, divorce him. He'll pay for it, I guess. Leave you everything. The house. The furniture. The car. He can go on off to New York with Miss Ophelia. Live with that nice plum-colored woman and help raise his son. Live a life of peace instead of bein saddled with a sour-mouthed wife who found it in her heart to forgive him. Ain't nothin worse in the world than livin with a woman whose every look keeps callin you a sinner."

A string of curses came through the window. Hot enough to burn up the screen. Worse than the ones I had just heard.

Uncle Willie sat back down, chin up, one eye closed against the smoke from the cigarette dangling from his lip. He crossed his leg, moving it slowly up and down, up and down.

There was a two-day lull. I went to visit Teeny. We worked on her sampler at her house. She had chosen a proverb: "Wine is a mocker." I drew it on linen and she drew a border like the one on my first sampler. We sat on the hill and worked steadily, talking and not talk-ing, laughing, then not laughing, content to sit and make crosses.

"Mama made me some dresses and I'm goin to town to buy some notebooks with the money Aunt Rachel and Uncle Avery gave me," I said one of the times we talked. There had been twenty dollars in the envelope she had passed to me, and I had stared in shock at the four five-dollar bills. I'd never held so much money in my life. Now I contin-ued. "I wonder who I'm goin to have for a teacher. I sure hope I don't have that Miss Richardson."

"She all right," said Teeny. "But she gets real mad if you don't do your homework." She handed me her sampler to inspect. "I'm goin back to Baltimore before I go back to school. Mama said I could go tomorrow night. I called Aunt Betty and she said she could come for me late. She likes to drive late at night so she misses all the traffic. She drives like crazy, girl."

Tomorrow night. I sighed. Just when we were getting used to each other again.

Teeny smiled sympathetically. "I'll bring you something back. I know! Ribbons for your hair. All colors. When I come back I'm gonna fix your hair a new way. You should wear it out, like mine. Not in plaits. Maybe your mother might even let you cut it. Ooooh, Belly, I bet if you cut it you'll have curls all over your head. I bet you would look so *cute*."

I laughed. Mama would not let me cut my hair. Besides, it was much easier to keep neat if I wore it in a braid. But I didn't tell Teeny that. She might not bring me the ribbons.

"I think Mama's glad I'm goin to Baltimore so I have something to do," Teeny continued. "She's afraid I might do somethin crazy again. But I learned my lesson."

"Your crosses are gettin better," I said, returning her sampler. Then I said, "What if when you're in Baltimore Robert Hawkins asks you to . . . you know."

"I wouldn't," said Teeny. Then she giggled. "Besides, ain't no place where we could. And Aunt Betty she watch us girls like a *hawk*."

I had to ask. Just to be sure. "And you don't miss your baby at all?"

Teeny became serious. "I admit I did at first, even though I told you it was best, but no, I don't miss him now. It's almost like, like none of it happened. Mama say that's spiritual healing." She paused. "How's Miss Rachel? Is she still mad at Mr. Avery?"

Although I had not discussed Aunt Rachel's affairs with Teeny (I was sure Miss Myra would) I did relate the incidents of the last few days. Not all, just enough to give her an idea of the turmoil at our house caused by Aunt Rachel and Uncle Willie.

"That Mr. Willie, he can make you feel bad. That's why I don't like to be around him sometimes. If I was Miss Rachel, I'd *leave*, rather than stay there and listen to his mouth."

Apparently Aunt Rachel had similar thoughts. The next evening she announced at the supper table that she was going to call Uncle Avery the next morning. He would probably be at our house on Monday.

Early Saturday morning she went early to Miss Myra's to make the call. Uncle Willie offered to drive her over, but she told him coldly that she preferred to walk.

"Walkin's good for you!" he called from the porch where we were watching her cross the field. "Clear some of them cobwebs out of your head!"

"Well I hope you're satisfied now that she's leavin," said my mother. "Just don't start no trouble when Avery gets here. I'm tellin you that right now. *Just keep your mouth shut.*" She turned on her heel and went inside, letting the screen door slam behind her.

"Hooo. I guess I got my orders," said Uncle Willie.

"Everything ain't a joke, Uncle Willie," I said with a sniff and followed my mother inside.

"Hooo!" said Uncle Willie. "Everybody's toucheous today. Guess it ain't nothin for a man to do but go fishin!"

Later in the morning Miss Myra returned with Aunt Rachel. "Teeny gone again, Belly," she said as they came onto the porch. She looked around. "Where's Willie?"

"Mama laid him out so he went fishin," I answered.

"Good," said Aunt Rachel. "Now we'll have some peace around here."

"Well," I sighed heavily, "I wish he'd come back. Then maybe he'll go to Jamison and get my piano."

I was not thinking when I spoke; Mama and Uncle Willie and I had made a pact on the way home from Jamison not to mention the piano. "Only cause some friction," Uncle Willie had said. I certainly did not want more friction. I can only attribute my slip of the tongue to weariness and boredom.

Aunt Rachel and Miss Myra looked at each other on elongated necks, then turned their heads and looked at me like two chickens eyeing the same worm.

"Oh, a piano!" said Miss Myra, her eyes darting from me to Aunt Rachel, then back at me.

Aunt Rachel was more direct. "What piano."

Miss Myra drew back as if she knew the answer but did not want to hear it.

I opened my mouth, but no words came.

"What piano," Aunt Rachel repeated.

My words were warped, slow. "When we were at Miss Ophelia's she said I could have her piano and Uncle Willie said he would bring it here."

"Well, that's nice. Especially since the one Miss Janie gave you got chopped up," said Miss Myra nervously.

"Chopped up!" said Aunt Rachel. "What fool would chop up a piano."

Miss Myra explained about Lewis and the piano. "But now Belly will be able to practice and make use of all those lessons she took in Jamison."

"Playin that monstrosity?" said Aunt Rachel. "It's a wonder Belly's fingers didn't double in size pushin down on them keys. Piano playin is supposed to be a pleasurable hobby, not manual labor." She stood back, hands folded across her stomach, frowning mightily at the thought of the Mahogany monster.

"It wasn't that hard to play," I said. "It made my fingers strong."

"And I don't know where you gonna put that big thing," said Aunt Rachel. "The parlor can't hardly hold the junk that's in there now."

Mama had heard the discussion and was now on the porch. "It can fit into the parlor, Rachel. Sit against the wall next to the dining room."

"Or she could put it in the dining room!" said Miss Myra, as if inspired. "Y'all don't use it anyway. You could make it into a music room for Belly and a sewing room for Lizzie since that's where she sews. And Belly could put her books—"

"My God, Myra," interrupted Aunt Rachel, obviously irritated by such an enthusiastic response to my news. "You don't need to jump through hoops. Let Lizzie put it where she wants. If they get it down here in one piece. When Mr. Love Senior died, Reba Lomax tried to play on it and the thing fell over to the right as soon as she touched it. I guess him or Eddie Junior must've propped it up with some bricks or somethin."

"If it gets here, it does. If it don't, it don't. Belly will get a piano from someplace," said Mama.

Miss Myra's eyes kept swinging from me to Aunt Rachel, from Aunt Rachel to me.

I, cowed by the look my mother gave me when she had stepped onto the porch, made myself small as I could in my chair and said nothing else.

Aunt Rachel sat, arms folded across her chest, and regarded me with flat brown eyes in a sour manila face.

So even though it was not her vacation, Aunt Rachel was in attendance at Third Sunday that summer. And she did not have to nag my mother into going. Something else was drawing Mama to church that day. Something that caused her to put on lipstick, which she seldom did, and be extra careful while she dressed. I watched her apprehensively, for I suspected the cause of this meticulous attention to her physical appearance.

When we got to the church, loaded down with a meal fit for several kings, my suspicions were confirmed. Mama had hardly stepped from Uncle Willie's truck when Mr. Henry Binns hurried to her side, not in the manner of a stranger, but an acquaintance.

"Good afternoon, Miss Lizzie," he said, flustered.

Miss Lizzie. Hmph.

"Good afternoon, Henry," said Mama, very unflustered.

Mr. Henry Binns vibrated like a reed in a light summer breeze.

"I don't know if you remember my daughter, Belly."

"Yes, I do," said Mr. Binns. "Hello, young lady."

"Hello," I said, looking him over, keeping my hands at my side so as not to shake the one he held out.

"You've been in Jamison for most of the summer," he said.

"Yes, sir. Visitin my Aunt Rachel."

"Yes, and Willie has to go back for her now," said Mama. "We couldn't all fit in the truck."

Mr. Henry Binns seemed delighted at that piece of news and seized the opportunity to ingratiate himself with my mother. "Miss Lizzie, I'd be happy to take you home." He turned to Uncle Willie. "Then you wouldn't have to make two trips."

"What a blessing," said Uncle Willie. He and Mr. Binns took the picnic baskets from the truck and placed them on a table that Mama pointed out, then Uncle Willie got back in the truck and drove off for Aunt Rachel.

I went in for the first church service. There would be two more during the day. I went to no more services, but stayed around for part of the all-day festivities. Once I noticed some white people standing on the edge of the crowded church grounds. A woman with red hair kept looking in my direction, and when I pointed them out to Uncle Willie he informed me that they were Andersons from Ohio. Some of my father's people.

"Why do they keep starin at me?" I said.

"Probably because you are the last Anderson in Pharaoh. Maybe they think if they're going to keep on comin down, they might as well get to know you."

I shook my head. "They ain't been to see us before. I don't want to get to know them if they passin for white."

"They ain't my people," said Uncle Willie. "They're yours and your father's. So, I guess it's up to you."

I was conscious of their eyes from that time on, and it was one of the reasons I went home with Uncle Willie when he left. Aunt Rachel and Mama stayed to get a ride home in Mr. Henry Binns's navy blue Oldsmobile.

That disturbed me.

Uncle Willie noticed and asked me about it. "You don't like this Mr. Binns fellow, hunh."

"Why's Mama got to come home with that man."

"Because she wants to, Belly."

"Why?"

We were on the porch. I had relapsed into my defensive position, rocking and reading.

Uncle Willie took my book away and put his hand on the arm of the rocker to keep me still. "I'm gonna say this today, Belly, because it needs to be said. Lizzie is a beautiful woman. She needs companionship. Now, she is also your mother. And she's a damn good one. She has given all her time to raisin you and seeing to what you need. But she's lonely. And after a while, why in six or seven years, you'll be gone to college—"

"I ain't goin to college."

"Oh, you goin to college. You might as well get your mind set for that!"

"You can't make me go if I don't want to."

"Belly, don't ever say that around Lizzie. That you don't want to go to college. You don't know what she give up for you to go."

"I don't care."

"I ought to jump over there—" Uncle Willie pulled his bottle from his back pocket and took a big swig. "We raised you too easy, that's what we did. Your mama did, anyway. When Tyler didn't come back, she almost went out of her mind. But she had you. That's what she used to say. 'I got Belly.' And she got over it. And she remembered how he used to say he was gonna send you to college. Give you a education. We used to laugh, because we sure didn't have no money. But when he got killed, she got the money. His GI insurance. She could've got a big car, or a new house, or some clothes. She could've spent it lots of ways. But no, she spent some of it on a bathroom." He shook his head ruefully. "And if the bees hadn't stung Rachel in the outhouse, we'd probably still be usin it." He took another drink. "But she never spent another penny of it. Went to work so she wouldn't have to. So you goin to college. Even if I got to drag you there kickin and screamin. And you'll meet some boy there and then get married. And you won't give a thought to your mother and her bein alone."

"Even if I go to college, I ain't never gonna leave home!"

"I ain't gonna argue with you about somethin that's not gonna happen for seven years."

"But Mama don't want no boyfriend! She said so! Look what happened with Miss Lucy Jenkins!"

"You comparin you mother to Lucy Jenkins? That woman ain't got no sense."

"No! But the man, he might be like Deacon Thompson—"

"Hold on, Belly. You judgin the man and you don't even know him. All men aren't like Deacon Thompson. And you act like your mother ain't got enough sense to know a good man when she meets one. Don't you trust her?"

I didn't answer.

"And I know you better trust me. I'll be around, lookin and watchin him. And what about you? Can't you tell the difference between people? Because if you can't you better learn. But you can't tell nothin about *anybody* unless you give them a chance to be around." Uncle Willie put his hand on my shoulder. "Your mother's lonely, Belly. But she ain't gonna have no man around that you don't approve of. So give them a chance."

She was lonely sometimes, she had told me that. I could feel my eyes watering.

Uncle Willie put his hand on my shoulder. "You scared, Belly. And jealous. You think if she loves somebody else, she won't love you as much. Well, Lizzie got a lot of love in her. A lot. I've known her a lot longer than I've known you. She got enough love in her for you, and me, and Henry Binns or somebody like him. She got enough love to put up with that simple Rachel."

Just then Mr. Binns's car turned up into the driveway. I wanted to jump up and run into the house. But Uncle Willie's last words were already taking effect. So I took a deep breath and stayed in my rocking chair. When everyone got out of the car and came up onto the porch, I smiled at them. Even at Mr. Binns.

C h a p t e r 25

Uncle Avery arrived the next afternoon. When I spied his black
sedan turning into the driveway, I jumped up from the chair where I
was reading and ran up to my room. I threw myself across my bed and
hid my face. How could I face him? What would I say? What would
he say? I tried to calm myself. I had faced Miss Ophelia. And Aunt
Rachel. It hadn't been so bad. After all, what did I know? Nothing. I
had seen Uncle Avery come down to Miss Ophelia's house and had
told no one about it. *No one knew what I had actually seen.* No one.
Yet why did I want to hide? Because I had peeped into a window and
seen—I closed my eyes and groaned. Ohh. I wanted to crawl into a
deep black hole.

But hide I could not. It was almost time for dinner. I would have
to go downstairs. I got up. I took the book I had been reading that
morning and slipped down the stairs. Everyone was on the front porch.
I went quickly down the hall to the back porch and lay on the cot.
If anybody came to look for me I would drop down and pretend I
was asleep.

But I did not give Uncle Avery enough credit. Perhaps he had
wanted privacy for this first awkward moment, too. He must have been

waiting for me to come downstairs. I had just opened the book when I heard footsteps and voices. He and Uncle Willie had come into the kitchen. Uncle Willie peeped into the porch. "Here's Belly. Head in a book as usual." He tactfully withdrew.

"Hello there, Belly," said Uncle Avery, stepping onto the porch. "Got your list ready for me?"

I kept my eyes on the page. "Not all of it."

"What! I thought all children liked money."

"I do like money. I started the list. I just haven't had time to finish it yet."

"Well. You don't have to finish it to get your money." He was quiet a moment. I still had not looked his way. "You ever finish that book you were readin when you were at the house?"

"What book?" I frowned and looked at him then. Then I remembered and flushed. *Silas Marner.* About the deacons being hypocritical. Oh, how I had run my mouth that day. "Yes, sir. I finished it." He was acting just the same. I was beginning to feel more at ease.

"What happened to the young man? Silas Marner?"

"Well, he moved to a little village and made linen and he got old and stingy. And then he found a little baby"—I stopped, then rushed on—"and he raised it and the real father came after her when she got big and wanted it." I was whispering now.

"Why didn't the real father come after her at first?"

"Well, he was married to another woman. I mean, he thought the little girl was dead. Then when he found out she was big, she decided to stay with her old father, Silas Marner." I stopped and sat miserably with my hands folded on my lap.

Uncle Avery did not seem to notice my discomfort. He was busy scratching a match to light his pipe. "Was that good or bad?" he asked after he lit it. He leaned against the doorjamb.

"Well, it was good for Silas Marner because"—I thought hard—"because she was all he had in the world to love, I guess. And her real father, well, he still had his wife."

Uncle Avery nodded. "Sounds like that book is worth a dime."

"It was hard! And I didn't understand all those big words." We were over the hump. Discussing the book made us more relaxed. Uncle Willie, who had been hanging in the kitchen, possibly listening, if I knew him, and having understood that it was important for us to meet alone first, came in.

"You gonna need another list, girl."

"I just started this one this morning," I said proudly.

"No better way to spend her time," said Uncle Avery.

Uncle Willie nodded toward the kitchen. "I think your mother and Rachel are ready to eat."

I sighed with relief. Everything would be all right. But as soon as we were all settled at the table and eating, I could see that everything would not be all right.

As Aunt Rachel passed me the rolls, she looked me in the eye and said, "Well, Belly, did you enjoy your trip to Jamison the other day?"

I jerked as if I had just been hooked. I looked over at Mama for a look to guide me. But somehow, today, she was not looking my way. What should I say? I shrugged. "It was okay."

"Belly's got a piano," said Aunt Rachel to Uncle Avery.

I winced as Uncle Avery fell into her trap. "Well, Belly. A piano." I remember having mentioned to him that I played on Miss Janie's piano, for he said, "Miss Janie give you hers?"

I swallowed. "No, sir."

Mama and Uncle Willie were concentrating on eating, not saying anything. The silence must have warned Uncle Avery, and just as he must have realized where this piano was coming from, Aunt Rachel said, "Ophelia gave 'er hers."

Silence.

Oh, how I wished Miss Myra were at the table. I remembered how she had helped us through the awkward moments when Aunt Rachel had first come.

Aunt Rachel went on. "Don't know where you gonna put that monstrosity."

Mama looked over at her. "Told you in the living room."

"Seems to me like we already discussed this, Rachel," said Uncle Willie.

"All right," said Aunt Rachel. "We don't have to talk about pianos or piano lessons," said Aunt Rachel. She buttered a roll. "Myra told me Teeny's back home."

"Yes, ma'am."

Uncle Willie and Mama exchanged glances. Mama looked hard at me and shook her head slightly, my signal to stay away from the topic.

"She told me about giving the baby up," said Aunt Rachel. "Best thing for her and the child. She's only thirteen. What do a thirteen-year-old know about bringing up a child." She went on and on about babies and sin and foolishness.

I hung my head. I could not look up. I was too embarrassed. What was wrong with Aunt Rachel? Is this what Uncle Willie meant when he said she would make Uncle Avery pay the rest of his life?

I looked quickly at Uncle Willie, then Mama. They were sitting as if poised on the edge of hell. I looked down at my plate again. Aunt Rachel's voice went on and on, rising, subsiding, rising. I don't remember her words. I only remember her voice. Biting. Sarcastic. Intolerable.

I heard a chair scrape. I looked up. Uncle Avery had left the table. His napkin lay next to his plate of half-eaten food.

I looked over at Aunt Rachel. She was daintily picking at her mashed potatoes as if she were looking for something she had dropped there.

"Rachel," said Uncle Willie, "you are wrong."

"Willie," said Rachel, "mind your business."

"Stuff that goes on at my table is my business," said Uncle Willie.

"And mine," said my mother. "If I put some rotten food in front of you, you'd have a whole lot to say. Right at the table in front of everybody. All right. So maybe you haven't come to terms with your husband yet, but you sat here at my table and said things in front of my child that she didn't need to hear."

"Child. Is that what she is. She's a sneaking lyin devil, that's what she is."

My mouth fell open.

"Don't sit there and look like you don't know what I'm talkin about, Belly Anderson."

"But I *don't*."

"You didn't know about my husband comin to Ophelia's house."

"He only came to see how I was doin."

"Which he sure should've done, Rachel," said Uncle Willie.

"That's not all that happened. That's not what I heard."

"Rachel," said Mama, "I've talked to Belly. I told you. And I told you to leave it alone."

"Alone."

"She didn't have nothin to do with Ophelia and Avery."

"But she knew about it."

"Knew what? That's what I asked you. And you couldn't even say."

Aunt Rachel looked at me. "Look at her face. She knew."

I shook my head. Water came to my eyes. "No, I didn't know."

"What are you sayin she knew about?" said Uncle Willie.

"The baby, fool."

"The baby!" Uncle Willie laughed. "Woman, you is a fool. That baby had to be conceived long before Belly came to stay with you. So what you tryin to say?"

"That when she went down there for lessons, she knew Miss Ophelia was gonna have a baby."

"So what if she did?"

"If she'd a told somebody—"

"By somebody you mean you."

"All right. Me. If she'd a told me, I might've—well, I could've—"

"Might've what."

"Helped her."

"Helped her what."

"I—"

"You could've helped her cover it up that she was gonna have a baby? She was doing that already. You mean you could've helped her leave sooner so she wouldn't have tripped down them steps and had that baby here in Jamison. Or you could've stopped Belly from goin to her for piano lessons. But you sure couldn't have stopped Ophelia from gettin no baby because that happened long before Belly went there."

"Willie," said Mama.

"Willie, shit." Uncle Willie threw his fork on the table. "I told her to leave it alone, but since she didn't we might as well clear this air. Right here and now today in Mason County."

"Clear it, then!" said Aunt Rachel. "Clear it then!"

"Or is you tryin to say that you would've helped poor Ophelia by helpin her have the baby in secret and then adoptin it. Not knowin that it was Avery's of course. Is that what you tryin to tell us? That you would've done this great Christian act back there before that baby was born?"

"I would."

"Rachel, I know you, woman. I know you. And you know I know you. And I know the only reason you want that baby ain't because it's Avery's. That's just an excuse. You want it 'cause you seen it and it ain't nappy-headed, walleyed, or black."

"That is a goddamned lie, Willie Walker." Aunt Rachel's words were slow and measured. "You say you know me. Well, I don't know what you know, but I know one thing. I know that baby is Avery's. And I know Avery is my husband. And I'm goin to do all I can to persuade him to take his own child. It's as much his child as it is Ophelia's."

As I listened to that speech and saw the depth of Aunt Rachel's anger, my heart leaped up into my throat. She was right. Uncle Avery was her husband. And a husband stayed with his wife unless she kicked him out. And most women did not do that, no matter what he did, short of murder. Maybe she could persuade him to convince Miss Ophelia to leave the baby with him. Miss Ophelia would do that if he asked her to. I had no doubt about that.

I thought of the child, of the warm, helpless bundle I had held the day before, of the little fist grasping mine, of Miss Ophelia's soft voice saying, "Do you like him, Isabel?" I thought of the child, I thought of Miss Ophelia, I thought of Aunt Rachel, when I fell down the steps. "Gal, is you a fool?" I thought of her distaste for music and books. Most of all I thought of her insensitive, harsh way of doing things, the way she spoke about people. Hatred swelled inside of me like a balloon when it's filling with air. It burst and I jumped up. Words flew out of my mouth past a bitterness in my throat. Jumbled, angry words, loud and biting.

"No! Uncle Avery ain't gonna let you have Miss Ophelia's baby! God didn't let you have none because you killed one you was gonna have 'cause you didn't know if it was his or that other man's. And you couldn't have no babies because you messed up your wound and now you had to have a operation 'cause you messed it up when you jumped out of that tree and now you want Miss Ophelia's baby!"

I stopped, aghast. I had not been aware of anyone, not Mama, not Uncle Willie, not Uncle Avery, who had come back inside when I started screaming. I saw only Aunt Rachel. Now we stared at each other as if we were in a hypnotic trance.

She came around the table, stiffly, like a zombie, eyes never leaving mine. Finally she stood in front of me, drew her lips back from her teeth in a snarl. "You nasty yallah hussy." She drew back her hand on that wiry Walker arm and brought it around with as much force as she could muster and slapped my face so hard I saw stars.

I screamed and grabbed at her hand.

She snatched it away and drew her arm back to slap me again, but Uncle Willie grabbed her wrist. "Woman! Is you lost your goddam *mind*?"

Hand to my face, I turned and ran shrieking upstairs.

I was in the bed for the entire next day. My face was swollen; my mother packed it with towels wrapped in ice. One time I got up and looked in the mirror. I looked like a lopsided chipmunk with an exaggerated wink. I got back in bed and cried myself to sleep. No one could persuade me to leave my room. And no one except my mother and Uncle Willie would I let in. Not Teeny, not Miss Myra, not Uncle Avery, who knocked on the door several times asking me to let him in. I would not answer.

That same day he and Aunt Rachel went back to Jamison.

For three days I sat and stared out of the window. I would read for a while, then cry for a while, then sleep for a while.

Uncle Willie said my body was readjusting itself. "You been through a lot this summer. Teeny. Miss Ophelia."

"Where is Miss Ophelia," I said through swollen lips.

"She's in New York City. She's gonna write to you."

"She's got the baby with her?" I said.

"Sure, gal. What do you think."

"I'm sorry if I got you in trouble, Uncle Willie. Tellin all that after I crossed my heart and everything."

"Well, I didn't care about Rachel. I just thought I'd explain to Avery because he was real upset about you. Real upset. I thought he was gonna slap Rachel, he was so mad. Him and me had a long talk. A long talk. Thing was, he knew she was seein that Looby fellow when she was supposed to be his girl. Heard about it in town. And why not, everybody knows everything around. But he didn't know she deliberately got rid of that baby. He thought it was an accident. Like everybody else. But I'm glad he knows about it. Now Rachel can't throw Ophelia's baby up in his face. He can walk around with his head up as high as hers, higher maybe."

On one of those sad days when I was in my room recovering from Aunt Rachel's slap, Uncle Willie and Malachi Green went to Jamison and brought back Miss Ophelia's piano. It loomed proudly on the truck as it rattled up the driveway. I ran downstairs, hands clasped joyfully together, to watch them unload the precious cargo. As they lowered the piano, it tipped over and broke into pieces. I didn't cry. For some reason I thought God was punishing me for what I had seen and kept secret.

One afternoon about a week after school began I came walking despondently up the driveway, feeling very alone. Teeny was making new friends. We were growing farther and farther apart. When I got on the porch, Uncle Willie's face was lit up with a grin. He took me by the hand into the parlor.

"Surprise!" he yelled.

"Surprise!" yelled Mama.

And surprised I was. Against the parlor wall stood Aunt Rachel's spinet, gleaming, dustless, waiting. I went to it and played a little song and for a moment I was happy. I'd like to think that she sent me the piano to make up for that slap. But deep in my heart I know that she removed it from her house because she wanted no reminder of that summer or Miss Ophelia.

During one of my crying sessions, I looked for a book and came across the package that Miss Ophelia had given me that day she fell down the stairs. I had forgotten all about it. I opened it up. Writing paper. Green with green satin ribbon wrapped around it. On top of the paper was a note from Miss Ophelia telling me her New York City address and urging me to write to her.

I wrote to her that very day. Not a very long letter. Just one telling her how much I missed her. I asked about the baby and hoped that I could come to New York City to see him. I did not realize the effect that distance would have on our relationship.

That was the first of many letters. In my second letter I questioned her about sending a letter to Uncle Avery along with the ones she wrote to me and in reply to that question she told me a secret I would never have guessed.

Uncle Avery could not read.

So I became the link between him and Miss Ophelia and his son. In those letters, once a year, she sent a picture of the child whom she had named after Uncle Avery's father. Every August when Uncle Avery and Aunt Rachel came down for their annual vacation (yes, I got over that slap) he would come up to my room and I would take from a box all the letters of the year and read them to him and show him the pictures of the boy, who looked more and more like him. I was the one who wrote messages to Miss Ophelia and the boy, I was the one who sent pictures of Uncle Avery, gifts from Uncle Avery, love from Uncle Avery; and always those presents to the boy signed *Your loving father*.

Miss Ophelia and I wrote to each other for seven years. Then her heart gave out. She went to sleep one night and never woke up, her Aunt Virginia wrote. None of us went to the funeral. All of that was over by the time Mama received the notice. I was away at school, and Mama wrote to tell me about it.

When I came home that summer, I took out her letters and pictures and looked at them for a long time. Then I put them away and through the years thought about her less often.

I saw the boy only once, when he was a grown man. He had come down for Uncle Avery's funeral. We were in the church. In the front pew. And then I saw a man come in, a man who looked much like Uncle Avery might have looked when he was very young. My heart stopped. I whispered to Mama. I wanted to go back and meet him, but she told me to wait. The man stayed at the back of the church. He did not come through the line to view the body. When we looked for him after the service, he was gone.

Mama had sent a death notice to Miss Ophelia's aunt but had heard nothing from her, so she hadn't expected him. One day not too much later when I was looking in the book of guests who had attended the funeral I came across a name written in a neat hand.

Henry Swann II. New York City.

I saw Aunt Rachel and Uncle Avery once each year when I came home, either in Jamison or when they were in Pharaoh. He became even quieter than he had always been. She became reclusive too. Whenever I went to visit them in Jamison, she would be in one room, he in another. I would converse with one, then the other. I do not remember having a conversation with them both in the same room at the same time, and I do not remember ever hearing them carry on a conversation with each other.

I never wondered why Uncle Avery had not left Aunt Rachel. With the rage she was in she was capable of butchering him and Miss Ophelia in front of the entire community. I'm sure some sort of pact was made between them. Avery would stay with Rachel, she would let Ophelia get out of Jamison without bringing him up before the Deacon's Board for adultery. Expose him and Miss Ophelia to the snickering whispers of the congregation. Get him kicked out of the church. From what I had seen at Pharaoh Baptist in the matter of Deacon Thompson, it would have been very ugly. Uncle Avery might have let Rachel do it, but he would not have exposed Miss Ophelia to that. Never. He had to let her go.

•   •   •

So many summers have passed since then. I remember very little about them. Yet I remember that summer so long ago with such an ache in my heart that it brings tears to my eyes. I see a young girl, rough and loud, smiling at a woman, soft and gentle. I see a man at peace, smiling softly, eyes closed, listening. I see a clumsy mahogany piano, I see sunlight slanting on the yellow keys, I hear music, singing, rising, falling, rippling, singing a dream of love.

And as I grew older and more unwise in the ways of love, one question always came to my mind. Why?

That word seemed to obsess me. The question that Aunt Rachel surely must have asked herself. The question that the neighbors on Randolph Street must have asked. The question I had hoped Miss Mattie could answer. I never considered that the reason might be one of those "natural" transgressions attributed to men that Uncle Willie had informed me about so many years before. What I remembered could not be reduced to mere lust.

Never that.

There had to be something more.

Now I sit here this afternoon, dreaming, and I remember a conversation with Uncle Avery about a year before he died. He must have been in his early eighties then. He was in a chair on Mama's front porch, one leg crossed, pipe in his hand. He had stopped smoking it years before. I had just finished playing "When I Grow Too Old to Dream," the song he always asked me to play whenever we were there visiting. I had joined him on the porch to watch my two children play horseshoes in the yard under the big maple tree.

He was frail. Frail. But he still had that slow sweet smile.

He was looking at the children. "You've got wonderful children, Belly. Well mannered. Intelligent."

"Different from me when I was their age," I said, laughing.

He looked over at me with a wry smile. "Not much. And look at you. You've turned out to be a good woman as well as a good mother. That's important, Belly. A good mother is a wonderful thing, especially for a child. They remember that all their life . . . Even though I wasn't with mine past the age of four, I still recall certain things about her.

The way she held me close to her . . . how warm she felt when she hugged me." He rested his head on the back of the chair and closed his eyes. "I remember her gentleness, and her goodness . . ." His voice was trailing off now. ". . . and I remember the smell of roses."

He stopped, as if the effort of speaking had tired him. I thought he had dropped off to sleep, but after a moment came words wrapped in a breath as light as that of a sleeping baby. "Her perfume always smelled like roses."

They are all memories now. Faded and sweet, like flowers pressed between the pages of a book. Memories recalled at odd moments of the day. Here in my mother's house, now mine, I hear the sound of my boisterous grandchildren drifting in from the yard. No readers there, yet. But I have found a young piano player. Here she comes now for her lesson on Aunt Rachel's gleaming piano. She sits on the bench beside me, then gets up on her knees to smell the yellow roses I have cut from the garden. She is almost eleven. A very tender age. I give her a hug and turn the page of the book to Hanon. She places her hands on the keys, and I place my fingers over hers and we play together for a while, this young Isabel and I. And when we have finished our lesson, I put on a record of Bach or Brahms or Chopin, and we retreat to the side porch, where there's always a pitcher of iced tea and a plate of homemade cookies. And we sit on the swing and dream and create memories.